LAST
First KISS

La Fleur de Love: Book Two

By
LORI LEGER

CAJUNFLAIR
PUBLISHING

Cover by Lori Leger

Copyright © 2011 Lori Leger

Third Edition

ISBN-10: 1940305241
ISBN-13: 978-1-940305-24-0
(Cajunflair Publishing 6X9 Regular print)

DEDICATION

To anyone who's ever grieved over the loss of a loved one—and survived by picking themselves up and going on with their lives.

ACKNOWLEDGMENT

As always, to the love of my life, Michael, thanks for everything, babe.

To James and Amy Otto for combining your efforts to co-write the perfect love song, *Last First Kiss*.

Thanks to Joan Granger of Simple Memories Photography for making me look so good in my author photo.

To the girls in my life: Kitty, Shelley, June, Carla, Sherri, Arlene, Jessica, Stephanie, Nova and Trish...I love you all. To my old co-workers, the *other* Designing Women: Barbara, Joan, Tina and Cat—thanks for reading my stories. To Angie Hebert and Tammy Broussard, whose enthusiastic praise gave me hope. To Jess Ferguson and Pat Marcantel, I feel like I've known you gals forever. Gina, because we've been friends forever, politics aside. To Margaret...sorry I wasn't there when you needed me. To my Angels and the gals in the old L.A. "B" Club: Karen (the first one to tell me to quit whining about my life and do something about it) Cindy and Henrietta. To Cathy Hanks and Sharla Bertrand--I don't get to see you ladies nearly enough, but I love you anyway.

And finally, for those we've lost . . .Most recently, my mom, Diana, my dad, Andrus, Gordon, Claudia T., Marlene, Lil' Gail, Dale, Gary H., Ms. Lucy, Mr. Fred, Bo, Cristel, Karen, James, Marc, Carl, and Russie. You are all missed so much.

Map of South Louisiana
Real and *Fictional* towns in book

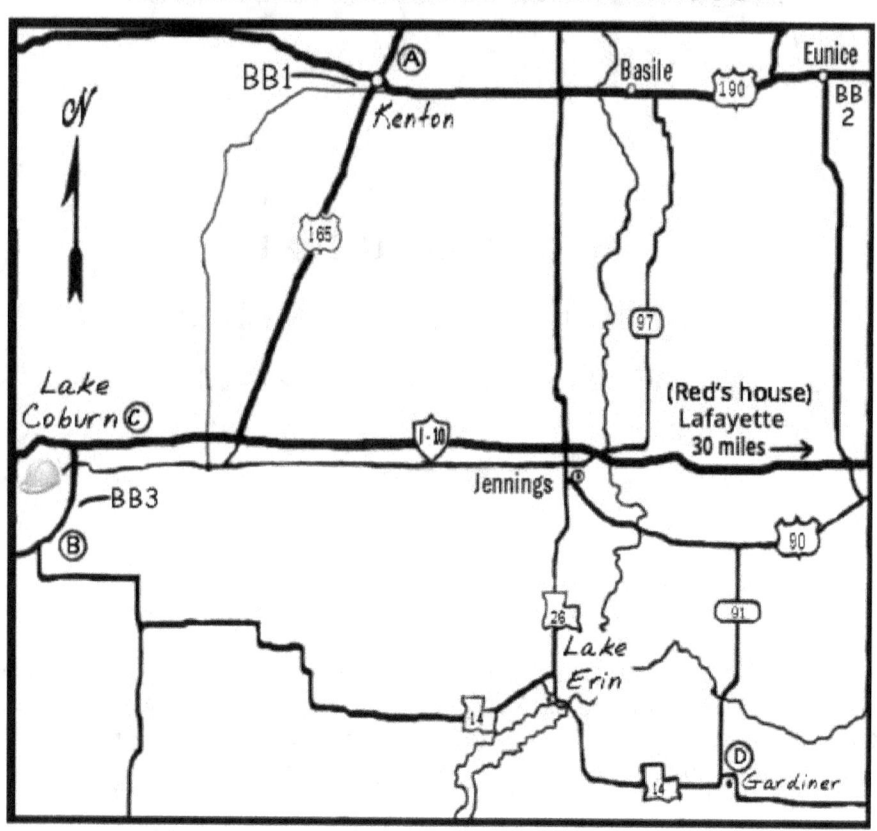

LEGEND:
- Ⓐ Giselle, Mac, and Lexie Granger's home
- Ⓑ Jackson Broussard's home
- Ⓒ Bill Broussard's home
- Ⓓ Carrie and Red's hometown
- ◌ Carrie and Jackson's Office
- BB1 Kenton Ball field
- BB2 Eunice Ball field (Mac's Tournament)
- BB3 Lake Coburn Ball field (Jackson's Tournament)

Chapter One

Early January

Jackson Broussard crawled through the gaping hole left by his blown out windshield. He struggled to his feet, wincing as pain shot through his left knee. Weak kneed and wobbly, he stood in place, trying to get his bearings. A lone observer standing in the midst of chaos. Within moments the shriek of sirens joined the wails and cries of other survivors.

He tensed as a fire truck's air horn jarred his traumatized senses, and then gasped and coughed, regretting the deep breath he'd taken. He choked on the acrid smell of burning rubber, and something else, a putrid odor that burned as it settled at the back of his throat. He fought the urge to vomit as he watched in horror, while inky fingers of smoke billowed skyward from several locations.

Jackson cringed at a woman's sudden hysterical screaming, not wanting to think about what she'd seen that made her lose control. Cries and moans of others joined in, collaborating to form a chorus of misery and death. The accident involved more vehicles than he could see or count. Male and female, young and old. Death would have no sympathy for the innocent.

He attempted to walk, but his knee kept buckling. Half dragging, half crawling, it took him another five minutes to find Chloe, his wife, where she'd landed after being ejected from his truck. Her face a bloody mass of bones and shredded tissue, her thin body bent, broken beyond repair.

He fought back another wave of nausea, knowing one seat belt could have made the difference between life and—this. As usual, she'd refused. Nobody told Chloe what to do. Law enforcement, or otherwise.

Should he believe she was gone? Or was it just another one of her cruel tricks to try and humiliate him? He studied her broken body again. No, there would be no coming back from this. He had to wonder. Would death bring her the peace she obviously lacked in her lifetime? God knows, there was no love between them anymore, but even so, he'd never stopped *trying* to make her happy for once in her dissatisfied, miserable life.

Jackson rose on shaky legs, allowing his mind to drift back to the moments before the accident. In typical Chloe fashion, she'd spent the last moments of her life berating him, screaming because his single act of kindness toward others had inconvenienced her. But . . . what act? He squinted against the throbbing in his head, the pain in his chest. What had he done to piss her off? Fighting off the dizziness, the sudden urge to pass out, he struggled with a missing piece of the puzzle, recognizing its importance to the completed picture.

Frustrated, he put both hands to his head, and willed himself to concentrate. Think. Retrace the events that lead to this moment: The stadium's malfunctioning traffic light after the benefit ended shortly past noon, him allowing several cars to turn in front of him, pausing to let one more vehicle pull out in front of him—the black Expedition and its occupants, and the last action, the catalyst for Chloe's steady stream of jibes that had escalated into increasingly ugly accusations.

He swung around, made himself dizzy as total recall caused a tightening in his chest. *Where are they?* Jackson spotted the SUV lodged against the guardrail and uttered a silent prayer as he stagger-crawled his way to Toby's truck. He forced himself to stand. His heart hammered in his chest when he saw his friend in the driver's seat. Just as quickly, it sank. The unnatural tilt of his head confirmed his dread. He reached through the shattered window, searching for a pulse, and found none. "Oh God, Toby," he groaned, despair stunning him for a moment as he realized one of his best friends was gone.

"Giselle!" Toby's wife slumped in the passenger seat, also buckled into place. He stumbled his way around to her, his heart plummeting at the blood pooled around the gouge on her forehead. Her chest rose and fell rhythmically as she labored to breathe. He ripped a piece from his already torn shirt to wipe the area clean, and allowed himself to relax once he saw the bleeding had already began to clot. He thought of the couple's two young daughters. What would happen to them if they lost both of their parents? Oh, God, she had to be okay.

Supporting himself on the truck he looked around. "Help. Somebody help!" he croaked, stepping away to find someone.

He staggered back to Chloe's body, swaying unsteadily, struggling through the pain and dizziness to remain on his feet. He fought the blackness closing in on him, determined to remain conscious until he made sure someone helped Giselle. Finally, two EMT's approached at a run.

"Sir, are you injured?" one asked.

He grabbed his head, squeezing his eyes against the sudden pain, then fell on his knees beside Chloe. "My wife is gone. You can't help her." He struggled to raise his hand, to point at the black Expedition. "My friend Toby didn't make it, but his wife has to live, for their little girls." He grabbed for the debilitating pain in his head again before collapsing onto the I-210 roadway.

He woke trying to scream, jerking away from the image of Chloe's bloody face filling his mind.

"It's okay Mr. Broussard, it's okay." The ER nurse spoke in a soothing voice.

Jackson blinked once, twice, and again to clear his eyes, and searched the nurse's face for clues.

She smiled down at him. "You're at St. Luke's hospital, and you've got a mild concussion. You'll be all right. How's the pain?"

He reached slowly for his head and felt. No bandages. He grabbed the nurse's hand as one particular memory rushed at him. "I need to find someone who was also in the accident."

"And I'll help you do that, Mr. Broussard. Is it a family member? Was there a passenger in the vehicle with you?"

"My wife was with me, and she—didn't make it." He sounded calmer than he felt. Was he drugged? "There was a black SUV with a couple in it. The driver was my friend and I—I think—I think his neck was broken. I couldn't find a pulse. His passenger, his wife, had a cut on her head, but she was breathing. They have two young girls and no other family. She has to be okay."

"I need her name and a description."

"Her name is Giselle Granger. She's tall and slim, about five foot eight, with shoulder length, curly, brown hair, and green eyes. She had a big cut on her forehead, right about here." He touched his own head above his right temple.

"I'll check, and be right back. You stay here, Mr. Broussard."

He grabbed her hand again. "What did they do with my wife? She—" He swallowed the bile as the image of her flashed in his mind again. "She went through the windshield."

The nurse gave him a look of sympathy. "I'm so sorry, Mr. Broussard. I'm not sure if they've transported her yet. I'll check on that for you, too."

She started to turn away then stopped. "If she's not already in the morgue, she will be soon, and we will need you to ID her."

He nodded, tried to sit up. "I can do that whenever you need me to, but can you help me find Giselle? She's a co-worker of mine and her husband was a close friend."

She nodded. "I'll see if I can find her."

"Ma'am, did I have a phone on me?" Jackson pulled his phone from the bag of belongings she handed him and made two calls. First, to his only living relative, his Uncle Bill, asking him to meet him at the hospital. The second call was much harder to make. He knew Toby and Giselle's girls were staying with another co-worker, a close friend of both his and Giselle's, Carrie Langley. He'd heard the two women making arrangements at the office yesterday. The phone rang several times before Sam, Carrie's husband, answered the phone.

"Sam, this is Jackson. Is Carrie around? I'm afraid I have some bad news." He struggled to control his emotions. In seconds, Carrie was on the line.

"Please tell me you weren't involved in that horrible accident, Jackson. At least fourteen vehicles, it's all over the news."

He cleared his throat. "I wish I could. God, you don't know how badly I wish I could. Toby . . ." He gathered his courage, spoke the words he hated hearing much less saying outloud. "Chloe and Toby—They're both gone."

Her next word came out in a single sob. "Giselle?"

"I'm waiting to hear." His voice broke.

"Oh, God. This is a nightmare," she groaned.

"If it was, we could wake up from it. As it is, well, if she—" he stopped himself and swallowed, unwilling to face the thought. "*When* she wakes up, she's going to need you here."

"I'm on my way."

He stared at the I-Phone, saw *Call Ended* flash across the screen. In his mind, he saw the picture Giselle kept of her girls in her cubicle at the office. He remembered well the devastating pain of losing a parent. He had lost both of his before his fifth birthday. In the same way, a car accident. Thank God for his one relative, his dad's brother, Bill Broussard. He hated to think what would have happened if he hadn't had Uncle Bill. Toby and Giselle's two little girls had no one else.

The nurse entered his room, jarring him from his thoughts.

"Mr. Broussard, there's a woman by that description upstairs, but I can't give you any information other than she seems stable. She's still unconscious. Do you feel like taking a trip to her room to verify her identity?" She pulled a wheelchair over to the bed.

"I can walk," he insisted. His knee was sore but definitely better.

"Not on my shift." Her tone demanded respect.

Jackson sat obediently, and gathered his thoughts on their way to the fifth floor. Before the elevator doors opened fully, he heard Giselle's hysterical pleading. He catapulted out of the wheelchair, limped toward her heartbroken cries, then stood in the doorway. He stared at the woman he'd worked with for five years, barely recognizing her through her tortured facial expressions. His heart ached as her cries rose in volume.

"Somebody tell me where my husband is! Is he alive? He has to be. Please, tell me. His name is Toby...Tobias Granger and he was driving a black SUV. Please tell me if he's okay—I have to know. He's got black hair, brown eyes, he's six-two and slim."

Jackson stood tall as stiff resolve seeped into his core. *Be strong for her.* "Giselle."

She swung her piercing green eyes in his direction. "Toby?"

As recognition dawned, Jackson watched her hope melt away like ice under hot tap water.

"Where is he, Jackson? Have you seen him? They won't tell me anything. Please, get them to tell me," she begged.

He spoke from the doorway, his voice steady, as calm as he could manage, given his heart was shattering at what was about to happen. "Giselle, try to calm down."

A doctor paused at the door before pulling him away. "Sir, are you a member of her family? We're trying to find someone to be with her when we tell her about her husband. He was DOA."

Jackson shook his head, his gaze reverting back to Giselle. "She has no family. Neither she, nor her husband had any living relatives, other than their two young daughters. She's a co-worker of mine, and her husband is. . ." He swallowed hard. "He was a good friend." He turned back to the doctor. Dr. P. Allemande, he read from the tag. "We were all involved in that accident. I'd like to be with her when you tell her, if you don't mind."

She gave him a slow nod and patted his arm. "Okay, but you need to get back in your wheelchair. You don't look too steady."

He sunk into the chair the nurse held for him and let her roll him into the room then next to her bed.

"Giselle," he said, staring up into huge, green, amber flecked eyes, now red-rimmed from tears.

She spoke in a voice hoarse with crying. "Jackson, where is he?"

"Mrs. Granger," Dr. Allemande began. "I'm so sorry to have to tell you this, but your husband didn't make it."

Jackson watched as she let her head fall back on the bed, her eyes squeezed tightly shut. "Giselle, I'm so sorry," he said, fighting back his own tears.

She lifted her head to meet his gaze with wild eyes. "You're lying."

He grabbed her hand as his own voice cracked. "I'm so sorry, Giselle. Toby was such a good man, a good friend."

"No! Noooo!" She pulled her hand from his. "You're lying! You're jealous, because we're so happy and you and Chloe aren't. It's a lie. It has to be. I can't live without Toby. I can't!"

He cringed at her heartbroken wail. "Giselle, I know how happy you were but you still have two beautiful daughters. Think of Mackenzie and Lexie." He gripped her hand tightly as the doctor moved in to give Giselle a sedative.

"Oh God. I can't do this without him. How can he leave me? How could he? I can't take this. I can't take it. I don't want to live without him." She crossed her arms in front of her face. "Please, God, Take me too. Why didn't you take me too?"

He felt her soul crushing misery. "Don't say that, Giselle. Toby wouldn't want that. He'd want you to be here for your daughters. Think about your girls. Your two beautiful girls—Mac and Lexie. Toby loved you so much and he would want you to live so you could take care of them."

Her body shook with hysterical, heartbreaking sobs. Jackson cried with her, repeating her daughter's names over and over, hoping she'd find some strength, some will to live for her and Toby's girls. Slowly, the sobbing lessened and she quieted. The drug seeped into her system, calming her. Giselle pulled her hand from his, and turned away, remaining silent through the continuous flow of tears.

Jackson felt a gentle touch on his shoulder and nodded as the nurse wheeled him out of the room and back into the elevator. The gentle whoosh of doors closing shut out the image of Giselle's crushed presence. He closed his eyes and zoned out, wanting to mourn for his friend properly, knowing he couldn't until Toby's wife and daughters were taken care of. And Chloe. Dear God, what the hell was he supposed to do with Chloe?

"Mr. Broussard?"

Jackson opened his eyes, shocked at the sign on a set of double doors three feet in front of him. The single word in thick, block letters, MORGUE, was a harsh reminder of his reason for being here. He nodded and the nurse pressed a button on the wall. Two seconds later, the technician opened the doors to let them inside. Within two minutes, he sat in front of a table as the tech lowered the vinyl sheeting to expose the body.

"Dear God." He covered his mouth with one hand, thankful for the shock he'd apparently suffered at the accident scene. Nothing could have prepared him for what lay before him. The last time he'd seen her, she'd been halfway clothed, and the other half covered with blood. This—this showed the ravaging effects of how her life had ended. It sickened him. The soft voice of the nurse reminded him he wasn't alone.

"Mr. Broussard, are you okay?"

He nodded, pushed himself up from the wheelchair to stand over the body of his wife, a woman he'd assumed the heavy burden of caring for. She'd made the last thirteen of their fifteen year marriage a living hell for him. Any love he'd felt had long ago been replaced with pity. But he'd never hated her.

Everyone thought he'd been crazy for staying with a woman who generated unhappiness like the sun gave off light. Her temper tantrums, violent mood swings, and overall nasty character had been hell to bear. But he knew the root of it—her inability to conceive the child they both wanted so badly. He'd seen what she considered to be *her* failure eat at her for years. The doctors couldn't find anything wrong with her, she'd said. He'd had all the necessary tests run, and his count was fine, his swimmers weren't lazy.

Friends had urged him to leave her, find someone who wouldn't torment him with false accusations, public displays of temper, and affairs she'd never admitted to, and he couldn't prove. He'd stayed in hopes that the baby they'd one day have would change her back to the woman he'd fallen in love with so many years ago.

Jackson's nod accompanied the solitary sigh of a man faced with the difficult task of closing the door on a part of his life. "It's my wife. Chloe Stansfield Broussard."

After filling out the necessary forms and releases, he gave them the name of a funeral home to contact. The nurse wheeled him back to his room where he called Chloe's mother in California. He'd just ended the call when the doctor came in to discuss his x-rays, and subsequently, release him.

Jackson made his way back to Giselle's room, and stood over her bed, watching her brow crease even in her drugged sleep. Remembering her cries from earlier. Even as his own personal hell had just come to a dramatic end, hers was about to begin. He reached out to touch the bandaged cut on her forehead, a minor injury compared to what could have happened to her. Her right hand was in a splint, but that, too, was minor. He stared at her perfectly symmetrical features, marred only by a light spattering of freckles along the bridge of her delicate nose and a tiny scar above one eyebrow.

A light touch on his arm disrupted his thoughts and observations. He turned to meet Carrie's worried gaze.

"Jackson, I'm so sorry." Teary eyed, she hugged him tightly. "I thought you'd be here, so I brought someone up with me."

Jackson caught the movement at the doorway and turned as his uncle walked in, Stetson in hand, looking unsure of what to say to him. He stepped toward the man who'd loved him since birth and treated him as his own for over thirty years. "Uncle Bill."

"Are you okay, Jackson?"

"A few bruises and a sore knee . . . nothing." He embraced his uncle, pulled away and shrugged. "It could have been a lot worse, obviously."

"I guess Chloe wasn't wearing her seat belt," Carrie said.

"She might be alive if she had."

Bill shook his head. "Senseless. Have you called her mother yet?"

Jackson grimaced at the memory of that particular conversation. "Oh, yeah. She said she was sorry for my loss but couldn't make it to the funeral."

Carrie gasped. "For her own daughter? Lord, it's no wonder Chloe was disturbed." She reached out to touch his arm. "Are you all right? I know how bad it was for you at home."

Jackson shook his head slowly. "I don't know how I feel yet. I mean, who are we kidding? We all knew Chloe was—difficult. I doubt either of us felt any love for each other in years, but to have her die like that." He lowered his head and squeezed his eyes shut. "God, I don't know if I'll ever be able to forget that. I wouldn't have known it was her if I hadn't recognized her clothing." He cleared his throat to keep his voice from breaking.

"I'm sorry, Jack." Carrie hugged him again.

Jackson held on to her, fighting back the tears that threatened. Besides his Uncle Bill, Carrie was the closest thing he had to family. At forty-eight years old, twelve years older than himself, she was more like an older sister to him than co-worker of ten years. She was his right hand at the office, and he'd vented to her often when life with Chloe seemed unbearable.

Carrie had also been his buffer zone when Giselle had declared him the enemy four years earlier. One careless moment of stupidity on his part and she still called him 'Satan' behind his back.

Her reaction to him walking away from an accident when Toby had not. No way would that be good.

Carrie's next statement jolted him to attention.

"Jackson, I'm fairly certain I'm not alone in this. But, I've seen you miserable because of Chloe for so many years. I can't help but feel that you're free now. I feel guilty about it, of course, but there it is."

He stared down at the woman who'd always been so supportive of him, even when he was a wet-behind-the-ear engineer, brand new to road design. "Have I ever told you how much I appreciate you?"

"Yes, but it's been awhile." She sniffed and wiped her eyes. "Seriously, Jackson. I'd love to see you happy."

"Thanks, Carrie." He turned to gaze at Giselle, sedated and sleeping. "I wish I hadn't been here when the doctor told her about Toby."

Carrie's jaw dropped. "You were here?"

"I volunteered to be here, but if I could do it over . . ." Then he remembered her asking God to take her too. Maybe he would do the same thing.

He walked out of the room, over to a window at the end of the hallway and stared blankly out at the parking lot below. "The doctor wanted someone present that she knew. She thought it might be a comfort, but I should have known better. I know she despises me."

Carrie put her hand on his arm. "What happened when the doctor told her?"

"It was terrible. They had to sedate her."

Carrie dabbed at her eyes with a tissue. "Toby's poor girls. It makes you wonder what God could have been thinking, doesn't it?"

Bill, who'd been quiet up to now, stepped up suddenly. "Wait a minute. Is that the wife of your friend, Toby?"

Jackson nodded slowly. "He died in the accident."

Bill's head fell forward. "I'm sorry, Son. I didn't realize. Isn't she the one you pissed off at work a few years back?"

"That's her," Jackson said, giving his uncle another nod. "She already didn't like me. After walking away from an accident that took Toby's life, she may never forgive me."

"She wouldn't hold that against you," Carrie told him.

He raised an eyebrow. "You didn't hear her." He shook his head and pushed away from the window. "She was right about one thing, though. She said I was jealous of their marriage. I was."

"Come on, Jack. Everyone was envious of those two. They were the perfect couple," Carrie said. "Now, you need to go home, take a couple of aspirin, and go to bed."

"I need to get to the Chevy dealership for a new truck. I can't drive Chloe's Vette around. I can't get comfortable in that thing. Are you ready, Uncle Bill?"

"Are you released yet?"

"It's taken care of. Will you be here all night, Carrie?"

"I'll be here until they release her." She reached up to touch a tender spot on his face. "I'm worried about you, Jack. You call me if you need to talk."

He leaned over to hug her. "If you need anything while you're here, let me know, and I'll get it to you."

"I've got your number. Get your new truck then go straight home. Bill, maybe you ought to stay with him tonight."

"I don't need a damn baby sitter," Jackson grumbled. He rose from the seat too quickly and winced at the pain in his knee.

Carrie clucked her tongue. "Now see? That's good for you, smart ass. Good luck, Bill."

Bill leaned closer to Carrie. "You can call *me* at home if you need anything, hon."

Chapter Two

The two men walked into the elevator. "So that's Giselle Granger." Bill pushed the first floor button as Jackson nodded. "Any children?"

Jackson had to swallow hard to keep his voice from shaking. "Two beautiful little girls, ages six and four."

"Bad ages to lose their daddy."

Jackson didn't trust himself to speak, so he nodded again. If anyone knew what those girls would have to endure in the coming months, years, decades . . . he knew. Thirty-one years after losing his parents, he still missed them.

They drove in silence as Jackson attempted to deal with the multitude of emotions bombarding him. He closed his eyes and saw Chloe's broken body, then pressed the palms of both hands up against his sockets, trying to block it out.

He let his head fall back on the dusty seat of his uncle's old truck as a sudden wave of sadness washed over him. He would have given anything to have a marriage like Toby and Giselle's, but Chloe had been difficult to live with, so imbalanced, that any attempt to relax around her turned futile. In the best of times, he felt pity for his wife. In the worst, he had prayed to be free of her, but never this way. Swamped with guilt, he ran his hands brusquely through his hair. He winced as his fingers snagged the strands, still blood-caked and stiff.

He had loved Chloe once. The first year had been good until she began developing symptoms of what became constantly changing diagnoses. Manic depression, chemical imbalance, schizophrenia, bi-polar disorder...one quack had even suggested she was an exceptional actress. Whatever her condition was, it had made his life a living hell. Her threats to kill herself if he left had seemed real enough to make him stay. He couldn't have lived with himself if she followed through. Jackson lifted his head as his uncle grunted and cleared his throat.

"So, that was Giselle Granger. Tell me again what it was you did to piss that little lady off so bad."

Glad, for once, to be talking about his major foot in mouth episode, he took a deep breath. "I accused her of being incapable of following directions during a plan in hand meeting." He puffed out his cheeks as Bill gave a low whistle. "I know. In a room full of engineers and consultants."

"What happened after that?"

"She...ah...told me I'd better search my steel trap of a mind to remember who I'd given those directions to. She walked out, straight backed, head high, holding a grudge from hell."

"Hell hath no fury..."

"Like a woman humiliated and blamed for something she didn't do," Jackson finished.

"Did you ever apologize?"

"I never got the opportunity." He stared at his uncle's incredulous gaze. "It's impossible to apologize to someone who avoids being in the same room with you."

"Difficult maybe, but not impossible."

"Whatever."

Bill gave him a deep chuckle. "Surely she has to discuss work with you."

"Yes, when others are present, and always very civil, very professional. Cold as an Arctic frontal system."

Bill shook his head. "I don't get it. How the hell did you and her husband get to be such good friends?"

"We met building Sam and Carrie's deck last year. I don't know, we hit it off right away. He knew she hated me. Said he'd set a personal goal to 'patch things up' between us."

"You think he'd want you to look after his wife and daughters until they come to terms with things?"

Jackson let his head fall back on the seat again as he thought of Toby and how hard Giselle and her girls would take his death. As much as he'd miss his friend, he couldn't even imagine how Toby's family would suffer over the months ahead. "I know he would, but that doesn't mean she'll let me," he admitted.

He suddenly found a reason to be grateful that he and Chloe's marriage had been so miserable. It wasn't fair that God spared him, but took Toby from the wife and children who desperately needed him. A shrink would probably call this survivor's guilt.

"Do you want me to go with you?" Bill asked, interrupting Jackson's thoughts.

He blinked as they pulled into his driveway. "No. Thanks for the ride, though."

"Call me if you need anything."

Jackson took the time to shower and grab a change of clothes. He grabbed the keys to Chloe's Corvette and popped a couple of pain relievers on his way to the dealership.

⚜

Jackson pulled his new truck into the garage and turned off the ignition. He sat quietly, listening to the sounds of the engine cool. His head fell heavily against the headrest as he fought to keep his eyes opened. His muscles ached, along with his head, and his eyes burned from exhaustion. Even so, he couldn't help but remember the last time he and his wife had arrived home together.

The trip to a newly opened restaurant began pleasantly enough, until Chloe accused their waitress of flirting with him. He'd never forget the horrified expression on the poor girl's face. His own face had burned with embarrassment while Chloe raged on; she had made certain all attention in the room had thoroughly focused on her. Management asked them to leave quietly, but Chloe never did anything quietly, especially when asked to.

On the entire trip home she'd ranted, raved, and rebuked him for apologizing to restaurant personnel, insisting she had deserved the apology instead. The rant ended with a typical snide remark. "Way to show your support—*loser*."

Ten minutes after getting home, she performed her infamous "Chloe"...the hundred and eighty degree mood swing that always left him confused and no matter how hard he tried not to be, annoyed as all hell. She had initiated sex for the first time in a month, and he knew turning her down would have caused an all-night bout of crying and suicide threats he'd been too exhausted to handle that night. Sex with Chloe had long since turned into a chore for him because of her emotional blackmail. The only way he could 'see it through' was to close his eyes and imagine someone else in his arms, and hope this time she would conceive the child that would make his life bearable. He couldn't help but wonder. Could she tell? He supposed he'd never know.

Jackson pushed open the kitchen door and threw the bag containing the Vette's contents on the table. He started a fresh pot of coffee before picking up the phone to call his lawyer. They'd made their wills a couple of months ago and she told him she'd left a letter for him with their attorney if she went before he did. When Neil Ellender answered the phone, Jackson informed him of Chloe's death.

"She did leave a letter," Neil commented. "She made me read it before it was sealed. You sure you want to see it?"

"I'm sure."

"I can't keep it from you, of course, but I wish you'd let me destroy it. Your wife was—quite disturbed."

Jackson snorted and rubbed his hands over his eyes. "You're not telling me anything I don't know. I still want to read it."

"To my recollection, it does contain her wishes concerning a funeral service—among other things." The attorney cleared his throat uncomfortably. "I'll bring it over now if you want."

"I'd appreciate that, Neil."

Jackson grabbed a bottle of water from the fridge and swallowed two more aspirins. He pictured Chloe in his mind, how she had worn her straight, blonde hair in a short, spiky style that made her light blue eyes look even larger in her gaunt face. She was into being thin; like, way too thin. Uncle Bill had taken to calling her 'Bones' when he referred to her. He didn't call her anything to her face. Jackson had never seen two people so effectively ignore each other as his uncle and his wife had.

He entered the master bath and faced another ghostly memory of Chloe. Just yesterday, he'd stood outside the closed door, listening to her retch. He'd knocked to see if she was all right.

"What do *you* think, genius?" No niceties there.

He had kept his cool. "Do you need any help, Chloe?"

"What could you possibly do to help but stand there and look stupid?" He'd become accustomed to her rudeness. "Did you eat something that didn't agree with you?"

"It's a bug or something. Just leave me the hell alone."

He hadn't thought about it at the time, but he wondered if she had caught a bug, or if it was something else.

Thirty minutes later Jackson sat reading the letter his 'loving' wife left for him. He clenched his jaw as he finished it, cocked his head, and emitted a mild snort. Fifteen years with that woman had lulled him into believing he couldn't be shocked by a damn thing she did anymore. Well, the hell if she hadn't gone and done it.

He folded the letter into a neat rectangle, and placed it inside his wallet. By the time he met his lawyer's gaze, he had already decided to put that part of his life behind him.

"I just made a pot of coffee. Would you like some, Neil?" He stood and walked to the coffee maker, feeling calm, considering this latest revelation about his dead wife.

Neil got to his feet. "No, thanks. As I said, she insisted I read it." He cleared his throat, uneasily. "I think she just wanted me to know what she was up to. I hope you realize that I will uphold the strict attorney–client confidentiality."

Jackson turned slowly toward the man who looked enough like Tim Conway to be his brother. "I know. I wouldn't give a rat's ass if she hadn't mentioned other people."

"Of course, I understand completely."

"Can you handle her cremation for me?" Jackson asked. "I don't care what it cost, I never want to deal with her again."

"I can do that. Do you have the name of a crematorium you'd like to use?"

"I don't know anything about crematoriums. I trust you to do whatever you feel is necessary. Send me the bill and have her ashes sent to her mother in California. No service, as per her wishes," he said coldly.

"You got it, Jackson. I'll see myself out."

After Neil left, Jackson looked around at his home, filled with the sterile, plastic, ultra-contemporary furniture and accessories Chloe had chosen. He hated it, and she knew he hated it. Hell, knowing what he knew now, she probably hated it too, and chose it just to make him suffer.

How the hell had he managed to throw away fifteen years of his life with that lunatic? He had to hand it to her—she had fooled him. She was that good. The irony of the situation suddenly struck him. It started with a low chuckle, and built in a slow crescendo to uncontrollable laughter. After five minutes of wondering if he had completely lost his mind, he finally calmed down and sat at the dining room table with his cup of coffee.

He glanced at the bag of items he'd removed from Chloe's car, opened it, and began to sort through them. He flipped through a stack of letters and saw there was one from a doctor there in Lake Coburn. Curious, he opened it. The letter, dated a week earlier, was from an Obstetrician's office congratulating her on her pregnancy and urging her to call his office to schedule her first pre-natal check up with him. The doctor also stressed the importance of pre-natal vitamins to insure the health of the fetus.

The letter fell from Jackson's hands to the floor. Elbows on knees, he let his hands support the weight of his head, taking deep gulps of breath until a wave of nausea passed. After all those years of waiting and wanting a child, Chloe was pregnant. Jackson wondered when she planned to tell him about the pregnancy. Considering what he'd just discovered in the letter, he wondered if she even planned to tell him. He supposed he'd never know.

Overwhelmed by the senseless loss, and so alone in his misery, he lethargically reached for the phone to call Uncle Bill. As soon as he picked up the handset it rang. He took a deep breath and barely croaked out a hoarse hello. A too-damn-perky woman on the other end of the line began speaking in an irritating sing song voice.

"This is the Family Planning Clinic of Beaumont and we are trying to reach Chloe Broussard about her missed appointment. We don't approve of 'no shows' but we do understand that sometimes things happen that are beyond our patient's control. If she is there we need to know if she wants to reschedule the procedure."

Jackson's breath froze as he made the connection. Nausea plus pregnancy plus an appointment at a clinic of this type equaled to one thing. No. She wouldn't. Would she? Then he remembered the letter. The hell she wouldn't.

He cleared his throat, needing to know for sure. "I'm sorry she missed her appointment, ma'am, but there's no need to reschedule the abortion." He held his breath, stilling clinging to the hope this woman wouldn't confirm his suspicion.

She hesitated briefly before continuing. "Oh. Has she decided to go through with the pregnancy? If that's the case, I'll remove her from the doctor's schedule."

Jackson swallowed the build-up of bile in order to answer, his voice steely with anger. "The bitch is dead." He ended the call, sat staring at the phone several seconds before letting it fall to the floor.

He covered his face. Chloe had been pregnant, and didn't want the child. His child. Or maybe not, considering the contents of the letter. Regardless, he'd have wanted the child, would have treated it as his own, showered it with love, making up for its horrible mother, protected it from her. But maybe once she'd had a child, she would have changed? Her condition—he clipped the thought short, remembering there was no condition. An act, all these years, a horrendous, cruel act on her part to keep him emotionally attached and sympathetic, even with the absence of love. She'd been incapable of love, obviously.

Jackson focused on the scene in the truck with his wife, recalling the few minutes before the accident. Her irrational anger at something so trivial had seemed normal at the time. Now, of course, he knew the reason behind it.

It had all started with her long sigh of impatient suffering. "What the hell are you doing, Jackson?"

As usual, he'd kept his voice low and reserved. He'd always endeavored to be the sedative influence during Chloe's bouts of unreasonable behavior. More often than not, it proved to be the calm before the storm. "The light is out on that side. I'm letting people exit."

"That's their problem. It won't kill them to wait."

"It won't kill us to be kind, Chloe."

She'd faced him then, her face twisted in rage. "I have things to *do*."

He'd turned to his wife as he let another vehicle turn onto the highway in front of them. "I'm sure they all do, too."

She'd glanced impatiently at her phone. "I couldn't care less about anyone else."

"Wouldn't hurt you to try."

She'd whipped her head around. "Did you say something, asshole?"

Jackson kept quiet as he let his foot off the brake and inched forward slowly.

"It's about damn time," she'd huffed, facing her window. But, his foot hitting the brakes had her whipping her head forward once more. "What now?"

He'd nodded toward the black SUV at the intersection. "That's Toby and Giselle. They're on their way to a party." He'd lifted his hand, grinning at his friend, Toby's enthusiastic wave of gratitude.

Chloe had jerked her head toward him in agitation. "I told you I have things to do, Jackson. Let's go!" The last two words had come out in a screech of uncontrolled rage.

He'd pulled out after the black SUV and followed them back toward the interstate, all the while enduring a continuous diatribe of insults from his dear wife.

Jackson stood slowly. An abortion. She had to drive to Beaumont for an abortion, and he'd been holding her up. She must have been frantic she'd miss her appointment. She'd missed it, all right. But for a reason totally beyond his control.

He walked over to the latest of many studio portraits taken of Chloe and picked up the frame. He studied the features of his dead wife; from her expensive, high-end haircut, her two hour make-up application, to the perfectly manicured nails. She spent more money monthly on her appearance than most people did on home mortgages. He should know, he'd paid for it for years. All that pretty on the outside had done nothing to improve her inside. What he'd mistaken for a medical condition had proven to be nothing more than a spiteful streak of evilness that made her the cold hearted bitch she was.

Jackson pitched the frame across the room, gleamed some satisfaction as it landed on the opposite wall and shattered. How he wished he could get his hands on her skinny little ass just for a moment. Just to tell her how he felt about her. To let her know he'd survived her hatefulness without letting it turn him.

He stood there, gasping for deep breath to keep from screaming, staring at the house that had never felt like a home. Chloe had damn well made sure of that. He picked up his keys, and stormed out, heading to the U-Haul business two streets over. When he returned thirty minutes later, his truck bed was loaded down with moving boxes and crates.

Jackson worked like a man possessed, stopping just long enough to call the local Salvation Army. He told them he had a houseful of furniture and clothes to donate that he would put to the curb tonight. Two men arrived within the hour and began to fill the truck with furniture and boxes containing Chloe's things. By eight p.m. he'd removed all traces of her. Not a single item remained to show that she'd even set foot in the structure, much less lived there for nearly eleven years.

He poured himself a highball glass of whiskey, dropped into the one chair he'd kept, a remnant from his college days he'd stubbornly refused to part with. He drank steadily for another hour, then made his way to the guest room with the stripped down queen-sized mattress and box spring, Throwing back the last swallow, he fell onto the bed, and descended into a deep, dreamless, abyss of drunken slumber.

Chapter Three

Jackson awoke promptly at six a.m. the next morning. Once he'd showered and shaved, he called Carrie. Her first thought was for him, and it made him smile.

"Hey, Jack, how are you feeling this morning?"

Jackson sipped at his cup of coffee. "I'm okay. How was her night?"

"It was rough. I wish Sam was here with me."

"Will I do? I'll be heading there, shortly."

"Don't you have to make funeral arrangements?"

"Nope, but at some point I'll need to buy a house full of furniture."

Carrie inhaled sharply. "What the hell's going on, Jack?"

"I'll tell you when I get there."

Jackson glanced up at the soft whooshing of elevator doors opening. Carrie stood there, arms crossed, and foot tapping. He ignored her look of impatience and brushed past her to look in on Giselle.

"Well" he said, as they exited the room again, "at least she's not curled up in the fetal position. That's what I'd do."

"She tried. Broken ribs wouldn't allow. Come on, I'll buy you a cup of coffee and some breakfast. You look like crap."

"Well, thanks a heap, Carrie."

"Anytime. When's the last time you ate anything?"

"Breakfast...yesterday."

She harrumphed. "That's what I thought. Let's get you some sustenance."

They stood in the breakfast line at the hospital's cafeteria, sliding their trays along the metal rail. Jackson placed a pastry in his tray. Carrie removed it, placing it back on the shelf.

He reached out for it. "I wanted that."

She slapped at his hand. "You haven't eaten in twenty four hours. You need protein in your system, not this crap. You know better than that."

Jackson opened his mouth to protest until he saw the tell-tale lift of her brow, a sure-fire-dare for him to disobey.

Carrie filled his tray with bacon, eggs, whole wheat toast, and a cup of fresh fruit. She dropped containers of juice and milk in his tray. "We'll need a carafe of coffee at our table," she told the cashier. She passed the woman her debit card.

Jackson grabbed Carrie's card and dropped it in her purse, then handed his card to the cashier.

"Pushy," Carrie said.

"That's funny, coming from you," he snorted.

They emptied their trays onto their table while someone brought the coffee. Carrie poured two cups and pushed one toward Jackson. "Sooo," she drawled. "Why are you buying furniture today instead of making funeral arrangements for your wife?"

He coughed on his sip of juice. "Jesus, you don't beat around the bush, do you?"

She pulled back the lid on a container of creamer. "Answer the question."

He paused several moments after taking another sip of juice then cleared his throat. "Chloe left a letter with our lawyer. She said she didn't want any kind of funeral service, and she wanted to be cremated."

"Oh." She looked over at him with narrowed eyes. "Please tell me you're not going to keep her in an urn on your mantle. That's so damn creepy."

"I don't have a mantle. I thought I'd keep her at the office where you could visit with her every day," he said dryly.

She dropped her fork, and glared at him. "Even with no loss of love between she and I, that is *so* not funny."

He grinned tightly at her. "She wanted them sent to her mother in California."

Carrie's mouth dropped in shock. "To the woman who was sorry for your loss but wouldn't attend her funeral. Really?"

Jackson shrugged. "She did me a favor." He felt his friend's gaze on him. "Long past time one of them did."

"Come on, Jack. I've known you long enough to know when you're holding back from me. This is not about funeral arrangements, is it? What's going on, here?"

He placed his fork on the tray and wiped his mouth with a napkin. He leaned forward, rested his elbows on the table, and met her curious gaze. "It's not about funeral arrangements."

"What else did she say in that letter?"

"She said that she had been on the pill the entire time we'd been together. She never wanted a child. Anyone's child."

"That can't be true. What about the depression when she got her period every month?" Carrie reminded him.

He pushed back in his chair. "You remember that quack doctor that tried to tell me she was putting on an act?" He waited for Carrie's nod. "It seems I owe him an apology."

Her face turned pale. "Are you sure?"

"I'm sure."

"You must be—I—I don't know what to say," she stammered. "I can't even imagine how you must feel. I'm so sorry." She wiped a tear from the corner of her eye.

"Don't cry over her, Carrie, she's not worth it."

"She's not, but you are. All the years you wasted on that spiteful, conniving. . ." She swore then released s deep sigh. "I shouldn't say that. I know you still loved her."

"I put up with her. But love? Not for a long time."

She stared at him for a minute in silence. "Did she say anything else?"

"Nothing that should ever be repeated."

Carrie shook her head in disgust. "I'd give my right arm to go one round with that skinny tramp."

He gave her a sad smile. "Aw, thanks hon, it means a lot that you'd be willing to whip her ass for me."

"It's not fair, Jack. You're a good man, and one day, you'll make a wonderful father."

He shook salt on his eggs. "Aren't you skipping a step?"

Carrie supported her chin on her clasped hands. "I think God has something special planned for you. I really do."

He dropped his fork in his plate and rested his elbows on the table to gaze at her. "I sure as hell hope you're right, Carr. It'd be nice to actually look forward to going home at the end of the day."

She nodded in understanding. "It happened for me after eighteen years. It'll happen for you, too."

He straightened and cleared his throat.

"So, what's the deal with the furniture?"

He told her how he had emptied his house of everything that reminded him of his wife.

"So you purged your home of Chloe."

"You could say that. Now I can buy some decent furniture."

"God, she had horrible taste in furniture, didn't she?"

He nodded, refilling his coffee cup. "So, how's Giselle? Does she hate me any worse today than she did yesterday?"

"She doesn't hate you. Maybe when she sees her girls, it'll be better."

"Do they know?"

"No, and they need to be told. I don't know what to do. I hate to take too much of this on myself when they have a mother, but she's still so out of it," she murmured.

"Do you have a photo of the girls here?"

"No, I have plenty at home. Do you think that would help? I could have Sam bring some over."

Jackson stood up and fished his truck keys out of his pocket. "I'll be back in thirty minutes or so." He ran to catch the elevator before the doors closed.

Giselle turned her head at the sound of a light knock on her door. Awake and subdued for the moment, she faced the wall again when Jackson stepped inside. "I don't want to see anybody," she said.

"I thought you may want to have this with you. Giselle, look at me."

She turned to him, focused on the photo of her girls She reached out with both hands. "My babies!" She pulled the photo close, as silent tears trailed down her bruised cheeks to fall onto the glass covering the photo. She glanced past Jackson to Carrie. "Do they know?"

Carrie sniffed and cleared her throat. "No sweetie. I didn't want to do anything without talking to you first."

"I'll tell them, but I want to do it at home. Do you think the doctor will release me soon?"

Jackson stepped forward. "What's her doctor's name?"

"Dr. Allemande - I saw her in the hall a few minutes ago."

"I'll find her."

Giselle didn't acknowledge Jackson's exit. After several minutes had passed, she turned to Carrie. "Why is Jackson here? Is Chloe in the hospital, too?"

"No, hon. Chloe died in the wreck. He's here because he wants to help."

"I didn't know," Giselle whispered. "We saw them just before the accident, you know."

Jackson re-entered the room and froze at her agonizing admission, afraid to make his presence known. The sound of Giselle's voice, heartbroken and tortured, droned on, as she explained about the malfunctioning light at the Civic Center. He smiled as she told Carrie how he'd let her and Toby cut in front of them in the long queue of traffic.

"You know," he heard her say, "If he hadn't, Toby and I would have missed the accident," Giselle murmured.

Jackson's breath froze as he heard Carrie's distressed comeback.

"Oh, honey, there's no way of knowing that."

"Think about it," he heard Giselle say, her voice lifeless and void of feeling. "Jackson let us out and Toby's dead. This may have happened because of him."

Jackson's heart plummeted to his toes. Miserable and unable to face anyone, he backed silently out of the room, and then caught the elevator to the lobby. He walked outside to his truck and pulled out his cell phone to call Carrie.

"Hey, I wanted to tell you that I found her doctor. She'll be in her room to discuss her release within a few minutes."

"Thanks, but where are you?"

"In my truck. I'm leaving."

"Why didn't you say goodbye?"

He paused for a moment. "I don't think she wants to see me. She really does hate me more today than she did yesterday." He waited through her prolonged pause then sighed. "I heard what she said."

"She didn't mean that."

He wiped roughly at his eyes. "That's not how it sounded."

"Jack—"

"I'll talk to you later." He disconnected, dropped the phone in his pocket.

Jackson sat in his truck, wondering what the hell to do. He felt stranded, with no place he could go. He didn't want to go home, now that he remembered how it echoed with emptiness this morning. He couldn't face it yet, not until there was at least the prospect of having furniture again. He opened his phone and redialed Carrie's number.

"Hey, Jack."

"I need some help."

"Anything," Carrie whispered.

"Where can I buy furniture on a Sunday?" Her quiet chuckle reached him.

"And here I thought you'd be suicidal."

"I would be if I had to go home to that tile covered mausoleum."

"I'm assuming you need a warehouse type that has everything you want in stock."

"Un huh. Preferably with same-day delivery."

"If you're willing to pay, they will."

"I'm willing."

"Are you looking for a particular style of furniture?"

"Hell, I don't know," he growled.

"Just go to that place on Highway 90 down the street from the office. I know they're open on Sundays. They have a huge selection of high quality furniture and dozens of displays set up. Walk around those displays until you find pieces you like. Tell them you want same-day delivery *and* set-up."

"Thanks, Carr, I knew you could help me out."

Jackson drove to the place. He stepped inside, got the immediate attention of a pretty, long-legged brunette.

She sidled up next to him. "Is there something I can help you with today?" she purred.

Jackson ignored the blatant "I'm available" signals the woman projected. He was used to ignoring women, having a wife like Chloe. If he'd shown the slightest bit of interest she'd have had his balls for breakfast, and the recipient either fired or embarrassed beyond belief. Jackson addressed her in a business-like manner. "Do you work on commission?"

She nodded. "Why, yes I do."

"That's good, because I'll be paying in full for a house full of furniture and I need guaranteed delivery *and* set up *today*. I'm willing to pay whatever it cost, since it's Sunday." He faced her fully. "Now, *you* tell *me*. Can you help me, or not?"

She lifted one finger and raised her phone to her ear. "Why don't you start looking around while I secure the delivery men? My name is Brenda and I'll be with you in one minute."

Jackson didn't know a thing about decorating, but he knew what he liked. As a result, he'd taken Carrie's practical approach and checked out each display. If he found one that looked tasteful but comfortable, he delighted Brenda with four simple words. "I'll take it all." *All* had included tables, end tables, lamps, and any accessories used for display purposes. It took one hour and a sizeable amount from his checking account, but he didn't care. Jackson walked out of the furniture warehouse with Brenda's card tucked inside his pocket and a promise for delivery by four p.m. Rather than going home to wait, he drove to his office and worked until nearly four.

By seven o'clock that evening, the deliverymen were gone and Jackson was testing out his new king size bed. It was massive, in rich, dark woods; masculine, without being overbearing, and long enough to fit all 6'4" of him.

He walked into his living room and surveyed his new furniture appreciatively. The sofa was of fine grained, soft as silk, Italian leather, distressed and slightly worn in all the right places, giving it a broken-in appearance. He stretched himself out on it, and again, appreciated the fact that it was long enough to accommodate the entire length of him. He also purchased two matching leather club chairs and an oversized chaise lounge chair, upholstered in a russet textured fabric.

The shopping trip had been worth every penny spent. After a decade of living in this house with Chloe's horrible choices in furnishings, he was finally comfortable in his own home.

He showered and dropped onto his comfy couch to watch some sports. His phone rang, he checked the screen and answered. "Hey Carrie, how is she?"

"Released and home. The doctor came in right after you left. Apparently, you made enough of an impression on her that she rushed to do your bidding. Must be that fantastically fit body of yours and those big blue eyes. I swear she kept looking for you the entire time she was in the room with us."

"Your ass...So how is she?"

"Better now that she's with her girls. You were right, it made all the difference."

"Have they been told?"

"Yes, I got her settled at home then brought the girls to her."

Jackson heard her pause and squeezed his eyes shut. Knowing how Toby felt about his daughters, it must have been horrendous. He didn't press her.

"Those poor babies," she said, sobbing quietly into the phone. "Mackenzie will be seven soon and she understands. Lexie is only four, almost five. I'm not sure if she realizes how...permanent this is."

"Believe me, if she doesn't understand everything right now, she will soon. That's the age I was when I lost both my parents." He rubbed a hand over his face. "Toby's girls..." he murmured. "Man, I'd give anything to have him alive and well." He heard Carrie sniff and pause before she answered.

"I know you would. He thought the world of you, you know. He was always trying to get Giselle to forgive you."

"No chance of that, now, is there?" he said dejectedly.

"I'm going to have a talk with her about that."

"Don't upset her, Carrie. She's been through enough."

"So have you. I won't let her hold that against you."

He sighed and ran his hands through his hair. "God, I'm tired, Carrie."

"Get some sleep, Jackson."

He considered whether or not to let her in on Chloe's secret. Finally he spoke, his voice coming out in a tortured whisper. "She was pregnant, Carrie. Chloe was pregnant. I found a letter from her doctor. And then..." he swallowed the disgust he felt for his dead wife. "She had an appointment for an abortion yesterday in Beaumont."

"I don't understand. If she was on the pill..."

"She took two rounds of antibiotics last month. It must have weakened the effectiveness of the pills," he explained.

"I'm sorry, Jackson. I know how badly you wanted a child."

There was an extended pause before Jackson began to speak again. "The thing is, I thought she was bi-polar all these years...manic depressive...chemically unbalanced...call it what you will, but I thought she couldn't help the way she acted, you know? She was adamant about not taking any medication as long as there was a chance she could get pregnant." He stood and began pacing with the phone.

"This may sound crazy to everyone else, but I thought if she could make that sacrifice for us, I was obligated to stay with her. I kept thinking if we could just have a child, she could get the treatment she needed and be normal." He burst into hysterical laughter. "Now, I find out it was all an act."

"What the hell are you talking about? What act?"

He thought about the letter tucked inside his wallet. "It was all an act, Carrie. She explained it all in her letter."

"I'm not saying I don't believe you, but I'd kinda like to read that letter."

"Maybe one day," he said. "Not now, though. There are things in it that are...too...personal."

"I'm sorry, Jackson. I know you have your reasons, so I won't ask again. I uh..." She took a deep breath. "I called to tell you about the funeral arrangements." She gave him the time and location of the funeral home in Kenton.

"She won't want me there.".

"I think you should be there."

"I don't want to upset her."

"You need to go. She'll hold it against you."

He closed his eyes and sighed. "She may hold it against me if I do." He heard her sigh in frustration. "All right, I'll go."

"I knew you'd see reason. Now get some damn rest."

"Aye aye, Captain," he said, with a snort.

"Don't make me go over there, smart a—"

"—Good night, Carrie." He disconnected and dropped the phone.

Jackson was laid back on his new couch, trying to concentrate on a ball game, when he heard the knock on his door. Suspecting it was his uncle, he rolled his aching body off the couch and limped over to open the door to let him inside. He stood tall, and nodded at Bill. "I knew she wouldn't let up on me that easily." He turned back toward the couch.

"Who?"

"You know who...Carrie." Jackson resumed his seat in front of the ballgame. "She asked you to check up on me, didn't she?"

Bill shrugged and pulled a cold, six-pack of long neck beers from a bag. He held one out to Jackson and put the rest in his fridge.

Jackson twisted the cap open and took a long swig of the ice cold brew. "That's good," he said, wiping his mouth on the back of his hand.

Bill stood staring at the results of Jackson's furniture shopping spree. "Damn, you've been busy, haven't you, Son?"

Jackson nodded, keeping his eyes on the television screen.

"What brought this on?"

"Don't try to act like Carrie hasn't told you all about it. I know her better than that," Jackson huffed.

"All right, I won't. So, you erased all traces of Chloe."

"That was the plan," Jackson said, lifting his beer again.

"Well, I can't say as I blame you. The place looks a lot better than before. I don't know how you lived in this place."

"I didn't. I only existed here, but not anymore."

"It seems like you should be grieving a little," Bill said.

"I am grieving, just not over her. Never again over her."

Bill sat in a club chair and sighed in appreciation. "Nice chair. I know what you overheard at the hospital."

"Never doubted it," Jackson snapped. "Carrie would never pass up an opportunity to discuss me with you."

Bill leaned forward in his chair. "I'm going to say this one time. Carrie cares about you as much as I do, so maybe you could show some appreciation. I raised you better than that."

Jackson sighed and swung his long legs over the edge of the soft leather into a seating position. He stood slowly and faced his uncle. "You did, and I do appreciate both of you. But, I'm hurting as much over losing Toby as a friend as I am about anything else. I keep thinking I'm going to call him and see what he thinks about this, but I can't. It's hard to accept." He grabbed the back of his head with one hand. "And if I'm hurting this bad," he said, his voice hitching, "I just keep thinking how hard it's going to be on Giselle and the girls."

"Are you going to the funeral home tomorrow morning?"

He gave his uncle a look that asked if he was serious. "If I don't, Carrie will send over the National freaking Guard."

Bill chuckled and agreed. "You mind if I go with you?"

Jackson watched him, curiously. "You don't know them."

"I'd like to go as a show of respect. I know how you felt about Toby," Bill replied.

Jackson remained silent, but nodded his head in agreement.

Chapter Four

Giselle made funeral arrangements in a fog of shock. A single thought rolled through her mind like her computer screen's marquee setting—*this can't be happening*. She faced the first morning of the wake, surrounded by a tight circle of friends; Carrie and her three daughters. With their steadfast love and support, she got through her first viewing without falling apart. Her girls joining her proved to be a completely different experience.

Her daughters stared at their daddy—sleeping until he saw them again—wearing curious looks on their faces. Her youngest daughter, in true Lex fashion, spoke first.

"Won't we see daddy awake again?"

Big sister Mackenzie threw her a piece of wisdom. "Not until we see him again in heaven, Lex." She turned to her sister. "It's okay, though. Remember? Mama said we can miss him, but we'll see him again one day. A long, long time from now."

Giselle watched her youngest child's mouth twist in contemplation, waited for the comment that was sure to raise a few eyebrows.

"I don't think I could do that now, Mac." Lexie gave her glossy curls a shake. "Mama says I haven't learned to keep still yet."

Giselle smiled, pulled her daughter close for a one armed hug as a rustle of low snickers passed through the group. "Oh baby girl. I hope you never do."

"Jee-zus! Who is *that*?"

"Which one?"

"Either. *Both*."

A third woman's voice joined the conversation. "Lawd, that's two of the finest looking men I have *ever* seen."

Carrie heard the increasing buzz of interest from several women in the gathering. She turned, knowing instinctively who she'd see. Sure enough, there stood Jackson and Bill Broussard. Jackson looked like a male model, handsome and sexy in his tailored black Ralph Lauren suit, with a dove gray shirt and dark gray silk tie. Bill looked equally handsome in a dark brown western cut suit, also tailored, and wearing a pair of immaculately clean high quality western boots.

Jackson had the slight advantage in height by maybe a half-inch difference. Both men had dark brown hair and blue eyes with straight noses and clean shaven, angular jaws. Both carried themselves well on broad shoulders with lean, muscular torsos, tapering down to narrow hips. At fifty-seven, Bill Broussard was handsome and healthy, foretelling of Jackson's odds of keeping his good looks and health for many years to come. They were the picture of rugged masculinity, resonating in sex appeal and quiet reserve.

She smiled, knowing for a fact that neither of them had the slightest idea how appealing they were to the opposite sex. She walked over and gave Jackson a hug. "I'm glad you're here." Then she turned to his uncle. "Bill, you look absolutely scrumptious," she said, walking into the man's big bear hug. "Honestly, you two boys have every woman in this room drooling."

"Your ass," Jackson murmured. "You look nice, though."

"She sure does," Bill commented, gracing her with a smile. "Where's old Sam? Is he ready to give you up, yet?"

Sam Langley walked up to the trio. He was an inch shorter than Bill, but just as broad shouldered and formidable of a man. He placed a possessive arm around Carrie's waist. "It's not up for discussion, Bill. Go find your own wife, this one's mine."

Carrie laughed and turned in to her husband's embrace. "It's no use, Bill. Sam has me spoiled beyond belief for any other man."

Bill gave Carrie a wink. "If he ever stops, let me know."

The three men shook hands.

"It's good to see you two." Sam gave his throat a gruff clearing. "I wish it were under different circumstances."

Jackson nodded before turning to Carrie. "How'd it go this morning?"

"Our three girls were here with her this morning, and I think that helped. They all had to go to work. They'll be back this afternoon. Are you ready?"

"Shouldn't we find out first if Giselle wants me here?"

Carrie placed a comforting hand on his arm. "Don't worry, she's expecting you."

They walked into the viewing area and stopped near the front. Giselle stood to one side of the casket, speaking with an older couple. They left her and she turned, gave him a weak smile.

Jackson approached her. "Giselle."

Giselle wiped her palms on her dress, seeming unsure of what to tell him. "I'm glad you came, Jackson."

"Are you okay with me being here? I don't want to upset you."

She bit her lower lip and nodded, sending a glance Carrie's direction. "Carrie told me you overheard what I said yesterday. I'm sorry, Jackson. I honestly didn't mean that."

He nodded. "Thank you. How are you, physically, I mean?" He reached out to pull her hair back from her forehead. "You got a good sized gash."

"The head is fine, but my ribs hurts. I'm taped up and the pain killer takes the edge off." She held up a braced right hand. "Guess I won't be going back to work anytime soon."

"Nobody expects you to. Take all the time you need."

"How about you? No broken bones?"

He shrugged it off. "Banged up knee and a few bruises."

Giselle touched his arm. "I'm sorry about Chloe, Jackson. If you told me, I was too out of it to remember."

"Not as sorry as I am about Toby. He was one of the best men I knew, and a damn good friend to me. I know for a fact, how much he loved his girls. All three of his girls."

Giselle blinked several times. For a moment, Carrie thought she'd crack. Instead, she wiped her eyes and smiled.

"Thank you, I appreciate that." She looked over at Bill and smiled. "I know you're his uncle, but you must have been his dad's twin, because y'all look so much alike. I'm Giselle Granger."

Bill shook her hand. "I'm Bill Broussard, ma'am. No, Jackson's dad, Jamison, was two years older. I'm sorry for your loss. Jackson always spoke highly of Toby. How are your girls?"

"I think we're in shock. It's difficult because there's no one but Carrie to help until I'm back to full speed. My girls are trying to be on their best behavior, but they're both so active."

Carrie grinned at the mention of Toby and Giselle's daughters. "If you haven't met them yet, you're both in for a treat. Ah, speaking of which . . ."

Jackson's breath caught at the sight of the two girls running to their mother. Both stunning in their own ways. The photos he'd seen of them didn't do them justice.

Giselle turned them one by one. "Girls, I'd like you to meet some people. This is Mr. Jackson Broussard."

"I remember him, mama," the younger of the two girls said, beaming at Jackson. "He was in that picture on our frij-rator until daddy took it down because you drew on it. He's the tall man that works with you, except . . ." She scrunched up her face. "I thought his name was Satan."

"Lexie!" Giselle whispered harshly, covering the child's mouth with her good hand, while the others attempted to smother their laughter.

Jackson chuckled. "It's okay, Giselle." He squatted low so that he was eye level with the tiny version of her mother, down to the curly brown hair and green eyes specked with gold. "Lexie, it's true that your mom called me that sometimes, but I'm hoping that if I promise to be really nice to her, she won't be mad at me anymore. Maybe if you just call me Jackson, your mom would too." He glanced up at Giselle.

Lexie turned a curious gaze up to her mother. "Mama?"

Giselle nodded sheepishly. "I think that's a great idea."

Lexie nodded, obviously accepting the proposal without question. "You're tall, Jackson. So is he!" She pointed at Bill. "They sure grow 'em big where you come from."

Jackson and Bill chuckled. "That's my Uncle Bill, Lex, but he's been like my dad for a long, long time."

Her small face turned serious. "But why?"

"I lost both of my parents in a car accident when I was the same age you are now." He placed a finger lightly on the tip of her nose. "I was lucky, because I had Uncle Bill."

Lexie's eyes grew large. "You lost your daddy *and* your mama? You must have been really sad. I know how sad I am that I don't have my daddy anymore. But I still have my mama."

Jackson glanced up at Giselle's trembling chin then back down to the adorable little girl. "You know, Lexie, your daddy was a great friend of mine and he always said how much he loved his girls." He placed the tip of his finger over her heart. "But you'll always have him—right here."

"Yeah, that's what mama says, too, but it's just not the same." Something caught the child's attention and as quickly as she appeared, she ran off, her curls bouncing with each step.

Giselle wiped a tear from the corner of her eye. "Jackson, I'm really sorry about that."

He rose slowly, the effort causing him to grimace. "Don't worry about it." *Damn knee.*

She placed her hands on the shoulders of a beautiful, female version of Toby. "This is Mackenzie."

He gazed down at the six year old, with her father's straight black hair and huge brown eyes. "Hello, Mackenzie. It's nice to meet you." He held out his hand and she shook it.

"It's nice to meet you, too, Jackson. Everybody calls me Mac. I knew you weren't Satan. My dad told me you were a good dude."

Jackson beamed. "Well, thanks Mac, that means a lot to me."

Her brown-eyed gaze landed on Bill. "Are you his Uncle?"

Bill nodded, his eyes sparkling with laughter. "I sure am. I'm his Uncle Bill."

Her gaze moved to Jackson, then back to Bill. "You don't look old enough to be his uncle."

His uncle's face broke out in a huge grin. "Well, thanks, little lady. You just made my day. I promise you, I am."

She smiled shyly at the older man before running off to meet her sister.

Jackson could see his uncle was obviously as taken with the girls as he was. "Photos don't do them justice, Giselle. They're beautiful, and you should be proud."

"I am, most of the time. Oh, but Lexie!"

He couldn't conceal the laughter from his tone. "That child is your clone, Giselle. She even has your mannerisms."

Giselle groaned. "I guess so." She glanced at Toby's casket then back at Jackson. "Are you ready?" she asked quietly.

He nodded. "I guess I've put it off long enough."

Jackson walked up to the casket that held the man who'd been as close as any brother for the past year. He only thought he was prepared.

Turned out he wasn't.

Seeing him there. Eyes closed, mouth sealed shut, his hands together and clutching a rosary. Well shit. Nothing could have prepared him for that.

"Oh, man. Oh, Toby." He pulled out his handkerchief and wiped his eyes. Jackson felt a light touch on his arm and turned to gaze down into Giselle's tear-filled eyes. "Giselle, I'm so sorry. He was such a good man."

"I know he treasured the time he spent with you, Jackson." She stared at her husband, her face crumbling on a quiet sob. "I just . . ." She shook her head. "I just can't imagine how to live without him."

Jackson led her to a chair in the corner of the room.

Giselle dabbed at her eyes with a tissue. "We were so happy, Jackson. I feel like God pointed his finger and said 'You! Time's up! It's someone else's turn to be happy.' I know I have my girls, and I'm thankful, but how can I ever be happy again—without him?"

Jackson lowered himself into the chair across from her. He leaned forward. "I know you two had something special, but I believe God will be generous enough to send happiness your way again. In the meantime, you have your friends, and I hope you consider me one of those friends, because I'd like to help. Anything you need done around the house. If you need help with the girls. I mean it, just ask."

"I appreciate the offer, but you have your own problems."

His gaze landed on the flower arrangement nearest to them. He could just make out the card—realized it was from his and Giselle's place of employment. He found himself wondering how he'd spend his evenings now that he didn't have to dread going home to Chloe. It seemed Giselle wasn't the only one who had to learn how to live again. "What I have now is a lot of free time on my hands."

She twisted the tissue in her hands. "I know Chloe was demanding. She seemed . . . you seemed . . . you didn't seem happy."

Jackson used one finger to trace the floral pattern on the chair's overstuffed arm. "I was miserable with her. The fact is, I'm just finding out how disturbed she was." He cleared his throat. "It's a long story, and we don't need to talk about it here." He stood and helped her to her feet. "People are starting to come in now."

Giselle scanned the room. "I don't see my girls. I hope they're not up to anything."

"I'll find them and try to keep them out of trouble for you."

"Thanks, I'd appreciate that," she said, turning to greet a group of visitors.

Sam and Carrie approached. "Thanks for talking her through that one, Jack. I'll be a basket case before this is over."

"Yeah, well thank you, too. I don't mind telling you, I was dreading the initial face to face with her."

"All I did was tell her you'd overheard her comment. By then she'd already concluded you weren't to blame."

"That's good to know." He searched the room, looking for Mac and Lexie. "I told her I'd keep an eye on her girls."

Sam leaned toward him. "They're in the kitchen with Bill. The bakery just delivered donuts."

Jackson made his way to the kitchen. As he got closer, he could hear the giggles of two little girls. He entered, spotted his Uncle Bill sitting at one of the tables with Giselle's daughters. Mackenzie was telling him about the latest teen diva, while Lexie ate jelly donuts. Jackson walked over and poured himself a cup of coffee before joining the other three occupants at the table.

Lexie graced him with a cheesy grin, her face covered in what he suspected was raspberry filling. "Hello Jackson!"

He couldn't keep from laughing. "Hello Lexie." He dampened a napkin at the sink. Lifting her chin, he gently wiped her face free of all traces of pastry. The sweet smell of glaze and raspberries, mixed with the scent of little girl, was something completely new to him. "I can't let your mama see you like this, Lex. She'll think I'm not doing my job and fire me."

Mac looked up at him, wide-eyed. "Mama gave you a job? Is she your boss now?"

Jackson grinned. "I told her I'd find you two and keep you out of trouble."

"Huh!" Mackenzie snorted. "Good luck trying to keep Lex out of trouble. Daddy says she's a trouble magnet." She frowned before continuing. "Daddy said a lot of things that made me laugh, and he made mom really happy. She said so all the time, and that she thanked God for him. Maybe God will send her someone else so she can be happy again."

Lexie turned innocent eyes on the older man. "What about you, Bill? You seem nice and you said you don't have a wife."

From the look on his uncle's face, the comment took him by surprise.

"Uh—I think I'm a little too old for her. Most men my age have children the same age as your mama. She may need someone a little younger."

Lexie suddenly turned toward Jackson. "How about you? Do you have a wife? I didn't see you with one."

"No. Not anymore."

"Lex, shhh!" Mackenzie hissed. "Don't you remember what Carrie said? His wife died in the same accident as daddy."

Lexie's brown furrowed adorably.

"If you lost her, why aren't you out looking for her? I lost my Barbie's horse once and didn't find it for two whole days." She shook her head. "But I never stopped looking."

Jackson bit his lower lip to keep from laughing as Mac slapped her hand over her own forehead.

"No! She's not lost. She's like daddy."

"Oh. She's sleepin', too. Sorry, Jackson."

He wiped his mouth and attempted to look somber. "That's okay, Lex."

"Were you and your wife as happy as mama and daddy were?"

Jackson shifted uneasily in his chair. "No, not really, Lex."

Mac locked her gaze on him, for a moment looking so much like Toby. "Why not?"

Lexie answered her sister's question. "Because she was a piece of work, wasn't she? I heard Daddy say that once. He said it just like that, too. "Jackson's wife is a piece of work." What does that mean?"

Jackson smothered more laughter. "It's, uh—it's kind of hard to explain."

Lexie's green eyes pinned him. "Was she mean?"

"Yes," Bill answered for his nephew.

"Uncle Bill, that's not necessary."

Mackenzie lifted her eyes to Bill, somehow realizing he was the one to ask. "Was she just mean to Jackson, or to everyone?"

"To everyone," Bill answered. "But she really liked to upset Jackson."

"Uncle Bill," Jackson admonished.

Lexie slapped both her hands on the table. "Well, I like you, Jackson. I'm glad she's not around to be mean to everbody and upset you anymore."

Mac threw her head back, rolled her eyes in exasperation. "Lexie! You shouldn't say things like that. Mom would be *upset* with *you* if she heard you."

Lexi seemed to weigh her sister's words. "No, she'd prolly be mor...mort...morti...What's that word she uses sometimes when I say things like that?"

The older child's brow furrowed in concentration. "I think it's mortified, or something like that."

Jackson choked on his sip of coffee, while Bill covered his mouth to keep from laughing.

Giselle chose that moment to enter the kitchen. "Come on, girls," she said. "There are some co-workers of daddy's who would like to meet you both. You want to come with me now?"

The girls nodded and climbed down from their chairs.

"Lex, have you been in those jelly donuts?" Giselle examined her daughter's face and hands.

"I'm clean, Mama. Jackson washed my face just like daddy does."

Surprised by Lexie's comment, Jackson met Giselle's equally shocked gaze.

Lexie's gaze moved from Giselle to Jackson and back to her mother. "Did I mortify you again, Mama?"

Giselle shook her head as Jackson and Bill worked hard to conceal their grins. "What am I going to do with you, Lex?" She herded the girls out the door, casting a glance back at Jackson. "I can only imagine what you four have been talking about in here."

Still chuckling over Lexie's comment, Jackson and Bill left the kitchen just as four young women entered the building through the front door. "That's Sam and Carrie's three girls and their daughter in law. Have you ever met them, Uncle Bill?"

"No, but I'd like to. Which ones belong to who?"

"That dark haired one is Sam's daughter, Amanda. Those two are Carrie's twins, Gretchen and Lauren. The tall one is Trina, their daughter in law. She's married to Nick, Sam's son." Amanda turned at their approach.

"Hey Jackson, we didn't expect to see you here. We're all so sorry to hear about Chloe." The other three added their condolences.

"Thanks ladies, I appreciate that. It's been awhile. This is my Uncle, Bill Broussard."

"Mr. Bill, didn't I hear Carrie say you recently retired?" Amanda asked.

Bill nodded. "Somewhat. I was part owner of a small oil drilling company, but I sold most of my shares and bought myself a small ranch and some livestock. Now I mostly ride horses and work cattle."

They all turned at Carrie and Sam's approach.

"Is Giselle still here, Mom?" Gretchen asked.

Carrie nodded. "She doesn't want to leave, but she needs to eat something so she can take her pain medication. I can tell she's hurting."

Jackson had suffered through a couple of cracked ribs before. He still remembered how bad it got if he didn't keep the meds rolling on schedule. He left the group to find Giselle. He caught her grabbing her side, wincing, as she walked away from a couple. He hurried over, offering his arm for support. "You need to eat something now, so you can take your pain meds."

She shook her head and placed a hand over her stomach. "Honestly, Jackson, I'm not hungry."

"Suit yourself, but if you take that pain medication without food, you'll be sorry. And if it wears off completely, you'll be miserable."

He led her past the others and straight into the kitchen area where he seated her, fixed her a plate of sandwiches, and pushed a bottle of water into her hand.

Jackson pushed the plate to Giselle. "Now eat."

She made a face. "I'm uncomfortable eating alone."

He placed four sandwich halves into a plate and grabbed another bottle of water, before sitting across from her.

Giselle smiled shyly at him as she nibbled at her sandwich. "What were you four discussing in here earlier?"

He cracked open his water and shook his head, unable to hide his grin. "Your girls are something else. That Lexie."

"You don't have to tell me. You cannot imagine some of the things that come out of that child's mouth."

He related the conversation as Giselle took her turn laughing and hiding her face in embarrassment.

She shook her head. "Lex should know that word *mortify* by now. God knows she hears me say it enough." She lifted her hand and let it fall. "Honestly Jackson, sometimes Toby and I would just look for a place to hide."

Jackson finished off his bottle of water. "At least she's a child. There's always hope she'll outgrow it. Besides, there's a difference between a child's adorable honesty and—well, a grown-up just being a pain in the ass. Believe me, I've lived through my share of mortifying moments." He stood to place his empty plate and water bottle in the trash receptacle. "And there was no hiding from Chloe," he added.

"Carrie said she left a letter leaving instructions for her arrangements."

He nodded. "An extremely informative little note, but there again, you don't need to hear about that."

"I'd like to, if you don't mind telling me. It would keep me from thinking about all this." She waved her hand.

He cleared his throat. "There was one thing that stood out. Her entire Bi-polar, depression because she couldn't get pregnant thing was an act. She was on birth control the entire time. Didn't want kids. Only did that to guilt me into sticking around. But . . ." he paused, considered not telling her the worst of it. He decided he didn't have damn thing to lose or gain at this point by telling her. "Something went awry with her plans, because she was pregnant when she died." He lifted his hand as Giselle gasped. "But had she lived, she had an abortion scheduled that very afternoon in Beaumont." He shook his head, still unable to fathom how someone could be so vile. "That's why she was so impatient when we left the coliseum the day of the accident. I stopped to let people out at the light and she was furious with me. Because she still had to make the drive to Beaumont."

"Let's go," Giselle murmured.

"Excuse me?"

"Toby and I saw her turn to you and say 'Let's Go'. It looked like she was screaming."

Jackson snorted. "See what I mean? Couldn't hide from Chloe. Not. Ever."

"Was it always that bad?"

"The mood swings and temper-tantrums started after the first year. I've discovered recently that she'd slept around since day one, even at our wedding with the 'not so' best man."

"Good Lord, Jackson. What kind of friends did you have?"

"He wasn't my friend. Wasn't supposed to be my best man. But, that's another long story. Maybe I'll tell you about it someday. Anyway, Chloe's gone, and I can't get myself to grieve for her. I think she did me a favor. I don't have to go through this hell."

"You've already been through your hell, Jackson."

"Maybe," he shrugged. "Those pain killers working yet?"

"Yeah, I think so." She took a deep breath. "I can breathe now. I need to find my girls and make sure they eat some lunch, if they're not too full on jelly donuts."

Oh, give 'em a break today, Mom." He helped her stand.

"I don't know, if I give them an inch . . ."

The two of them walked to the front. Jackson, limping because his knee had stiffened while he sat. Giselle, with one arm clenched up to her side and the other clutching Jackson's arm. She passed the first row of chairs where Carrie and her girls sat, gripped one side of Toby's casket.

"Hey, Baby," she whispered.

Jackson turned away, leaving her to speak her mind to her dead husband. No doubt whispering words of endearment even as she wondered how to go on without him.

Again, he couldn't help thinking that if he had the chance to speak his mind to Chloe, it'd be on an entirely different level.

Chapter Five

The morning of Toby's funeral, Giselle woke to the sound of rolling thunder and a steady downpour of rain. The sound of overflowing gutters and rain hitting the window panes called to mind memories of the previous Friday morning. She and Toby had awakened to identical weather on what would turn out to be their last workday morning together. She'd rolled over, snuggled against her husband's chest.

Toby had pulled her close with one arm and buried his face in her hair. "Mmmm, babe. What do you say to staying home to play hooky?" he had murmured, pulling her closer. "I don't have anything pressing. Do you? We could send the girls off to school and spend the rest of the day making love."

Torturing herself further, she recalled the entire conversation—the pitiful excuse she'd used to turn her husband down.

"I can't babe. We have that deadline and Carrie and Jackson both worked late last night so I could go to the girls' dance recital. I can't leave Carrie to deal with 'Satan' all alone."

He'd groaned. "Carrie doesn't think he's Satan. You're the only one who does. Don't you think it's time to drop that ridiculous grudge you have against him? Jackson's an okay guy once you get to know him," Toby had insisted.

"He's a grumpy ass, even if he is the best engineer we have in our department," she'd countered. "He's only grumpy because of that bat shit crazy, she-bitch wife of his."

While Toby never missed an opportunity to defend his friend, *she* pressed her case. "Chloe's depressed, like I'd be if I had to live with that man."

"To forgive is divine, Babe. Maybe it's time you try some of that."

"I will, just as soon as he apologizes to me."

She could still see the look on his face as she slipped out of bed to get ready for her workday. He'd put one arm behind his head to watch her dress and grinned as she stuck her tongue out at him.

"You're sexiest when you're being stubborn, you know that? Come back to bed, Giselle."

"I can't sweetie. But it's Friday. Save that thought for tomorrow night. The girls will be at Carrie and Sam's for the night and we can do whatever we want once we leave the charity function."

Giselle threw her arm over her eyes and suppressed a sob. She'd blown the last chance to make love to her husband. Toby hadn't seen tomorrow night.

But she had, though she barely remembered it. Her doctor-prescribed, drug-induced, state of semi-consciousness had subdued her screams and hysterical sobs. Even then, it hadn't stopped the soul-crushing ache of loss that had been her constant companion since that earth shattering moment. The moment she'd heard her husband was gone.

Giselle wiped her eyes, thinking regrets were all she had left. Regret she hadn't made more time for Toby; regret for how she'd treated Jackson; regret that she'd never again be able to look into the gorgeous brown eyes of her husband. She never imagined it was possible to act so normal while feeling so completely lost inside.

Dear God, please give me the strength to get through this day. Please let me be strong for my daughters. Please send the help we need to get through this.

Then I can fall apart.

Giselle sniffed loudly, then attempted the most difficult and painful physical act she'd gone through since the accident; getting out of bed after sleeping through the night without a painkiller. She tried to sit up, but was in so much pain she broke out in a cold sweat.

She rolled out of bed. The action produced a wave of nausea so severe she had to sit until it passed. She finally maneuvered herself out of the door toward the end of the hallway, leaning against the wall for support while taking shallow breaths. Her daughters sat at the breakfast table eating—chattering with Sam, Jackson, and Bill.

She finally managed to gasp a single word. "Help."

Jackson shot out of his chair to reach her before she collapsed.

"Sam, get her pain killers, two of them, and a glass of milk." He helped her to sit.

Lexie's voice rose in panic. "What's wrong with mama?"

Jackson spoke, his tone calm and soothing. "It's okay, sweetie. Your mom just slept through the night and doesn't have any pain medication left in her system. Here, Giselle, take them with milk and when you feel like you can eat something, let me know."

Giselle chased the two pills with a swallow of milk. She held on to the glass with shaking hands, and leaned to one side as she fought a wave of dizziness.

"Whoa, where do you think you're going?" Jackson took the glass and sat beside her to support her.

"I guess-I need-to set my alarm-to take a dose during the night." Her breath came in shallow pants.

"That may be a good idea for the next week or so. Try to drink the rest of this." He pushed the glass of milk at her.

She pushed it away. "Don't want it."

Jackson faced off her irritated gaze with a look of warning. "Pain killers on an empty stomach? Ever had dry heaves with a broken rib, Giselle?"

Giselle thought about it, hating to admit he was right. Reluctantly, she downed the rest of the milk then stared at the men. "What's-going on?"

"I took Carrie's place this morning," Sam explained. "Then Jackson and Bill showed up with breakfast."

She checked out the spread, glanced at Jackson. "You brought- breakfast?"

"I stopped off at Shoney's and got an assortment from the breakfast buffet: scrambled eggs, sausage, bacon, grits, hash browns, mushrooms in butter sauce. What'll it be, madam?"

"A little of-everything. Don't want-dry heaves."

Jackson prepared a plate of food and sat it before her.

"You forgot to tell her about the pancakes with strawberry sauce and whipped cream. They're awesome, Mom," Mackenzie added.

Giselle frowned. "You holding-out on me?"

"I didn't know if you could handle anything sweet."

She thought again of dry heaving and shuddered. "Right." Giselle looked at Lexie's face, covered in strawberry sauce and whipped cream. "Lex. Did you-get any inside-your mouth?"

Bill chuckled. "Don't worry, she's eaten plenty."

Jackson leaned forward to address her. "Do you want coffee or juice?"

No contest. "Coffee."

He brought it to her. "Now eat."

She pointed her fork at him. "You're not-the boss-of me here," she gasped. "What time is it?" She attempted to bring a small bite of scrambled egg to her mouth, only to have it fall off the fork she had gripped in her trembling hand.

"A little before seven." Jackson commandeered the fork to bring a bite of egg up to her mouth. She glared at him, mouth closed tightly. She relented after his better than average imitation of dry heaving.

"Looks like-you're no stranger-to dry heaves," she gasped, accepting another forkful of food.

He shrugged. "I went to college."

She nodded and concentrated on eating as the meds began to kick in. After several minutes the hitch in her side eased enough to speak a full sentence

"Why are you two up so early?" she asked her daughters.

"I got up to pee."

"Lex. It's use the bathroom," Giselle corrected.

Lexie gave a drama queen sigh. "I got up to 'use the bathroom' and I heard them all talking. I was so happy to see Jackson, I stayed up and told Mac that Bill was here. Jackson's my favorite, but Bill is hers."

Giselle barely suppressed a snort as she glanced at the two men.

Jackson shrugged. "We can't help it if we're irresistible to women."

She scowled. "Not all women."

"To the only two who count," Bill added.

"I could get used to being somebody's favorite." Jackson hugged Lexie.

Giselle remembered her prayer asking God to send them help. Maybe these two men were the answer for her girls. Nobody could ease her pain over losing Toby, but if her children didn't suffer, she could bear it easier.

Thank you, God. I owe you one.

As soon as the thought formed, the pills seemed to take effect, and the pain eased off immediately. She took her first deep breath since waking this morning.

I guess I owe you two.

Jackson leaned close and spoke in a low whisper. "Percocet kicked in?"

She nodded. "Does it show?"

"Significantly. Think you can feed yourself now?"

"Yes, thank you." She sat a little straighter and finished her breakfast as her daughters shamelessly manipulated the three men at the tale. Giselle shook her head when Lexie went to give Jackson a kiss and burped, most unladylike, in his face, making him jerk back with surprised laughter.

"Whoa! That's a first," he said.

Lexie giggled through an apology. "Sorry Jackson, that was on a asscident."

"Not a problem, Lex." He laughed and accepted a kiss from her anyway. When Lexie attempted to climb up on his knee, Jackson swung her easily onto his lap.

"She'll get strawberry sauce all over your nice suite," Giselle said. "She makes Toby late all the time . . ." She froze, as the reality of no more Toby hit her full force. "I mean, she made him late. He'd have to change his shirt—" She paused, having to swallow the lump in her throat to finish. "Before he could leave the house in the mornings," she finished in a whisper, wiping a tear from the corner of her eye. "Excuse me, I have to get ready."

Sam reached for his cell phone. "Do you need me to call Carrie?"

"No, I'll be fine. Could someone clean Lexie up, please?"

"I got that," Jackson said, getting up to wet a paper towel and beginning to wipe the child down. "Between the three of us, we could probably get the girls ready for you and give you and Carrie a break. I can't do their hair, though."

"Mac can do her own hair, and I'll tend to Lexie's."

"Mom, can you braid my hair today?" Mac asked, running up to her mother. "Daddy liked it in one long braid, and I want to look nice for daddy."

"Sure baby, when I'm done." Giselle gently smoothed the child's bangs back away from her forehead. She suddenly pulled her daughter's head close to her own body and hugged her tightly. "Daddy will like that." She placed a kiss firmly on the top of the dark silky head that was so much like Toby's. The action made her remember that she would never again feel Toby's hair against her lips, and it brought tears to her eyes. She wiped at them hastily, and released her daughter before turning toward the hallway. "I'll lay their clothes out for you."

"I wish mama wasn't so sad."

"I know, Lex. She'll be sad for a while, but it won't last forever," Jackson said, capturing one of her silky ringlets between his fingertips.

"Maybe God will send her someone else to make her happy."

"Maybe so." He carried her to the sink.

"I don't think I'll like not having a daddy. You think he could send her someone who could be a good daddy for us?"

Jackson wet another paper towel and gave Lexie's face a second cleaning. Considering the sticky level, she may even need a third. "Maybe he will one day, Lex, but you can't rush something like that. You and Mac and your mom—you all loved your daddy a whole lot. It would be hard for someone to step in and take his place."

She lifted her pixie face, stared at him with huge green eyes. "What about you, Jackson?"

He tackled a missed spot of sauce under her chin. "What about me?"

"You already hug and smell like a daddy. Could you take his place?"

Jackson's hand froze in midair. "I do?"

She nodded enthusiastically, sending her ringlets bouncing.

He lowered his hand, completely aware that this conversation had garnered Sam and Bill's undivided attention. "I'm kind of curious, Lex. How do daddies hug and smell?"

Her little forehead scrunched up in concentration. "My daddy always smelled good and so do you, but in a different way. And when daddy hugged me, I felt all warm and comfable. That's how *you* make me feel." Her eyes widened as she stared up at him. "Did I 'splain it good enough, Jackson?"

Jackson blinked quickly then cleared his throat. "Yeah, Lex, you explained it fine." He kissed her lightly on the forehead. "I believe that's the nicest thing anyone has ever said to me."

The group entered the funeral home, shaking the water from umbrellas and shedding raincoats. Toby's girls were dressed in their finery, and hoped he approved from wherever he watched.

A somber Giselle dreaded the inevitable. She would never again run her fingers through the black silkiness of Toby's hair, or gaze into the mesmerizing sexiness of his beautiful, brown eyes. Her daughters seemed to sense her distress, and abandoned their 'favorite' men to remain by her side for the service.

All too soon, it ended, and the occupants of the funeral home vacated the viewing room, leaving only family members behind.

Giselle faced the final moment with her daughters pressed closely to her side.

God give me the strength to do this.

She stood for her final viewing of the only man she'd ever loved. She stared at the face she adored. "Hey baby, I guess it's time to give you up now." Her chin trembled. Her entire body shook with the effort to control her emotions. She reached inside the casket. Touched his hair one last time. Leaned in to place a gentle kiss upon his unresponsive mouth. She patted his chest, straightened his tie, and touched each button on his shirt, anything to avoid leaving him. Her quiet sobbing grew in intensity as the pain of losing him became the harshest and cruelest of realities. She leaned over his casket to rest her face on his chest for the last time; the pain in her side nothing compared to the agony of her heart shattering.

Carrie and her daughters joined forces to support Giselle through the traumatizing transition of letting go. At some point her daughters had abandoned her for the comfort of Jackson and his uncle. Once she'd gained control of her emotions, Jackson lowered Lexie to the floor and she and Mac rushed to her side again.

They somberly left the room to wait outside while the six pallbearers prepared to carry Toby to his final resting place. The five male members of Carrie's family had known him for nearly seven years and thought of him as an older brother, or a son, in Sam's case. The sixth was Toby's co-worker and close friend, Gordon.

By the end of the church service, the weather had grown less ominous. The rain diminished to a light drizzle by the time they arrived at the graveyard. People left their vehicles and began the walk to the tent, the snaps and pops of opening umbrellas punctuated the otherwise somber silence. The graveside service was a heartwarming tribute given by Father Mitch, the local priest, another friend of Toby's. By his conclusion, the rain had stopped, the skies cleared.

"You see?" Father Mitch said, pointing to the sky. "Toby doesn't want his girls to get wet." The comment actually brought a smile to Giselle's face. It was just the thing needed to lighten everyone's mood. Giselle hugged Father Mitch, and thanked him for the beautiful words that she knew had been difficult for him to say without breaking down.

Giselle stood next to the casket, both hands splayed over the glossy mahogany, her head lowered, and filled with the scent of the gorgeous spray Carrie and her family had donated. She finally straightened, and plucked three roses for herself and her girls before pulling away from the casket. As soon as she stepped from under the covering, several shafts of sunlight broke through the clouds like spears through tufts of cotton.

Mackenzie pulled on her mother's hand as she pointed upward. "Mom, look at that!"

Everyone turned and gasped at a perfectly defined rainbow on the horizon.

Lexie's little voice squealed in delight. "Did Daddy send it for us, Mama?"

"I bet he did, baby. I bet he asked God to send us that rainbow so that we wouldn't be so sad. He's still taking care of us, isn't he?"

"That's just like daddy to do that for us," Mac said.

"Yep, it sure is," Lexie agreed. "Mama, can we go home now? I heard Carrie tell Bill that some daughters have brought a lot of food to our house, and I'm getting hungry."

Jackson heard the comment and laughed.

Giselle grinned at her daughter. "She's probably talking about The Catholic Daughters, some nice ladies from our church."

"Oh." Lexie spun around. "Jackson, are you and Bill coming to our house to eat some food the Calflick Daughters brought?"

"We don't want to impose," he said, when Giselle faced him.

"You're not imposing. The girls would be upset if you and Bill weren't there." She put her hand to her side and winced.

Jackson walked quickly over to support her. "Do you have your pain pills with you?"

"No, I forgot them at home, and it's time, too."

"Let's get you home then." He helped her into the limo and loaded the girls inside for her so they could leave.

The atmosphere inside Giselle's home was light-hearted, largely due to her youngest daughter. Once Lexie realized she had a captive audience, she kept everyone laughing with the antics and 'Lexi-isms' she was famous for.

"Mama, did you know that Bill has a ranch, and he has horses, and cows, and even some little piggy goats that don't grow very big at all."

"I think he may have Pygmy goats," Giselle corrected.

"I guess so. Anyway, he also has a big pond on his ranch where we could go fishing. He wants to cook us all a barbeque when your ribs don't hurt you anymore. He said our whole family could go—Carrie's and Sam's, and our school friends, too. Can we go, Mama?"

"Maybe by the time school ends I'll be feeling better and we could plan a day like that."

"Can't we plan it now, Mama?" she pleaded.

"Lex, you're putting poor Bill on the spot."

Bill stepped forward, lowered himself into the chair beside her. "It was my idea. As a matter of fact, Mac told me she and Lex both have birthdays coming up in July. One's on a Friday and the other is the next Tuesday. How about planning a joint party for them on the Sunday? I'd love it if you'd say yes, Giselle. It would give this old man something to look forward to."

She gazed into kind blue eyes, feeling a distinct connection to this generous man. Maybe it was because he and Jackson were as alone as she and Toby had been since the deaths of their adoptive parents. For whatever reason, her girls had bonded with these two men.

She nodded. "All right." Mackenzie brought the kitchen calendar to her so she could mark the date. Her two girls jumped around excitedly, telling anyone who would listen about their upcoming birthday party.

Jackson looked up from a conversation with Bill and Sam as Carrie joined them on the patio. "How's she doing?"

"I just got all three of them tucked in for an afternoon nap. I thought you two went home an hour ago."

He shook his head. "We've been discussing maintenance issues for this place. I told Sam that if the rain stops, I'll come over on Saturday to do her yard work. He's been showing me some things that I can take care of for her. She's got some branches on those trees that need some trimming."

She glanced in the direction he'd pointed and nodded. "I'm sure she'd appreciate that. You know, I've been thinking how rough it'll be on those girls not to have their dad around for ball games. He's gone to every tee-ball game since Mac's been in it. This is Lexie's first year, and I know Toby looked forward to watching her."

Jackson rubbed his hand over his jaw. "You think Giselle would mind if I made some of their games?"

"I'd like to make some, as well," Bill added.

"I don't see why not," she said.

"The girls would love it," Sam added. "You know, I always thought it was odd that Toby didn't play baseball, as much as he loved other sports. I guess you knew he was a star running back for L.S.U. How about you, Jackson? You look athletic. You ever play baseball?"

Jackson shrugged. "I played some."

Bill chuckled. "Jackson pl—"

"So when does ball season start around here?" Jackson shot his uncle a look of warning.

"It starts the end of March, about a month away. Opening day's a big deal here," Sam added. "Think you guys can make it?"

Jackson nodded. "We'll be there." He looked at his uncle. "You ready to head out?"

"Let's go."

They said their goodbyes and settled into Jackson's truck for the drive home.

Bill buckled his seatbelt and turned to his nephew. "I played some? What the hell was that all about?"

"It was high school and a little bit of college."

"A little bit of college?" Bill asked incredulously. "You had scouts for the major leagues watching you."

"Keep it to yourself, Uncle Bill. Nobody wants to hear about any of that, or why it didn't happen." He shifted uncomfortably under uncle's gaze.

"What could it hurt, Jackson? It's not like you've tooted your own damn horn about it all these years. And that bitch, Chloe, isn't around anymore to kick you down about throwing your shoulder out before you hit the big time."

His jaw clenched involuntarily at the mention of *her*. "Don't say her name around me. That part of my life is over with, and so is baseball."

Bill lowered his sunglasses to look down his nose at his nephew. "You know, this system of yours—of not dealing with things—not wanting to talk about it to anyone. Well, hell, boy. That can't be healthy."

"Healthy or not, it's how I deal."

"I'm just saying, maybe it'd do you some good to vent a little about all the crap you've put up with over the years."

"Vent? It's not like you don't already know what a cold-hearted bitch she was."

"I don't know. Maybe you and Giselle could vent to each other. Kind of a mutual commiseration thing. A group therapy for just the two of you."

Jackson glanced at his uncle, wondering if he'd lost his mind.

"Maybe let her read that letter your lawyer brought over. You know, the one you won't show anybody? There's bound to be something eye opening in that thing. Something that'll set you free from all that pent up hatred."

He hit the brakes at the four-way stop and gave his head an emphatic shake. "Trust me, Uncle Bill. That's one thing that will *never* happen."

Chapter Six

The rest of the week rolled by in a succession of cold, drizzly, bleak days. Every morning, Giselle woke early to the sound of deep rolling thunder and rain pounding on the roof of her home. Every morning, she thought of Toby then rolled over and reached for the Percocet. She swallowed a pill with the glass of milk Carrie placed on her nightstand then went back to sleep for another two hours.

Jackson called Carrie every morning that first week, asking how things were going. As of yet, her reports to him all sounded exactly the same. The girls were fine, although they missed their dad terribly, but Giselle was not so good.

On Friday morning, the rain finally stopped, allowing the sun to break free in a brilliant display. Carrie got the girls off to school then went home to do a few things while Giselle slept. As she pulled up into her empty parking spot beside Sam's truck, he came out to meet her.

"Hey Sugar," she said, thrilled at the sight of her husband.

Sam pulled his wife into his arms. "I miss you, Babe. Going to bed without you brings back awful memories."

"I know, babe. Maybe by Monday she'll feel well enough so that I can come home at night. Right now there's no way she can handle the girls. I'd tell you to come meet me, but I'm sleeping on the sofa because the mattress in the master bedroom is so bad."

"Giselle's still camped out in the guest room?"

Carrie nodded. "I was hoping she'd have tackled that by now."

"She may need a little more time, hon. That house is so full of the feel of Toby. That's got to be difficult for her to live with."

"It's learning to live without it that's difficult for her." Carrie took her husband's hand and walked inside.

By the last week in March, Giselle was better physically, but, according to Carrie, still wallowing in depression. Carrie and her girls visited often and tried to get her to come out of the house, but she wouldn't budge. Carrie had confided in Jackson that the melancholy atmosphere of their home began to take a tremendous toll on Mackenzie and Lexie.

Jackson and Sam took turns doing Giselle's yard work the first few weekends, but with the approach of ball season, Sam was busy getting the park's baseball fields ready for play. As a result, Jackson had spent the last two Saturdays working in Giselle's yard.

Mac and Lexie, drawn to anyone who paid them attention, usually spent the day helping him out in the yard. Jackson's heart ached for the little girls he'd grown so fond of. He knew they missed the life they had before their father died, and he tried to compensate wherever he could.

The day before Kenton's opening day of the summer league season, Carrie walked into Jackson's office and plopped down in a chair across from his desk. She kicked off one heel and leaned over to rub her foot, before catching his curious gaze. "Are you and Bill still interested in making Mac and Lexie's ballgames?"

He stacked the set of plans he'd been studying on top of another set. "Absolutely. Tomorrow is opening day, isn't it?" At Carrie's nod he continued. "You don't think Giselle will mind, do you?"

She slipped her shoe back on and stood up. "I can't imagine why, but I guess it wouldn't hurt to call her."

"I've got a conference call scheduled in a few, but I'll do it as soon as I get a chance."

The chance didn't come until nearly noon. He waited nervously for her to answer and took a deep breath.

"Giselle, its Jackson. How are you?"

"I'm okay."

"I know your girls have games tomorrow for opening day. Would it be okay if Bill and I go to watch them?"

"Oh." She paused briefly. "I'd forgotten about opening day. I don't know. I guess so. I don't think I can handle that right now, Jackson."

"Bill and I will take care of them for you, Giselle."

"Everyone's already doing so much for us around here, I feel like such a burden."

"You're the only one that thinks that."

"I just . . . I just wish things could be like they were," she said, barely above a whisper.

Jackson was quiet for a moment as he ran a hand through his hair. "Believe me, we all wish the same thing," he murmured, before clearing his throat. "If it's dry enough on Sunday, I'll mow your lawn."

"You don't have to keep doing that; I can hire someone."

He stood up and walked nervously to the window of his office to look outside. "Look, I've got all this free time on my hands, remember?" He listened as she released a long sigh before speaking again.

"That's fine, I don't care."

The connection ended suddenly. Jackson stared at the dead phone in his hand, shocked at the magnitude of zombie-like waves of despair transmitted through her tone. As it happened, his wife's varied performances over the years were nothing compared to the genuine article.

At the end of his workday, Jackson drove to his gym. His membership had been a birthday gift from Chloe, whose gifts to him always contained a not so hidden barb. This one had come with the snide comment, "Love handles on men your age are never attractive, Darling." Even though he hadn't the slightest hint of love handles, he'd tried to work out twice a week, despite Chloe's demands and tantrums. Now that he had free time on his hands, he was able to go every day or night of the week that work didn't demand his attention. He didn't see any difference in the way he looked yet, but he felt remarkably better at the physical activity.

With the dawn of Saturday morning came the promise of a beautiful day. Jackson and Bill entered the ballpark at a quarter to eight, amazed at the multitude of people already there.

"Damn!" Bill said. "Kenton's serious about their summer league. Look at this crowd."

"Sam said that everyone shows up for opening ceremony but it thins out as the games begin. Mac and Lex each have two games to play today, but I'm not sure about the times." Jackson stared at the groups of kids running around in uniforms. "I can't pick anyone out. They all look alike to me."

Bill laughed. "That's why I'm looking for Sam. That big boy will stand out in a crowd, no matter what he's wearing." He pointed. "There he is at the concession stand."

Sam looked up as Jackson called his name. "Hey, I'm glad you two could make it," he said, exchanging handshakes.

"Mac and Lex wouldn't have let us live it down if we hadn't. Did Giselle come?"

Sam shook his head while opening a case of chips for the workers. "No, she wasn't feeling up to it. Carrie said she'd be checking up on her all day in between catching up with some things that she had to do at the house. The girls are here already. They'll be excited to see you two."

Jackson gazed into the throng of people. "Where the hell do we look?"

Sam pointed to a spot in the stands and they walked in that direction. Within seconds, Jackson heard his name being called as Mackenzie, Lexie, and four other children ran up to him.

Lex threw her arms around his legs. "My Jackson's here! You came to watch us play?"

He leaned over to hug both girls then reached down to lift her in his arms. "Of course. I said we would, didn't I?"

"Mama doesn't feel well, so I'm glad we have you."

"I'm glad too, Sweetie."

Mac beamed as Bill placed his hand gently on her head and pulled her to him for a hug. "Now, who are all of these kids?" Bill asked.

Mac introduced them to Cathryn, Allie, Emmelia, and Gage, all grandchildren of Sam and Carrie's, and all in uniforms. Their mothers,

Amanda, Gretchen, and Lauren approached shortly after to hug the two men and say how glad they were to see them there.

As soon as the ceremony was over, Lexie's team took to the field. Jackson and Bill spent the next three hours watching the morning games of all the children, whooping and hollering when any one of them made a good play.

"I've never had so much fun in my life," Jackson exclaimed, after the last morning game. "How many of the group have second games?"

"They all do. The second round starts at one-thirty. We have two hours to feed this mob," Lauren said.

"Head on over to our place," Sam said. "Carrie cooked lunch for everyone."

Within ten minutes the group arrived, bubbling with excitement and starving. Jackson approached Carrie, who was in the kitchen preparing the spread for chili dogs with all the fixings.

"Hey! So, what'd you and Bill think of opening day?"

Jackson sent her a huge grin. "I can't wait for the second round to start. I'm having a blast."

"I'm glad you two are enjoying it. I grilled hot dogs for lunch. Grab a plate and serve yourselves, buffet style." She pointed to a cooler. "Canned drinks are in there."

"Thanks, Carrie." Jackson leaned in close. "How's Giselle?"

Carrie shrugged and opened a pack of hot dog buns. "She's about the same, and I'm starting to worry. She wasn't the least bit interested in today."

"Has she tackled the master bedroom yet?"

Carrie shook her head. "She won't even open the door."

"Maybe she needs more time."

"Maybe she needs to be reminded that she has two daughters who need her," she said. "I was going to bring the girls back home to rest for a while until it's time for their next games. Would you and Bill want to bring them after lunch for me?"

"We'll do that as soon as we finish eating."

Mac and Lexie dragged the two men through the kitchen door of their home.

Giselle looked up from where she sat with a cup of coffee. Dark circles accented her pale, thin face. She looked childlike without her makeup, but so tired and unbearably sad, it nearly broke Jackson's heart. The girls demeanor turned noticeably subdued the moment they saw their mother.

Bill sat beside Giselle at the table and took her hand. "Hey Hon, how are you feeling?"

"Hi Bill. I'm okay." She turned to her daughters. "How were the games?"

"They were good, we both won," Mac said, quietly.

"Yeah, we both won," Lexie repeated. She lifted her shoulders and let them drop, as she released a deep breath.

In all fairness, Giselle made a valiant effort to smile at her daughters, but Jackson couldn't help but notice that the smile she gave them never seemed to reach her eyes. No doubt her daughters did too.

He sat at the table across from her. "Maybe by next week you'll feel well enough to make one of their games."

"Maybe so."

"Mac hit two home runs, and I hit the ball off the tee twice, mama," Lexie told her.

"That's great, sweetie."

"Jackson said that daddy was watching, so we did it for him. Ouch!" Lexie turned, ready to fuss at her sister for jabbing her in the ribs. She stopped when Giselle suddenly left the table. Within seconds, she'd disappeared into the guest bedroom, closing the door behind her.

"I told you not to talk about daddy," Mac hissed at her sister. "It makes her cry."

Lexis's little face crumbled as she turned to Jackson for comfort. He picked her up and seated her on his long legs as she turned her face into his broad chest and sobbed. He held her close, gently running his fingers through her silky curls, inhaling the scent of her children's shampoo. "Don't cry Lex. Your mom's just hurting right now."

"I'm s-so-orry Jackson, I th-thought she'd b-be happy that daddy was w-wa-watching us-s," Lexie sobbed into his shirt. "I won't s-say d-daa-dd-dy a-g-gain."

"Maybe, just for now, Lex," Jackson told her.

Bill grunted and gave his nephew a disapproving look.

"Uncle Bill," he warned sternly, "Not now."

Bill sighed then turned to the older child. "Mac, do you think you'd like to rest?"

She nodded, walked to her bedroom, and closed the door.

"How about you, Lex?" Jackson whispered softly into her ear. "Think you could take a little nap for me?"

"I want to st-stay with y-you," she sniffed.

Jackson exchanged a look with his uncle, both clearly at a loss as to what to do. Finally, he got up with her and asked if she wanted to sit next to him on the sofa.

"C-Can I get M-Mac?"

He nodded and put her down so she could get her sister. When the two girls came back into the room, Lexie snuggled up next to Jackson, and Mac took the spot next to Bill. Within a few minutes, both girls had fallen asleep on the large, comfortable sofa. Jackson followed Bill out to the back patio so they could talk without disturbing them.

"They shouldn't be afraid to talk about their dad," Bill seethed. "They should be talking about him so they can remember him without mourning. Giselle has to face this."

"We can't do anything, Uncle Bill. They're her girls."

Bill sighed, and agreed to disagree on the matter for the moment.

About five that afternoon, Jackson stopped loading his truck to embrace Lexie as she launched herself at him.

"Jackson, I don't want you to go!" she wailed.

He lifted her, hugged her tightly. "Aw Lex, you'll see me tomorrow, sweet girl. I have to do your mom's yard work tomorrow, remember?"

Lexie's eyes grew wide as she turned to her sister. "Mac, We get to see my Jackson two days in a row!" she said, squealing in delight.

Mac lifted her face to Bill, her eyes bright with hope. "Are you coming back to watch us play again?"

Bill touched her nose with the tip on one finger. "I wouldn't miss it for the world, Mac."

Long after the two of them parted the girls' company, the thought of Lexie's comment brought a smile to Jackson's face.

"What are you grinning about?" Bill asked.

He uttered a single syllable as explanation. "Lex."

By the time he pulled his gaze from the roadway to face his uncle, Bill was wearing the same ear to ear grin.

The next morning, Jackson awoke to rain and disappointment that he wouldn't get to see 'his girls' as he'd begun to think of them. When he called Giselle to tell her he wouldn't make it because of the weather, she said it was fine, and hung up before he could ask to speak to either Mac or Lexie. He spent the day missing the children he'd grown so fond of, wishing he had another excuse to see them other than yard work.

By Tuesday afternoon, he was missing them so badly, wild horses couldn't have kept him away from Mac's game. He saw them again for Lexie's game on Thursday. Giselle attended neither.

The next Saturday, Jackson arrived at Giselle's around nine a.m., to the delight of both children. Before he even got out of his Avalanche, the two excited little girls ran out to greet him. He hoisted Lexie into the air and hugged Mac as she wrapped her arms around him.

"Are you two ready to get to work? Maybe if we get mom's yard looking good it'll make her feel better."

"Maybe she'll want to come outside with us when we're finished. We used to spend a lot of time on the patio with Mama and Daddy. We'd even eat out here," Mac said.

Jackson ruffled her hair. "It's worth a try, sweet girl."

Carrie walked out of the house to greet him.

"Hey, I didn't expect to see you here," he said.

"I came by to see if she needed anything this morning. She's up and dressed, and there's coffee in the kitchen if you want some. Those two monkeys have been up since the crack of dawn waiting for you to show up."

Jackson beamed at the two girls playing on the patio. "How's Giselle?"

Carrie climbed into her Explorer. "Physically, she's fine. Mentally," she lowered her voice to a whisper. "Well, that's an entirely different story. I surely thought she'd have pulled herself out of this by now."

"It's only been . . ."

"I know it's only been three months, but those poor girls, Jackson. The sadness in that house." She wiped a tear from the corner of her eye. "It's overwhelming. I hope she snaps out of this soon, because her girls need their mother. They're all hurting so badly right now."

She started her truck and put it in drive. "Make sure she eats and see if you can get her outside for a little sunshine."

"I'll do my best," he said.

By eleven o'clock, he was finished with the mowing and trimming. By eleven thirty, Giselle's yard, porch, and patio were all in pristine condition, thanks to the hard work of Jackson and the girls.

"Who's hungry?" he asked.

"Me!" Lexie threw her hand up in the air.

"Me too!" Mac called out to him.

"What are y'all hungry for? It's my treat, because you two did such a great job at helping me."

Lexie wanted McDonald's and Mac wanted pizza, so Jackson decided to compromise. "How about if we order pizza then get some chicken nuggets for Lex before we pick it up? What do you think your Mom will want to eat?"

The girls grew ominously quiet before exchanging looks. They turned back to face Jackson.

"Mama doesn't eat anymore," Lex said.

"Only when Carrie makes her," Mac added.

Lexie turned her green gold eyes on him. "If Carrie's not around, she won't eat at all."

"Well, then, we may have to call Carrie in. I'd rather have your mom mad at me than Carrie."

They entered the kitchen through the back door. When they walked inside, Giselle looked up from the crossword puzzle she was working.

"Giselle, I thought I'd order a couple of pizza's from the place here in town. Do you have the number?"

Giselle gave him a vacant look. "It's in the phone book on that table. Look up the Pizza Depot."

He found the number and addressed her again. "I like everything on mine, but what do you order for the girls?"

"That's fine," she said, not looking up.

As Jackson reached for his phone, Mac pulled him down to her level, whispering something in his ear. He nodded and kept an eye on Giselle as he dialed the number. He ordered one pizza with everything, and a second with no jalapenos, a standard topping, unless otherwise requested.

He ended the call, and turned to her. "Giselle, is it okay if I bring the girls with me to pick up the food?"

She nodded without making eye contact.

Jackson got the girls buckled into the back seat and started his truck, planning his first stop. A comment from Lexie jerked him from his thoughts, leaving him breathless.

"Mama doesn't care about us anymore, Jackson."

Jackson swallowed hard before answering. "That isn't true, Lex."

"Yes, it is," Mackenzie agreed with her sister. "She knows we can't eat those peppers because they're too hot. We always ordered one with everything for daddy and one without peppers for us."

Jackson gazed back at the two girls, not knowing quite what to tell them. They both looked so sad and dejected he wanted to cry for them. He backed slowly out of the driveway onto the street, driving slowly so they'd have time to talk. "Girls, do you know what it means when someone is depressed?"

"I think it means they're sad," Mac answered.

"That's right, but it's more than that. It's a sadness so bad that sometimes they can't get back to their lives. Sometimes they don't even realize they're acting that way. Your mom is depressed about losing your dad."

Mac's eyes narrowed angrily. "But, shouldn't she be thankful that she still has us? Like me and Lex were thankful that we didn't lose both mama and daddy. We're still here."

The bitterness in her tone shocked him. *Sheesh. Out of the mouths of babes.*

"Mac, that's one of the symptoms of depression. She can't help what she's feeling."

"If daddy had lived and she had died, he would have taken better care of us than she is," she said.

Jackson turned in his seat to face her. "Mackenzie, don't ever think that and don't say that again. Your mom loves you two more than anything. She just needs a little help right now. I think she needs to see a doctor."

"You can go to a doctor for being sad?" Lexie asked.

"You sure can. Just like if you were sick or had a pain in your foot. You could go to a doctor for help. It's the same way with depression. A doctor can give her medicine that would help her not to feel so sad.

Lexie looked up at him with those beautiful eyes, so much like Giselle's. "Can you bring her, Jackson?"

"It's not my place to talk to her about it, but I bet Carrie can. You know what might help?"

"What?" they asked, in unison.

"If you both said a prayer for your mom and asked God to help her get through this."

Lexie's little face scrunched up in wonder. "Jackson, can God hear me praying even if I whisper?"

"You know, I've always believed that God is so powerful, he can hear you even if you think it to yourself."

"He must have really good ears!" she said, clearly impressed.

"Oh yeah. He has the best hearing in the world."

Both girls got quiet for a few moments and when Jackson checked out his rearview mirror, he saw that Lexie had her eyes squeezed tightly shut and her lips were moving in silent prayer. He looked over at Mackenzie's head, also bowed in prayer. He smiled before sending his own prayer to the man above.

Jackson purchased what they needed to lay out the meal then went to McDonald's and the Pizza parlor for their food. Once home, Mac and Jackson set the patio table while Lex filled cups with ice. After they had laid everything out on the table, the three of them went in to let Giselle know lunch was ready.

Giselle looked up at them from her same spot at the end of the sofa. "I'm not hungry."

The girls faces deflated in disappointment. No way in hell was he letting this one go without a fight. He walked over to Giselle and stood over her with his hand out. "Come on Giselle, you are not getting me in trouble with Carrie. I'm under strict orders to make sure you eat and get some sunshine today, in that order. Besides, the girls went through a lot of trouble to make sure it looks pretty for you." He brushed off her protests. "No excuses now, take my arm."

She glared up at him with angry eyes. "You're not my boss here. Quit trying to make me do something I'm not ready to do."

He looked over at the children. They stared at their mother as though she were a complete stranger. "Girls, go outside and wait for us, we'll be there soon." When they walked outside and closed the door behind them, he turned back to Giselle.

"So, what you're telling me is you're not *ready* to share a meal with your children? You're not *ready* to spend a few minutes with your daughters, who are also hurting because they've lost their father?"

She lowered her head. He immediately felt guilty for upsetting her. "Come on, Giselle. Just a bite of pizza. It'll do you good to get a little sun." He felt encouraged as she pulled herself up off the sofa. He followed her to the door and opened it for her, hoping she'd give her girls the reaction they so desperately longed for.

Giselle barely noticed the table, beautifully set, with flowers they'd picked and tied together to form napkin rings. She didn't see the freshly picked flowers placed in a clear plastic cup they used as a centerpiece; and she didn't notice that every place setting was set with forks and knives, arranged carefully next to the clear plastic dishware.

The only thing she noticed was Toby's absence. It wasn't Toby who had painstakingly mowed the lawn, or carefully trimmed around the sidewalks, shrubs, and flower beds, then swept the sidewalk free of dust and grass clippings. She and Toby had always done the yard work together, rewarding themselves and the girls afterwards with a meal out on the patio. Sometimes they grilled it themselves, sometimes picked up something quick—like pizza or McDonald's.

Her eyes clouded with tears. "Is this some kind of cruel joke?"

"What? No!" Jackson said.

"How could you do this?"

"Gis—"

She cut him off. "Shut up, Jackson." She turned to her daughters. "How could you let him do this? You know. You both *know*!"

Every sight, every smell, every sound reminded her that Toby wasn't there and never would be again. Her heart ached. She nearly fell to her knees from a fresh onslaught of sadness. Jackson's voice, rife with anger, cut into her misery.

"My God, Giselle. How could you?"

She turned on him then. "How could *you?*"

Chapter Seven

Jackson spun her roughly away from the girls, who sat there, both heart-broken that their mother hadn't appreciated their effort for what it was. He closed the door and turned on her.

"What the hell is wrong with you? Can't you see what you're *doing* to them?"

Wordlessly, she turned away from him. He stared after her as she walked to the room she had occupied since Toby's death, and closed herself inside.

He followed her, then stood helplessly in the hallway listening to her heartbroken sobs coming from the other side of the door. Now he knew what Carrie meant about the overwhelming sadness in this house. It consumed everything in its path, like a dark shadow eating away at the light, the life, that used to be present here. He felt the sting of frustration and helplessness, knowing that Mac and Lexie could do nothing but watch their mother sink further into the abyss of loneliness and despair.

He squared his shoulders and walked outside to meet the two beautiful little girls who were sure to need comforting. He dropped into a chair between the two of them and sighed heavily, waiting for them to say or do something.

Lexie looked up at Jackson with tear-filled eyes. "Maybe God can't hear me, Jackson. Maybe I need to pray louder."

Mac wiped her eyes with the back of her hand and sniffed. "I think God's too busy to help Mama."

Jackson opened his arms wide and both girls went to him. He pulled them close and kissed the top of their sun-warmed heads, then their wet-with-tears cheeks. He hugged them both tightly, deeply inhaling the scent of hard work and sweat and sunshine on their skin, clothing, and hair. He finally spoke in a voice that cracked with emotion.

"I love you, girls. Do you hear me? I love both of you so much, I can't believe it. I love you enough for both your mom and dad, until your mama is feeling well enough to show you again. She still loves you both so much. She's just too sad to show it right now, that's all. But, I promise—I *promise* you this. She will again."

Both girls dissolved into more tears, shaking and sobbing loudly into his shirt. For the first time in his life, Jackson knew what it must feel like to be a parent with a child who is suffering. He knew how it felt to be helpless and unable to ease their pain and discomfort. Inadequacy didn't come close to what he felt. He'd do anything to take the pain from them if he could. He let them cry, Mackenzie with her arms around his neck, and Lexie with hers wrapped around his waist.

Their tears finally slowed, and then eventually stopped, leaving in its wake the sniffling and hiccupping that happens after a good cry. Jackson dried their eyes, wiped their noses with paper napkins, and finally kissed them both on the cheeks. He looked into their faces as he cradled their heads gently with his hands.

"Better now?" he asked, drawing two nods from the girls. "Good, because, I tell you what," he said comically, "All this crying is hard work isn't it? It's made me hungry. How about you two?" They nodded. "Well, then, if you want any pizza or chicken nuggets, you'd better hurry up and eat because I'm hungry enough to eat everything on this table." He reached over to the food with both arms.

"No! I want my pizza!" Mackenzie shrieked.

"I want my chicken nuggets!" Lexie yanked the box out of Jackson's grip, even as she emitted a high-pitched giggle.

"Well, I guess I'll have to make do with one measly, old pizza with jalapeno peppers," he said dramatically. "But if it even *looks* like you aren't going to eat enough, I just may decide to eat more than my fair share."

Mackenzie picked out two slices of pizza, put them on her plate, and pointed her finger at Jackson. "Look, just because I'm starting out with two slices does not mean I won't want one more when I'm done with these. Don't eat the rest yet, okay?"

"Okay," he said in his best Eeyore imitation, causing the girls to break out into fits of giggling.

Lexie held out her box of nuggets. "I'll share with you, Jackson."

He gazed adoringly at the miracle in miniature of Giselle, and thought his heart would burst with the love he felt for her and her sister. He brushed her hair away from her forehead and planted a kiss on her nose. "You go ahead and eat first, baby girl. If there's any left, I'll take one if I still have room."

Lexie nodded, rewarding him with a big cheesy grin. He started to take a bite of pizza when Lexie stopped him.

"Wait! We have to say the blessing first!"

"Lex," Mac whispered. "Maybe Jackson doesn't do that. Mom said not everyone does, and if we were around someone who doesn't, just to say it to ourselves."

Jackson put the pizza back on his plate. "No, that's a great idea. Would either of you like to say it?"

"I will. I learned one from catechism class," Mackenzie boasted. "We all have to hold hands first." She and her sister joined hands and each grasped one of Jackson's. "It goes like this. *Bless us, oh Lord, for these, thy gifts which we are about to receive, from thy bounty, through Christ, our Lord. Amen.* Was that good, Jackson?"

Jackson beamed proudly at her. "That was perfect, Mac."

"Do you know any?" she asked. "Daddy only knew one."

"The only one I ever learned was this." He put his hands together reverently and spoke in a somber voice. "Rub a dub dub—thanks for the grub."

Mac and Lexie's mouths gaped open in awe. They looked at each other then back at him. "That's daddy's too!" they chorused.

Jackson put his head back and burst into laughter, while the girls doubled over into fits of giggles.

❧

Carrie watched the threesome, unseen, from the corner of the house. She'd arrived during the first bout of crying, held back her own tears at Jack's profession of love for Toby and Giselle's little girls. She'd kept her silence, waiting to see how he'd handle the heartbroken, sobbing little girls. She couldn't help but be pleased, and knew their father would be also. Toby couldn't stand to see his girls, any of his girls, suffer.

She remembered the day he'd called her from the local hospital, begging her to meet him there because Mac needed stitches after falling off her bike. Giselle was out of town for a three-day training class. It'd torn him up to see his daughter getting stitches. Mac ended up comforting her dad, and telling him it wasn't his fault she'd gone too fast on her bike.

Carrie smiled at the memory. Then took time to marvel at how perfect this threesome before her looked. Well, almost perfect, anyway. Seeing the patio table all set for a meal, she didn't have to ask where Giselle was. She wiped all traces of tears from her eyes and finally made her presence known.

"What's so funny over here?"

The girls turned her way and continued to giggle.

"Aw it's just a private joke, Carrie," Jackson said. "Would you like some pizza?"

"Nope, Sam and I ate lunch already and Sam's passed out in his recliner at home. I told him if he was going to spend the day sleeping, I'd just as soon bring these two munchkins to watch a movie in Lake Coburn."

"You think Mama would let us?" Mackenzie asked, her face filled with hope.

"Sure, eat your pizza. Here's a schedule." Carrie handed a computer printout to Jackson. "See if you can help them agree on a movie please, Jack." Carrie walked in to check on Giselle, dreading what she'd find.

She opened the bedroom door quietly and entered, seating herself on the side of the bed. Giselle turned, giving her a vacant look. Carrie sighed and brushed her friend's hair back from her forehead. Gazing into her eyes was like looking into a hope chest that had once been full, but had been stripped of every item; every last shred of, well—hope. "You need to eat something Giselle. I'm not fooling around here, either. I'll feed you my damn self if I have to."

"Where are the girls? With him?" Giselle asked, her voice cold and angry

"Him? You mean Jackson? Yes, your daughters are outside eating with *him*. Which is where you should be, spending time with your girls and getting some sunshine." She took a deep breath and exhaled loudly. "Did he try to get you to eat?"

Giselle nodded silently.

Carrie turned Giselle's face toward her. "Let me guess, the sight of the table, all set for dining like that reminded you of how you all did that with Toby after finishing the yard work."

Giselle nodded silently and squeezed her eyes shut.

Carrie nodded. "I understand that you're upset, but he didn't know. You need to eat, and you will eat. He only did what I asked him to do."

"He's not my boss over here. I don't have to listen to him," she sneered.

"You sound like a child. *He's not the boss of me!*" Carrie stood, getting angrier by the minute. "I tell you what, honey. Maybe you don't have to listen to *him*, but you will damn well listen to *me*. We're all bending over backwards to help you, and we don't mind doing it, but it's time you start helping yourself. Now get up out of that bed."

"I don't feel like it right now."

"Look, Giselle, I figure losing a man like Toby merits three months of feeling sorry for yourself, but your children are suffering too, and neither I, nor Jackson, is a good enough substitute for their mother." She turned and walked back to the door. "As soon as they're finished eating I'm going to clean them up and take them to a movie in Lake Coburn."

Giselle threw her hand over her eyes. "Good, as long as you leave me in peace."

Carrie turned, eyes narrowed. She left the room, a plan already formed in her mind.

Jackson had just helped the girls settle on a feature when Carrie came out to meet them.

"Jackson, how would you like to take these girls to a movie?" She didn't miss the little girls gasps of delight.

"Sure, you need some help?"

"No, I mean you bring them while I stay here with Giselle. Would you two like that?"

"Oh Jackson, please!" Lexie pleaded.

"Say yes! Please say yes!" Mackenzie bounced like frisky puppy.

"I'd love to, but, did you clear it with Giselle?"

"You leave her to me. Have you all eaten enough?"

Mackenzie looked down at her plate. "Can I put a slice of pizza back? I want to save room for popcorn."

"I ate all my chicken nuggets, but I'm still going to want popcorn."

"Good, let's get you cleaned up. What time does it start?" Carrie asked Jackson.

"In an hour and a half, but I need to go home and shower. I kind of reek." He pulled his shirt away from his torso and made a face. "Would that be okay?"

She nodded as she herded the girls into the house. "I'll get them ready. You want to come in and cool off?"

"I may not be welcome in there right now," he whispered.

"Giselle's in the bedroom. It's safe for now."

He nodded, then rose from the table as she went inside with the girls. Jackson boxed up the pizza and left it on the kitchen counter then cleaned up outside. As he waited at the door, he noticed a digital picture frame on the countertop. He reached over to turn it on and a slide show began of the Granger family in all kinds of candid moments. He laughed aloud when it got to shots of Toby dressed up in full princess regalia. His daughters had obviously draped every one of his upper extremities with dance costumes from their closets. Toby was grinning out from behind pink and purple feather boas, boasting a pair of pink, plastic, clip on earrings. Lexie was dressed in a lion costume and Mackenzie in her ballerina costume. There were shots of him in dance positions with his two girls, and shots of him tending to the gas grill set up in the back yard. Giselle must have set the timer, because she was in the last shot with her family, smiling and happy. Would she ever be that happy again?

Lexie ran to up him. "Jackson, can you buckle my shoes?"

"Sure, put your foot up here." She did, and he buckled her sandals for her. Then he took the hairbrush and brushed her hair for her. When he'd finished, Mackenzie walked up and turned her back to him, expecting the same. He brushed her hair until it resembled black, glossy layers of silk.

Carrie watched the interaction between the three, in amazement. It looked as though they had been around each other for years instead of a few months. She stepped up and cleared her throat. "It looks like you're ready to go. You girls be good. Don't fill them with too much candy, Jack."

He got them both buckled into the back seat and climbed back in to the driver's side. "We're going to the two o'clock feature at the mall." He leaned over to Carrie. "You sure she's alright with this?"

"She'll be fine." Carrie leaned in and gave him a hug through the door of his truck. She started to release him then hugged him tighter. "You're a Godsend, Jackson Jamison Broussard."

She watched them drive off then went to Giselle's room.

"Okay, Giselle, I hope you're hungry. There's plenty of pizza left."

Giselle rolled away from her. "I'm not hungry."

"That's too damn bad, because I outweigh you by a good sixty pounds, and I say you're going to eat anyway."

"Leave me alone, Carrie. I just—I just want to die."

"Do you?" she asked, not bothering to hide her anger. "Do you really? Think about what you're saying, Giselle. I understand your grief, but those girls are part of Toby. Do you really think he would want you to lie here and waste away while you force his daughters to watch?" She pulled Giselle's shoulder so that she partially faced her. "Do you really want them to be left alone in this world?"

"They wouldn't be alone, they'd have each other," Giselle said, without meeting her gaze.

Carrie released her and straightened. "I cannot believe you just said that. That falls unbelievably short of having a mother who loves you, don't you think?"

Giselle met Carrie's gaze. "They'd have you and Sam."

"Sam and I have raised our children and we babysit enough for our grandchildren as it is. As much as we love your girls, we're not looking to start over." She reached out, grasped Giselle's arm, and pulled her to her feet. "You're eating, and you're going to do it outside on the patio. You need sunshine."

They walked to the patio door, where Giselle hesitated until she established they were alone. She flinched as she stepped into the sunshine for the first time in three months. It took a few minutes before her eyes adjusted to the blinding whiteness of the scrubbed concrete patio. The sunlight reflected off the spotless glass-topped table. She finally made her way to the table and sat in one of the chairs.

Carrie brought her a plate with a slice of pizza and a glass of tea. Giselle began to nibble slowly while Carrie sat across from her with a cup of hot tea.

"Where are my girls?"

"They went to the two o'clock feature at the mall."

"Who'd they go with? One of the twins?"

Carrie lowered her cup. "Jackson took them."

Giselle met her friend's gaze head on. "He's got no business taking my girls anywhere without my permission."

"I asked him to."

"You had no right!"

"Would you be as upset if they'd gone with Lauren or Gretchen?"

"No."

Carrie shrugged and leisurely picked a piece of lint from her capris. "Then I don't see a problem. It was either this or wake Sam to come babysit their mother. But my husband worked hard this week, and he deserves a rest. Besides," she gave Giselle a self-satisfied smile, knowing she was about to cross a line. "Jackson was already here. He was more than happy to take the girls." She took some satisfaction at the angry narrowing of Giselle's eyes. Anger was better than nothing.

Carrie decided to push the envelope. "Well, look at it this way. After you starve yourself to death, Jack would be all too willing to adopt those two. They're crazy about him, and God knows he adores them. They'd miss you of course, but they'd get over it with the love of a good father-figure like Jackson."

An angry flush infused Giselle's face. "Those are *my* children. *I'm* their mother."

Carrie cocked her head. "I'm glad you finally remembered. Maybe now you'll start acting the part again." She put on her glasses and cleared her throat. "Now finish your lunch so I can go spend time with my husband. He actually likes having me around."

Carrie's temporary feeling of guilt vanished completely when Giselle finished a slice of pizza then took another from the box. She knew Jackson would catch hell over this, but if that's what it took to bring Giselle back to the land of the living, there was no help for it. She'd get over it.

Carrie left her friend sitting at the patio table working a crossword puzzle, and drove home to meet Sam.

Sam seemed surprised when his wife walked into the door. "I didn't expect to see you so soon."

"It seems I've stumbled on the right motivation to get her up and moving. Too bad I had to piss her off to do it."

"What did you use to motivate her?"

Carrie grimaced. "I used Jackson, and he won't be pleased about it."

Sam nodded when she explained the situation. "Sounds like you did what you had to do. Something had to give."

"I think so. I just hope I haven't done anything to damage Jackson's cause."

"I wouldn't worry about him. That young man can take care of himself. Those girls are all the motivation he needs to keep on plugging away at it."

Sam wrapped Carrie in his arms. "It's amazing how quickly Mac and Lex took to them."

"I know, right?"

"And God knows he and Bill are crazy about them."

"Noticed that, have you?" Carrie grinned at her husband. "Now if their mom would soften her heart towards him, it may do them both some good."

Jackson pulled his Avalanche up into his driveway. "Here we are."

As soon as he unlocked his door, the girls ran inside. Mackenzie surveyed the living area and gave him a brief nod. "I love your house, Jackson.".

"I love your sofa! It looks so big and comfable for you. Is it?" Lexie asked.

He laughed. "Yes, sweetie, it's very comfortable for me."

"I like this one." Mackenzie climbed into the oversize lounger. "We could all fit in this chair."

Lexie ran down the hallway, paused to inspect the guest bedroom, his office, and then gasped as she made it all the way to his bedroom. "This is the biggest bed I've ever seen!"

Mac joined her sister. "Oh my gosh, Jackson, it's beautiful. Did you pick it out, or did your wife?"

"I picked it out. The bed I had before was small and ugly. It didn't fit me."

"Because you're not small or ugly," Lexie said.

"No, you're big, and tall, and very handsome!" Mac's comment had attitude to spare as Lexie agreed.

"Well, thank you very much ladies, I appreciate the compliment. Now let's get you two set up watching some tv in the living room while I shower and change." He turned on his equally impressive large screen television set, and they watched the cartoon network while he took a quick shower and changed into some clean clothes. He entered the living room a short while later to find his uncle seated between the girls, watching cartoons.

Mac met his gaze, her eyes sparkling with delight. "Bill is coming with us."

Jackson figured his uncle didn't need much convincing. "I thought you were out of town, or I'd have called you to help me. I'm kind of new at this stuff."

"I got back and came straight here. Where are we going?"

"The two o'clock feature at the mall. Let's go."

"Are they out already?"

Bill turned in his seat to check on both the girls. "Yep. Out like a couple of just fed kittens. All that laughing must have worn them out."

Jackson nodded. "That, along with a little emotional upheaval earlier today. Poor things must be exhausted."

"What happened?"

"Giselle happened. I never thought I'd get to the point where I'd actually lose patience with her. But her treatment of those girls this morning . . ." He stopped, shook his head. "Poor babies."

"You gonna tell me what the hell happened or leave me hanging?"

Jackson made sure the girls were completely out before filling in the blanks for his uncle. He finished and wiped his face, as if by doing so, he could wipe out the memory of those couple of minutes when Giselle had uttered those ugly accusations at her daughters and then him.

"The girls were heartbroken. I'm talking total devastation."

"Shit."

"Yeah. Shit."

"What'd you do?"

"Whatever I could to smooth things over. Not with Giselle, of course. She crawled back into her hole, and cried. I hugged the girls and tried to make them laugh. Eventually they did. Carrie came over to take them to the movies. She went to tell Giselle and next thing I knew, I'd agreed to take them for her." He tapped his steering wheel with the heel of his hand. "I mean, I know she's sad. She's lost a good man, the love of her life. But she's missed out on three months of her daughters' lives. They need her."

"It's past time she got some help," Bill growled. "Hell, I'm surprised she let you take the girls to the movies after that episode."

"Seriously, I doubt she cares one way or the other who takes them where right now. I expect after her little outburst, she cried herself to sleep, and woke up as completely despondent as she has been for the last three months."

Only later would Jackson realize his mistake. Somehow, in the few months of spending time with Mac and Lexie, he'd grown lax. Let his guard down. Somehow, he'd forgotten the harshest lesson he'd ever learned from his miserable existence with Chloe.

Always expect the unexpected.

Chapter Eight

Jackson pulled his Avalanche into the driveway at 5:15.

Bill opened Mac's door, unbuckled her seat belt, and roused her from her nap. He kissed her on the forehead and lowered her to the ground so she could walk sleepily to the kitchen door. She waited at the door, almost as if she didn't want to go in to face her mother alone.

Jackson released Lexie's seatbelt before waking her. Still half asleep, she automatically reached for his neck, wanting him to carry her inside. He smiled and kissed her cheek as he carried her to the door where Mackenzie waited for him.

Mac had just gripped the door knob when it was ripped out of her grasp from the inside. The door swung wide, and Giselle appeared, looking like she was ready to spit fire. Mac backed away from the door, sidled up next to Jackson as though seeking protection from the one person she should never fear.

But Giselle's angry glare was aimed directly at Jackson—her animosity concentrated at maximum force—as though he'd just committed some unspeakable crime.

"Who the hell do you think you are?"

Jackson shifted Lexie in his arms. "Excuse me?"

"You had no right to take my children out of town without my permission!"

"Carrie asked me to take them to the movies. I didn't have anything else to do so I said yes. I thought she cleared it with you."

"She didn't clear anything with me. She told me after the fact, when it was too late to do anything about it."

He pulled his phone from his pocket. Waved it in front of her. "You have my number, Giselle. All you had to do was call. I would have brought them back immediately."

"I shouldn't have to. You should have asked me first."

Jackson spoke calmly. "I had no idea Carrie didn't, and I'm sorry." He lowered Lexie to the floor. She joined her sister, both of them hiding behind him from their own mother.

"You're damn right you are. You can't be their father, Jackson, they already have a father."

"I'm not try—"

"Yes, you are. And I don't give damn what Carrie asked you to do. I'm telling I don't want you to see them anymore. No more movies. No more ball games." She grabbed her daughters' hands and jerked them into the house.

"Mama, nooo!" Lexie wailed.

Mackenzie turned pleading eyes to her mother. "We love Jackson and Bill. Please don't make them stop coming to see us. They're all we have!"

"You have me." An icy glare aimed at Jackson accompanied her vicious reply. "Now say goodbye, girls. You won't be seeing him again."

Mackenzie pulled free from her mother and cried out. "Noooo! I hate you!" The outburst finally got Giselle's notice. Rather than shrink from her mother's undivided attention, Mac let loose on her. "You don't even love us anymore. You should be glad that Jackson and Bill want to watch us play ball and take us to movies. I bet daddy's glad! Daddy would have wanted us to be happy. Daddy wouldn't have minded if we said your name. I wish—I wish—"

Jackson's stomach lurched, knowing what was coming. "Mac! Don't."

But Mackenzie was past listening. "I wish it had been *you* to die instead of daddy!" she screamed.

Giselle grabbed her oldest daughter by the shoulders and leveled a glare at her. "Not half as much as I wish it."

Jackson watched in horror as Mac twisted out of her mother's grip, and ran crying to her room, slamming the door behind her. Lexie stood there sobbing, and when he reached out to comfort her, Giselle clasped her shoulder, pushing her back and away from him.

"Go to your room, Lex."

Lexie's gaze swiveled frantically from him to Giselle, then back to him, her eyes wide, her lashes wet with tears, her plump cheeks covered with them. He could see her reluctance to either leave him or disobey her mother. Her eyes pleaded silently for him to do something, anything, to make it better. Jackson clenched his hands into fists to keep from reaching out.

"It's okay, Lex. I love you."

"J-J-ackson . . ."

For the second time that day, his heart broke for her.

"Your room, Lex. Now." Giselle issued the command through clenched teeth.

Her little mouth quivering, and without another word or glance in her mother's direction, Lexie ran to her bedroom in tears.

Sick at heart, Jackson stared down at Giselle. "Please don't take this out on them. Can't you see they're hurting as much as you are?"

"I doubt that. Because of you they don't seem to even remember their father. You've made sure of that, haven't you?"

Insulted by her accusation, his voice rose in anger. "Oh, they remember him, Giselle. Didn't you hear Mac? They remember exactly what a wonderful father Toby was."

She shook her head like a mad woman. "You're trying to replace him. They don't even talk about him anymore!"

He walked to her and grabbed her shoulders, longing to shake some sense into her. "They *can't* talk about him here. Those girls are terrified to speak his name around you, because when they do you run to your room and hide."

"It's because of you!" She pulled out of his grip and tried to close the door.

Jackson pushed the door wide and glared at her. "For God's sake, Giselle, are you so wrapped up in your own misery that you can't see their pain? Or is it the fact that they turned to *me* for comfort that upsets you so much?"

"Don't try to turn this around on me. This is your fault! Now, I mean it, Jackson. Don't you come around my girls again." She slammed the door in his face, and as an added insult, locked it.

Jackson stood there, shocked, silent, completely stunned. His hands clenched, his entire body tensed, with his mouth open. How the hell had this happened? He placed both palms flat on the door, wanting to knock, desperate to make her see reason. Bill appeared beside him, his voice deep, calm, speaking words he barely comprehended through his fog of despair.

"Don't, son. You'll only make it worse. You can't reason with her now."

Jackson turned his tormented eyes to his uncle. "Did you hear what she said? What Mac said?"

Bill nodded.

"Lexie tried to come to me, but Giselle wouldn't let her. She was crying, they both were, and I couldn't do a damn thing about it. I feel so—so frustrated and—helpless."

Bill nodded. "I know you do, and so do I, but we can't fix this tonight. Let's go home and sleep on it. I'll drive."

He nodded, climbed zombie-like into the passenger seat of his own truck. Jackson stared blankly out the window all the way home, seeing nothing, hearing nothing, saying nothing.

They arrived at his place and Bill left immediately in his own truck. Jackson dropped on his sofa and pulled out his phone. He waited for Carrie to answer.

"What the hell did you do, Carrie?"

"You saw Giselle?"

"I saw her."

"She was pissed?"

"Oh yeah."

"I'm sorry Jack. Those girls needed a break from her. Giselle was talking like she wanted to die, serious enough so that I didn't want to leave her alone. I had to do something. I ended up having to piss her off to get her to eat, and I used you to do it."

Jackson plastered his hand over his queasy stomach, fearing the worst. "What did you tell her?"

"I told her when she was gone, you'd probably want to adopt the girls because you were so crazy about them."

"Oh God, you didn't really say that, did you?"

"I'm not proud of it, but I couldn't help myself. It worked too, because she had two whole slices of pizza and sat outside to eat it."

"But now she hates me, Carrie. Has forbidden me to see the girls."

"You saw her, didn't you? The woman was starving herself to death."

Jackson groaned and grabbed the top of his head with one hand. "She was already pissed at me."

"Maybe you should tell me why."

"She hurt the girls' feelings today. Broke their hearts, really. I lost patience, kind of yelled at her."

Carrie exhaled loudly. "I wondered why the thought of you taking the girls to the movie upset her so much."

"There must be something we can do," he groaned.

"She hung up on me earlier and won't answer her phone or the door. I'm sure she'll cool off by tomorrow."

He gave a hysterical laugh. "Well hell, Carrie. I wish I was as sure of that as you are."

"Trust me, Jack. This will all blow over."

He snorted. "Yeah, right. Because we have a history of blow overs, right?"

"Ja—"

"Hanging up now. I've got a date."

"What?"

"With a bottle of Crown. Don't worry, I won't be driving. I'll just be here, alone in my house, drinking until I pass the hell out."

Jackson hit the end call button and dropped the phone on the chair. He went to his bar and grabbed his Crown, thought about mixing it with coke, but instead filled the highball glass with the amber liquid and downed it. He refilled the glass, brought the bottle with him. Dropped on the couch Lex had, just four short hours ago described as 'comfable'.

He felt a lump in his side, reached back for it. Pulled out the stuffed pony that she'd left for him in his truck on opening day at the ball park. He crushed the toy to his chest, remembering how he'd arrived at the Kenton ballpark a few days later to find her seated in the bleachers beside Sam. He'd greeted Sam quietly so Lex hadn't seen him yet. Clearing his throat, he'd spoken. "Has anyone here seen a pretty little girl named Lexie Granger?" Lex spun around, her expression that of an innocent child's joy—pure unadulterated, uncontaminated.

Lexie had scurried to the top row in the low bleachers and thrown herself into his arms.

He'd hugged her tightly. "How are you, Lex?"

"Fine, now that you're here, Jackson."

"You know, somebody left a stuffed pony in my truck last Saturday. Was it you, by any chance?"

"I left it so you would have somethin' to 'member me by when I'm not with you. Did it work?"

"Uh huh. It must be a magic pony, because every time I pick it up, I think of you."

Lexie's adorable pixie face had lit up as she nodded. She hadn't left his side throughout the entire game.

And now. Now Giselle wouldn't let him or Bill see the two little girls they'd fallen so hard for. Engulfed with frustrated helplessness, more severe than anything he'd ever felt with Chloe, he replayed the previous, terrible scene. Giselle's cutting words to him. Mac's awful words to her mother. He didn't know who he hurt more for—the child or the mother. Lexie's tiny, tear covered face swam before him, her chin quivering before she ran to her room. The sound of her cries joining with Mac's would haunt him forever. He covered his ears and groaned, blocking out the memory of their heartbroken sobs.

Jackson put his head in his hands and sat, feeling as miserable and alone as he hadn't since the night he lost both his parents.

He threw back the whiskey and stared at the empty glass, turning it in his hands. And filled it to the brim.

Bill stormed into his house and threw his keys onto the counter top, still sick with what he'd witnessed less than an hour ago. He'd been shocked, had never expected that. And Jackson—good God. His nephew, even living all those years with that lunatic wife of his, hadn't been the least bit prepared for that.

But then, Jack had never really loved Chloe. Hell, Bill had known that as far back as the wedding. No way had his nephew totally invested his heart into that woman. Oh, the potential had been there, at first. But Chloe had crushed that with a lie and her demand for him to make a choice. His nephew, ever the gentleman, ever gallant, had chosen wrong. Despite that, his commitment to his wife had remained steadfast, loyal to the end.

But Mac and Lexie—those two little girls had crawled into both his and Jackson's hearts, found their spots and taken up permanent residency. Jackson had only been trying to help. Trying to fill a void. Not the void left by their father's death—but their mother's. Because sure as shit, taking a blow like that to your soul, losing someone *that* close to you, your other half—well, that *was* like dying. Worse than dying, for a while.

His nephew didn't know that.

But Bill did.

He picked up his phone, punched in a number, and waited. He heard the voice on the other line and took a deep breath.

"It's time."

Her doorbell rang at 8:00 a.m. the next morning. Giselle peeked through the window of her kitchen door, uttered a low growl at the sight of Carrie's SUV parked in her drive. She opened the door, and stood staring at Bill Broussard, her "I don't want any lectures" speech frozen on her lips.

Bill stood tall, straight, hat in hand. "Hello Giselle."

She shot him a suspicious glare. "Bill."

He slapped his Stetson nervously against his thigh. "Honey, I've got something to tell you that may help you to gain a little perspective—."

She raised her hand. "Don't say you know how I feel, because you couldn't possibly."

Bill gave her a sad smile. "You don't know how badly I wish that were true. What I'm about to tell you, I've not told to another living soul in close to four decades. How about you let Carrie take the girls to her house for a while?"

The sadness in his tone, more than anything, had her curious about what he wanted to say. Sensing their presence behind her, she turned to her daughters, who stood waiting like somber little porcelain dolls, and gave them a nod.

Mackenzie approached Bill for a hug, sending her a glare, a dare to stop her—a true act of rebellion for the good natured child.

Lexie stopped before Bill and stole a glance in her direction. When he leaned closer for a hug, she whispered something in his ear.

He gave her a big smile and brushed his hand lightly over her cheek. "He already knows, but I'll tell him anyway."

Her lip trembled as she nodded, setting her golden curls into motion.

She'd earned their animosity, the wary looks they gave at her approach. She knew that. She'd no doubt spend the rest of her life trying to erase those five minutes of a memory from hell from her daughters' minds. Probably unsuccessfully.

Carrie stepped forward to give Giselle a hug. "I don't know what he's got to say, but hear him out, honey. I know he's got your best interest at heart, or he wouldn't be here." She turned toward her truck, pausing long enough to squeeze Bill's arm and whisper a hasty "Good luck."

Alone in the kitchen with Bill, Giselle offered him a seat and handed him a mug of steaming coffee. She settled herself across from him at the kitchen table and waited. He began to speak in a deep, mesmerizing tone that she found mysteriously comforting.

"When I was eighteen, I decided to work my way across the United States—do some travelling. Up until then, I hadn't been out of the state of Texas. I'd already registered for the draft, and I figured if they were going to ship my butt to Viet Nam, I was gonna see my own country first. As it turned out, the draft board never called my number, and though I would have gone if they had, somewhere along the way I discovered I wasn't the volunteer type.

As a result I'd lived in and worked in thirty of these states by the time I turned twenty years old. I ended up in Washington state, working as a lumberjack. I fell head over heels in love with a pretty girl named Lorraine Stubbins. She felt the same way, and two short months later, we married."

Bill put his cup down and smiled. "It was heaven. We lived in a two-room shack, and loved every minute of it. Lorraine came from a wealthy family, but she never complained a day about our little shack. Neither did her folks, because they started out the same way, and knew we would do better for ourselves, eventually."

"It only took a couple of weeks to get her pregnant, and man, was I ecstatic. I couldn't wait to have a little girl who looked just like her mama." He gave his head a slow shake before he continued. "I got a steady job with better hours and we started putting a little money aside for when the baby came. Lorraine was healthy, and I treated her like a queen. We couldn't wait for the baby to come so we could give him or her as much love as we had for each other." Bill paused, smiling at the memory, and looked for a moment as though he was completely lost in the past. He lowered his head and continued, his voice tight, controlled.

"In her sixth month, I dropped her off on my way to work so she could visit her folks all day." Bill scooted his chair out suddenly, leaned forward, his head down as he rested his forearms on his thighs. "When she started hemorrhaging, they rushed her to the hospital in Seattle."

He faced her then.

"Both she and our baby died and I never got to say goodbye." He put his head down for a moment to wipe his eyes. "I lost them two days before Christmas."

Giselle choked on a sob, raised her hand to cover her mouth.

Bill continued in a monotone voice, lost in the past. "Those were my days of hell on earth. I wanted to die. I couldn't see a reason in the world to live. My in-laws were as distraught over my condition as they were about losing their daughter and grandchild. Over the next two and a half months they watched me deteriorate. I couldn't eat, I couldn't work, and they knew something had to be done. My father in law called my brother, Jamison, and he drove up to Washington state to pick me up."

"When we got back home, I met my sister in law, Elise. It seems that while I was gone, Jamison had also fallen in love and married. They had a baby boy, just two weeks old, named Jackson Jamison Broussard, and they were every bit as happy as Lorraine and I would have been, had she and our child lived."

"As soon as I got to their little home in Pasadena, Texas, Elise sat me down and place that child into my arms. I guess it looked like I didn't know what to do with the baby, because it damn near scared Jamison to death. He tried to take him from me, but Elise stopped him. I'll never forget her words. She took my face in her hands and looked me in the eyes when she spoke. "There is no kind of pain in this world that an innocent child can't heal, Billy" she said. "Now you hold your nephew. You're the only family he's got besides his mama and daddy. He's going to need you." She was alone in this world also, and knew how important it was to have family."

Bill stood up and walked to the window overlooking the back yard. "That sister-in-law of mine was some kind of smart, because that child did heal me. I fed him, I changed his diaper, and I even gave him his bath some days. It didn't take me long to realize the needs of that baby had to come before my grief. My nephew and I had a strong bond. Five years later, when Jamison and Elise died in a car accident, there was no question that I would raise him." He exhaled and wiped his eyes with his handkerchief.

Giselle couldn't choke back her sobs. "I'm so sorry, Bill."

"My boy would be two months younger than Jackson. We were going to name him William Clayton Broussard, Jr., because Lorraine insisted that any boy with that name would be destined to grow up as fine as his daddy."

His voice broke slightly and he wiped his eyes again. "It's always a part of me, Giselle, but I had to move on. I had to leave it behind me so I could live the life I knew she wanted for me. I guess that's why I never bothered telling Jackson."

She wiped her eyes and sniffed. "Jackson doesn't know?"

"As he got older, I didn't see the need. And after his folks died—well, it was him and me, and that's all that mattered. He was my boy after that. I've never let him forget either of his parents. They were wonderful people. Jackson doesn't remember much, but he remembers some." He placed a hand over his heart. "He knows enough to keep a part of them here, where they belong."

"Did he grieve for them?"

"Oh sure. We both did, but there's nothing as bad as a child losing his, or her, parent. You see, that's why Jackson relates to your girls so easily. He understands that they need to be able to talk about their dad, so that when they think of him, they can remember the joy he brought to their lives. Now, I never met the man, but from what Jackson says, he was a wonderful father and husband. You owe his daughters the chance to remember him with love.

So, you see, I *do* know your grief. I know you've lost the love of your life, but you're not done living. You'll find love again."

Giselle shook her head. "You didn't."

"I never found anyone willing to put up with me and Jackson in those early years, and he had to come first. Once I went in with a pal of mine and started a new oil company, I got too busy to settle down. That's not to say that I haven't had my share of female companionship, but no one serious enough to settle down with."

He flipped his hat to examine it. "I been thinkin' lately, maybe it's time I find someone. One of these days, you will too. Hopefully, it will happen sooner for you. Until then, you take care of those girls. In time you'll think about Toby and it'll hurt less. Eventually, you'll only remember the good times and none of the pain. In my opinion, the Lord does that so we don't die of sadness." He paused to sip his coffee.

Giselle reached out to touch his hand resting on the table. "I'm sorry, Bill."

"It's alright, hon. I just want you to understand that God puts people in our paths for a reason. I know the reason he put Jackson and I in yours was so we could help your girls through this. When they're with us, they talk about all the fun they had with their daddy. We allow them to remember him with love, with joy in their hearts. And isn't that what you want for them?"

She choked up at his words, able only to nod at him.

"Then, for God's sake, don't make them feel like they can't speak of him in their own home where you were all so happy. Put *their* grief before your own, and yours will disappear."

Giselle's head dropped forward on the table as she cried for those left behind—Bill, Jackson, her girls, and finally herself. Her tears, quiet at first, progressed into long, loud, body-wracking sobs. The kind that free the soul of suppressed sadness and excruciating pain.

Bill wrapped her in his strong, comforting arms, and held her while she cried.

Her sobs subsided eventually and she wiped her swollen eyes. "My babies," she groaned. "What have I done to my poor children?" She turned tear-filled eyes to Bill for answers. "*How* can they ever forgive me?"

Bill handed her a box of tissues. "Hon, they'll be so glad to have their mama back, they'll forget everything else."

"Mac said she hated me. She was right, too, when she said Toby would have taken better care of them if I'd been the one to go. He never would have let this happen."

"What happened was meant to happen. It's all tiny threads woven into the fabric of your life. It's all part of God's plan and you have to trust he knows what's best for you. Mac didn't mean what she said any more than you meant what you said."

"I pray you're right, Bill." She groaned again. "I said such awful things to Jackson. How can I ever face him?"

"Don't worry about the rest of us. We all know what you were going through. He just wants to see you back to your old self so you can tend to your daughters. Those girls of yours sure have found a place in our hearts."

Giselle wiped her eyes. "I know you both mean a lot to them, and you two are welcome to be a part of their lives."

"Thank you for that." His voice deepened with emotion. "I know they don't have a grandpa of their own, but I'd be honored if you'd let me treat them as if they were my grandchildren."

She gazed at the kind man before her, knew they'd bonded over this moment. "Are you sure, Bill? What if Jackson meets someone and has children of his own? Wouldn't you want them to think of you as your grandfather?"

Bill stood, stretching his tall frame to his full height. "Of course I would. Giselle, people have more than one set of grandchildren all the time; by blood, by marriage, or by adoption. I have enough love to spare for as many grandchildren as I'm blessed with." He placed his hat back on his head. "And for God's sake, please give me a reason not to be so damn jealous of Sam Langley."

Giselle slapped her hand over her mouth to stop the laugh that popped out of her. She looked up at Bill, unable to suppress it any longer, and let it burst forth. Surprised that she could laugh so soon after her bout with tears, she held her side as tears of laughter streamed down her face.

Gaining control, she sat back in her chair and dabbed at her eyes with a tissue. "Oh, that felt good," she said, giving Bill's hand a tight squeeze. "I don't know how to thank you." She was silent for a moment before grinning up at him. "How would you like it if my girls started calling you Grandpa Bill?" Her smile broadened as his blue eyes sparkled with delight.

"Make it 'Paw Paw' and you've got yourself a deal."

She nodded. "Paw Paw, it is."

"Paw Paw Bill—I do like the sound of that. Thank you hon, you've made me one happy old man today. Just wait until I tell Sam."

"You're not old, Bill. As a matter of fact, Carrie's said on countless occasions if Sam hadn't stolen her heart, she could really go for some Bill Broussard, but you didn't hear that from me."

Bill sucked in his breath and grimaced. "Playing second fiddle to Sam Langley isn't quite the ego boost I was looking for, but I guess it'll have to do." He sat back down in his chair and stretched one of his long legs out in front of him. "What's the story with those two? Why didn't they ever have any children together? They've been together long enough."

"By the time they met their children were older. Carrie couldn't have kids anymore. Those two really do have their own love story, though. Maybe she'll tell you about it someday."

Bill gave her a nod. "I bet that's a story I'd find interesting. Should we call her back now?"

She nodded and made the call. Within five minutes, they'd heard the slam of car doors in the drive.

Bill stood and gave her a hug. When he pulled away, she placed her hand on the face so similar to Jackson's. "Thank you, Bill."

"You're welcome, hon." He turned to the door. "I'll leave, so you and those girls can have some privacy."

"Oh, but can you wait around for a few minutes? I want you and Carrie to be here after I straighten things out with Mac and Lexie."

He nodded. "I'll send the girls in to you."

Bill met Carrie and the two girls in the patio, closing the door behind him. Mac and Lex went to him, both casting cautious looks at the door.

Bill cradled both girls close to him and tried to reassure them. "Everything is okay now, girls. I promise. Go on, your mom's waiting for you." He watched the girls disappear into the house then turned to Carrie. "She'll be fine now."

Carrie reached out to cover his hands with her own. "I don't know what you told her, but I know it had to be difficult for you, and I'm so thankful."

He gave her a sly look. "Enough to leave Sam for me?"

She pushed his hands away and laughed. "Be serious, Bill."

"It don't cost a thing to ask, and all you can do is turn me down one more time."

Carrie wiped tears of laughter from her eyes as she gazed up at him. "You and Jackson should put a patent on those sexy grins of yours, you know. They're absolutely irresistible."

He raised a brow as he pulled the patio chair out for her. "Have you reconsidered?"

"Okay, nearly irresistible," she threw in, shaking her head as she sat and waited for him to sit across from her. "I've already found the love of my life, but that doesn't mean we can't find someone for you. You interested?"

He pulled his hat off and placed it on the glass topped table. "You know, I've been thinking maybe it's time. Got anyone in mind?"

"I'd have to think on it." She leaned her elbows on the table and tapped her tooth with a fingernail. "Hmmm...What kind of woman would be right for you?"

"I could do with a young grandmotherly type, kind of like you," he said, giving her a wink.

Carrie chuckled as she shook her head. "I appreciate the compliment, honey, but, you can do better. Have you thought about someone young enough to give you a child of your own?"

Bill's brow furrowed as he pondered the question. "I'd like that, but I really didn't think it was an option for me."

"Why not? You're healthy, aren't you?"

"My doc just told me I had the heart of a man twenty years younger. I don't smoke, I lift weights, and swim laps every day to keep in shape, I only drink occasionally, and I do all my own work around the ranch."

Carrie leaned back in her chair and crossed her arms loosely. "At the risk of inflating your ego, you and Jackson are two of the finest looking men I've ever known. When it comes to sex appeal, you easily hold your own against men half your age."

"You really think so?"

"Yep, and I think you should consider children," she said.

Bill sat back in his chair. He ran a hand through his hair and released his breath in a slow hiss. "All right then, let's do it. My life is in your hands. What do you need me to do?"

She smiled and gave his hand an affectionate pat. "Sit back and watch the gears turn, Bill. I'll take care of you."

The door suddenly opened as Mac and Lexie burst through, giggling and grinning from ear to ear. The two little girls ran to Bill's outstretched arms, as squeals of "Paw Paw!" filled the air.

Giselle watched through tear-filled eyes as her daughters hugged the man who'd promised to become an even bigger part of their lives.

"Is it true?"

"Are you our Paw Paw now?"

Bill beamed down at them. "I am if you want me to be," he said, to even more high pitched shrieks of joy.

"We've never had a Paw Paw before," Lexie said.

Mackenzie raised hopeful brown eyes to Bill. "Would that make Jackson our uncle, or our daddy—" She spread her hands, "Or what?"

She caught the amused look Bill sent her direction. "How about if you just call him Jackson, for now?" she offered. "I'm sure he'd be fine with that."

"We have a Paw Paw Bill, *and* a Jackson!" Mackenzie squealed. "I can't wait to tell everyone that my birthday party is going to be at my Paw Paw Bill's house."

"Paw Paw Bill's *ranch*," he corrected her.

Mackenzie's eyes grew large with excitement. "Lex, our Paw Paw has a real ranch with cows and horses.."

"And mini horses and piggy goats," Lexie added, her voice rising to an excited crescendo.

"And a pond we can fish in," Mac finished.

"I also ordered paddle boats for your party," Bill added. "They'll be ours to keep so you can use them anytime."

Mackenzie threw herself at him again. "I can tell already, you're going to be the best Paw Paw in the world." She turned to her mother. "Can we call Jackson? I can't wait to tell him we're his family now."

Giselle sucked in her breath as she made a face. "Um, not just yet. I think I need to speak to him first then I'll let you talk to him. You two go inside with Bill and Carrie, okay?"

As Bill and the girls vanished through the door amidst giggles and laughter, Carrie turned to Giselle. "Do you have his number?"

"Sure do," she said, flashing her I-phone.

"I've been calling all morning and he hasn't answered. Maybe he will, if he sees your number," Carrie said.

Giselle took a seat at the patio table and pulled up Jackson's number, then lifted her face to soak up the glorious morning sunrays while waiting for him to answer. She finally heard a gravelly voice croak a single word.

"Yeah."

"Jackson. It's Giselle."

"What do you want?"

"Are you okay?"

"If you mean miserable, heartbroken, and hung over, then yeah, I'm damn near perfect," he said, the sarcasm pouring forth from her phone's speaker.

"Oh, I'm sorr..."

"What the hell do you want? You want to rip my heart out? Blame me for Toby's death again?"

"If you'd let me expl..."

"You know, I didn't ask for this crap, and I sure as hell can't help the way I feel. Leave me the hell alone."

Giselle heard the distinct click of disconnection and stared, dumbfounded at the phone. She hit redial and waited. He picked it up and disconnected without a word. The next time she hit redial, she got a busy signal.

"Well, crap," she murmured. "How am I supposed to apologize if you won't answer?" She stood abruptly and went inside.

Lexie turned her hopeful face toward her. "Did you talk to Jackson, Mama?"

"No sweetie, he must still be sleeping. I'll call him later."

Lexie's face crumbled in disappointment. "I bet he's still appressed after yesterday. Can we go see him?"

Giselle brushed her daughter's bangs back from her pixie face. "I think I need to talk to him first before you see him again, Sweetie."

"Can you hurry, Mama? He looked so sad the last time I saw him."

"I'll keep trying, Lex, I promise." After Lexie ran off, Giselle turned to Bill. "I think I need to go over there," she said, repeating their brief conversation.

She caught Carrie's cautious glance in Bill's direction. "I don't know if that's such a good idea. The last time I talked to him, he said he was on his way to an all-nighter with a bottle of Crown. Sounds like he accomplished his goal."

"Jackson hardly ever drinks. He had to be hurting to pull one that bad," Bill said.

Giselle chewed on the corner of her thumbnail. "I can't stand this. I need to apologize to his face."

Carrie's gaze shifted from Giselle, to Bill, then back to Giselle. "I really wish you'd let him sleep it off."

Giselle paced the floor between her fridge and her guests. "I feel guilty, Carrie. Can you understand that?"

"You could follow me over there," Bill suggested. "That way I can be there to make sure he's okay. He was some kind of upset when I dropped him off."

Giselle turned pleading eyes toward Carrie. "Could I bother you one more time to watch the girls for me? You can bring them to your place."

Carrie released a long sigh. "All right, but this goes against my better judgment."

Giselle clasped her hands together. "Thank you. Let me get my purse."

Chapter Nine

Bill pulled into Jackson's drive thirty minutes later, followed closely by Giselle. He rang the doorbell several times without getting an answer. Using his key, he let himself and Giselle inside.

"Wow. I love what he did in here," Giselle whispered.

Bill collected the nearly empty bottle of aged ninety proof whiskey he'd given Jackson for Christmas. "New furniture. Old whiskey. Said he was gonna save it for a special occasion." He turned to Giselle and sent her a grin. "Congratulations." She had the decency to look ashamed. He sniffed at the half empty glass on a sturdy end table and made a face. "Straight," he said. *Oh. Shit.*

Bill turned to her, prepared for the worst. "Might be a good idea for you to wait outside. I need to see what kind of shape he's in."

She gave him a silent nod and stepped outside.

Giselle tensed up when she heard the deep, menacing, growl behind her. She turned to see a huge Doberman, its teeth bared in a snarl, at the end of the sidewalk. She backed cautiously to the door, blindly feeling for the knob; thankfully, it opened for her and she backed into the room. She cleared the door in just enough time to screech and slam it in the fast approaching dog's face. Giselle breathed a sigh of relief as she rested her forehead on the door then turned. She froze, her breath catching in her throat, at the sight before her.

Jackson shut off the shower and stepped out onto his newly tiled bathroom floor, dying for a big glass of ice water. His mouth was dry as the Texas panhandle in the middle of a drought. He could have used another hour or two of sleep, but Giselle's call had ended all hope of that. Just hearing her voice had twisted his insides into a painful knot. He wrapped one towel loosely around his hips and grabbed another for his hair. Bill's voice rumbled from the opposite side of the door. He pulled it open and stared at his uncle.

Freshly shaved and showered, with his hair still dripping water, he began toweling his hair. "Excuse me. I'm thirsty as hell," he growled, brushing past Bill.

Jackson was almost at the end of the hallway when he heard a feminine screech, accompanied by the slamming of a door. His neighbor's damn Doberman barked incessantly outside the front door of his home. He cleared the hall and froze in his tracks at the sight before him. What the hell was

Giselle doing in his living room? And why was she standing there with her forehead resting against his front door?

Almost as though she felt his presence, she turned slowly to face him. Their gazes locked, her eyes seemed to double in size. Any second now, she'd turn away from him.

She didn't.

Giselle didn't speak, didn't give him reasons for being there, didn't even blink, for that matter. She just stared. Hard. Her gaze took a leisurely path across his upper torso, down to his mid-section, and past that to his lower extremities. It continued with a slow tour upward again, revealing a tick of her left eyebrow, a slight lift—as though she'd seen something she particularly liked—picked up its trail over his arms and shoulders until her lips parted. Her breathing grew shallow, somewhat labored. Still she didn't turn away.

He stood there, observing her reaction to him. She licked her lips, liking what she saw. Then caught her lower lip on her teeth, scraped until it popped out. Wet. Swollen. Effective. Seriously. If a lab could find a way to bottle that move, no man would ever need to take a little blue pill. Ever.

And if he didn't get the hell out of that room *now*, she'd have something new to stare at.

He spun on his heel and walked away from her, back to his bedroom.

"See about Giselle," he growled at Bill. "I think the neighbor's Doberman attacked her." Bill rushed out, leaving Jackson alone with his dilemma. He shut the bedroom door and took several deep breaths, trying to regulate his heartbeat. The unexpected sight of Giselle staring him down—and looking as if she liked what she saw. That wasn't something he'd forget anytime soon. He caught sight of his reflection in the full length mirror, the evidence still there, undeniable, in no way lessening. He re-entered his bathroom, stepped inside the shower, and flipped the shower tap to cold.

Jackson stood there, fresh from a shower, obviously, in nothing but a towel wrapped loosely around his hips. In his right hand, he still clutched the hand towel that he'd been using to dry his hair. She lifted her gaze to his well-defined chest and abdomen, covered with a fine dusting of dark, silky hair. Her eyes followed the trail of hair down past his belly button to where the towel covered up the rest of him. Her gaze traveled to one side of his hips, then the other, noting that sexy pad of muscle there on both sides. She dropped past the towel to thickly muscled calves, then back up to his long muscular arms and shoulders. Giselle stared at the torso rivaling that of a Greek god's, and felt her face infuse with heat. She licked her parched lips, thinking she could slap someone for a long, cool, drink of water. Just as she lifted her gaze to his stunned face, he turned and headed down the hallway.

The rear view of Jackson was almost as captivating as the front. She watched, fascinated, as the muscles in his broad, tanned back and shoulders worked and rippled with every swing of his arms. She stared at the towel that clung tenaciously to his narrow hips, willing it to fall off so she could get a glimpse of what it hid. Giselle watched it shift from left to right, with every step Jackson took, craning her neck to keep him in sight. She heard him mumble something to Bill, who barreled out of the bedroom door and down the hallway toward her. Her shocked gaze locked onto Bill's as she heard the slam of a door in the distance.

Slightly dazed, she pointed over her shoulder toward the front door. "There's a dog. A big dog."

"Are you hurt? Did he bite you?" Bill walked toward her and the door.

"N-no-no," she stammered.

He gently moved her away from the door then jerked it open. "Get out of here you son of a bitch!"

The offensive animal ran off.

"Every stinking time I come over here, that dog's loose. I kicked it in the face once so he's got enough sense not to come after me."

Giselle's gaze locked on Jackson's as he re-entered the room, wearing jeans and a white T-shirt, feet bare, hair tousled, looking damn near as good as he had wearing nothing but that towel. She jumped at Bill's angry bark.

"That damned dog is a menace!"

Jackson stopped within three feet of her. "Are you okay?"

She nodded, averted her gaze as heat rose from her neck, inching its way upward.

Bill continued his rant, thankfully, drawing Jackson's attention from her rapidly flushing face.

"Who's that damn Doberman belong to, Jackson? That's the third time this month I've seen him out of his yard and off his leash, and I don't even live here."

Jackson's gaze finally wavered, then focused on Bill, thank God.

"I've been meaning to talk to my neighbor about him."

"What if Mac and Lexie had been here?" Bill demanded.

Jackson's gaze travelled from Bill, to her, then back to Bill. His tone grew hard. "Why would the girls be here?" His gaze landed once more on Giselle. "Come to think of it, why are *you* here?"

She met his gaze for a split second before allowing herself the chance to absorb the sight of him. Giselle had worked with Jackson for five years and had never seen him in anything more casual than Dockers and a Polo shirt at the office. She'd barely noticed him when he showed up to work in her yard the past three months. Yet, here he stood, in a pair of faded jeans that fit snugly over his muscled thighs, hugging his hips. He wore a clean, white, V-neck T-shirt that clung nicely to every dip and bulge of his beefy chest. And he was barefooted. Her senses firing on all cylinders, she swallowed.

Giselle lifted her gaze to his clean shaven face. Several locks of damp, chocolate brown hair curled enticingly over his forehead. Dark circles peeked out from under his eyes, remnants of his night of drinking, no doubt. It jogged her into remembering the reason she was here.

"Jackson, I came to tell you how very sorry I am for saying those awful things to you." She searched for Bill, for some form of backup. He'd somehow managed to slip out of the room, maybe out of the house. She took a deep breath and began her explanation.

"I know you were only trying to help. You and Bill have been so good to the girls. I couldn't see past my own hurt and ended up hurting them, and you, too. I'm sorry."

He released the breath he'd been holding, seemed to relax for the first time since she made her appearance. He took two steps closer, spoke in a voice deep, and a little husky—maybe from whisky?

"What does this mean?"

His breath was sweet, a blend of minty toothpaste and either mouthwash or whiskey. She couldn't concentrate with his gaze planted on hers. She focused on his broad chest instead. "I'm sorry for trying to stop you from seeing the girls, and for being such a—for being so unreasonable. Whether you like it or not, you'll be seeing a lot more of them from now on." Giselle's breath caught in her throat as he cocked his head and lifted one corner of his mouth in a lopsided grin.

"Oh yeah? Why's that?"

"Bill asked if he could be their honorary grandfather," her voice trailed off.

He leaned in closer. "What was that last part again?"

She gave him a weak smile, for the first time, wondering if he'd mind. "He wants my girls to call him Paw Paw Bill from now on. I hope you don't mind."

He was so near, she could smell the fragrance of his soap, a clean, masculine scent, tantalizing her nostrils, tempting her to lean closer. Oh God, she'd missed being this close to a man.

Jackson shook his head, clearly confused. "Why would I mind? Don't you realize how I feel about those girls?"

She heard the sincerity in his statement. "I do now."

He lowered his head, looking pensive for a moment. "Giselle?"

"Huh?" *Focus on the chest. Just the chest.* She fought the urge to run her hands over the fabric of his T-shirt, it's material stretched tautly over the sculpted surface of his pectorals.

"If Bill is their Paw Paw, what does that make me?"

She blinked, as if awakening from a trance. "You're Jackson. Just Jackson." Her eyes darted up to his face. He gave her that crooked grin again, the one that must have made the girls melt when he was about seventeen.

"Just Jackson, huh? That's fine by me. Do you mind me asking what brought on this change of heart?"

Giselle nodded. "Your Uncle Bill and I had a talk. He's a very smart man, you know."

Jackson snorted, his irritation obvious. "God, I hope you didn't tell him that; he already thinks he's right about everything."

She grinned slyly. "Is he? Always right about everything, I mean?" Her stomach flipped at his low rumble of laughter.

"Always, and it annoys the living hell out of me." He shook his head. "I've got a Master's Degree in Engineering, and he's never spent one day in college. He's still smarter than I am."

Giselle chuckled. "That must be a gigantic blow to that big, bad engineer ego of yours."

"No," he sighed, dramatically. "Just a small one."

"What's the matter, Jackson? Did the big, tall man hurt your widdle biddy, feelings?" She pushed out her lower lip.

His brow furrowed. "Okay smart ass," he growled. "Don't push your luck." He reached out to place his hands on her thin shoulders, and locked his gaze on hers. "Are you okay now, really?"

Giselle felt heat infuse her face at his close perusal. She looked away shyly and lifted a shoulder. "I think so. I'm not saying I won't have some bad days, but the worst is over."

"Giselle." He gave her shoulders another light squeeze, urging her to look at him. "Are *we* okay?"

Reluctantly, she met the piercing blue-eyed gaze. "You tell me. I'm the one who came here to apologize." She pulled away and shifted one foot to put some distance between them. "You could have saved me a trip if you hadn't hung up and taken your phone off the hook."

He gave her a halfhearted shrug, "What can I say? I had a rough night." Jackson pulled her into a hug that probably would have been short and sweet, had she not wrapped her arms tightly around his waist.

"Thank you, Jackson," she spoke into his chest. "You and Bill have been lifesavers for the girls, and for me too."

He pressed her head to his chest, gently cradling her as his right arm tightened protectively around her shoulders. "I'd do anything for Toby's girls."

She turned her face and pressed her nose up against his shirt. Her senses fired on all cylinders, overloaded and exploding. She had the strongest urge to flatten the palms of her hands over the cottony fabric, to push it tight against the twelve pack abs. She inhaled deeply, breathing in the scent of freshly laundered cotton, lifted her face until her nose cleared the V-neck collar.

Intoxicated by the scent of pure, masculine Jackson, she forced herself to loosen her grip on his waist. When he released her, she grabbed the opportunity to back away.

"I'm glad you're better, Giselle."

"Thank you." She coughed and cleared her throat.

"That dog didn't bite you, did he?"

She shook her head, her face heating again as she remembered the sight of him in that towel. "Bill told me to wait outside, but that dog came after me. I ran inside and when I turned around, you were there. And, uh, sorry about that," she finished lamely.

"I'm sure I'm not the first man you've seen in a towel."

"No. I just never expected to see my boss in that state of—undress." She fanned her face. "Is it just me or is it kind of warm in here?"

"It's just you." He turned and tried, unsuccessfully, to hide the grin that covered his face. Oh yeah, he was enjoying this.

"Speaking of work," he said, clearing his throat. "I heard an ugly rumor that you may not go back."

She took two steps back and turned away from him. "I'm considering staying home, now that it's just me and the girls. Toby picked up a lot of slack for me around the house when we were trying to meet project deadlines."

"I could make sure you wouldn't have to work any overtime."

"That wouldn't be fair to Carrie or anyone else, Jackson."

"Anything you couldn't take care of during your regular work hours, I'd do for you. Other than the girls' ballgames, it's not like I have anything better to do," he added.

"Not now, maybe, but you could in the future. Besides, I don't want anybody doing my job for me. If I can't handle it, I'll resign, so you can hire someone to replace me on our team."

"Can you afford to quit working? Are you okay, financially, I mean?"

She nodded. "I never did work for the money. Toby was a good provider. It was just to have someone to relate to other than the two kids. Once the insurance companies settled, we were all set for life. Trust funds and college funds for the girls. Toby took care of us." She smiled wistfully.

"Of course he did. He was a good man. And a great friend to me."

She nodded, wiping a tear from the corner of her eye, then shook it off. She looked around suddenly. "You've made some changes since I was here last."

His brow rose, curiously. "You've been here before?"

"It was for a Christmas party about a month after I started at B & L." She walked over to the furniture to examine it. "Toby and I came over with Sam and Carrie. I remember your furniture was—it was—well, this is better."

"Thanks. Chloe's taste really sucked, if truth be told." He waved his hand. "I bought all this stuff after—after the wreck."

"You picked it out yourself?"

"Yes, all by myself," he boasted.

"You're such a big boy. Yes, you are," she teased.

"Oh, you're a riot," he said, dryly.

"This place looks like you now. Is this all you bought?"

"I got a new bedroom set, too. Oh man, my new memory foam mattress is fantastic. If you're ever in the market, I recommend one like that. I love my bed," he said with a deep sigh.

"Really? Our mattress was shot. Do you mind if I check it out? It's down here, right?" she said, walking toward the end of the hall. Giselle pushed open the door and gasped in unconcealed pleasure at the sight of the huge bed. "Jackson, this is gorgeous." She ran her hand along the satiny rich wood grain, appreciating the fine quality. She fingered the rich woven fabric of the comforter and walked over to run her hand slowly along the drapes. She knew he'd followed her to the room. "Is all of this new?"

"Yep, I got it all from the display."

Giselle nodded slowly. "Excellent choice. Now what's so special about this mattress? Is it a pillow-top?"

He nodded. "It's unbelievably comfortab—" His breath caught when she sat on the edge of the bed, kicked off her sandals, and stretched out across it.

"I don't know how you can stand to leave it. It cradles you," she purred. She curled into a fetal position and released a low groan. "This. Is. Fabulous."

Jackson froze in the doorway of his bedroom. The sight of Giselle, lying on his bed, moaning in pleasure, was too much for one sex-starved man to bear. For the second time in under a half hour, he had to turn away from her. He cleared his throat loudly as he walked away. "I need to hydrate. You want some water or anything?"

"No, I'm fine."

"You sure as hell are," he mumbled under his breath.

"What was that?"

He grimaced as he got to the end of the hallway. "I said, are you sure?"

"Yeah, I need to go. I've imposed on Carrie enough."

"You drove by yourself?" he asked, hoping to change the subject to something mundane. "Where the hell did Uncle Bill go, anyway?"

She followed him into the living room. "I think he went outside. Do you think that Doberman's still out there? I'm not usually scared of dogs, but that one is pretty big, and mean looking."

Jackson opened his door then stepped out in his bare feet

"Nope, I don't see him. Maybe Bill took care of him for you."

Giselle rushed to the door. "What do you mean, took care of him? He wouldn't shoot it, would he? It's not the dog's fault it's not penned up."

"I just meant he'd go talk to the owners. But he did leave. His truck is gone. Come on, I'll walk you to your car. How's it running, anyway?"

"Okay, I guess."

"Does it need to be serviced anytime soon?"

"I don't know. Toby took care of all that."

He opened the driver's side door and checked the sticker on the windshield. "He had everything done mid-December. See? It even shows when the next service is due."

She moved in to take a closer look at the windshield. "I remember now. He shows me that every time he gets—I mean—he showed me that every time he got it done." The sparkle receded from her eyes. "That's the difficult part for me, you know, trying to remember to speak about him in the past tense. It still feels like he's going to walk through the door, or pull up into the garage, or—"

"Or call or text you from his cell phone," he added. "I keep waiting for him to call me to set up a game of basketball."

She sniffed and wiped a tear from the corner of her eye. "It's the little things that set me off, you know?"

He nodded. "I do know. During that first month, I caught myself looking at the calendar because it would have been the beginning of Chloe's cycle. That's when she'd get really depressed and difficult. Of course, now I know it was all an act, but the habit is ingrained."

"How long do you think it'll take before we stop thinking that way, Jackson?"

He shrugged. "I'll let you know when it happens, okay?"

She smiled as she buckled her seatbelt and started her vehicle. "See ya."

"Careful going home, Giselle. Thanks for coming by."

"It was the least I could do."

All the way home, Giselle couldn't rid herself of the mental image of Jackson wearing nothing but that towel. Who knew that body was hiding under those suits, slacks, and dress shirts? Toby had always been in excellent shape, but Jackson—dear God—Jackson's body was magnificent. Catching sight of Toby's photo on her sun visor, she suddenly felt a wave of guilt.

"Oh, baby, I'm sorry," she whispered to her husband's image. "I guess I'm a little needy right now. It's been over three months since we made love, and you know how much I enjoyed it, Babe. If you can see me and the girls, watch out for us, will you?"

By the time she got to Kenton, she felt the consequences of both a sleepless night, and her morning outing.

Carrie took one look at her and sent her home for a nap. "Come back after you've rested. Sam's barbequing and all the kids will be here for lunch."

Giselle gave her friend a hug. "What would I do without you and Sam, and the rest of the family?"

"We're all just happy you're feeling better, hon. I don't mind telling you what a huge relief it is to have *you* back."

Once she was home, Giselle walked down the hallway to the master bedroom. She opened the door, stood in the doorway staring at the bed she'd shared with her husband.

She entered the walk-in closet, ran her hand along the rows of neatly hung slacks, shirts, blazers and jackets. She flipped the tie carousel, sending the banners of silk into a blur of colors. She lifted the lid on the hamper. Gasped when she found the Dockers and Polo shirt he'd worn to work the day before he died. That was the day she'd come home from work and found him dressed up like a princess, courtesy of Mac and Lexie. She smiled at the memory and thought of the shots she'd taken with her digital camera. She'd plugged the memory card directly into the digital picture frame in the kitchen but hadn't had a chance to view them. *I'll watch it with Mac and Lex later this afternoon.*

She picked up Toby's shirt and carried it with her to bed, teary-eyed and smiling, as she picked off bits of pink feather boa from the navy blue shirt. She curled onto her side and raised the shirt to her face, breathing in his lingering scent before closing her eyes. She let the tears flow freely, quietly mourning the loss of her husband.

Would she ever feel love again? Maybe, but there's no way she would never feel what she had with Toby. The absolute certainty that they were created to complete each other. Her tears stopped after a few minutes, and she drifted off to sleep, think of a soft bed; one that cradled her and made her want to stay in it forever.

She and Toby were making love, and it was so wonderful. When she opened her eyes, instead of seeing Toby's sexy brown eyes, she gazed into smoldering, piercing blue eyes. It was still Toby, but with those intense blue eyes. She'd been confused at first. But those eyes, those fabulously sexy eyes lured her in. By the time she knew she wanted more of those eyes, they began to fade away. All of it, the face, the gorgeous eyes, the long, muscular body that had covered hers, filling her completely—vanished. She awoke feeling alone, empty, not to mention confused, and sexually frustrated.

She sat up, searching out the familiar surroundings. The sense of Toby was so strong in the room they had shared together since before the birth of their daughters. They had discussed whether or not to sell their home and buy something larger with more living area. They'd even talked about buying a few acres just outside the city limits and building their own home. He'd mentioned drawing up a floor plan one day, but she didn't know if he'd had a chance to complete it. Maybe there was something in his office.

Toby's office. She hadn't been since the accident, and Gordon, his partner, hadn't pushed her, but it was time to clean it out. Giselle stretched and winced at the familiar kinks caused by this old mattress. Definite candidate for replacement.

A quick glance at the clock told her she'd slept for two hours. She rose from the bed to tweak her make-up and hair, and slipped on a pair of sandals. Snatching her keys from the counter, she walked outside. As soon as the glorious warmth of the midday sun touched her face, she decided to walk the two blocks to the Langley's home.

During the walk, her thoughts returned to the dream. Those deep, sensual eyes that replaced Toby's brown eyes continued to haunt her. It didn't make sense, but she could still see them—piercing and blue, mesmerizing, and sexy as hell. God, she'd like to get one more look at those eyes. She pushed aside her feelings of guilt. *It's just a dream, Giselle.*

She approached the Langley home, its driveway street front packed with vehicles. She hit their walk, but the sound of laughter from the backyard had her bypassing the front door. She turned, instead, for the south side of the house—lured by the laughter and happy chatter.

Giselle rounded the corner at a brisk walk, and collided with a large body as firm and solid as a brick wall. A body whose magnificent masculine scent stirred her senses as well as her memories.

She glanced up as two strong hands reached up to balance her, keep her from flying on her backside. She looked up, then froze. Her apology ready but silenced, as her gaze settled on a pair of sexy as hell blue eyes.

Chapter Ten

"Did I hurt you?" Jackson stepped back to examine her.

"N-n-no. I'm," she stammered, then let her voice trail off as the sudden realization hit her. Jackson's eyes?

She inhaled sharply, her gaze locked onto his eyes. His sensual, sexy, piercing blue eyes. The ones from her dream.

"Oh. Oh. My. God"

"What? Are you alright? I'm so sorry. I should have been paying closer attention. I was on my way to your place. Carrie had just asked me to go check on you."

"I'm okay."

"Good. Did you have a good rest?"

She nodded, unable to tear her gaze away from those eyes. Finally, feeling a blush start to rise, she forced herself to look away and tried to move around him. "Is everyone back there?"

"Yes, but hold on, now." He grasped both of her arms in a gentle hold. "Are you okay?"

"I'm fine. I'm anxious to see everyone, that's all." She crossed her arms self-consciously.

He looked around for her truck. "Did you walk here?"

She nodded and attempted to walk past him again.

"Wait..." He grabbed her wrist.

"What, Jackson? Jeez!" she said, desperate to get away from those eyes.

"Was the walk too much? Do you need something for pain?"

She closed her eyes, thinking it would be foolish to pass up an opportunity to explain her strange behavior. "Maybe I pushed it too far today, but I already took something. I'll be fine in a bit."

"Okay." He relented, but held her arm protectively as he escorted her to the back yard. "Look who's here, everybody."

Lexie got to her first "Mama! Jackson and Paw Paw came."

Giselle stole a glance at Jackson before answering her daughter. "I see that, Lex. Have you eaten yet?"

Mac approached. "No, Sam just finished cooking the barbeque."

"Mama, guess what," Lexie said in a whisper loud enough for Jackson to hear.

"What, sweetie?" Giselle brushed her daughter's curls away from her eyes.

"We almost had to eat our barbeque like daddy use to cook it. With that black stuff on it."

Jackson gave Giselle a curious look. "Did he use some kind of blackened seasoning?"

Giselle suppressed a snort of laughter as Lexie raised her scrunched face toward Jackson. "Is 'burned to a crisp' a kind of seezning?"

"Oh," Jackson led Giselle to a chair. "I get it, now."

Despite her uneasiness, Giselle laughed over her daughter's comment. "Toby couldn't grill a thing without burning it."

Jackson laughed and shook his head. "He always told me he was a master griller. You want to eat inside or outside?"

"Outside, I think. It's nice today."

He nodded. "I'll bring your plate to you. Do you want anything in particular?"

"I'm hungry, so some of everything."

As soon as he disappeared into the house, the younger women of the family swarmed her. "What's going on here today? Is it somebody's birthday?"

"It's for you, chick," Gretchen said.

"Is it?"

"Because we're all so glad you're feeling better," Lauren added.

Giselle placed one hand over her heart. "I'm so touched."

Carrie spoke from behind Giselle. "We celebrate family and you and the girls are part of it."

Jackson appeared with her plate and glass of sweet tea. "Here you go."

"Thanks Jackson."

"Ladies, are the other men attending to your needs?" he asked the other women.

Carrie waved him off. "We're fine, Jackson. But Lexie won't let anyone but you fix her plate, so you'd better get in there."

"I'm on it," he said, grinning.

Once he'd left, Trina let out a low whistle. "Honey, he can attend to my needs any day of the week."

"That's what I'm talking about," Gretchen agreed.

"Either Jackson or Bill, for that matter," Amanda added.

"Neither of them act big headed about their looks," Lauren said.

Carrie shook her head. "I think they're completely unaware they have that effect on women."

Giselle kept her silence, but groaned inwardly. *Oh Lord, please let him be unaware.*

She felt a little self-conscious with all the attention, particularly since Jackson seemed to be catering to her. She didn't need any prolonged contact with him, especially after that dream. Forget dream interpretation. It didn't take a genius to tell her she was attracted to the man. She stared at his bulk filling the doorway. It took less of one to see why. He wore a blue Polo shirt tucked into a pair of dress khaki shorts that fit snugly around his hips. A nice look, but it didn't hold a candle to him draped in a towel.

Giselle turned as Carrie cleared her throat, caught her friend watching her. She shifted her gaze quickly to her plate.

The after dinner conversation gravitated to baseball, especially since seven of the eight children in attendance were playing in the summer league.

Jackson took the empty lawn chair beside Giselle. "Are you feeling up to making some of the girls' games yet?"

She glanced at her daughters playing with the other kids and nodded. "I'll make them from now on."

"And speaking of baseball," Carrie announced, "I heard this year's Summer Sizzler tournament has been scheduled for the second Saturday in August. Sam, they want you to call the games. You up to umpiring in hundred degree heat again this year?"

"I guess I'll live for one day," he groaned.

Jackson leaned forward. "How are the teams formed?"

"Area contractors form teams by cities," Sam explained. "I've seen years when we have five or more teams, and I've seen some lean years when only two showed up. I know the Lake Coburn team could use some new blood."

"You know," Bill said, "Jackson played some college ball. Are you going to play this year?"

"You played college ball? Where'd you play?" Amanda's husband, Joe, asked.

Jackson cleared his throat and mumbled an unclear reply.

"I'm sorry, I didn't understand you, Jackson. Who'd you play for?" Joe repeated.

"L.S.U." Bill answered. "Louisiana State University."

"Really? What year was that?" Joe was showing some real interest now.

"I only played one year, and it was nearly 20 years ago."

"But it was a hell of a year," Bill said, his eyes shining with pride.

"What position?" Joe asked.

"I pitched, until my injury."

"Wait a minute! Around that time, my step dad and I went to watch L.S.U. play," Joe said. "They had a freshman pitcher who blew his shoulder out after pitching a no-hitter the last regular game of the season. He was a Broussard, and real tall. Was that you?"

"Afraid so," Jackson admitted.

"All this time you've worked with Carrie and Sam and we didn't know. Man, you were a hell of a player. That shoulder injury of yours was a tragedy."

Jackson shrugged. "It was unfortunate—not tragic."

"So, that was it. You never played again?"

"Nope. That ended my short lived career. After I had the surgery and completed physical therapy, they wanted me to play first base, but all I'd ever wanted to do was pitch. Besides, they already had the best first baseman." He shrugged. "That's when I changed my major to engineering. I hadn't really thought about what I was going to do with my life until then."

"So, if you hadn't blown out your shoulder, we never would have met you," Carrie said. "So, are you thinking about playing?"

"I just might. Do they call practices? I'm kind of rusty," Jackson admitted.

"Practices!" Sam laughed. "No, they just show up and pray they don't hurt themselves. Relax, you're in good shape."

Amanda coughed. "Understatement," she said, as a ripple of laughter ran through the women. All the women except Giselle, who was trying like hell not to picture him wrapped in that towel.

Inspired by all the talk of baseball, Sam and the rest of the guys hit the storage shed looking for surplus baseball equipment, which Sam had plenty of. Before long, nearly everyone was out in the huge yard, playing a game of softball.

It didn't take long to discover that Jackson hadn't lost his touch when it came to hitting or fielding. Even the women got into the game, all except for Carrie who sat with two year old Ava, and Giselle, who sat next to her to watch the game and cheer. When it was Jackson's turn to bat, he stood solemnly for a moment then pointed out to right field, drawing hoots and hollers from the other players. He shuffled his feet at the makeshift base and swung the bat a few times to loosen up. He let Joe's first and second pitches go by, but the third one came right over the plate. Jackson's bat met the ball with a loud crack and sent it exactly where he'd pointed, over the fence. Lex and Mac screamed with excitement as he trotted leisurely to the bases and finished by stomping on home plate.

"Might be worth going to watch that game this year," Carrie mentioned. "What do you think, Giselle?"

"Huh? Oh, yeah, maybe so," she stammered, trying to hide the fact that she enjoyed watching him move. She'd been totally engrossed in watching his powerful arms when he hit the ball with enough force and control to send it just where he wanted. She couldn't tear her gaze from him as he ran the bases with the obvious grace of a natural athlete. She smiled as he easily scooped her two daughters up in his arms for hugs.

She turned, finding Carrie staring at her. The gleam in her eye, along with the satisfied expression had Giselle blushing down to her sandals.

Carrie smiled. "Don't beat yourself up over this, Giselle."

Giselle concentrated on the monumental effort of brushing a ladybug from her knee. "I don't know what you're talking about."

"You're not thinking anything different from any other woman out here."

Giselle shook her head, unable to face her. "God, Carrie, I haven't looked at another man since Toby. I loved my husband."

Carrie nodded. "We all love our husbands. It doesn't mean we can't appreciate the physical qualities of a man like Jackson. And it sure as hell isn't cheating on Toby. Besides, you're still so young. You have needs. Trust me, once you get over the initial shock of 'seeing' Jackson in that way, you'll remember soon enough that he's just a man."

"This morning," Giselle began uneasily, "I, uh, saw him with nothing but a towel wrapped around his waist. Long story—involved a dog coming after me," she said, as Carrie's mouth pursed. "Toby had a good body, but Jackson . . . He's a freaking Adonis under those business suits."

"Is he?" Carrie made a show of rising from her chair. "Think if I bring a towel out here he'll model it for us?"

Giselle grabbed her friend's arm. "You'd better sit your ass down right now, lady."

Once their laughter subsided, Giselle grew quiet. "I slept in my bed when I got home this morning."

Carrie nodded, remaining silent.

"His clothes from the last day he worked were still in his hamper in our closet." She left out the fact that she'd fallen asleep clutching the shirt still covered in her husband's scent. "I guess I should box everything up. That's what people on television do, isn't it? Box it up and give it to Goodwill or Salvation Army? And then they move on with their lives."

Carrie leaned toward her. "I think we know it isn't that simple. It can wait. I'm glad you slept in the room, though. Did you sleep well?"

"I woke up stiff," she said, making a face. "That mattress is shot. The guest bed is a lot more comfortable."

"You don't have to tell me. That's why I slept on the sofa when I was there."

Giselle nodded. "Something that won't wait for too much longer is Toby's office. I need to clean it out one day soon."

"If you need help, call me," Carrie said.

"Thanks, but I think that's a solo job." After a few moments of watching the ball game, Giselle turned to Carrie. "Did you know Jackson got all knew furniture?"

"Uh huh. He did it the day after the accident. He purged Chloe from the house."

"Come to think of it, I didn't see any sign that she'd ever lived there. No wedding pictures, no photos of them together, no snapshots on the fridge or anything like that."

"Oh, she never displayed any pictures of Jackson."

Giselle whipped her head around to stare at her friend. "You're joking, right?"

"I wish I was. That—" She covered her granddaughter's ears before continuing. "That self-centered bitch had glamour shots and studio shots of herself everywhere, but not a single picture of Jackson on display. No wedding, high school graduation, college graduation, especially when he played ball for L.S.U. Nothing. It was like he didn't exist. Chloe was one giant ego trip unto herself."

"Oh my God. What a horrible thing to do to your husband."

Carrie shook her head. "I always told you there was stuff going on in his home life that you didn't know about. That's why I stayed on your case to cut him some slack."

"And there I was, giving him hell at work, too. I feel so bad about that, now."

"Let it go, Giselle. He certainly has. So, how's the new furniture? Bill said it's nice."

"Beautiful! A huge improvement over what was there before. Very masculine, sturdy pieces, but all just beautiful and in good taste. It all looks right for Jackson." She nodded, her mind pulled toward the massive bed. "You wouldn't believe how comfortable his bed is."

"Oh, really?" Carrie leveled a gaze on Giselle.

"Oh stop! I tried it out to see what it was like. I swear, sometimes you're so twisted."

"I know," Carrie chuckled. "You can blame Sam. He's rubbed off, and not in a good way."

Giselle laughed and turned back to watch Jackson stretch one long, muscular leg, then the other. His fluid movements brought back the image of him walking away in that towel. "Yeah," she said, barely above a whisper. "I'd never want to get out of bed if I had a mattress like that . . ."

Jackson pulled in to her drive around 4 p.m. that afternoon, and walked Giselle and her girls to the door. He couldn't help but notice that she seemed a little quiet.

"You sure you're okay?"

Giselle nodded, rubbed her side gingerly. "It was a wonderful day, but I'm a little tired."

"It'll get easier now that you're moving around more. You'll feel better in a week or so."

"I hope you're right, I'll need stamina with those two. They only have six more weeks of school."

"Then we'll be out for the summer!" Lexie cried, darting between Jackson and Giselle to run through the open door.

Giselle turned to face him, but took a while longer to lift her gaze to meet his.

"I-I guess I'll see you at Mac's game on Tuesday."

He gave an adamant nod. "Absolutely. Would you like Bill and I to pick you and the girls up on our way in?"

Her gaze darted to the cement, to the patio table, to Mac bouncing a rubber ball. "Yeah, I guess that'd be okay. A little before six?"

"We'll be here." He smiled, not that she saw it.

Biting her bottom lip, she mumbled a quick goodbye, stepped through the door, and closed it behind her.

Jackson stared at the door for a second. Seeing his uncle watching from the truck, he lifted both arms and dropped them, completely stumped as to what he'd done to upset her.

He climbed in behind the wheel, still troubled at her behavior, and backed out of the drive.

"What's wrong?"

He turned to his uncle. "I have no idea."

"What do you mean? Did she say we couldn't go to the game on Tuesday?"

"No, we're picking them up on our way in."

"What is it, then?"

"I don't know. She won't look me in the eye."

Bill's gaze sparkled with amusement. "She keeps seeing you in that towel."

"I doubt that," Jackson mumbled, even as his uncle's low rumble of laughter reached him.

"I'm telling you, she keeps seeing you in all your glory. Didn't you see her ogling you? She couldn't force herself to turn away. The temperature in that room must've jumped twenty degrees. Got so hot I had to leave the premises."

Jackson turned on him. "Yeah, we noticed you'd left."

"Humph. I'm willing to bet it took a while. The two of you were so deep in it, I could have been doing one of Mac's cheers in a corner and you wouldn't have noticed."

Jackson shook his head. "It's got to be something else that's bothering her."

Bill dissolved into side-splitting laughter. "Whatever you say, Jackson."

Chapter Eleven

The next morning, Giselle was busy doing some light dusting and housekeeping, feeling uplifted by her recent phone conversation with her co-workers. The self-dubbed 'Designing Women' were a close knit group, more like friends than co-workers. They'd called her, wanting to plan one of their afternoons of dinner and a movie. She had agreed to the next Friday, and found herself looking forward to it. She'd just made a mental note to find a babysitter in case she got home late, when the ringing telephone interrupted her thoughts.

"Hello" she answered cheerfully.

"Mrs. Granger?" asked the voice at the other end.

"Yes, this is Giselle Granger."

"This is Delores Touchet from Kenton Jewelry and Gifts."

"Yes ma'am, what can I do for you?"

"Mrs. Granger, I was terribly sorry to hear of your husband's passing, he was such a nice man."

"Thank you Mrs. Touchet," she said, still waiting to hear the purpose of the call.

"Well, there's no delicate way to put this. Your husband purchased something for you with specific instructions for engraving. It was meant to be a Mother's Day gift and we've been holding it here. I'd actually forgotten about it. Mr. Granger paid for it in advance, and I just wanted to let you know that you could pick it up anytime you felt like it."

Giselle stood there, unable to speak for several moments. She finally managed a reply. "Yes, Mrs. Touchet, I'll pick it up now. Thank you for calling."

Once she reined in her emotions, she grabbed her purse and car keys, and drove to the jewelry shop on Main Street. She entered the store and accepted the bag with a box tucked inside. Giselle thanked her and left.

She drove home with a lump in her throat and her heart pounding like a set of kettle drums. Dropping the bag on the table, she stared at it a few minutes before sitting down to slay that particular dragon. Separating the delicate folds of tissue, she pulled out a black velvet case. She opened the lid to find a lovely silver filigree locket in the shape of a heart, about an inch in diameter. She pressed the catch and it popped open to reveal a photo of her and Toby on one side and another of the girls on the opposite side. The frame with the girls' picture also swung out to reveal a flat surface behind it. On that surface were the words Toby had engraved:

Love You Forever, My Girl – Toby.

Giselle's face crumpled. "You always knew my heart," she whispered, through her tears. She passed her fingers lovingly on the color snapshot that Carrie had taken of them at a Christmas party in mid-December—two people, happily unaware of the tragedy waiting to happen less than one month later. She placed a soft kiss upon it, then did the same to the photo of the girls, dressed in festive Christmas finery, she'd taken the same night.

It was beautifully constructed and attached to a sturdy chain. He knew how hard she was on chains. He knew her, everything about her, inside and out. How would she ever find someone who knew her as well as Toby did? She put the necklace on and smiled as the weight of the silver heart settled above her cleavage.

When her phone rang, she wiped her nose with a tissue and answered it, sounding slightly nasal.

"Giselle?" Carrie's voice filled with immediate concern. "I was calling about the Designing Women dinner date, but are you all right?"

"I'm fine. The jewelry shop called a little while ago. It seems Toby had purchased something for me. They'd sent it off for engraving and were holding it for me. I just opened it." She heard Carrie's gasp.

"The locket! Oh Giselle, he told me about it. He asked me for some pictures." Her voice warbled with tears. "I'm so sorry you had to go through that alone. Do you need someone there?"

"I'm okay. It was just a shock, you know? Did he tell you about the engraving?"

"N-no, he didn't."

Giselle swallowed before repeating the inscription.

"Oh God, that sounds just like him," Carrie said. "Are you sure you're okay?"

"I'm fine."

"I'm proud of you, Giselle."

She lifted the locket, held it close and smiled. "Thanks, I'm proud of me too."

Jackson and Bill picked Giselle and her girls up for both games the next two weeks. It had taken a few hours but she'd finally relaxed enough around the two men to develop an easy banter with them. She cherished the way Bill lavished affection upon his 'adopted' granddaughters. And strangely enough, as much as Mac and Lexie loved Bill, they were even more attached to Jackson. She was amazed at his ease with her girls, especially for a man unaccustomed to being around children.

Giselle was seated on the patio when the girls got off the school bus the last day of the school year. They ran to her, both dragging their overstuffed backpacks behind them.

"Mom, our teacher gave us a party!" Mackenzie said. "We got candy and gifts—we forgot to buy our teachers gifts this year, but mine said that she understood."

Giselle's face twisted in a grimace. "We sure did. How about if we send them both nice gift certificates in a card?"

"A gift certificate for what?"

"Mmm...I'm thinking the spa in Lake Coburn."

Lexie hauled her bag up to the patio chair. "Have I ever seen a spa, Mama?"

Giselle laughed and adjusted the barrette in her daughter's curls. "No, you haven't, sweetie. A spa is a place where ladies like to go to relax. You can get a massage, or a manicure, or even a pedicure for your feet."

"That's perfect," Mackenzie said. "I heard my teacher say she needed to relax after this past year."

"I'll bet she does," Giselle said with a knowing grin.

Lexie faced her mother. "Miss Melanie didn't say anything about relaxing. She just said she needed a good stiff, drink."

Giselle burst into laughter. "Trust me sweetie, it means the same thing. Now, let's get you two dressed and ready for your team pictures. Gretchen, Cat, and Allie are picking you up in a bit."

Lexie pulled on Giselle's shirt. "Mom, Allie asked me if I could spend the night with her tonight. Can I please go?"

"I have a better idea. How would you like Allie to spend the night here with us? We can all go to supper after the game and rent a movie."

"Could Emmelia come too?" Mac asked.

"Sure." Giselle called Gretchen and Amanda, and within minutes, their evening plans were set.

By the time Jackson rang her doorbell later that afternoon, Giselle was alone in her house.

She greeted him with a smile. "Hey, Jackson."

He gave her a huge smile. "Hey yourself. Y'all ready to go or do you need a few minutes?"

"I'm ready." She pulled the door closed behind her.

He looked around. "No Mac and Lexie?"

"They went earlier for group pictures. It's just little old me. Can you live with that?"

"I'll manage," he said, grinning as he opened the passenger door of his truck for her.

"No Bill today?"

"He had some business to tend to in Houston. Can *you* live with that?"

She grinned. "I'll manage," she said before buckling herself into the plush leather seating. "I have to tell you Lexie's latest."

He laughed at the 'stiff drink" comment. "How long has she been coming up with those?"

"Her vocabulary kicked into overdrive around four. That's about when she started popping out with the most embarrassing things."

"Mama, did I mortify you again?" he mimicked, in as much of a little girl's voice as he could manage with his baritone.

"Exactly! Get the picture now?"

He chuckled. "I believe I do."

They slipped into a rather uncomfortable silence, when Jackson suddenly spoke up. "I was thinking, since the game won't be over until after seven, how about if I take you and the girls to a restaurant for supper afterwards?"

"Allie and Emmelia are coming over to spend the night with my girls tonight, kind of a 'no more school' party. I told them I'd take them to a restaurant then rent some movies afterwards."

He nodded. "Oh, it's no big deal. I thought I'd keep you from having to scrounge up supper for them. Do you think you'll be able to handle all four girls?"

"I'll be okay. It's better some days, and nights, to keep busy." Her left hand worked at the locket as she kept her eyes focused on scenery outside the truck window.

Jackson reached over and turned the radio on to hear the number one song on the country chart playing.

"Ooh, I love this song," she said. "Do you mind?" She reached over and turned up the volume.

Jackson began to rummage in the console storage compartment. "I just bought the CD. Have you heard it?"

"No, I planned to. Is it good?"

"I like it. It's kind of rock/country cross over." He found what he was looking for and handed her a couple of CD cases. "I picked these two up at the same time."

"Marc Broussard," she said, looking at the second case, "He's from around Lafayette, isn't he?"

"He's from Carencro, Louisiana—near Lafayette...hence the name of the album. I like his style—down and dirty, rhythm and blues. You won't believe his voice."

"Is he any kin to you?" she asked.

He grinned at her. "Not that I know of; Broussard's are a dime a dozen in this state. I've downloaded those and converted them to MP3's already, so you can keep those if you want."

"Thanks," she said, studying the cases.

Jackson pulled into a parking spot near the field. He grabbed two chairs from the bed of his truck and set them up near the dugout.

Giselle seated herself as Mac's team began to prepare for first bat. Jackson walked back from the concession stand with two bottles of water and handed her one, as Lex ran over to him.

"Hey baby girl!" He scooped her up and kissed her forehead.

Lexie hugged him tightly then kissed his cheek. "Did you hear we're having a sleep over, Jackson?"

He nodded. "Your mom told me. I bet you're excited, and I know I can trust you girls to be good, right?"

Lexie's curls bobbed as she nodded. "We're going to watch movies and eat a lot of popcorn."

"Clean up your own messes?"

"Yes sir!"

"Very good. Make me proud."

"I will Jackson, you and Daddy."

He smiled tenderly at her. "Your daddy told me all the time how proud he was of you, your sister, and your mama."

"He did?"

He touched the tip of her nose. "Sure he did. He loved the three of you a bunch. He called you his 'three girls'."

She smiled and cocked her head to the side. "I sure do miss Daddy. I wish I could tell him."

"He knows you do, sweetie. He can tell what's in here," he said as he pointed to her heart. As soon as he put her down, she ran off to play. He sat down and stared ahead for a moment, then turned toward Giselle. "What?"

She grinned from behind her water bottle. "Have you ever been around little girls before?"

"Nope. If we were invited to anything where kids were included, Chloe always came up with an excuse not to go." He shrugged and shook his head. "I always thought . . ." His voice trailed off.

"That she was upset because she couldn't get pregnant," Giselle finished.

He nodded. "It pisses me off—the way she manipulated me—no—the way I *allowed* myself to be manipulated. If she was still alive, I could tell her how I've felt nothing but pity for her for years. Because I knew she'd never be happy with anyone or anything. But, she's gone, and I can't . . ." He slapped the arm of the chair in frustration.

"You can't get closure."

"I guess that's it."

"You need to find a way to deal with it."

"I have dealt with it. I've removed every trace of her."

"Maybe that's just denying it. Maybe you need to face it, like Bill made me face Toby's death."

He turned in her direction. "How do I do that, Giselle? How do I let a dead woman know that I regret our marriage? I wasted fifteen years of my life. How do I deal with that?"

His outburst proved how sensitive he was. He felt pain and frustration, just as anyone else would. It gave Giselle a jolt to realize that she actually saw him as a man, rather than her supervisor. Of course, she had already *seen* him, in the literal sense of the word. But, this man was confused, hurting, frustrated because he didn't know how to handle his dead wife's horrendous betrayal. His analytical, engineer mind was probably telling him there was a logical way to deal with it, but Giselle knew there wasn't.

She reached over to lay her hand on his. "Maybe Bill could help you," she suggested. "You should ask him." Her breath caught as his fingers curled around hers. She sat back in her chair, taking her fingers with her.

Jackson stared at the arm of his chair. "No doubt Bill has some mind-blowing revelation that'll reinforce his sense of superiority over me." He faced Giselle wearing a pitiful, hound dog expression. "Please don't make me do that."

She laughed. "You hate it when he's right, don't you?"

"The annoying old fart loves throwing it in my face."

"Don't you call my honey an old fart," she said.

"He's not your honey, he's Carrie's honey. I swear, if Sam ever messes up with her, she'd be my aunt in no time flat. He's got a thing for her."

"Yeah, well she likes Bill and all, but Carrie's got a thing for Sam." She laughed at Jackson's exaggerated sigh of relief. "But, you could have an aunt and even a younger first cousin before it's all over with."

His brow rose curiously. "You know something I don't?"

"Carrie's looking for a younger woman for Bill."

Jackson frowned. "How young?"

"Young enough to bear children; he's not too old, you know, and Bill's in great physical shape. There's no reason he can't start a family right now." She wondered at Jackson's puzzled expression. "Would that upset you?"

"What? No, not in the way you mean, anyway. I've told him for years he needed a wife and kids of his own."

"You did?"

He took a swig from his water bottle and recapped it. "Sure, I know he calls me Son, and I think of him sort of like a father, but, before my parents died, he and I were already tight. He was—Uncle Bill. It's kind of hard to explain."

"I can understand that, but you look a little upset."

"I guess I'm wondering if he passed up opportunities because of me."

"I don't think so, Jackson. He told me he never met the right woman. It may take some time to find someone good enough for Bill."

Jackson rolled his eyes and huffed in disgust. "Would you take him off of that pedestal? He's no saint, you know."

She laughed again. "What about you? Should we be looking for a woman for you?"

He pinned her with his gaze. "Where the hell did that come from?"

"Well, you're obviously good with kids. It would be a shame if you didn't have any of your own someday."

He nodded. "I feel the same way. Unlike Chloe, I have always wanted children."

"Well, then maybe we should start looking around for a girl for you. Someone worthy of you who can give you a couple of precious little miniature Jacksons," she teased.

Jackson cleared his throat as his head swiveled slowly in her direction. He dipped his head tantalizingly low to peer over the rim of his sunglasses. "I'm a big boy, Giselle. I don't need any help finding a woman."

His words sounded serious enough, but hidden within the deep baritone of his voice, there seemed to be just a hint of tantalizing mischief. Or was it a promise? She suppressed a shiver, wondering at the methods he'd use to find one.

"Mom!"

Giselle jumped at Mackenzie's bark. She turned to see her daughter, on deck and preparing to bat.

"Knock it out of the park, Sweetie."

She nodded, and adjusted her cap with one hand. "Hi Jackson, where's Paw Paw?"

"He couldn't make it today, but he sends his love."

She smiled brightly as the batter in front of her hit a double. Jackson and Giselle watched with pride as she jogged easily to the plate. She took a few practice swings then got into her preferred batting stance, ready and tensed. She swung the bat and hit the ball off the tee, hard and straight, right between second and third bases. Mac ran all the way to third before someone threw the ball in to home.

"Good hit, Mac!" Gretchen yelled, as she approached them, dressed in her work scrubs. "Hey, you two," she said, giving them both hugs. "Giselle, if four little girls are too much for you to handle, it's not too late to back out."

"It's fine," Giselle insisted.

The next batter hit a double that brought Mac safely home. She ran by the three adults grinning broadly as they cheered and clapped.

Mac and Allie's team easily won the game, and when it was over, Jackson rounded up the girls to bring them all back to Giselle's house. He placed the chairs in the back of the truck as the three little girls climbed inside.

"I'm hungry, Mom. Can we go somewhere I can have some fried shrimp?" Mack asked Giselle. "Are you coming too, Jackson?"

"No, I think your mom wants to have some girl time."

"Mom, can he come with us?" Lex pleaded.

Giselle climbed inside the truck. "Sure he can, I just didn't know if he could handle five females at one time."

He grinned. "How can I pass up a challenge like that?"

She buckled her seatbelt and smiled. "I guess you can't, but don't say I didn't warn you. We're picking up Emmelia on the way."

Within ten minutes, they'd corralled the four boisterous little girls into the local seafood restaurant. Giselle brought them to the restroom to wash their hands before sending them back out to the table. She'd gone into one of the stalls when the door opened and someone occupied a stall at the end. The door opened again and two women walked into the restroom. She immediately recognized the voices of Suzette Simon and Isabelle Allen, neither of them high on her list of favorite people.

Isabelle, or Izzy, as she insisted people call her, had never missed the opportunity to throw herself at Toby. She'd even made a pass at him at a Christmas party two years earlier. This particular town tramp had a reputation for chasing married men, and getting them. With the help of a few weak willed men, she'd instigated the break-ups of more than a couple of marriages along the way. Giselle remained in her stall, hoping they'd leave soon.

"Who is that *fine* hunk of man with Giselle Granger tonight?" Suzette asked.

"I don't know, but you can bet your ass I'm going to find out. My God, he is gorgeous, isn't he? One thing's for sure, that tramp didn't wait very long before throwing herself at another man, did she? Poor Toby's only been in the ground for five months."

"Honestly, I don't know what he ever saw in her," Suzette said. "He could have done so much better."

"Uh huh—like me!" Izzy's high-pitched cackle bounced off the walls. "I would have worn Toby down eventually. He was just beginning to show some interest. What a waste. Let's go, Suz. There's a Bloody Mary with my name on it at the club."

Giselle sat in silence as the two women walked out. She didn't need to look in the mirror to know her face was on fire. Her stomach knotted with tension as she left the stall and approached the sink. She washed her hands and took a moment to splash her face with water.

Just when she thought her humiliation could not be more complete, the door of the last stall opened. Jeanette Ross, Amanda's mother-in-law, approached her, her face flushed with rage.

The other woman washed her hands then gave her a hug. "Honey, everyone in town knows how happy you and Toby were together. He never would have looked twice at Izzy, I hope you know that."

Giselle nodded. "I know that, Jeanette."

"Don't you dare waste one tear on those two tramps, now come on."

Giselle walked out in front of Jeanette, just in time to see Izzy exit the restaurant, wearing a barely-there top and a come-and-get-it mini-skirt. She thanked God for small favors, knowing she wasn't up to facing either of the women. They approached the table where Jackson sat with the four girls.

"That's my Granny!" Emmelia stood to hug Jeanette.

"It is?" Jackson stood immediately. "You must be Joe's mom. I'm Jackson Broussard."

"Yes I am, Jeanette Ross. It's nice to finally meet you. I've heard good things about you. I'd talk longer, but I've got to get my husband back home now. Emmelia, you be a good girl for Giselle."

"Yes ma'am, I will."

Before leaving the group, Jeanette gave Giselle a comforting pat on the shoulder.

She tried her best to have fun, but felt self-conscious about everything Jackson said or did for the remainder of the night. She pushed her grilled shrimp around on her plate, until she finally set it aside, and asked for a 'to go' box.

Tired of dodging Jackson's curious glances, she nearly cried from relief when they finally got up to leave. Completely distracted, she nearly walked off without her purse. When Jackson handed it to her, she thanked him quietly and remained silent during the drive home.

Back at her place, Jackson helped her to unbuckle the girls. She clamped her jaws tightly as Lexie pleaded with him to watch the movie with them. His decline had her shoulders sagging in relief.

"I appreciate the invite, Lex, but I have to work tomorrow." Whining their disappointment, the girls hugged him and ran into the house with their friends.

Giselle murmured a low volume goodbye and tried to close the door. She had no choice but to face him when he put an arm out to keep it from closing.

"Something happened in that restaurant," he said. "Did I do something to upset you?"

"No, it wasn't you. I can't talk about it right now," she said, fighting to control her emotions.

"We're friends, Giselle...Talk to me," he pleaded.

"Go Jackson, I'm just a little emotional, that's all." She wiped her eyes with the back of her hand. "Thanks for supper, Goodnight." She closed the door softly in his face.

Chapter Twelve

Still confused fifteen minutes later, Jackson answered his ringing cell phone to speak to Carrie.

"Jackson, how was Giselle when you left her?"

"Not good, and I have no idea why. She went into the restroom with the girls, and when she came back, she was on the verge of tears. She was nervous and distracted the rest of the night. I don't know what happened."

"I do. I got a phone call from Jeanette, Joe's mom. She told me about something they overheard in the restroom."

Once he heard what had upset Giselle, Carrie had to convince him not to go to her.

"Jackson, trust me, she won't want to see you right now."

"I have to call her."

"Let me talk to her first. I just didn't want you thinking you'd done anything wrong. I'll call and let you know what's going on."

"Call me soon, Carr. I'm already going crazy."

"I will."

Giselle turned toward the tapping on her bathroom door.

"Open the door, honey."

She reluctantly opened up the door to let Carrie in then turned quickly away from her.

"I know what happened at the restaurant," Carrie said. "Jeanette called me, furious with those two tramps. You are not going to let what they said ruin your night, are you?"

Giselle stared at her own reflection in the mirror, puffy-eyed from crying, and feeling foolish.

Carrie got a wash cloth out of the cabinet, wet it with cold water, and handed it to her. "Here, put this over your eyes—it'll help."

Giselle took the wash cloth and met her friend's gaze. "Is that what people are saying? That Toby's only been dead five months and I've already moved on?"

"The only two people that have said it are the ones you overheard in that restroom, and they're the two biggest tramps in Kenton. You know, of course, that Toby never looked at Izzy Allen."

"I know that, but Jackson hanging around as much as he does, coming to the girls' games. People may think..."

Carrie released a sigh rife with exasperation. "Damn, but you are determined to feel guilty about something, aren't you? Those two men are here to help your girls through a bad time, and I think they're doing a wonderful job. Jackson has his own issues to deal with, so maybe helping your girls is helping him. He didn't have it easy, you know. He had to learn the hard way just how little his wife cared for him."

"I know that, we talked about it at the park." Giselle stood and wiped her eyes. "Carrie, this has made me see things from another viewpoint. I can't be seen anywhere alone with Jackson Broussard or any other man, even if he is just a friend. You know gossip in this place spreads like wildfire. I won't have people thinking I loved my husband so little that I've moved on and left him behind already. The way I feel now, I may never move on. Toby was the only one for me."

Carrie placed her hands on Giselle's shoulders. "You two had a wonderful relationship, and it would be the sincerest form of flattery to Toby if you were to remarry. He'd want you to find that happiness again, hon."

"I can promise you it won't be anytime soon. I'm still so much in love with him."

Carrie nodded. "I know you are. All I'm saying is, one day you may decide you have feelings for someone else. If it happens, don't push him away because of some misguided feelings of loyalty to Toby...he wouldn't want that. Now, I've got to go home. I have to work in the morning."

Giselle stood up and rinsed the wash cloth again. "I suppose you're going to call Jackson so you can tell him everything that we discussed?" Giselle and Carrie's gazes locked in the mirror.

"I won't if you call him. He's worried sick about you."

"I guess I'll do it—it's the least I can do."

"Don't wait too long to call."

"I'll do it as soon as you walk out the door, I promise."

As soon as Carrie left, Giselle picked up the phone and dialed Jackson's number. As proof of how upset he was, he answered on the first ring.

"Hello."

"It's me," she mumbled.

"Are you alright?"

She heard the anxiousness in his voice. "I'm better, but, I've made a decision and I don't want you to think it's because of anything you've done."

"I'm listening," he said, bracing himself.

"Look, Jackson, you and Bill are welcome to spend as much time with the girls as you want, but I think I need to distance myself from you for a while. I can't have people thinking...things like that about us."

"Giselle..I wasn't trying to..it wasn't a date or anything. It was just a meal...with four little girls," he stammered.

"We both know that, but in small towns like this, people gossip. It's better this way."

"What about the ballgames and their birthday party?"

"You're welcome at the games, and the party is still on." She heard the relief in his voice.

"Thank you, Giselle. I'm sorry you were upset, but thanks for calling."

She knew he assumed that very little would change, but by the time Lexie's game rolled around on Thursday, he discovered the truth of the situation.

Giselle refused his offer of a ride and drove to the next game. She sat in the stands next to Gretchen and Lauren, and spoke to him only if he asked her a direct question. She made sure she was never alone with him, and the easy camaraderie they'd developed seemed to vanish overnight.

After a solid month of hurt feelings and frustration, Jackson finally spoke to Carrie about it.

"When is this going to end? I feel like I've lost another friend." He walked over to his window and stared out of it, his hands shoved deep into the pockets of his slacks.

"This is temporary, Jack. She doesn't want to give anyone the wrong idea. As time passes it'll get easier."

"Easier for her, but more difficult for me," he growled, then stopped to roll his sleeves up over his bulging biceps.

"Good Lord, have you been working out?"

"With no Toby for basketball, no Chloe to chase after, and Giselle avoiding me like the plague, working out is all I have." He turned to face his friend. "You don't know how bad I dread the end of baseball season."

"Maybe you should slow down a little."

"I can't. It's the only thing that keeps me sane."

"You need a hobby," she commented. "Get a dog."

"I don't want a dog," he snorted. "I have decided to build a patio deck, though, and I ordered a motorcycle."

"What'd you order—a Harley?"

"Overdone and screams middle aged crises. I went with America's first motorcycle." He turned to Carrie and froze at her horrified expression. "What's wrong?"

"Please tell me you didn't order an Indian," she managed to spit out in a hoarse croak.

Jackson cocked his head to the side. "Yeah, but how do you know about Indian motorcycles?"

"My dad had one a long time ago. It was second hand but from what Mom said, he loved that damn thing." She released an anguished groan and slapped both hands to her head. "Do you realize what you've done to me?"

He gazed at her in confusion. "Apparently not."

"Sam has wanted one for years!"

"I know...that's where I got the idea."

"You knew that. And you ordered one anyway," she said in dry tone. "Some friend you are."

"Am I missing something?"

"I'll never hear the end of it. My husband is going to whine endlessly for one just like yours. He'll bitch and complain until he wears me down and I tell him to buy one just to shut him up. You men and your expensive toys."

Jackson splayed his hands in front of him. "You just told me to get a hobby." She sighed in seemingly reluctant acceptance before she turned to exit his office.

"Why didn't you just get a damn dog?"

"Too much trouble," he called out, before she gave one last snort of disgust.

The Saturday before the girls' birthday party dawned bright and sunny. Jackson and Bill were halfway to Mackenzie's tournament in a nearby town when Jackson got an unexpected call from Giselle.

"My truck won't start," she said, sounding frantic. "I tried to call Sam, but I can't get a hold of him, and everyone else is either on vacation or at the tournament already."

"Sam and Carrie are in Gardiner for the day, I know that for certain," he told her. "It's probably just the battery. We're only a few minutes from you, so just hang tight."

Jackson lowered the hood of her truck. He placed the dead battery in the bed of his pick-up, then turned to her. "If you ride with us to the tournament, we can pick up a new battery for you and install it when we get back later this afternoon." He reached inside his truck for a package of wipes to clean his hands. "You should be safe enough," he muttered, as he sent her an accusing glare. "Bill will be with us the entire time." It came out sounding sharper than he meant, but he wasn't about to apologize.

Giselle stiffened her back as she pushed Lexie ahead of her to his truck. "Thank you, we'd appreciate the ride."

To Jackson's satisfaction, Lexie insisted that 'Paw Paw Bill' sit in the back with her. He watched Giselle, tight-lipped, and stone-faced as she slid into the front seat.

"I guess it's a good thing I sent Mac along with Gretchen this morning,"

He nodded, but remained silent as he put the truck in reverse, and backed out of the driveway. He attempted to ignore the furtive glances Giselle sent his direction. They got as far as the end of the city limits before he confronted her. "Is there a problem?"

Giselle had noticed the difference in Jackson the second she'd seen him. He'd always had good muscle tone, even more so at the towel incident when she'd lost her good sense. But now his arms, neck and shoulders bulged with added bulk—far more definition. He hadn't neglected his lower body, either. His muscular thighs strained against the material of his shorts. She should know. She'd been stealing covert glances at him since he'd arrived at her door. *Adonis has been working out.* She tore her gaze from him, stared straight ahead, put into play every method she knew to regulate the rapid pounding of her heart. *Deep breaths, Giselle. In and out. Slow and steady.*

"Giselle?"

"No problem. I was just-I was wondering how you've been, is all. I haven't talked to you in forever, it seems."

Jackson stared ahead at the road. "Only doing what you asked," he mumbled. "But I'm all right. Trying to stay busy."

She heard Lexie and Bill talking excitedly about the upcoming birthday party. "You need help with the party?"

He kept his eyes on the road. "Nope, Bill has everything under control."

"I made them hold it down to twelve invitations each. That, along with Carrie and Sam's family, adds up to a lot of people invading Bill's property."

"He's been looking forward to this for months. He's as excited about it as the kids are." Jackson glanced at her then turned back toward the road.

They got to the ballpark and found the field where Mac's team was playing. The previous game hadn't ended yet, and Mac, Allie, and Gretchen were standing off to the side of the bleachers, waiting for their team to take to the field.

"Aw hell, I forgot the chairs in the back of the truck," Jackson growled before turning back to get them.

Giselle turned to follow him. "Do you need some help?"

"No!" he said sharply, stopping her in her tracks.

She was still standing there, watching him walk back to his pick-up when Gretchen joined her.

"Has Jackson been working out?" the twin asked, as she stared at his retreating form.

Bill crossed his arms and grunted. "It seems like every time I call him, he's at the gym."

"Who do they play this morning, Gretchen?" Giselle asked, wanting to change the subject. Jackson's new physique had affected her more than she wanted to admit, even to herself.

"Eunice, and they're good, too. That's the team that beat everyone yesterday." She looked up as her twin sister, Lauren, walked over with Gage and Ava, carrying her own chairs. "There are Lauren and the kids," she said.

Lauren walked up to them and dropped her folding chairs on the ground then reached over to give Bill a hug. "I just saw Jackson on the way back to his truck. He's definitely been working out!"

Bill chuckled. "He's trying to stay busy—I guess it keeps him from thinking about things too much."

"Here he comes," Gretchen said, as they all turned to watch him. He walked up, loaded down with at least six strapped bags containing folding chairs, no sign of breathing hard or breaking a sweat.

"Who wants a chair? I brought everything I had."

"I'll take one," Gretchen said. "Let's set them up under the tree for some shade."

Jackson set the chairs in a line and sat down in one on the end. After everyone else had taken a seat, Giselle took the remaining one next to Jackson. He got up immediately to go to the concession stand. He came back with several bottles of water and passed them out, then whispered something to his uncle. Bill stood and moved to the far end next to Giselle and Jackson sat in the chair he'd vacated.

Giselle smiled at Bill, trying to ignore the hurt of being snubbed by Jackson. He's only doing what you asked, she reminded herself. She listened, without seeming to, as he got into an animated conversation with Allie, Mac, and Cat about baseball. Within minutes, Lauren's little girl, Ava Grace, made her way over to Jackson to flirt shamelessly with him. By the time the game began, the toddler wouldn't sit with anyone but him.

"Would you look at that," Lauren said, observing her daughter. "Ava already has him wrapped. He's so good with kids; I sure hope he has a couple of his own someday."

"Me too," Bill agreed.

Jackson, who had been engrossed in conversation with Ava, glanced up to find them all staring at him. "What?"

They all laughed and he turned back to Ava. "They're jealous because you love me more than them, aren't they?" She gave him a cheesy grin and nodded, her curls bouncing. He tapped one side of his face and she kissed his cheek.

"Giselle, video that, would you? Bryan won't believe his baby girl loved up on another man. Who is that, Ava?" Lauren asked her daughter.

"Das Jackson!" the toddler chirped. She leaned over, grabbed his face in her two chubby little hands, and gave him a kiss right on the lips.

"Thank you so much, Ava!" He let her wrap her arms around his neck for a big hug.

"That is so sweet," Gretchen said.

Lauren chuckled. "It won't be sweet about two hours from now, when she's all sticky and sweaty and snotty from that summer cold she probably just gave you, Jackson."

"That's okay. Some things are worth it, aren't they, Ava Grace?" The child nodded and beamed at him.

Giselle watched the exchange with a smile on her face while she caught it all on her digital camera. "Yeah, I told him we could find him a wife so he could have some of his own, but he told me he could find his own woman."

"That's right," he said. "When I'm ready to move, I will. Don't you worry about me." He riveted his gaze on Giselle.

She felt herself coloring as she adjusted her sunglasses and looked away. "Speaking of which, ladies, we need to find someone for this fine looking gentleman on my left."

Lauren spoke up. "How about Ms. Clair Bertrand."

Gretchen leaned over to look at her twin. "Ms. Clair from admitting? She's too old for Bill. We need to find somebody younger, who can give him children. right, Bill?"

He shrugged. "I'd like kids, but if it doesn't happen I'll be satisfied to have someone of my own. I've got Mac and Lexie, and I'm sure Jackson will furnish me with a great niece or nephew one day."

"Hmph. Don't count on that happening anytime soon," Jackson mumbled under his breath.

"What was that, son?"

"I said I hope that happens real soon, Uncle Bill." He winked at Lauren, who grinned at his comment.

"Until then, I'll just keep Ava." Jackson leaned over to the toddler seated contentedly on his lap. "How about it, gorgeous? You want to come home with me?"

She nodded adamantly, causing her golden brown curls to bounce and glisten in the sunshine. "I go with Jackson!" She climbed down from his lap and waved to her mother. "Bye Mommy!"

Everyone laughed as Jackson tried to tell Ava he wasn't leaving. She reached up for him until he picked her up again. He looked over at Lauren. "Tell Bryan he's been replaced."

Giselle watched and listened to his remarks, remaining silent. She turned her attention to the field, shifting uncomfortably. All this talk of Jackson finding someone else and starting a new family had her feeling a little confused. What if he found someone? How would she feel?

She hadn't told anyone about her recurring dreams about him. It was easier not to see him. She tried to push all thoughts of the dreams aside, but every time she heard his voice, she saw the image of those deeply intense, sensual blue eyes. By the end of the day, she was a bundle of nervous energy.

On the way home, she insisted on sitting in the back seat with Mac and Lexie. Jackson and Bill installed the new battery in her truck, and she thanked them both when it cranked up easily. She couldn't look Jackson in the eye, but hugged Bill before she went inside her house, closing the door behind her.

Jackson waited for Bill to climb back into the truck.

"Well, that's interesting," Bill said, buckling his seatbelt.

"What's that?"

"She can barely look you in the eye."

Jackson shifted to reverse and backed slowly out of her driveway. "Noticed that, did you? I have no idea what I did to piss her off this time."

"You didn't do anything. She's attracted to you."

Jackson hit the brakes at the intersection and turned to face his uncle. "You are so off the mark on this one, Uncle Bill. That lady can't stand the sight of me."

Bill released a loud sigh and shook his head. "One of these days you're going to learn to listen to me. I'm telling you, she's attracted to you. And don't even try to deny you feel the same way."

Jackson glared at his uncle. "She's the widow of a good friend. I only try to help her out when she lets me, and only because Toby would want me to."

"Bullshit! You can lie to yourself if you want to, but you can't lie to me. I know what I see."

Jackson jumped when a car behind him blew the horn. He eased off the brakes and took a right to head for the highway. He glanced at his uncle, who sat there wearing a shit eating grin. "Fine, dammit. I'm attracted to her—a fat lot of good it does me. Are you happy now?"

Bill gave a loud guffaw of laughter. "I was right."

Jackson snorted in disgust at his uncle. "You always are, you old coot. And it's damned disconcerting, if you want to know the truth."

"Dis..con..what? Talk English..I'm just a simple man."

"It's ass-chapping, okay? It chaps my ass, the way you're always right."

"I'm just older and wiser in the ways of the world."

"Yeah. What the hell ever."

Bill put his head back and laughed. "It's like Sam always says, Son. There's all kinds of smart."

"Maybe so, but I think you're wrong about Giselle being attracted to me. If she is, she's got a hell of a way of showing it. I'm about fed up with her damn attitude."

"An intelligent man would try to see it through her eyes. Think about it, Jackson. Toby's been dead for just over seven months and she feels guilty for being attracted to another man, not to mention terrified of what others will think. If you'd been sitting where I was, you'd have noticed she was a bundle of nerves by the end of the day." He shook his head. "Your generation has mastered the art of wasting time. I'd have thought you and Giselle would see the senselessness of that after what you'd both gone through. By the way, you hurt her feelings when you switched chairs on her."

"I didn't do it to hurt her feelings. I just didn't want to embarrass myself. There's no way I could stare at those long, tanned legs of hers all day and not—you know." Just the thought of her had him adjusting himself. Bill responded with a low chuckle that escalated into a knee slapping belly laugh. Jackson adjusted the adjustment, more than a little annoyed at his uncle's joviality over his excruciating predicament.

Jackson gripped the steering wheel with both hands. "You don't know, man. Every time I see her lately, it's agony. You have no idea how much I dread tomorrow." He shook his head slowly. "For me, the only thing worse than seeing Giselle—Is *not* seeing Giselle."

Chapter Thirteen

The first luminous rays of dawn broke on a cloudless sky, promising a glorious day for Mac and Lexie's party. Guests started arriving around eleven thirty to food tables, loaded down with barbeque and side dishes. Servers urged everyone to line up, buffet style.

"Paw Paw!" Mac and Lexie ran to Bill, with Giselle following closely behind them.

"There are my two birthday girls!"

"We wanted to come and thank you for doing all of this for us," Mac said. "I can't wait for the paddle boat rides."

"We'll start them right after lunch, so you'd better go eat," he told the girls as they ran off.

Giselle gave him an appreciative hug. "Bill, the girls are thrilled. I don't know what kind of day they would have had without this." *Their first birthdays without a father.*

He placed his hands on her shoulders. "Jackson and I would do anything for you three. You know that, right?"

"I do, and I love you for that."

Carrie joined them. "Come on, you two, let's get in line."

As they settled down at a table with their plates, Jackson and a pretty woman named Gwendolyn Perry approached. He pulled the chair out next to Giselle for Gwen, then sat next to Bill right across from her. "Does everyone here know Gwen?"

Gwen, who had a seven-year-old named Alyssa in Mac's grade, took the initiative and introduced herself to Giselle. "Hi, you're Mac and Lexie's mom, right?"

She nodded. "Giselle Granger, nice to meet you, Gwen."

"Same here. Alyssa was thrilled with the invitation to the party. Thank you so much."

"Sure." Giselle had seen Gwen occasionally at school events, but had never actually met her. She assumed Jackson had previously, because within minutes, he and Gwen were deep in conversation. She fought off an unreasonable wave of jealously, and wondered if there was a Mr. Perry.

"So, Gwen," Giselle picked up a barbequed rib, "Where's Alyssa's father? Is he at home?" The question, successful in bringing an effective halt to Gwen and Jackson's dialogue, had the same effect on the entire table. All conversation came to a dead stop, followed by an uncomfortable silence, as all eyes turned toward Giselle.

Gwen cleared her throat before elaborating on that particular line of questioning. "I'm actually Alyssa's aunt, Giselle. Her father was my younger brother, David. He and his wife were killed in a boating accident six years ago and I've raised her since then. She calls me mom because she doesn't remember her parents."

Giselle felt the heat of a shameful blush as she stammered her apology. "I'm so sorry. I didn't know. Do you have family around to help?"

Gwen shrugged. "My father died when I was in grade school, and my mom passed away from cancer three years ago. I've never been married. I was engaged at the time of the accident, but my fiancé said he didn't want to raise another couple's child. That was that," she said.

Jackson gave a low grunt. "I bet it's been rough for you two."

"It's not always easy," she said. "I mean, I do okay financially as a single parent. I work as an accountant at the Kenton Hospital. The pay isn't great, but at least I'm home at a decent hour for Alyssa." She turned to Giselle. "You know how it is. I wish I could be home more for her. Do better for her."

Jackson reached out to place a comforting hand over her wrist. "Maybe one day that'll happen for you."

Was he trying to tell her he was interested? That he was available? Giselle winced at the unaccustomed pain in the pit of her stomach. Gwen was gorgeous; fair complexioned, with hair a shade or two shy of black, and eyes the same shade of blue as Jackson's. She was around her own height, but voluptuously curved. Probably just the type of woman Jackson was looking for. She pushed her plate away, unable to eat another bite.

Conversation picked up immediately. Within minutes, she knew that Gwen was thirty-nine years old, and dreading her fortieth birthday, which was just around the corner.

"Don't dread forty—forty was fabulous!" Carrie said.

"Not when you're husbandless, without children of your own. I thought by forty I'd have all that tucked neatly under my belt. Don't get me wrong, I love Alyssa as if she's my own daughter, but I didn't get to experience childbirth. I feel like I'm running out of time."

"You're still young," Carrie insisted. "There are still good men out there who wouldn't mind starting a family."

"Not in my experience," Gwen confessed. "The few guys I've dated don't seem thrilled when they find out about Alyssa, and she has to come first right now."

Giselle's heart plummeted at Carrie's next comment, spoken as she faced Jackson.

"You'd be surprised at the method God uses to bring two people together."

"This food is wonderful, isn't it?" Giselle said, a little too forcefully. Carrie's blatant attempt at matchmaking hadn't gone unnoticed, and it certainly wasn't appreciated—not by her, anyway.

"It sure is. Who'd you hire to cater?" Sam asked Bill.

"A business that does all of our oil company's parties. They're used to serving large numbers of guests, so this was easy for them."

Jackson sneezed into his napkin, turned his head and sneezed again. "Excuse me, must be allergies."

Carrie grinned. "You're probably getting Ava's cold. I heard how you let her kiss on you at the ballpark yesterday. That child is shamelessly rotten."

"I told Lauren to tell Bryan he's been replaced."

Carrie grinned at Jackson. "You obviously haven't seen her with her daddy yet."

"I bet she has Bryan wrapped, with that curly hair and those big brown eyes," he commented.

"Are you talking about that adorable Shirley Temple look alike running around here?" Gwen asked.

"That would be Ava Grace, our granddaughter," Sam answered. "She's only one of seven grandchildren."

Just then two of them picked that moment to make an appearance. Emmelia ran up with Allie and Lexie. "Can we go on the boats now? Is it time yet?"

"I want to see the little mini horses!" Allie said.

Lexie jumped up and down. "I want to see piggy goats!"

Emm looked confused. "What's a piggy goat?"

The adults laughed before Bill explained again about the animals. "Pygmy goats are goats that stay small. I'll tell you what kids, give me five minutes to finish eating, and then we'll start showing everybody the animals."

"Okay," Lexie said, before the three of them ran off.

"I didn't know there were animals like that on this place," Gwen said. "Who owns this ranch?"

Bill raised his hand. "That'd be me."

"Cattle or horses?"

"A little of both," he answered. "Do you ride?"

"Not in years, but I used to practically live on a horse."

"I never would have thought that by looking at you," Jackson said. "You don't seem like that type of girl."

"Afraid I am," she said, flashing him a dimpled grin.

He returned the smile. "It's been awhile for me, too."

"Don't let him fool you," Bill said. "He's a natural horseman, and you don't forget that."

Jackson shook his head. "No, if you want to see a natural on a horse, it's that man right there." He pointed to Bill.

Gwen turned to Bill. "Did you teach your son everything your knew about horses?"

"Jackson's my nephew, my brother's son. But yes, I tried to teach him everything I knew," he said, wiping his mouth on a napkin. "About riding, anyway."

Gwen's gaze flash back and forth between uncle and nephew. "My goodness, you two look enough alike to be father and son, but I guess you've heard that before."

"My older brother, Jamison, and I looked a lot alike." Bill jerked his head toward Jackson. "Our story is similar to yours and Alyssa's. Jackson's parents were killed in a car accident a couple of months before his fifth birthday; I've thought of him as a son for thirty-three years."

"How old were you at the time?"

"I was twenty-four."

"But, that would make you fifty-seven years old." Gwen shook her head. "There's no way you could be that age—I thought you were in your mid-forties."

Bill beamed at her as he stood and made his way around to her. "Looks like we have a lot in common," he said, sounding pleased with himself. "How about we go find those girls, along with your Alyssa, and show them some animals?"

She backed away from the table and reached for the hand he held out to her. "I'd love to."

Giselle breathed a little easier watching Bill and Gwen's departure, totally engrossed with one another. Why did she feel like she'd just dodged a train wreck? Carrie's comment jarred her from her thoughts.

"Well, how about that? Looks like you didn't move quick enough, Jackson. I guess old Bill didn't teach you everything he knew."

"You think?" Jackson asked smugly. "He taught me how to use reverse psychology. I brought her here for him." He winked at her and grinned.

"Have I told you lately how brilliant you are?" she gushed.

He stood, giving her an exaggerated sigh. "It's been awhile—slacker."

"Well, let me say now, that was brilliantly played out."

He bowed at the waist. "Thank you very much."

The four of them paired off for the walk to the barn, Carrie and Sam took the rear behind Giselle and Jackson.

Giselle chanced a look at Jackson. "Gwen and Bill seem to have a lot in common, don't they?"

"Yes, they do."

"How long have you known her?"

"I only met her today."

She turned to him, shocked at his admission. "Really? The way you two were talking, I thought—that is—you seemed so relaxed with her."

Without a pause in stride, he spoke, his tone icy. "Only because she allowed me to be." Suddenly, he veered off in the direction of Bill's ranch style home.

Giselle watched him stalk off, as Carrie and Sam caught up with her.

"Where's he going?" Sam asked.

"I don't know," Giselle said.

"Is he upset about something?" Carrie asked.

Giselle kept her eyes on Jackson. "I think so, but damned if I know what set him off."

Jackson trudged over to Bill's house, muttering and cursing inwardly the entire way. What the hell did that woman want from him? Why is it okay for her to initiate a conversation, but when he tried it, she treated him like a pariah? His heart ached at the sight of her, but it had taken a beating and he was damned tired of being her whipping boy. Hadn't he put up with enough crap from Chloe for fifteen years?

Jackson grabbed a bottle of tea from his uncle's fridge and stood there until he'd downed the entire thing. He gave himself a few minutes to cool down before returning to the party, more determined than ever to avoid Giselle.

He walked over to the barn where everyone had gathered to pet the miniature animals raised on Bill's ranch. He walked over to where his uncle and Gwen each held bridles of a pair of Shetland Ponies attached to two carts. The younger children lined up for the cart rides while the older ones were petting the tiny pygmy goats and horses, all well supervised by various friends or employees of Bill. He'd also rounded up the new calves and foals, placed them in two portable holding pens, to separate them from their mothers.

"Uncle Bill, where do you need me most?"

"You go on in with either the calves or foals right now, Jackson. Bring a few people in at a time so that the animals don't get spooked. We need to get this part of it done quickly so they don't miss their feeding times with their mamas."

Jackson entered the horse pen and crossed to where Lauren and Bryan stood with Gage and Ava. "Hey, Ava," he said. "You remember me?"

Ava, who was firmly attached to her daddy's hip, looked at Bryan. "Das Jackson, Daddy!" she crowed.

Bryan nodded at his daughter. "Uh huh, I heard how you gave him all those kisses yesterday at the ball park. That's not cool, baby girl. Not cool at all," he groaned, as Jackson and Lauren laughed.

Jackson looked down at Gage, Ava's big brother. "Come on in here, Gage." Gage scrambled under the tubular fencing, as Jackson reached over to get Ava from Bryan. The child reached out to him and he brought her over inside the fence and placed her on his hip. He walked over to one of the more docile foals with the two children, gave Gage a sugar cube, and showed him how to feed the horse.

"Did you see, Mom? He licked it off my hand!" Gage said.

"Yes, I took a picture of it, too," Lauren said.

"Ava, you want to feed the horse?" Jackson said.

"No!" She pulled herself away as he neared the animal. "I want Daddy!"

Jackson pretended to pull a dagger from his heart. "Aw, and here I thought I'd replaced that ole daddy."

Bryan grinned as he reached for his daughter. Once again happily ensconced in her father's arms, Ava looked at Jackson and as she patted Bryan's face. "Das my Daddy," she said, before planting a kiss firmly on her daddy's mouth.

Jackson shook his head even as laughter rumbled deep in his chest. "Maw Maw Carrie said I couldn't steal you from your daddy. I guess she was right." He waited for them to cross into the pen then used Lauren's camera to take several shots of the family feeding the animals.

Mac and Lexie were next in line. When the two girls joined Jackson inside the pen, Giselle stayed put outside to take some shots of the three of them. He squatted between Mac and Lexie, right next to the foal while Giselle took the shots.

She helped her girls from the pen. "Thank you, Jackson."

"You're welcome," he said, turning quickly away from her to assist a beautiful, dark haired child with bright blue eyes and a pixie grin. "Hello there."

"My Mom and Mr. Bill told me to come ask you to show me the foals and calves," the little girl said shyly.

"Is your name Alyssa?"

She nodded and grinned.

"It's nice to meet you Alyssa. I'm Jackson. Bill is my uncle."

She smiled, revealing a gap where she'd recently lost a bottom tooth. "He's nice. It's nice to meet you, too."

He got one of the two photographer's Bill had hired to come over and get several poses of Alyssa with the animals. The next hour went quickly as tried to make sure every child there had pictures taken with the animals.

Bill approached him. "You start rounding the kids up for boat rides, Jackson. I'll have the men get these babies back to their mamas."

Jackson called everyone to the four canopied paddleboats docked at his fish stocked pond, each one able to seat four people. The boats began to fill up with children and adults as they all took to the water, paddling leisurely around. They agreed on fifteen-minute rides until everyone had taken turns.

To pass the time while waiting for boat rides, children played in one of the two inflatable fun jumps rented for the occasion, one with a huge slide attached to it. His uncle had spared no expense when it came to Mac and Lexie's birthday party. Jackson had known his goal from the onset of its planning stage—to assure that Toby's daughters didn't have one moment of sorrow during their party. By the looks of it, Uncle Bill had succeeded.

By the end of the day, after most of the guests had gone home, Giselle approached Bill, looped her arms around his waist, and hugged as tightly as she could. "I'm overwhelmed, Bill. You've made this day so special."

"Well, the three of you make me feel special every single time we see each other. It feels good to be able to return the favor," he said, as Mac and Lexie ran toward them. He leaned over to catch her girls, lifted them easily in his arms.

Mac laid her head on his shoulder. "Thank you for the best day ever."

"This was the best birthday party I've ever had, Paw Paw. I love you so much!" Lexie hugged his neck tightly.

"I love you too, my girls. The animals, the pond, and the boats are always here for you. You can come over anytime and bring your friends, too," Bill said.

Mac lifted her head. "Even my new friend, Alyssa?"

"Sure you can." He gave Giselle a wink. "And tell her pretty mama to come along, too, while you're at it."

Mac's eyes widened with childish curiosity. "Do you like Miss Gwen, Paw Paw?"

Bill gave her a nod. "I sure do. Do you think I have a chance with her?"

Lexie nodded vigorously. "I heard her tell Carrie you were a fine looking hunkaman," she whispered excitedly in his ear. "I don't know what a hunkaman is, but I think it means she wants to be your girlfriend."

"Do you really think so?" They nodded enthusiastically.

"I think you need to marry her," Lexie whispered.

A deep chuckle rumbled through Bill's chest as he set both girls on the ground. He removed his straw Stetson, and passed a hand through his dark hair before leaning toward Lex. "How about if I ask her on a date first? You know, just to make sure we're compatible?"

"Okay, but you better hurry, Paw Paw," Lexie warned. "Some other guy might start to think she's patable too."

Bill tweaked her nose. "I wouldn't want that to happen. Thanks for looking out for me," he said, before they ran off.

"They're something," Bill said.

Giselle poked him in the chest. "Well, they happen to think you're something, Paw Paw Bill. And so do I, but—I have to wonder how Gwen's going to handle being called Maw Maw."

He sucked in his breath. "We'll cross that bridge when we get there—if—we even get there."

She stood back and studied the man before her, thinking Gwen would have to be crazy to pass up a man like Bill Broussard. And Gwen didn't look a bit crazy to her. "I think I'll put my money on when, rather than if, Bill." She gave him a conspiratorial grin. "Good luck, Mr. Broussard."

"Thank you, Giselle. But I don't believe in luck. I do, however, believe in skills."

She was still grinning when they met up with the remaining members of Sam and Carrie's family. It was six o'clock. The children were all exhausted from playing hard, pink from too much sun, and quickly running out of fuel.

"Bill, this was a blast," Carrie said. "I'd have never guessed this was the first little girl's birthday party you'd hosted."

He waved off the compliment. "All I do is write out the checks and delegate all the real work." He removed his hat and looked around. "Has anyone seen Gwen?"

"She was hanging around waiting to speak to you earlier, but you were busy," Carrie said. She pointed to the parking area. "Look over there. She and Alyssa are nearly at her car, but I bet you can catch her if you hurry."

"Excuse me, but I've got some 'patability' issues to iron out." He winked at Giselle then jogged toward Gwen and Alyssa.

Gwen felt a sharp stab of disappointment at not being able to tell Bill goodbye. She'd waited around as long as she could, but he'd been busy, and

Alyssa was too exhausted to wait any longer. She'd just helped her into the back seat when she heard someone calling her name.

Gwen turned, her stomach flipping in excitement at the sight of Bill jogging towards her.

He slapped his hat on his jeaned leg. "Now, I'd have been real hurt if you and Alyssa left here without saying goodbye."

"Hey, Bill. You seemed busy—I didn't want to interrupt."

"Never too busy for you. Did y'all have a good time?"

"We had a wonderful time, didn't we sweetie?"

Alyssa nodded then gave a huge yawn.

"Whoa, she'll be out before I reach the end of the drive way." Gwen looked up at Bill. "I had fun, too. It was nice meeting you." She smiled and held her hand out to him.

He took her hand, but held it and stepped up closer. "Gwen, would it be a waste of time if I called you for a date?"

She looked into his sexy blue eyes and seemed to lose her voice. All she could do was to shake her head.

His eyes sparkled with amusement. "Does that mean 'No, I wouldn't be wasting my time' or 'No, I don't want to date an old man like you.'"

Gwen's eyes widened as she took a hard swallow and finally found the nerve to answer. "You would not be wasting your time, and I can think of several ways to describe you, but 'old' isn't one of them."

He smiled and pulled out his wallet, then handed her two business cards. "There's my phone number if you ever need to get in touch with me. I'd appreciate it if you'd write your number on the back of one of those so I could call you."

She reached into her purse, pulled out one of her business cards from the hospital, and handed it to him.

He gave her a crooked grin. "Even better."

She looked closely at his card. "Don't you have a mobile...a cell phone?"

"I never needed one before, but—" he swept his hat from his head and stepped closer, "—if you promise to call me, I'll buy one tomorrow."

She nodded. "I promise." She heard a sound from the back seat and they both looked down. Alyssa had already fallen asleep and was snoring. She laughed quietly. "I need to get her home." When she turned back around, Bill had moved in so close she could feel his breath on her face as he spoke to her.

"Well," he said, as the deep baritone vibrated in her ear sending chills down her spine. "I'll talk to you later." He leaned over and kissed her on the cheek then pulled back a bit. He moved back in and kissed her lightly on the mouth then hovered for a moment over her lips before he looked down at her. She'd closed her eyes and when she finally opened them, she saw him watching her. She raised a hand to her face, knowing by the heat that it was pink and flushed.

Bill cleared his throat before speaking again. "Gwen, I think I should tell you that I've waited a long time to look for a lady to share my life with. Once I think I've found her, I plan on moving ahead quickly. I'm not getting any younger, and time is too precious to waste. How do you feel about that?"

She gazed up into his sober, blue eyes. "I feel the same way, but..." She placed her hand against his chest when he attempted to move in for another kiss. "I don't want to waste my time either, so...I do have a few questions."

He raised his hand and rubbed his thumb softly along her bottom lip. "Fire."

Her body immediately flooded with need. No kidding. "Are you looking for a long relationship?"

"I'm looking for a rest of my life relationship."

She closed her eyes and calmed herself. "Would you have a problem with Alyssa?"

"Absolutely not, she's a wonderful little girl."

She swallowed hard before asking the final question. "How would you feel about having more children?"

"All for it...As many as you want...As soon as you want."

"Oh, dear God," she said, in a sudden release of breath.

He leaned in and kissed her again, this time holding nothing back. When he finally pulled away, they were both drawing in ragged breaths and trembling. He rested his forehead against hers. "Just so you know, I'm okay in all departments."

Gwen raised a brow at his devilishly handsome grin. "I bet you are." She pulled away from him and situated herself in her car. After turning the ignition with shaky hands, she lowered her window and looked up into his piercing blue eyes.

Bill folded his long, lean body over, and rested his arms on the opening. "I'll give you a couple of hours to settle in before I call."

"That would be perfect." She closed her eyes as he leaned into the window to kiss her again. Once he straightened, she placed a trembling hand on her gearshift, and put it in drive.

Bill watched the red tail lights of her Chevy disappear in the dust, knowing that wasn't the last he'd see of Gwendolyn Perry. He wanted her in his life, wanted to make life easier for her and Alyssa. He turned away from the dust trail and started the walk back to the barn. "Bill, ole boy...it's time to get your game on," he mumbled.

Bill met up with Sam and Carrie on his way back to the barn. He tipped his hat to them. "Carrie, Sam, I hope you had a good time."

"We had a great time, thank you," Sam replied.

"Did you enjoy yourself?" Carrie asked smugly.

He gave her a wide grin. "Best damned day I've had in a long time, hon."

She gave him a hug. "Good for you, Bill."

They headed back to their truck, both chuckling as the sound of Bill whistling a snappy tune carried to them.

"That old dog," Sam said, grinning at his wife. "The Lord sure works in mysterious ways. I didn't even know our girls knew Alyssa."

"They didn't, but they do now," Carrie hinted.

Sam looked confused. "They must have if they invited her."

"Maybe they didn't invite her." She gave her husband a wink. "Bill and Gwen are perfect for each other, don't you think?"

Sam stopped walking and stared at his wife. "Well, I'll be damned."

Carrie laughed. "Just try to keep up, babe."

Chapter Fourteen

Giselle stared at the pond, now placid and peaceful after the afternoon of activity it had hosted. She tried to calm her nervous stomach, hoped to ease the tightness in her chest. She'd been tense and edgy all day. No use asking herself why. Even knowing her uneasiness centered around Jackson, she couldn't pinpoint the *why* of it. She turned at the sound of approaching footsteps and gave Bill a half-hearted smile.

"What are you looking so serious about, darlin'?" he drawled.

She stuck her hands in her back pockets and forced herself to relax. "I was just thinking what a good day it was, that's all."

"It was, wasn't it? The girls are tuckered out, but they don't want to give it up just yet."

Giselle smiled as she watched her daughters trying to skip stones in the pond, something Jackson had shown them earlier. "I know. I've been trying to get them to leave for ten minutes. I'm sure you're tired of seeing us by now."

"No hurry," he said. "This place is gonna be too damned quiet after you leave."

"I know what you mean," she said, thinking about how quiet the house would be once she got her girls home. She'd be lucky if they stayed awake through their baths.

"Those boats sure look nice," she said as she pointed to the paddleboats. "There was so much going on today, I didn't have a chance to take a ride in one."

"Well, we can remedy that. Come on girls, your mom didn't get a turn on a paddle boat!" Bill called to them. "Hang on just a minute, hon."

Giselle stood at the edge of the pond, staring out at the sunset, waiting for Bill to get back.

"I heard someone's ready for one last boat ride?"

She turned, surprised to see Jackson walking over to the nearest boat, as her girls ran to him like metal shavings to a magnet. "Oh. I thought it would be Bill—"

"He asked me to so he could attend to his hired hands," Jackson's tone seemed gruff, to the point. "Well, come on then." He pulled the boat closer to the dock so they could step in easier.

Giselle situated herself in the back to the right of Mackenzie and let Lexie sit up front with Jackson. He began a leisurely trek around the water's edge, paddling with his muscular legs. Giselle tried to stay focused on the glorious sunset reflecting off the glasslike surface of the water, but her gaze continued to return to Jackson. From her vantage point at the back of the boat, she was able to observe him unnoticed as he pumped up and down at the pedals. His arms rested on the steering wheel of the small craft, but even in his relaxed posture, she could see the definition of muscles and tendons in his upper body.

Her gaze moved from his shoulders to the angular profile of his face. She had to admit, he was nice to look at, especially when he wasn't aware that she was watching. Even if he turned around to face her, her dark sunglasses wouldn't reveal her target of sight.

Mac and Lexie's heads nodded as both struggled to stay awake through the sound of water being dispersed by the paddles.

Giselle gazed at the tranquil beauty of the pond and the array of colors it reflected from its surroundings. "It's beautiful here," she murmured, then turned back towards Jackson.

He nodded, staring out at the sunset. "It's the best time of the day to be out here."

She spoke quietly, afraid to disturb the solitude of the moment, but for some reason, longing to hear the sound of his voice. "Did you grow up on this ranch?"

He shook his head slowly. "Naw, Bill didn't buy this place until after Chloe and I were married. He said he wanted to be ready when we had kids." He snorted, "You can see how well that turned out."

"Best laid plans and all that."

"That's right." He sighed deeply, then looked over to the right of him and smiled. "This one's out like a light."

Giselle looked to her left. "Mac is, too." She gazed out at the blazing sunset. "Are you angry with me, Jackson?"

He stared straight ahead and waited, as though he were considering how to answer.

"Not so much angry, as disappointed in your actions, I guess. I thought we'd become friends, but then you distanced yourself."

"I told you why—"

"I know why you did it, but it doesn't make it hurt any less, especially when you change the rules to suit you."

She turned to face him. "What do you mean by that?"

He shrugged. "First you totally ignore me, then you're friendly, then you ignore me again. It's hurtful and confusing. Frankly, I'm fed up with your attitude."

"What attitude?" Her voice rose more than she intended.

He cocked his head and faced her. "If you're friends with someone, you're always friends, not just when it suits you."

"I don't want people talking about me, and insinuating that I didn't love my husband enough," she insisted.

"Give me a break, Giselle. Anyone who knows you also knows how much you loved Toby. I can't believe you'd shut me out just to satisfy a couple of sluts, one of which wanted to get her hands on your husband."

"Now she wants to get her hands on you." She spoke in a low murmur, more to herself than to him.

"What was that?"

"Nothing."

"What'd you say?" he demanded.

She turned to him, irritated that he wouldn't let it go. "I *said* Izzy wants to get her hands on you now."

He froze, bringing the boat to a quiet halt on the far edge of the pond. "Did this Izzy person tell you that?"

"That's what she said that night. She said she didn't know who you were, but she was damned sure going to find out," Giselle admitted.

"Did she really?"

The slightest hint of a devilish grin revealed itself, and she suddenly wanted nothing better than to slap it off that handsome face of his. "Do you want an introduction next time you're in town?" Her tone dripped with sarcasm.

"It depends. What's she like?"

"What you're really asking is what does she look like, right?" She snorted in disgust as Jackson shrugged and took his sunglasses off to give them a leisurely cleaning with the edge of his T-shirt.

"I guess she's pretty enough, if you like that type. She has big boobs, thanks to one sugar daddy or another, and lots of curves in all the right places. Let me think, I didn't actually see her that night, but the last time I did, she was blonde, but that varies. She wears lots of eye makeup—that never varies, and always, always wears a ton of jewelry. She's in her early to mid-thirties I believe. It's kind of hard to tell, because she has that classic, slutty, rode-hard-and-put-up-wet look about her, you know?"

Jackson nodded and gave a grunt of understanding.

"Izzy's responsible for several separations and divorces in Kenton. Her and those weak-willed husbands that couldn't keep it in their pants," she added.

He slid his sunglasses back on. "She sounds interesting."   Her eyes narrowed to angry slits. "Did you say you were interested?"

"I said she sounds interesting, but I guess I'm not quite weak-willed enough. That's not what I'd look for."

"What type are you looking for?"

"I'm not looking at all, actually."

"Does that mean you don't want another woman right now, or that you've already found one?"

"Is this really any of your business?" he snapped.

"It is if you're going to be bringing her around my girls."

He swung his head around, ripping off his sunglasses so fast they flew to the bottom of the boat. "What the hell gives you the right to insult me like that? Have I ever acted in any way that would make you think I'm irresponsible enough to bring some tramp around these girls?"

She slipped off her own sunglasses. Their gazes clashed, one full of intense anger, the other full of self-righteous indignation—until she realized that his anger had been fueled by hurt.

"Answer me, dammit!" Lexie jerked slightly in her sleep at the intensity of his bark.

She tore her eyes away from his handsome, but furious face and looked out toward the sunset. "No, you haven't. I'm sorry. I shouldn't have said that."

"You're damn right you shouldn't have."

"Look, I said I was sorry." That's as far as she'd go when it came to throwing herself on his mercy.

He resumed his pedaling but veered the boat toward the bank.

Apparently she'd irritated him enough to cut their ride short. "Bill and Gwen seem like a good match, don't they?" She followed her attempt to change the subject with a statement that tasted like bile on its exit. "Maybe she's got a friend for you. You and Bill could always double date."

"I'm not Uncle Bill," he growled. "I don't need help finding a woman."

"What do you mean?"

"I meant I don't need to be 'set up'. Someone invited Gwen here for him. Was it you?"

She cocked her head in concentration, trying to remember. "I wrote invitations for twelve of Mackenzie's classmates, but I don't remember writing one for Alyssa. I've never even heard Mac talk about an Alyssa. I wonder who invited her."

"Gwen said she'd been surprised to get the invitation since Alyssa has never been in one of Mac's classes. Carrie probably invited her. She's just enough of a busybody to do something like that," he insisted.

She smiled as she pictured Bill and Gwen together. "Well, they seem perfect for each other. I don't know her, but Carrie and Sam both like her. Maybe this will be good for Bill, for all of them."

"I hope so." He wiped his brow with the back of his hand. "Bill was married a long time ago, you know. They were both very young and his wife died in childbirth, or miscarried, or something like that. I think it nearly killed him."

"You know about that? I don't think he's aware of it." She shook her head. "Amazing. How is it that two men, who are as close as you and Bill are, have never discussed something as important as that?"

"For one thing, I was an infant when it happened. We're not chicks. We don't feel it necessary to bare our souls about something that happened nearly four decades ago." He was pensive for a moment. "Besides, I never told him I knew. I didn't see any point in it. I always figured if he didn't want to bring up the subject, he must have had his reasons. When did he tell you about that?"

Giselle stared at the back of his neck, where his sweat dampened hair met smooth, tanned skin. She swallowed and forced herself to speak. "That Sunday morning before Sam and Carrie's barbeque. He credits both your parents with saving his life, but mostly your mom." She stopped to think about the kind of woman Elise Broussard must have been. "You know, Jackson, your mother's words and actions, thirty-six years ago, helped me to understand what I'd been putting my own children through. In a way, she helped me to snap out of it enough to take care of Mac and Lexie. Bill must have had a great deal of respect for your mother."

She paused, and closed her eyes, letting the peacefulness of the summer afternoon envelop her. The boat drifted, aided only by a subtle breeze.

"Do you remember much about your parents, Jackson?" She opened her eyes to watch his reaction as she waited for his answer. His gaze fixed on the sunset as crickets chirped from the banks of the pond. She heard the call of a mockingbird in the distance, then the gentle whinny of a horse in a nearby pasture. Had nearly given up on a response from him when he finally spoke.

"I remember a few things, like how my mom tucked me into bed at night and taught me my prayers. And how when my dad carried me on his shoulders, I thought I could touch the sky. I remember how he clowned around with Uncle Bill, and I remember watching my mom and dad dance in the kitchen to the radio. They did that a lot. But this one time it was to that Van Morrison song, *Into the Mystic*. I stood there watching until I realized I wasn't alone. Uncle Bill had walked up behind me, and he was watching them too. Then he put his finger over his mouth to keep me quiet and pulled me away. When we got to another room, he explained that mom and dad been dancing to *their* song and we shouldn't interrupt. You know . . ." He paused to wipe his brow with the back of his hand. "Even as a little kid, I could see it. I could feel that my parents were so in love that nothing would ever separate them." He shook his head. "I always figured God knew it too, and that's why he took them at the same time."

Giselle watched Jackson's face as he let memories from his past wash over him. She could see the need in him to find his own connection with another person, the kind his parents had with each other. She concentrated so hard on his expression that his next words made her jump.

"Just before my folks died, I overheard my mom telling Uncle Bill that he needed to find another wife. He said he'd lost a wife and child on the same day and couldn't even think of replacing her. She said it wouldn't happen unless he let it." He cleared his throat then. "That same night, my parents put me to bed and kissed me goodnight. Uncle Bill stayed home with me so they could go dancing for New Year's Eve. They hardly ever went out and mom was so excited. She looked so pretty."

Jackson laughed quietly. "I remember my dad saying 'See you next year, my boy'. I got a sick feeling in my stomach, because that sounded like a long time to me. My face must have shown it, because dad laughed and said they would see me the next morning." Jackson took a deep breath and let it out slowly. "I never saw them again. Not alive, anyway."

Giselle covered her mouth to quiet the sob that built in her throat.

"I guess that's why that conversation my mom had with Bill stayed so clear in my head all these years. It was almost the last words I ever heard her speak. I was two months shy of my fifth birthday."

She swallowed the lump in her throat. "Do you miss them?"

He nodded. "Every day. Bill was good to me, and I love him, but I still remember what it was like to have all of them—my mom, my dad, and my Uncle Bill. We were a family. I want that, Giselle. I've always wanted it. To be part of a family again—kids arguing, babies crying, chaotic holidays and family gatherings . . ."

"Like Sam and Carrie's, with enough people to play baseball?"

He nodded. "Just like that. I wanted a houseful of kids, and one day grandkids."

"You could still have that. You could meet someone."

"I'm thirty-six years old, Giselle. I need somebody soon who'll be willing to help me have all that. I'm tired of waiting for it, and I'm frustrated as hell." He released a long, deep sigh and began pedaling toward the dock.

The silence in the boat weighed heavily on Giselle's mind, filled her with a melancholy.

Jackson helped her get the two sleeping girls to her truck. Once everyone was safely buckled in and settled, she started the engine. She paused to glance up at him through the open window. "Thanks, Jackson—for everything."

He lowered himself to pass a glance over the two girls in the back seat. Then his gaze found hers. He placed his hand over the arm she had resting on the window opening. His next words seemed finite, almost as if it were more than a simple farewell. Caused an uneasy stirring in her heart.

"Take care, Giselle," he said, then turned and walked away.

Jackson met up with Bill in the stables. "Well, you had yourself a good day, didn't you?"

Bill leaned on the pitchfork he'd been using to meet Jackson's amused gaze. "Yep. A very productive day."

"Are you going to see Gwen again?"

Bill grinned. "As soon as I can. As often as she lets me."

"Do you really think you should be moving that quickly?"

"Son, it's like I told her, I'm too old to be playing games. That's just a waste of time and it's too precious to me now. Besides, as it happens, she feels the same way."

"Well, you're a big boy and a good judge of character, so I won't bother with the usual precautionary words." Jackson slapped his uncle on the back. "I hope everything works out for you."

"Me too, but I need to bother you for some advice, son."

Jackson grinned. "Like how to date in the new millennium?"

Bill chuckled. "What the hell would you know about it? You haven't been on a date since the nineties. Don't worry about me, I can still teach you some things about women."

"Then why haven't you dated recently?"

"Who says I haven't dated?"

"I haven't met any of them."

Bill turned toward his nephew. "Why should you meet them?"

"It seems like you'd want to introduce them to your family," Jackson mumbled.

Bill snorted. "They weren't exactly the type of women you bring home to meet your mama." He cocked an eyebrow. "And even if they were, you ain't my mama."

"Oh." Jackson wasn't about to go *there*. "What kind of advice do you need, then?"

"Who's the best carrier for a mobile phone?"

"I thought you didn't have any use for one," Jackson said, once he'd recovered from the shock.

"I didn't before. Now I do so Gwen can reach me."

"Welcome to the new century, Uncle Bill."

"I'm also buying a new truck tomorrow."

Jackson's eyes widened in disbelief. "You're seriously getting rid of that old Ford?"

"No, I'm going to hang onto it for farm work. But the first time I go pick Gwen up for a date, I want it to be in my brand new truck."

"Oh Lord, I can't believe it took a woman to get you to come into the new age. Good for you, old man."

Bill laughed and continued his previous chore of shoveling hay into horse stalls. "You know what they say, you're only as old as you feel—and today I don't feel a day over forty. So, how was your day?"

"Confusing as hell," Jackson growled, as he picked up a second pitchfork and joined his uncle in tossing the fresh hay into the nearest stall.

"That's because you won't listen to me."

"Your ass," Jackson snorted. "I let loose on Giselle in the boat when she made a comment I didn't care for."

"And that ended how, exactly?"

"She apologized. I told her I could find my own damn woman and I didn't need to be set up like, well, like you."

Bill stopped shoveling hay and looked at his nephew. "I figured as much when Alyssa and Mac met for the first time today." He wiped his brow and released a low chuckle. "I asked Carrie to find me someone. It's nice to know she's taking care of me."

They worked in companionable silence for a while, just the two of them in the barn with the animals. After debating whether or not to broach the subject, Jackson finally spoke up. "You know, Uncle Bill, I know about the wife and baby you lost a long time ago."

Bill leaned on his pitchfork. "You do? It wasn't a big secret or anything, I just didn't see any reason to bring it up. How'd you find out?"

"I overheard you and mom talking about it the same day she and dad died. She was telling you it was time to find another girl."

Bill smiled at the memory. "Elise was always trying to set me up with some friend of hers." He faced the west, toward the setting sun. "New Year's Eve— Jamison was taking Elise dancing." He passed a hand over his face. "That was a bad time for both of us."

Jackson nodded, and leaned against the wall. "I told Giselle I'm tired of waiting for a family. I must have used up my reserve of patience on Chloe."

Bill leaned over to pick up a length of rope and slowly wound it into a coil. He walked over and hung the rope on a hook near Jackson's head. "Maybe you're just tired of denying your feelings for Giselle."

Jackson met his uncle's gaze. "I've already admitted that I'm attracted to her."

Bill shook his head, "I'm not talking about physical attraction. I'm talking about the fact that you're in love with her. Are you ready to admit that?"

Jackson pushed away from the wall. "Don't start. Her husband was one of my best friends. I would nev—"

"You would never have acted on it as long as Toby was alive. Believe me, son, I, better than anyone, know that."

Jackson let his head drop and closed his eyes. After a few moments of silence, he met his uncle's sympathetic gaze. "I've loved her for so damned long. I *wanted* what she and Toby had. But *I* wanted to be the man who had it with her. I've loved her for three and a half years of my life now, Uncle Bill." He lifted his arms, let them fall heavily to his sides. "I don't know how to go on if I never get the chance . . .Dammit!" He kicked an empty bucket and sent it flying noisily across the wooden floor of the tack room.

Bill walked over to where the bucket landed, and picked it up. "What is it you're so upset about?"

"Now that you know and I've accepted it, well, shit!" he snapped. "What if?"

"What if, what?"

"What if she never returns the feelings? What do I do then?"

"Then, you do what we've been telling her to do for months. You move on, look for someone else to fill the void."

Jackson groaned and walked away from his uncle until he was outside of the stables. He paced slowly, both hands clasped at the back of his head.

Bill followed him out. "Don't worry, I doubt if anyone else besides me and Carrie know about this."

Jackson stopped and faced his uncle. "Carrie knows too?"

Bill shrugged. "We haven't discussed it, but I'd bet my last dollar on it. She's worked with the two of you forever." He placed a hand to Jackson's shoulder. "You don't die from disappointment, son, or a broken heart over unrequited love. Believe me, I know."

Jackson thought of the years he'd spent loving Giselle. Wanting her. "Every time I looked at Chloe, I wished for Giselle. I knew it wasn't right, but hell, I couldn't help myself. Throughout everything, I kept hoping that if Chloe had a child, things would get better."

Bill grimaced at Jackson's words. "I know I probably shouldn't say this, but the thought of Chloe alone with an innocent baby always scared the living hell out of me."

Jackson shook his head slowly. "I know, but I'd have protected it, would have raised it alone if push came to shove." He shook his head. "My feelings for Giselle kept me going. Pitiful, ain't it? Carrying around a torch for a woman with two kids and already in a wonderful marriage. I didn't see the harm in holding out for a miracle." He rested one hip against the opening of the barn door. "The day I met Toby it threw me for a freaking loop, I tell you. To make matters worse, he turned into my best friends for the entire last year. Hell, I was happy they were so good together. But even then, I wanted to be the one Giselle loved." He crossed his arms against his chest and stared at his uncle. "You have no idea what that's like."

Bill got a misty look in his eyes. He took his hat off and slapped it against his thigh, sending particles of hay and dust flying. "Oh, I think I can empathize with you some. You see, a year or so after my wife died is when your Elise started her mission to get me married off again. The night you overheard us, I'd have said anything to get her off my back. I knew I couldn't have feelings for anyone else. Just like you with Giselle, I'd fallen in love with your mother."

Jackson's gaze clashed with his uncle's.

"And just like you, I never acted on it. I would never have dreamed of telling her or your dad. I was every bit as happy for your parents as you were for Giselle and Toby." He looked at Jackson. "I'm only telling you this so you'll know, that I understand exactly what you went through then—what you're going through, now."

Jackson stared at the man who had been so good to him, his mind working furiously to process this new information.

Bill must have taken his silence for something other than what it was. "I hope you don't think less of me."

Jackson snapped out of his musings. "Of course not. But I'm just realizing now that you've lost the most in all this. You've lost two women you loved, as well as a child, and a brother. No wonder it took you so long to move on. Jesus Christ, Uncle Bill. How the hell did you manage?"

"I had you, son. You put everything into perspective for me. You always have."

Jackson thought of Mac and Lex and how he'd been willing to do anything it took to keep them smiling. It made perfect sense to him. He gave his uncle a brief nod before pulling out his wallet. He handed Bill a business card. "Here's the carrier I use, and I can't wait to see the truck you buy to impress Gwen. I sure hope you find happiness with her, because I can't think of another person who deserves it more than you do."

Bill glanced at the card, slipped it into his shirt pocket. "Oh, I don't know. I can think of one other man who's sure as hell due for some."

Chapter Fifteen

Jackson released a long whistle as he walked up to Bill's new truck, a beautiful Super Duty Ford F-350, ready for towing, bronze in color and trimmed up in chrome. The King Ranch accessory package dressed up the eye-pleasing, luxurious interior. The seats were tan saddle leather, heated for wintertime comfort, with front and back climate control. The truck boasted a built-in GPS and a premium sound system. "Gwen will be impressed. I promise you. Hell, I'm even impressed. You're making me regret my Avalanche."

Bill took off his hat and passed his fingers through his dark hair. "I just want her to be comfortable."

"She will be. I nearly forgot. My new bike is coming in tomorrow, so I'm taking the day off," Jackson explained. "They're delivering it to my place tomorrow morning."

"What'd you get?"

"An Indian Chief Road Master. It's the motorcycle version of that truck." He cocked his head toward Bill's new wheels. "I'm hoping it'll be the perfect distraction to keep my mind off Giselle." He spotted Carrie approaching. "Look who's coming. This is going to blow her mind."

Carrie beamed at Bill as she approached. "If you're trying to impress a certain Ms. Perry, this should do it. It's not necessary, but a good looking man like you belongs in a truck like this." She glanced inside the open driver's door and gasped. "This is *so* Bill Broussard."

Bill leaned over to hug her. "I haven't had a chance to thank you properly, for Gwen, I mean."

"You're welcome, honey. I heard her story and knew God put her in my path for a reason, and it had to be you. I only want credit if it works out, though."

"How about if I buy you lunch?"

She shook her head. "Not today, I've got errands to run. She called me this morning, you know. I hear you two had an interesting talk last night. A two hour phone call?"

"Sure did," Bill admitted. "That much less to say next time I see her."

"A little less talk and a lot more action?" she teased, as Bill gave her an enthusiastic nod.

Jackson scratched his head. "Two hours? Hell, I can't get you to talk for five minutes on the phone."

His uncle gave him a wink. "You don't look like Gwen."

Carrie grinned and turned to him. "Jack, are you going to lunch with Bill?"

"Yeah, we're going to choose a wireless phone and a plan for him before lunch."

Carrie's mouth dropped in obvious shock. "Next thing you know, you'll be setting up your own web page and surfing the net from your smart phone."

"I don't know about all that. I just want Gwen to be able to get a hold of me when she feels like talking. It's going to be rough not to be around her twenty-four, seven, now that I've found her. I've waited a long time for this."

"Oh yeah." Carrie sent him a knowing smile. "I remember those days. Not wanting to be separated from Sam for one single night. Good times ahead for both you and Gwen. I'm happy for you, too." She headed for the office, giving them a wave. "You two boys have a good lunch."

Jackson's bike was a far cry from the Honda 750 he'd ridden when he was in college. He pulled into the park the next afternoon for the Tuesday ballgame, an impressive sight, judging from the appreciative stares he got upon his arrival. He had just dismounted and taken his helmet off when he heard a sharp whistle.

Sam approached, his eyes glowing with admiration. "You got an Indian. Man, I am so freaking jealous right now, it ain't funny."

Jackson grinned at Sam. "Yeah, when I told Carrie I'd ordered one she got pissed. She said you had always wanted one, and that you were going to whine about it until you wore her down. So, you know what to do, don't you?"

Sam nodded, and spent the next minute drooling over the bike. "Damn, and my wife's here today, too. I think I'll start that whining right now," he said.

"You didn't hear that from me," Jackson added.

"Not a word," Sam said as they walked over to the stands. He approached Carrie, who sat on one end of the bleachers. He tapped her arm. "Babe, look who's here."

She turned to face them. "Hey Jack, I wasn't sure you were coming today since you'd taken the day off."

"He came on his new bike, babe. Look, he got an Indian."

Her gaze flew to the bike, then back to Sam who already wore the face of a deprived child.

"Babe, can I have one, please?" he pleaded.

"Stop it, Sam." She climbed down from the bleachers and poked a finger in Jackson's chest. "I blame you for this."

"Yes ma'am, I'm sorry," he told her.

"No, you're not, don't even try to pull that crap with me," she scolded.

He grinned. "You're right. I love my bike."

They walked over to examine it, and Gretchen and her girls joined them.

"Who's this fine bike for?" Gretchen asked.

"It's mine," Jackson admitted.

"How's it ride?" Sam knelt before it, almost reverently.

"Like a dream."

"Oh for God's sake, get up off your knees, Sam," Carrie chided. "You look like you're worshiping the damn thing."

"But, that's the one I've always wanted," Sam groaned.

Gretchen laughed. "Oh, here we go. Mr. Sam won't stop whining until mom lets him get one."

Jackson cracked up at Gretchen's astute comment, knowing by the look on Sam's face that it was spot on. He stifled his laughter as Carrie's glare seared him.

"You see? She knows how he is. This is not funny to me, not at all. That's the price of a mobile home, Sam. Or that really nice RV we agreed we couldn't afford."

Giselle and her girls approached the group, all standing around in obvious admiration of one of the most beautiful bikes she'd ever seen. "Wow, who's bike?"

"It's Jackson's, dammit!" Sam growled, as everyone laughed—everyone except for Carrie.

"Is it really yours?" Giselle faced Jackson, thinking how good he probably looked on it.

"Yep, it was delivered this morning."

"It's so big, and it's pretty!" Lexie said.

"I like the fringes on the seat," Mac said. "Can we ride?"

"No sweetie, not just sitting behind me. It wouldn't be very safe. Sam, you want to take it for a spin?"

Sam's eyes lit up at the prospect. "Will you be here for a while?"

Jackson nodded. "I can be here for as long as you need me to be."

"Then I'll take it for a spin after the game."

They headed to the bleachers as a group. Giselle turned to Jackson, who'd taken the last seat below her on the end of the bleachers. "I never took you for the motorcycle type.".

He shrugged. "I'm sure there are a lot of things you don't know about me." He stretched one of his long legs out on the bleacher in front of him. "I had one the entire time I attended LSU. It was a hell of a lot easier to find parking spots."

"Toby had a bike too, before we got married, but it wasn't very practical for us as a couple. We had to sell it and buy a car." She sighed, remembering the last ride they'd taken before they let it go. "I loved that bike." She found herself imagining what it would feel like to be behind Jackson on that bike, the wind blowing in her face. Her hands wrapped around his waist—the feel of those well-defined, rock hard abs under her hands. Those abs, with the perfect amount of dark feathery hair leading down the happy trail path to that—towel. That damned towel.

His long leg welcomed her to feast her man-starved eyes upon him. Feeling suddenly hot, she tore her gaze from the sight of him and used her hand to fan her face. Toby had always looked better in preppy clothes than dressed down in jeans. But damn if Jackson didn't wear them better than any male model she'd ever seen. Who the hell knew her former supervisor could look so freaking *hot* in a pair of faded jeans. She sent him another covert glance, thinking Jackson Broussard would look just as comfortable working on a ranch as sitting behind a desk with a computer in front of him. She looked quickly away, unable to escape her thoughts. *He'd look hot as hell dressed in black leather and riding a big, beefed up bike—or better yet—nothing at all.*

Unable to resist his masculine presence, she turned back to watch him from beneath her dark glasses. He drew one long leg slowly up to shift his position, having to pull up on the jean material above his knee to adjust them over his bulging thighs. He stretched the opposite leg out in front of him and bending the leg closest to her at the knee. She bit her lip as her heat level rose, pushing its way further her neckline to her ears, and beyond.

Oh damn.

With concentrated effort, she pooled her will power and forced herself to turn away from the flesh and blood Jackson. She congratulated herself at her personal victory.

Especially since she'd long since stopped turning away from the dream version of the man.

Halfway through the game, Jackson rose to stretch his legs. "I'm going to the concession stand. You ladies want anything?" Though he'd asked them as a group, his gaze lingered on Giselle, who'd been unusually quiet during the competition.

She glanced at him, smiled, but turned quickly away again.

Several other "I'm goods," preceded her mumbled "No thanks, I'm okay."

Carrie was waiting at the concession stand window when he walked behind her and goosed her in the side.

"Hey!" She turned, her hand up, ready to slap someone. "Oh, it's you," she said, obviously expecting to see her husband, who'd teased her non-stop about the bike since he'd seen it. She pointed at him. "I'm still a little pissed at you, you know."

"I gathered."

She wiped a hand across one cheek, her fair skin pink from the heat. "It's hot today. God, I hate summer time."

Jackson nodded. "It was hot as hell on that bike." He grinned, waiting for it. Wasn't disappointed by her accompanying snort.

"No sympathy here, asshole. Not one damned bit."

"Carrie, is that any way to talk to your boss?" he teased, backing up in case she decided to take a swing at him.

"Not here, you aren't," she growled. "This is my turf—"

"Ooh honey! Is that your gorgeous bike over there?"

Jackson cringed at the irritating screech that erupted from behind the two of them. He turned, to see a youngish woman, although questionable as to whether she was a lady; blonde, obviously bleached, wearing a pair of tight shorts, and a skin-tight, low-cut tank top. She wore huge, dangly earrings and several metal, bangle style bracelets on her wrists that jangled when she moved. And she moved—a lot. She could have walked right on to a Kabuki theater stage with the amount of eye makeup she wore. His nose wrinkled involuntarily, overpowered by the sickeningly sweet smell of whatever perfume she'd bathed herself in. The woman's single-minded vocabulary apparently had no acquaintance with two words: subtlety or moderation. She reached over and latched onto his arm like a leech in marsh water.

"You want to take me for a ride, cowboy?"

Jackson didn't have to wonder who she was. Giselle's more than accurate description of 'Rode hard and put up wet' told him he was in the presence of the infamous Izzy whatever-the-hell-her-name-was.

"My name's Isabelle, but everybody calls me Izzy." She pushed her considerable bust right up against his torso. "And who are you?" She cracked her chewing gum loudly.

All Jackson could think when he looked at her was the heartache this woman had caused Giselle, and the months of frustration she had caused him. He wanted to shake her until her teeth rattled, but his uncle had raised him to be a gentleman. "Excuse me, please." He turned to walk away but Izzy was persistent, as well as loud, brassy, and no doubt, easy as hell.

She grabbed his waist with both hands. "Oh come on now, don't go away just yet. Don't you want to ride me on your big, bad motorcycle? I can show you a real good time." She slid her hands down his stomach to his crotch.

He grabbed her hands, and jerked her to a halt. "Honey, you don't have a damn thing I want," he growled, before pushing her hands roughly aside, then turning to leave.

"Uh! Forget him." Izzy turned to her equally trashy sidekick. "He must already be screwing Giselle Granger."

Jackson stopped in his tracks and turned to glare at her. By the time he closed the distance between them, Carrie had her by the arm, and was pulling her behind the concession stand. Izzy's sidekick looked as though she would assist her friend, until Jackson's icy glare made her dart off in the opposite direction.

Jackson walked back up to the window and paid for three waters, then waited around for Carrie, just in case she needed any assistance from him. A minute later, a terrified Izzy stumbled out from behind the building. When she saw Jackson, she tried her best to salvage what little dignity she never had. She flounced off, wagging her ass, jingling loudly with every exaggerated step and pronounced swing of her arms and hips.

Carrie appeared next, grumbling to herself. "That tramp has got some nerve."

Jackson stared down at her and grinned. "I can say, without a doubt, I've never been *that* hard up."

Carrie shook her head, that left eyebrow of hers lifted as she considered his comment. "No, I wouldn't imagine you had been. Come on stud, let's go watch the game."

Mac and Allie's team finished off the opposition in an easy win. The group migrated over to Jackson's bike, and soon stood watching Sam drive off on Jackson's motorcycle.

"Crap, I'll never hear the end of this now," Carrie complained. She headed to her car, but not without giving Jackson the evil eye.

"Do I have to bring him back home?" he called out.

"No, his truck's here. I imagine he'll be back when he gets hungry enough. Serves you right, troublemaker!" she snapped.

Jackson waved Carrie off and turned to find Giselle waiting to speak to him.

"Um, Jackson. I wanted to let you know that Lexie's game has been cancelled for Thursday. The coaches are going on vacation, and I'm taking the girls to New Orleans. We won't see you for a week."

He nodded, and kicked at nothing with his boot. A week without seeing the girls—or her. That's gonna suck. Bad.

Giselle watched him scuff and kick at the dirt. He looked younger, standing there with his hands shoved deep in the pockets of his just right tight jeans. His red T-shirt, bearing the name of the bike dealership, hugged his torso just enough—a perfect showcase for his muscular body.

"You don't have to wait here with me, Giselle. I'm fully capable of staying by myself until Sam gets back."

"Lexie's team is practicing over there." She pointed to a practice field. "They figured they'd get one in before everyone goes on vacation and hope the kids retain a little."

He gave her a sheepish grin. "Sorry, I hadn't noticed."

"What happened with Izzy?"

"What do you mean?"

She grinned. "Gretchen and I saw her walk away from the concession all upset. What happened?"

"She asked me to give her a ride. I said no, and when I tried to leave—she—grabbed at me . . ." he finished, lamely.

She leaned forward to hear him better. "She did what?" He cleared his throat and actually turned a shade of red.

"She grabbed at my crotch. I told her I wasn't interested."

Giselle snorted in an effort to hold back the laughter. "And then?"

"Uh, I think Carrie chewed her out."

"For grabbing at your crotch?"

He shook his head. "For what she said after I said no."

"Which was . . ."

Jackson cleared his throat uncomfortably. "It's not important."

"Go on, you can tell me," she urged.

"She suggested to her equally trashy friend that you and I were already...You know," he said, obviously reluctant to finish. "Who the hell dresses like that for a ballgame, anyway?"

Giselle chuckled. "She wasn't here for the game, she was here for you. She said she'd make it her business to find out who you were. People see you and Bill here, and—well, the two of you kind of stand out in a crowd. You're both so—tall." She supposed it wouldn't do to expound on his and his uncle's exceptional drool-worthy qualities.

"I guess so." He cocked his head, squinting his eyes against the setting sun. "How'd you know she was here? Did she say something to you before that?"

Giselle giggled. "Are you kidding? She sounds like one of Santa's reindeer with all that jingling and jangling." She waved her arms and shook her butt in a comic imitation of Izzy that had Jackson in stitches. "Did you hear what Carrie said to her?"

"No, but I can guess."

She grinned. "Me too. I'm glad she's in my corner."

They made their way over to the batting cages. Lifting his arms, he hooked his fingers in the wire fencing above the gate. Giselle watched his muscular arms flex and strain, and wondered again how one man could look so damn good in faded jeans and a tee shirt.

She tore her gaze away from bulging biceps long enough to speak. "How's the fledgling romance going? Have Bill and Gwen spoken again?"

"Oh yeah. It's all fireworks and phone calls that last for hours. Did you hear he bought a new truck and cell phone yesterday?"

"I did and I'm impressed. Gwen's accomplished a lot in a short time with Mr. *I don't need no fancy cell phone and my old truck is just fine*," she said, in a near perfect imitation of Bill.

Jackson laughed again then tweaked her nose. "You're pretty good. Maybe you should take that act on the road."

"Yeah, right," she snorted. She looked up at him and sobered. "I'm happy for him, though. He's such a good man. And Gwen seems really sweet. They make a good match."

"I know, right. He said he feels twenty years younger. I predict they'll be married soon and working on adding to the family."

She couldn't keep from smiling at a particular mental image. "I can see Bill with a new baby. Can't you, Jackson?"

He nodded. "Yeah, I can."

She hesitated a moment. "I can see you with one, as well. Maybe Gwen will produce that friend for you, after all."

"Are you that anxious to see me married off?"

Was she? "I'm-I'm j-just saying. I know it's what you want, and you want it soon, and I—I think you deserve to have children—of your own. You deserve to be happy."

Jackson seemed to weigh her comment before replying with one of his own. "And what about you, Giselle? Don't you deserve to be happy again?"

"I *am* happy—happy enough." Thankfully, Sam chose that moment to return with Jackson's bike. She spun around to watch him turn into the park entrance. "Here's your ride."

She waited for Sam to park the bike and climb off. "How was it?"

Sam slipped off the helmet. "Handles like a dream. My bike is a real smooth ride, but this is like a Rolls Royce in comparison."

Giselle leaned in to get a closer look at Jackson's bike. She could see her reflection in chrome that was buffed to a high polished perfection, smoothed her hand over the custom painted tank. She nodded, able to appreciate the machine's beauty.

"Looks like someone wants a ride," Sam spoke from behind her.

She glanced back, giving him a hopeful look. "I really would." She met Jackson's gaze and for a moment she thought he might volunteer to give her a ride.

He gave her a one shouldered shrug. "Sorry, I have to get back to Lake Coburn. Maybe another day."

She gave him a nod and straightened, wiping her hands on her shorts. "I understand completely. See ya next week, Jackson." She headed for Lexie's practice.

Jackson watched Giselle walking over to Lexie's field.

Sam's comment jolted him. "You know, Jack, if Carrie were here she'd ask if you'd lost your freaking mind."

Jackson mounted his bike and adjusted the straps on his helmet. "Not yet, Sam. But with *her* seated behind me on this thing? I may have lost my mind by the end of the ride."

Chapter Sixteen

A week later, Giselle, Gretchen, and Lauren sat in the bleachers waiting for Allie and Mac's game to begin.

"Are Jackson and Bill coming?" Gretchen asked.

Giselle gave her a nod. "Jackson should be here on his bike and Bill's picking up Gwen and Alyssa along the way."

Lauren leaned forward in her seat. "How's that going?"

"I don't know. I haven't seen anyone in a week. We were in New Orleans for four days." The sound of a motorcycle entering the park had the group of women facing that direction. Jackson fit his bike into a spot near the front of the park and dismounted. He started the walk to the bleachers wearing his standard uniform of faded jeans, and white T-shirt, his Ray Bans pushed up in his hair, and his helmet tucked under his arm.

An older woman seated next to them gasped. "My God, who is that?"

The three women exchanged knowing looks as Lauren explained his identity.

"Honey, I may be sixty-five years old, but I'm not too old to appreciate a fine looking man when I see one."

"Yeah and he's got an uncle that looks just as good," Gretchen told the woman. She pointed Bill out, arriving with Gwen and Alyssa. "There he is now."

The woman groaned as she shook her head in disappointment. "Damn, the good ones are always taken."

The women scooted over at Gwen and Alyssa's approach to make room for them, while Bill and Jackson hung back.

Jackson sauntered up to the team dugout to speak to Mac then turned back toward the bleachers. "Hello ladies." His gaze lingered longer on Giselle. "How was your trip, stranger?"

She shrugged. "It was okay, I guess. We'd been before, but I couldn't work up the nerve to go any further. I don't feel comfortable traveling without—well—with just the girls and I. I don't feel safe, you know? I hate driving in traffic."

Before Jackson could respond, Lexie called out to him. He turned in time to catch her launching herself into his arms. "Hey munchkin, I missed you. Good Lord, you must have grown two inches since I saw you last." He hugged her tightly then put her down so she could run off to play.

"We just got back from San Antonio," Lauren told Giselle. "That's where you need to take the girls. There's so much to do there, and the drive wasn't that bad."

Gwen turned to her. "Bill, Alyssa, and I are planning on going the first weekend in August. Why don't you and the girls come with us? It would give Alyssa some company."

"I don't want to impose like that, Gwen. The three of you are trying to bond right now." She bit her bottom lip as she remembered something. "That's where Toby and I were supposed to take the girls this summer. We'd never been."

"I went five years ago, but it was a bust," Jackson said.

"What happened?" Lauren asked.

He shrugged. "My wife had a way of turning every vacation into a living hell."

Gretchen leaned forward. "What did she do, Jackson?"

"The usual—found fault with everything. We changed rooms three times." He slid onto the bleacher beside Giselle.

Giselle slid over to make space for him. "What was wrong with the rooms?"

"Not a thing, as far as I could tell. I suspect she did it just to piss me off. She thrived on childish public displays of anger."

"Did it work?" Giselle asked with a hint of tease.

He leaned back and swiveled his head slowly to look at her through his dark tinted sunglasses. "What do you think?"

Giselle studied his expression for a moment then leaned back to meet his gaze head on. "I think you took it all with a grin, just to piss *her* off." She grinned slyly at him.

Everyone waited patiently for Jackson's answer. He finally smiled and nodded. "You know me too well."

Giselle laughed softly. "Was she upset?"

"Extremely upset. We finally cut the trip short and just came on home. I'd love to go back, but I doubt it'd be any fun alone. I wouldn't mind driving if you and the girls wanted to come with me. I could get us separate rooms in the same hotel Bill and Gwen are staying."

"There you go," Lauren said. "Sounds like the perfect solution, Giselle. You'll have a blast. There's the water park, the caverns, Sea World, The River Walk, the wax museum, Ripley's Believe It Or Not—All kinds of things to do."

Giselle nodded slowly, contemplating the possibilities. "Let me think about it."

Once their team ended the game with a narrow win, Giselle asked everyone to follow her to her truck. She and her girls passed out the gifts they'd brought everyone from New Orleans. Mac and Lexie saved Jackson's gift for last—a gold tee shirt, with a tiger riding a motorcycle on the back and LSU on the pocket.

"This is the coolest shirt ever," he said, clearly pleased with his gift.

At Lexie's urging, he slipped out of his shirt to try on the new one. The circle grew quiet at the sight of a bare chested Jackson.

"You sure have a lot of muscles," Allie said, giggling.

Giselle's face remained stony as Lauren nudged her in the rib and whispered in her ear, "He certainly does, doesn't he?"

Every woman there had seen the flash of tan skin and his muscular display in the few seconds it'd taken to change shirts.

Jackson smoothed the shirt down and tucked it into the waistband of his jeans. When he was done, he turned around for the two little girls and posed. "How does it look?"

"I like it!" Lexie said.

Mac nodded. "You look very handsome. Do you like it? When I saw it, I knew we had to get it for you."

"I love my shirt," he said, lifting them both easily for a group hug. He turned to their mother. "I really do. Thanks for thinking of me, Giselle."

"You're welcome," she murmured.

Gwen placed her hand on Giselle's arm. "Are you going to take Jackson up on his offer for San Antonio?"

She nodded. "It sounds too good to pass up, doesn't it?"

Gwen turned to Alyssa. "Mac and Lexie are coming with us on vacation. Won't that be fun?"

The three girls began to jump up and down excitedly.

Giselle looked up at Jackson. "Are you sure you don't mind? They can drive you crazy on trips."

"I'm preconditioned to crazy, hon." He gave her a wink. "I got this."

The next two weeks flew by as Jackson and Giselle prepared for their trip. Bill took care of the rooms, booking four at the same hotel, one of the nicest in the city. Giselle scoured the internet researching and scheduling things for them to do while they were in the city. They planned to leave as soon as Lexie's game was over on Thursday evening and spend the weekend. Monday they would drive home so that Gwen could go to work on Tuesday.

Thursday, day of departure, Giselle managed to squeeze in some last minute shopping in Lake Coburn before Lexie's ballgame. She'd cut it close shopping, time-wise, and skipped lunch. Too rushed to hit a fast food chain, she grabbed a sandwich at the same convenience store she tanked up her small SUV on the way home. By the time Lexie's game started, she was feeling a little nauseous.

"Are you feeling okay, Giselle?"

She chanced a look at Jackson, and pressed a hand to her stomach. "Not really. I think something I ate is disagreeing with me." She stuck it out for two more innings. At the top of the third, Jackson leaned in close.

"What exactly did you eat? You're looking a little rough."

"A ham and cheese from a convenience store cooler."

He took her elbow and helped her to her feet. "I think you should go home—now."

Too sick to argue, she nodded. "I think you're right."

"I should get that in writing."

"You're funny."

"Yeah? Well, you're green. Need me to go with you?"

She waved him off. "No, I can make it."

And she did—just barely—make it to her bathroom before emptying the contents of her stomach into the toilet.

By the time Jackson and her girls joined her, she'd emptied a lot more than that, suffering from cramps and nausea so violent she thought she would crack her rib again.

Another hour of more of the same had her realizing she was in for a long night of it. After the latest bout with nausea, she turned to her self-proclaimed caretaker.

"Take the girls to San Antonio, Jackson. I don't want their weekend ruined. They're looking forward to this."

He shook his head. "I'm not leaving you but I knew you'd feel that way. I've already called Gretchen and Caleb. They've agreed to go in our place. Is that okay with you?"

She managed a weak "Yes," before succumbing to another round of dry heaves.

Gretchen entered Giselle's bedroom around 8:00 p.m. "How's the patient?"

Jackson stood, looking down at Giselle. She lay there, still as death, with a cold wet washcloth over her eyes. "Not good."

Gretchen shook her head. "This will probably last into tomorrow, and probably still won't feel worth a damn until Saturday. Keep her hydrated."

He nodded. "I will." He handed her a prepaid Visa. "This should take care of all your expenses. You've got two adjoining rooms, already paid for. Just make sure your bunch, along with those two monkeys have a great time." He rested one knee on the floor and reached out to Mac and Lexie, who stood at the door, looking uncertain. "Come here girls. You be extra good for Gretchen and Caleb, okay? Mind your manners."

"But, what about mama?" Lexie turned her tear-filled eyes toward her deathly still mother. "Who's gonna take care of her?"

Jackson gave her a hug. "I will sweetie, don't you worry."

Mac's big brown eyes watered. "You won't leave her, will you, Jackson?"

"I promise I won't leave until she's feeling better. But we want you girls to have enough fun for both of us. She'll feel better soon. Now give mom a kiss. You've got to get going so you can have a great time."

Giselle made the effort to acknowledge her daughters, paid for it dearly with another wave of nausea. Jackson left to see her daughters leave, returned in time to hold her head with one hand while she threw up in a bucket he held for her. Under normal circumstances, that would have mortified her.

Tonight, as sick and weak as she felt, she was glad not to be alone, even if it meant having Jackson seeing her at her absolute worst.

To his credit, he kept his promise to her girls. He never left her side for more than a few moments. All throughout the night and into the entire next morning. When it finally ended, she fell into an exhausted sleep.

Giselle woke up a little lost. A glance at her clock told her it was almost seven o'clock. The light filtering through her curtains told her it was p.m. and not a.m. She picked up her cell phone from the nightstand, managed to catch that it was Friday evening before it died on her.

She took her time rolling out of bed, cringed at her reflection in the full length mirror, and staggered to the bathroom. A shower did wonders to make her feel better. As did a fresh set of clothes. She'd just passed a brush through her blow dried hair, when she caught a whiff of something appetizing enough to make her stomach growl.

Exiting her bedroom, she tiptoed down the hallway toward the kitchen, stopping to watch Jackson stir a large pot of something. He had the stereo on low and she listened, in amazement, as he began to sing along with Josh Turner to the tune of Your Man. He'd also showered, judging from the dampened locks of black hair semi-curling at his neckline. He wore work out shorts, and a sexy as hell sleeveless shirt that revealed every line and ridge of his bulked up arms.

The sight of him, along with seven months of celibacy, awakened feelings of need as he put his head back to sing a few lines of the song. His deep, resonant voice sent shivers down her spine as neurons sizzled, making it impossible to ignore the blatantly sexual signals oozing from the man.

How had she gone so long without seeing this side of him? How had she ever been able to sit next to him and not feel the intense magnetism he projected? She was starved for the touch of a man, but now she could admit to herself that it wasn't just any man she wanted touching her. She wanted the touch of this particular man.

Jackson danced his way to the counter in a smooth and graceful two-step, his back perfectly straight, and his head held high.

She sucked in her breath. All of *that*—and he could dance, too?

He chose that moment to execute a perfect spin on his left foot and discovered her watching him. He gave her a bright smile. "Hey, are you feeling better?"

She nodded, as she walked in and lowered herself onto a stool at the island. "Much better, thanks. What smells so good?"

He lifted the lid on the pot and showed her the contents. "Homemade chicken noodle soup. Carrie says it's the cure for everything."

She put a hand to her belly. "I'm famished, is it ready?"

"You're probably a better judge than I am. It's been simmering for an hour and a half."

She walked over and checked out the soup. "Oh, yeah, it's done. I've got to have some of this."

He got two bowls off the shelf and handed her one.

She poured heaping ladles of the steaming soup into the bowls, and they each brought one to the island to cool.

She took the opportunity to ask about his moves. "So, you dance?"

He shrugged. "Chloe and I took lessons. She wanted to make sure I didn't embarrass her in front of her friends."

"And you sing too?"

He froze. "Uh. No."

She swiveled in her chair to face him. "Yes you do. I heard enough to recognize talent when I hear it. Why doesn't anyone know?"

Jackson grimaced. "I guess I haven't had much to sing about in recent years."

She stared at him, thinking of the life he'd led with Chloe. "I guess not."

Jackson turned away from her. "Toby used to tell me how much he loved hearing you sing, though. Have you ever sung in front of an audience?"

"In high school chorus and now my church choir. Have you?"

"I think I'd freeze up singing in front of other people." He turned to her with a gleam in his sexy, brown eyes. "I'd sing for you if you asked me to, though."

She bit her bottom lip, and forced herself to turn away from him. "The soup should be cool enough to eat now."

"Maybe you'll sing for me one day," he said.

"Maybe we could sing together," she answered in a rush before changing the subject. "Do you want some crackers with your soup?" She reached up for a box from the pantry.

"That sounds good. I hope it's seasoned enough." He seated himself at the island and placed some crackers on the plate next to his bowl.

She sat across from him, took a bite, and rolled her eyes in pleasure. "It's just right. God, I'm so hungry."

"You haven't had anything in your stomach in over twenty-four hours." He picked up his spoon. "So, did you learn anything from this experience?"

She gave him a crooked grin. "No more sandwiches from convenience store gas stations for me."

Jackson chuckled. "I'm just glad I was here to help."

She gazed up at the sincerity in his face. "Thank you, Jackson. Holding someone's head while they puke in a bucket is going above and beyond the call of friendship."

He gave her a gracious nod. "For you, anytime."

Jackson dropped the spoon in his empty bowl—his second of the meal. "I've done all the damage I can do for tonight. How about you?"

"I'm done too, but it was delicious. Thanks for cooking for me."

They cleaned the kitchen together, soft country music playing in the background. Her sudden request took him by surprise.

"I'll take that song now, Jackson."

"What song?"

"The one you said you'd sing for me if I asked you to."

"You said we could sing one together," he reminded her.

"Did I?" she asked, as he nodded.

She got up from the island and went to her computer. He stood over her while she was searching for a particular song.

"Do you know Another Try by Josh Turner and Trisha Yearwood?"

"The song, not the lyrics," he said.

She went online and printed out the lyrics. "Here, listen to it once with the lyrics in front of you. Then we'll play it again and sing it. It's easier to sing a duet than solo."

He tensed up immediately. "I don't think I can do this."

She placed a comforting hand on his shoulder. "Come on Jackson, you'll never conquer your fears if you don't try. It's easier if you close your eyes."

They listened to it once then she started it over. Jackson closed his eyes, and at his cue to start singing he hesitated slightly then began. He could hear he was singing in pitch, but he couldn't manage to get the volume up.

After the first four lines, Giselle joined him, harmonizing in a sweet, clear voice. It lifted him, gave him the courage to continue, and by the end of the duet, his discomfort had all but vanished. At some point, she'd stopped her own singing and stood watching him as he finished the final stanza as a solo.

The music rolled to a stop and he stood there, refusing to fidget under her gaze. He raised his right hand slowly to cup her chin and push lightly to close her gaping mouth. "Are you that shocked that I can do something other than piss you off?"

She seemed to snap out of her daze and straightened her spine. "I'm sorry, but I was so impressed that I forgot to jump in," she stammered. "You sing beautifully, Jackson."

"Thank you, Ma'am. So do you." He gently pushed a strand of hair away from her brow. "Now, What should we do for the rest of the weekend?"

Her brow lifted at his reference to 'we'. "I don't know."

"Someone else is enjoying our vacation, so we may as well have some fun. God knows you've earned it," he added.

She nodded, made a show of looking around. "Do you see the phone anywhere? I really want to talk to my girls." He handed her the phone and she plopped herself on the sofa to call Bill. They were at a restaurant on the River Walk so she kept the conversation brief, told them she loved them, and hung up. She was quiet afterward, and shrugged when Jackson caught her wiping a tear from her eye.

He crouched next to her, placing one hand gently on her shoulder. "Hey, you okay?"

She nodded once before giving a contrasting shake of her head. "They didn't even sound like they missed me," she said, sobbing quietly into her hands.

Jackson laughed as he grabbed a tissue and handed it to her. "They missed you. They called here three times while you were still passed out."

She nodded and wiped another tear away. "I guess I'm just a little lonesome. I've never been away from them this long before." She wrung her tissue and looked around. "And I'm wondering what I'm going to do while I'm alone in this big empty house for the next two days."

"I'll keep you occupied. You think you'd feel up to a bike ride tomorrow?"

Her face lit up with excitement. "Could we?"

He laughed at her reaction. "I can swing by and pick you up tomorrow morning."

Her brow furrowed. "I'd rather meet you at your place."

Jackson nodded, wondering much of her suggestion had something to do with her not wanting people in Kenton to see them together. "There are lots of great roads out by Uncle Bill's."

"What time do you want me there?"

"It's cooler in the mornings, so how about around nine?"

"I'll be there." She gave him a huge smile.

"Great, I need to get home to take care of some things." He walked to the utility room to get his clothes from her dryer.

"It's a good thing you had extra clothes," she said.

"I keep extra sets of workout clothes in my truck." He stepped into her guest bathroom to change.

He walked out looking sexy as hell in his jeans and tee shirt, his hair slightly tousled. Giselle reached up to smooth his dark locks and their eyes met for a brief second.

When he opened the back door, she looked past him. "Why is Carrie's car here?"

"We didn't want your nosy neighbor to talk, so Sam drove it over and brought my truck to his house. Your reputation is intact, m'lady."

"That was considerate of you, but she's out of town all week. I owe you big for this one, Jackson." She wrapped her arms around his waist and squeezed.

He hugged her. "Next time I'm nauseous, I'll call you. You can hold *my* head while I puke in a bucket."

She smiled into his tee shirt. "You got it."

Jackson placed a hand on her head, and pressed her gently to his chest. "Besides, I promised Mac and Lex I wouldn't leave your side." He placed a gentle kiss on her crown before resting his chin on it. It felt far too good having her in his arms this way. He took a deep breath, forcing himself to pull away from her. "I've got to go," he murmured, heading for his truck. He buckled up, returning Giselle's brief wave before she closed the door behind her.

The ride home was quiet, too damn quiet, without her presence. He could only wonder about tomorrow's bike ride, and its possibilities of eventually leading to more—if God was willing. He couldn't help but smile at the thought.

Chapter Seventeen

Jackson heard the ruckus from his living room. The neighbor dog's vicious snarling and barking accompanied by a feminine screech. He ran to the door, hearing his own name being screamed, jerked on the door just in time for Giselle to run into his open arms. He spun her away from the snapping and snarling, and yelled at the dog until the animal ran back to its own house.

"Hold on, I'll be right back." Ready to spit fire, he stalked to his neighbor's house and punched the doorbell several times. Finally a younger man of about twenty-five or so answered, shirtless, and wearing boxers.

Jackson jabbed his finger in the man's face. "The next time *your* dog attacks someone in *my* yard I'm going to do something about it. I'm not telling you again, either. You keep his ass chained up, or else."

The young man stepped out onto the porch full of congenial bravado. "Dude! Brutus is harmless. He's all bark and no bite."

He backed the younger man up against the stucco exterior of his porch, his face inches from the younger man's. His voice lowered to a menacing level. "My name is Jackson Broussard. You can call me Jackson . . . Mr. Broussard . . . Or sir, if you prefer. But don't you ever call me *dude*. From here on out, whenever I see *that* dog—" He pointed at the animal cowering inside the doorway, "—he had better damned well be on a leash, and *your* ass had better damned well be on the other end of it. You got that?"

The man swallowed. "Y-Ye-Yes sir. I'll keep him chained up from now on," he stammered.

Jackson headed back to his own front porch, passing Giselle, who'd watched the altercation from the steps. He stopped at his door, letting her go in first.

"I'll kill that dog if he comes after you again."

Giselle placed a calming hand on his arm. "Don't kill the dog because of the owner's stupidity. I'd feel terrible."

"Yeah? Well you'd feel worse if he bit you, don't you think?" he said, irritably. "I wouldn't hurt the dog, but I'd have him picked up. What if it had been Lex or Mac?"

A look passed over Giselle's face. "Then I'd hurt him."

"You see? It's not right that it's allowed to run loose, and that guy doesn't seem to give a damn."

She smiled. "Do you feel better, now that you've vented?"

He shook his head, and grinned sheepishly. "Yeah, but I miss my old neighbors."

"Was it a family with kids?"

"No. Just old. Did you not hear me say "my old neighbors"?"

His comment earned a snort along with a well-timed, "Smart ass," from Giselle.

"And they didn't have a mean-ass dog." He grinned at her eye roll. "I've got something for you if you're ready." He pulled a helmet from his utility room.

She made a show of it. "For me?"

"Safety first. I guessed at the size."

She slipped it on and adjusted the strap. "Perfect fit. How do I look?" She took two exaggerated steps and spun, a move worthy of any runway model.

He grinned. "A hell of a lot better than yesterday."

In less than five minutes, they turned onto the highway that led out toward Bill's place. Jackson pushed the bike a little harder, picking up speed, forcing her to hold on tightly. He reveled in the feeling of her arms wrapped around his waist. Her long, tanned legs pressed up against him. How the hell was he supposed to be in her presence all day and not go crazy from wanting her?

They drove for an hour, up and down winding country roads. They passed fields of rice, nearly ready for harvest, and pastures with peacefully grazing cattle. She pointed out a pasture full of horses. He pulled the bike over, so they could watch a foal run on its spindly legs.

Giselle checked her shoulders for burning and pulled a small tube of sunblock from her pocket.

Jackson watched her apply the sun block to her shoulders and arms. No problem. Once she began rubbing it on her long legs, it was a different story. Her hands, moving in long, slow strokes, up and down her upper thighs and calves, seemed almost erotic. So erotic that he had to walk away.

"Jackson?"

He turned, seeing her holding the tube out to him.

"Could you put some on my back, please? I don't want to get a tan line."

"Sure." How difficult could this be? She turned in front of him and he squeezed some lotion into his palms. He rubbed it onto her upper back, bared from the tank top she wore, and slid one finger slowly under the edge of the top to spread the lotion evenly. Determined to torture himself further, he applied more lotion to his fingers and pushed her straps out of the way to spread it on her bare skin.

The sight of goose bumps rising on her bare flesh caused a hitch in his breathing. As his breathing stopped, hers increased to accommodate her quickening pulse. He stared at the spot on her neck, thinking he wanted nothing more than to cover it with his mouth.

He cleared his throat and turned away. *More difficult than he imagined.*

Jackson handed her the tube and swung his leg over the bike. Feeling her gaze on him, he started the ignition and waited for her to join him, thankful the helmets shield hid all evidence of churning emotions.

They rode on for another hour, until they came to a century old oak tree with a plaque near it. He pulled up slowly and turned off the ignition, then used the kickstand to rest the heavy bike before they both dismounted.

Jackson set both their helmets on the seat and walked slowly to meet her. "You're not hurting, are you?"

She rubbed her backside and made a face. "My butt is sore, but I'll live. My body has gone through some changes since I last rode a bike."

"It couldn't have changed that much."

"After two children, you bet your ass it has."

Jackson released a feral sounding grunt. "If that's true, I wish I'd known you back then." Tantalized by the blush staining her cheeks, he forced himself to be a gentleman and redirect the conversation. "What did you think of that Marc Broussard CD I gave you?"

She nodded. "I love his style. And his voice—he's got this deep, bluesy sound—very unique. It works for him."

"You know, he's playing in Lafayette tonight."

She nodded. "I did hear that he's going to be at some club called Red's. I thought about trying to see him, but we weren't supposed to be here this weekend."

He nodded. "But we are, aren't we?"

Giselle grinned. "Yes, due to my inability to read convenience store sandwich expiration dates—we are here."

"It's the club's opening tonight, and I hear it's a nice place. I have a personal invitation from the owner, if you're interested. It happens I'm an investor."

"I never thought of you as the type to invest in a club."

"The owner, Red McAllister, is a college buddy of mine. Great guy, and brilliant businessman, I trust him. You want to go with me?" It surprised him to see the spark of excitement in her eyes.

"I haven't danced in a while, so I may be a little rusty. What time would we leave?"

"Doors open at 7:00, since it's opening night, but I imagine it won't start kicking until 9:00 or so. But I'd like to get there a little early to get in a quick visit with Red before he's pulled in all directions. Can you be ready by 5:30?"

She nodded, and looked at her watch. "That's doable, but I'd have to do some shopping here in Lake Coburn. All I have in my closet are mom clothes and Mardi Gras ball gowns. How about if we grab a bite to eat then you take me to my truck so I can hit the mall?"

"Sure, I don't mind letting you go early if I get to see you later this evening." He took a deep breath as a blush infused her lovely face with color. The fact that it happened over his words was such a huge boost to his morale. Not to mention a turn on.

He brought her to a small mom and pop diner for a relaxing lunch. They made plans for the evening, deciding to stay in Lafayette for the night.

"I'll book two rooms as soon as I get home. The best hotel in Lafayette is only a few blocks from the club."

They rose from the table and Giselle turned to him. "I'm excited about this. I haven't been clubbing in forever. Thank you, Jackson."

He gave her a gallant bow. "It's my pleasure," he said. For once he didn't doubt it would be.

Giselle found the perfect dress. A slinky black number with gold metallic threads woven throughout that draped and hung in perfect folds. The dress had a halter neckline, and a daring low cut back, necessitating a trip into Victoria's Secret. Her mani and pedi were still fresh, as was her haircut.

She spent the rest of the afternoon preparing for the short trip to Lafayette. By the time Carrie knocked at her door around 5:15, she was dressed and ready, black clutch in hand and bags at the door.

Giselle welcomed her friend inside. "I was just about to call you to let you know my plans."

Carrie's mouth opened in surprise. "Well, I'm assuming you feel better. You look wonderful. What's up?"

"Jackson and I are going to a club opening in Lafayette."

Carrie nodded in approval. "You're going to the opening of Red's place. Give him my love when you see him."

Giselle quirked her brow. "How do you know Jackson's college buddy?"

"Scott McAllister, or 'Red', as everyone calls him, is originally from my hometown of Gardiner, and I used to babysit for him. His mom and I are second cousins. He's the sweetest guy, and I know you'll love him. You two have a blast, and please be careful driving home tonight in that horrible Lafayette traffic."

"That's what I was about to call and let you know. We've got rooms at a hotel in Lafayette."

"Perfect. I won't have to worry about you. Dance a couple for me."

Jackson checked his screen before answering his mobile. "Hey Carrie, what's up?"

"Hi Jack, I just left Giselle's place. I see you took excellent care of her, and I'm thrilled you two are going to Red's together."

"Are you?" He held his breath.

She was quiet for a moment. "I know how badly you want this, Jackson."

He took a deep breath and released it slowly. "You know, don't you?"

She released a low chuckle. "For a few years, now."

He frowned. "Who else knows?"

"No one at the office. Sam knows because I don't keep anything from my husband. But, I'd bet money Bill knows."

He coughed out a surprised laugh. "What the hell is it with you two? He said the same thing about you."

"Hmm . . . Great minds and all."

Thoughts of Toby suddenly filled his mind. "Do you think he'd mind, Carrie?" He had to wait a bit for an answer.

"Sam and I both believe that if Toby could have chosen any man in the world to take care of his three girls, he would have chosen you."

Jackson blinked several times to clear his eyes. "Hearing that from you means a lot to me."

"I know." She sniffed. "I just wish I could be there when you see Giselle."

Jackson sucked in his breath. He knew that tone. The tone that said she knew so much more, but wasn't telling. "That good, huh?"

"Have fun, Jack."

Giselle's breath hitched at the sight of Jackson looking GQ sexy. Black dress slacks and a long sleeved burgundy shirt, with a black and burgundy patterned tie.

He interrupted her shocked silence with a long, slow whistle of approval. Giselle beamed at him and turned slowly for his inspection.

"Jesus. You look like a million bucks, Giselle. Really beautiful."

Once again, she blushed down to the roots of her hair before thanking him. "You look very handsome, yourself," she said, flipping his tie.

He smiled, then grabbed her bag. "Is this all the luggage you have?"

"I travel light, whenever possible," she returned.

"I see that. Chloe would have filled up the back seat."

She stopped to look up at him. "Let's establish here and now that I'm not Chloe."

He gazed at her for a moment. "No, you're not, and I'm not Toby, either."

They nodded at each other, forming an unspoken agreement not to mention the names of either spouse the rest of the night.

By the time Jackson ushered Giselle into the classy looking club, it was nearly 6:45. A large dance floor dominated the center of the room, with a smaller, more private one off to the side. The bandstand was situated between the two. The two separate bar areas were glorious concoctions of lights, mirrors, and granite countertops. Leather stools lined each bar, and tables dotted the large areas situated around the dance floor, each one surrounded by four swivel chairs constructed in the same style as the stools.

"This place is beautiful. Your friend has excellent taste."

"I think you'll like Red."

"I'm sure I will."

"Just don't like him too much." He gave her a wink.

Giselle looked up as a man about the same height and build as Jackson walked through a side door. He had a shock of dark auburn hair, but it was his startling blue eyes that commanded her attention.

He grabbed Jackson's hand in a firm shake. "Hey buddy, you don't know how much it means to me to have a friend in my corner tonight." He turned to Giselle. "And who is this lovely vision? Scott McAllister at your service, ma'am, but please call me Red." He smiled, flashing straight, white teeth.

Red McAllister may have briefly had the opportunity to be considered an *average* looking man. Not nearly as handsome as someone with Jackson's GQ looks. But the genuine smile, the sincere kind that crinkled the corners of his eyes, dashed that to hell. She couldn't help thinking that a man with his type of rugged good looks belonged in the Scottish highlands. He should be wearing a kilt . . . and nothing else.

"Red, this very special lady is Giselle Granger," Jackson said, his voice sounding a little stilted and stiff.

"Red, it's wonderful to meet you," Giselle said. "I'm thrilled to be here tonight. You've done a beautiful job with the club's design."

Red flashed a grin at her. "Thank you, Giselle."

"Was any of this here already, or is it all new?" She was genuinely interested in the layout.

"It was a club, previously, but I didn't like the floor plan. I gutted it and started from scratch."

"We could use one like this in Lake Coburn, you know," Jackson admitted.

"That's my next location, so keep an eye out for property."

Giselle glanced around. "Is your plan to have a nationwide chain of clubs?"

"Nothing that grandiose," Red answered with a low chuckle. "My plan is to open several more here in Louisiana—New Orleans, Baton Rouge, Alexandria, and Shreveport. Louisiana's a great place to live and I'm tired of hearing everyone give it a bad rap. I may have a Scottish last name, but I've got Broussard and Hebert bloodlines, and I'm proud as hell of my Cajun roots."

Giselle remembered Carrie's message. "Speaking of Cajun roots, Carrie asked me to give you her love."

Red's eyes lit up. "I love Carrie. Did she tell you she used to babysit for me and my siblings?"

"She said she babysat for you, but she didn't mention anyone else."

He winked at her. "That's because I was her favorite."

"I'm sure that's it." She chuckled at his comment.

He laughed as he turned to Jackson. "How's Uncle Bill?"

"Ate up with a woman right now."

"No."

"Oh yeah," Giselle added. "Bill is in love."

Red's face blanched. "He can't be. He's my role model for perpetual bachelorhood."

Jackson laughed. "You'll have to find someone else; he's met a wonderful lady named Gwen, who's raising her seven year old niece. Gwen's brother and his wife were killed in a boating accident six years ago."

Red nodded solemnly. "They have that in common."

A ruckus at the side door drew their attention. "Hang on, there's the band." Red walked over to speak with them, pointing out various doorways. The band went off and Red came back to meet the couple.

"Look Red, we know you have a lot of responsibilities as the owner," Jackson said. "Just tell us where to sit."

Red escorted them to the section around the smaller dance floor. "This is the VIP section, and that's my table," he said. "That's where I want you two. I have some things to take care of before we open the doors, but I'll be back later."

The server came to the table to take their drink order. Giselle surprised Jackson by ordering a beer. He smiled, saying he'd take the same.

While waiting for their drinks, she saw him grinning at her. "What?" she asked.

"Sam Adams? I expected you to order a white wine, or something."

She fiddled with the latch on her purse. "I don't drink often, but when I do, I prefer beer and I prefer it made in America. Sorry to disappoint you."

"I'm not disappointed at all. I'm pleased."

By 7:30 people were pouring into the new club. Tables filled quickly, as did the bar. The house DJ kept the tunes rolling, priming Red's customers for the band's appearance at 8:00.

Giselle finished her second beer and sent a glance in Jackson's direction. "I know you can dance, Jackson, and I sure as hell didn't come here to sit all night."

Jackson jumped to his feet as the DJ kicked off a favorite of his. "I was waiting on you to tell me you were ready." He extended his hand. "I hope you can keep up."

She gave him a wink. "I'll try."

If Jackson seemed surprised that she was just as skilled at dancing as he was, he didn't let on. When the Texas two was over, the DJ swung them right into a country waltz. The third selection was a Cajun style jitterbug, and Giselle, a novice to Cajun dancing, very easily followed Jackson's lead. By the third dance, she needed a rest.

Red joined them at the table. "You two have some nice moves out there." He turned to Giselle. "Could I steal one from you later on?"

"If you let me catch my breath, first." She sent him a wink. "Jackson's just set that bar pretty high, though. He must have been an excellent student."

Red grinned, obviously recognizing the challenge. "I come by my talents naturally. No lessons necessary."

Jackson rolled his eyes at Red's jab, before turning to her. "You're an excellent dancer yourself. How'd you learn?"

"I actually worked my way through college teaching dance lessons."

Jackson jabbed his finger in her direction. "I *thought* dancing with you felt vaguely familiar. I ended up with my instructor as a partner."

Giselle frowned. "But, what about Chl...um...I mean your *regular* dance partner?"

Jackson grinned smugly. "She stormed out of the first lesson because I couldn't learn to dance her way—with two left feet—so I continued the lessons on my own."

"Aw, that's too bad."

He made a face. "I was a lot better off, trust me."

Giselle gazed at him, thinking again what a foolish woman Chloe had been.

Red cleared his throat. "You'd think, being the owner of this place, I'd have been able to find a date."

Giselle turned to their host. "You don't seem the type to sit still long. Did you stop long enough to ask anyone?"

He shook his head. "Too hectic. The last minute details are always hell."

"They can't accept if you don't ask."

Red frowned. "You sound like my mother. She keeps saying if I don't procreate before she dies, she'll haunt me."

Giselle waved her hand with a flourish. "Well, it'd be a tragedy to have all of that wonderful DNA go to waste."

"See, that's what my Mom says all the time."

"Of course she does."

His brow rose in question. "Are you offering your assistance, by any chance?"

Jackson's low growl of warning suddenly cut through his antics. "Red . . ."

Strangely turned on by his reaction, she answered Red, though unable to pull her gaze from Jackson's. "No, but I'll be on the lookout for you."

Red waved off her offer. "I don't have time for that right now." When the DJ started up an old country classic, Red succeeded in pulling her out on the floor. After proving he was as good on his feet as Jackson, he met with disappointment when he tried to lead her into a second.

Jackson gave his friend a surly glare before pulling Giselle out of Red's arms and back into his own.

"Where's the love?" Red asked, feigning hurt feelings.

"Go get your own date!" Jackson threw over his shoulder.

Chapter Eighteen

Red McAllister grabbed the mic and after a brief introduction as the owner, he welcomed everyone warmly. "I'd just like to remind you all that anyone lighting up in any shape or form will be escorted to the parking lot and refused re-entry into the building. This is my promise to you: When you leave any club of mine, you may smell like sweat from dancing, but you'll never smell like a dirty ashtray." His promise was met with cheers and applause. He introduced Marc Broussard, the local favorite, who'd made it big, to more applause, then left the singer to introduce his own band.

By the time Red made it back to the table, the band was already into the first beats of Home, in Giselle's opinion, one of the best dance songs on one of his earlier albums.

Giselle grabbed both Jackson and Red's hands and pulled them out to the floor. "Come on guys."

Jackson watched in amazement, as Giselle, mother of two, shimmied, and ground her hips to the driving beat of the song. She put one arm up behind her head and turned seductively, first toward him, then toward Red. He didn't blame Red for reaching for Giselle's waist, but still couldn't keep from wanting to throttle his friend. Thankfully, before Red made any contact, another woman jerked him away to dance with her.

He jumped at the opportunity to pull Giselle closer. She lifted her gaze to his, lost in the hard driving rhythm and grinding lyrics of the song. Marc Broussard cranked out line after line about long hot days, losing control, and drowning in a sea of soul.

Jackson ran his hands down Giselle's waist, landing on her hips to pull her toward him. She wound her arms around his neck, waited several beats then pulled him down by his tie until they were face to face. Her green eyes were slightly glazed, almost as though she were in a trance.

Her breath brushed his face and lips, nearly overwhelming him with the urge to kiss her. He moved in, stopped, forced himself to resist—determined more than ever not to screw this up. Giselle wasn't a drinker and she was totally out of her element here. No way would he allow alcohol to be a determining factor in her making a decision she could regret in the light of day.

No. Hell no.

He wanted her coming to him of her own volition, with a sound mind and completely free of Toby's ghost. He had too damn much riding on this.

He turned her until she faced the opposite direction, somewhat safer, he supposed, since he wouldn't be tempted to kiss her. He grabbed both her hands, linking his fingers through hers, lifted them above her head. In return, she shimmied . . . slowly . . . sensuously . . . driving her hips back and against him. She lowered one of his hands on the flat of her belly, covered it with her own, and began to swivel her hips seductively.

Jackson brought his other hand around until it rested on her waist, pulled her tight. "Sweet Christ," he groaned, certain his words got lost in the blaring music. He lowered his head to the crook of her neck, barely brushing his lips over her skin. He longed to taste her, to shock her with the touch of his tongue, but somehow he held on to his self-control. There was no way in hell she couldn't feel his arousal, but still she gyrated and swiveled her hips wantonly.

"God, give me strength," he whispered into her neck.

Giselle couldn't hear his words, but his breath on her neck brought a chill to her skin, despite the heat from his nearness. Just as quickly, it sobered her—made her acutely aware of her surroundings. Here she was, a mother of two young daughters, bumping and grinding her way around the dance floor with—exactly who the hell was Jackson to her? Was he her dead husband's friend? *Her* friend? Her *boss?* It hit her suddenly that she'd never be able to work in the same office with this man after tonight. She also knew, without a doubt, that she was exactly where she wanted to be at this moment. In the arms of Jackson Broussard.

The song finally ended and the band picked up with another of her favorites from a newer album. A slow and sultry ballad. Every nerve ending in her body already on sensory overload, she attempted to walk away.

Jackson wouldn't have it. He grabbed her hand and pulled her back into his arms. "Don't run off. This is my favorite."

Their gazes locked, and heat infused her face, yet again. Why couldn't she quit blushing around this man? *Thank God for dim lighting.*

Not dim enough to hide the need in his eyes. A reflection of her own feelings. One so strong that, for the life of her, she couldn't see her way around it. In her heart, she still felt it was too much, too soon. But her body wanted it *now,* and that had her heart clenching in terror. She shook her head slowly, and finally managed to croak a single word. "Jackson . . ."

They stood motionless, surrounded by other dancers as the man's sex appeal taxed her resistance to the breaking point. The man oozed confidant masculinity from his pores. With one touch he could wipe the word 'No' from her vocabulary, and she damned well knew it. This night had all the potential for hot, gritty sex followed by a morning of regrets and guilt. She could practically see Jackson's mind spinning, weighing the odds, calculating the pros and cons of an explicit night together and the conflict it was sure to cause.

Nerves won out as her knees buckled from under her.

Jackson tightened his hold, supporting her. "I've got you," he said.

"You do. But I'm afraid."

He shook his head slowly. "You don't have to be, Giselle. We're only dancing."

She struggled to breathe, tried to keep up with the pounding of her heart. "Is that all we're doing?"

He took a deep breath, as though to fortify himself. "If that's all you want this to be, that's all it is, I swear."

She nodded, let him cradle her head softly to his chest as they finished the slow dance. Thankfully, the next number was snappy enough for a good distraction. Jackson whirled her around the perimeter of the dance floor.

By the time the band took its first break, Giselle was out of breath, but completely at ease and enjoying herself tremendously with Jackson and Red.

When the DJ kicked off a slow request, Giselle closed her eyes and groaned. "I love this song."

Jackson smiled, and stood up, pulling her along with him. They began to dance slowly, never taking their eyes off one another. He pulled her closer, wrapping one arm tightly around her waist as he tucked her hand close.

"Sing to me, Jackson."

He lowered his mouth close to her ear and indulged her. She closed her eyes and melted at the dulcet tones of the melody, along with his sensual delivery of lyrics. As the last notes of the song drifted away, they stood in the center of the floor, their gazes locked.

Someone bumped her it gave Giselle the presence of mind to excuse herself. She entered the ladies room on shaky legs and leaned against the wall. She placed her hand over her pounding heart, willing it to slow as she let her head fall back against the cool porcelain tile.

Breathe in. Breathe out. Repeat. She was still fanning herself when a younger woman walked in and did a double take.

"Honey, you have got yourself one hell of a man out there. I've got two questions: Where can I go to find myself one like that? And does he have a brother?"

Giselle laughed, and leaned toward the mirror to inspect her make-up. "I used to work with him, and sorry, but he's an only child."

The woman's face fell in disappointment. "The good ones are always taken. Is he as good inside as he looks on the outside?"

Giselle met her gaze in the mirror. "Even better."

The woman grinned. "Good for you, honey."

When she got back to the table, George Strait's oldie *The Fireman* was kicking off.

Red walked up to her with his hand out, ignoring Jackson's glower. He took her hand and turned to his friend. "Take a break, buddy, it looks like you could use one."

Giselle couldn't help but laugh at Jackson's dour expression as she followed Red to the dance floor. Immediately after the dance, Red walked her back to the table to meet a grim-faced Jackson.

"Seriously, Red," Jackson snapped, "Next time we come here, you'd better have your own dance partner."

It was one a.m. before the two of them readied to leave the club. Exhausted, Giselle turned to Red. "Congratulations, Red. It looks like this place is a huge success."

"Thanks, and I hope you come back soon."

"I'll be back; if Jackson's willing, that is."

"Honey, you come by anytime, whether he's willing or not. There will always be a spot for you at my table. He gave her a wink that earned him another glare from Jackson.

She excused herself to visit the ladies' room before leaving the club.

"God, you're a lecherous son of a bitch," Jackson growled at his friend.

"Give it a rest, bro. I've heard you pine for this woman forever. You seriously think I'd hit on the love of your life? I'm not Tanner Collins, you know."

Jackson reached out and put a hand on Red's shoulder. "I know that, it's just that when I look at her, I see the possibilities." He wiped a hand across his forehead. "I want this so damn bad."

Red punched his friend playfully on the shoulder. "Hey, if you marry her, can I come to the wedding this time?"

"If I marry this one, you're the best man. No question."

Jackson pulled up under the valet awning of the four star hotel around one fifteen. Immediately after checking in, he carried their bags upstairs. Each entered their adjoining rooms.

Within seconds she heard his side of the adjoining door unlock then open. She'd already reached to unlock her side when he gave it a light tap. Giselle opened it and stood there hoping she didn't look as exhausted as she felt. He smiled, looking slightly worn, but just as good as he had when he'd first arrived at her door that afternoon.

"If anything happens, you come get me," he said. "I'll leave my side unlocked and you can lock yours."

She gave him a tired smile. "I think I'm going to take a long, hot, shower, and try to work the kinks out ahead of time. I know I'm going to be sore tomorrow." She placed her hand on the knob and gazed up at him.

"There's a dining room downstairs. Call when you're ready for breakfast and we'll go down together," he said.

She nodded.

Jackson loosened his tie. "I generally wake up early."

She nodded again but kept her silence.

He fiddled with his shirtsleeves. "Thanks again for coming with me tonight. I can't remember the last time I had that much fun."

She nodded once more, so hungry for his touch, she could barely stand it.

"Good night, Giselle."

After he closed his door, she stood staring at it for several moments. She reached up and knocked gently. He opened it and stood there, his blue eyes locked on hers, questioning.

He'd already unbuttoned the top three buttons of his shirt, revealing a dusting of dark chest hair. God, she wished she could unbutton the rest for him. Wished she could fan her hands over the sculpted abs she knew were hiding behind those buttons.

Instead, she approached him, pulled his face gently down to her level with both hands. She stared into his eyes before planting a light, chaste kiss upon his mouth. Judging by his sharp intake of breath, it took him by surprise. She kissed his cheek next, and then whispered into his ear. "Thank you, Jackson." She backed into her own room, and closed the door . . . without locking it.

Jackson woke early, a blessing really, since he'd tossed and turned all night. It had taken every bit of resolve he possessed to close his door after hers. Once he'd closed it, he knew he could resist her. But, between wondering if she'd come to him in the middle of the night, and wishing she would, he tossed and turned most of the night. What little sleep he'd had was riddled with dreams of long, tanned legs wrapped around him, greenish-gold eyes staring into his, and Giselle's sweet lips on his own. He'd been tempted to go to the pool to get some relief, but didn't want to be out of his room in case she needed him—for any reason.

It was eight a.m. before he got a phone call from her.

"Good morning, Jackson."

"Good morning, did you sleep well?"

"Not really, I was kind of restless. How about you?"

"Very little," he admitted.

"I'm exhausted and hungry. Are you ready?"

"Let's go," he said.

Jackson heard the door opening on her side of the room, and he went to open his. They stood gazing into each other's exhausted faces. She walked up to him, wrapped her arms around his waist, and laid her face on his chest. He hugged her tightly. "Good morning, beautiful" He placed a soft kiss on the top of her head.

"Good morning, handsome." She squeezed his waist.

They stood there silently, swaying back and forth for a full minute. Finally, Jackson spoke. "Does this mean anything, Giselle?"

She nodded, but remained silent.

"I need you to tell me what it means," he urged. "I don't want to say or do anything I'll regret the rest of my life."

"It means that I'm attracted to you, and I'm getting really tired of acting like I'm not."

"Is that all?" He damned well felt more than physical attraction for her. Wanted her to feel the same. His heart leapt when she shook her head.

"What else does it mean?" He waited, praying for deliverance of some kind.

"I can tell you that over here, away from home, I feel free enough to be able to do something like this, and to dance with you the way I did last night. But, when I get home, I'll still be worried about what people think." She paused before continuing. "And, as much as I'd like to, I still think it's too soon to take it any farther."

Strangely, he felt both exhilarated and disappointed by her admission. "If that's how you feel, I'll respect your wishes. We won't take it any farther, as much as I'd also like to." He set her away from him so he could gaze down into her face, still beautiful even lined with exhaustion. He cupped her chin and leaned in to give her the same type of chaste kiss she'd given him the previous night, before putting some much needed distance between them. "Let's get some breakfast."

She nodded. "I'm starving."

"Me too." He followed her into the hallway, biting back the words to the additional thought running through his mind.

In more ways than one.

Chapter Nineteen

They were on their second leisurely cup of coffee in the dining room, when Jackson answered a call from Red, inviting them to spend the day with him and have lunch. Jackson relayed the message to Giselle, and she agreed. They finished their coffee and went up to the rooms to pack. By ten o'clock, they were on their way to Red's place.

"I don't know if you brought a swimsuit or not, but he's got a fantastic pool," Jackson told her.

"As a matter of fact, I did bring one I'd bought for the San Antonio trip. Just in case." She twirled a lock of hair around her finger and stared out the window. "I nearly talked myself into taking a dip in the hotel pool around four a.m. I couldn't sleep for some reason."

"I thought about doing the same but I didn't want to leave in case you needed me—for anything," he said.

"Really," she murmured, turning to stare at his profile, catching the faint scent of his cologne. The one that made her mouth water. "That would have been something if we'd both ended up there."

His breath released in a rush as he whipped his head around to face her. "Yeah." He faced the road again. "That would have been something."

She couldn't help but stare at his lips. A ghost of a smile played at the edges of his kissable mouth.

"Your suit, is it, um, is it a one piece or two?"

Her left brow lifted at his curiosity. "It's a one piece." She turned away, adding in a soft murmur, "But just barely."

Red lived in a rather exclusive, older subdivision on the east side of the city. They pulled into the driveway of a very nice, single story Craftsman style home with a well-manicured yard, and gorgeous landscaping. Giselle climbed out of the truck, toting her leather shoulder bag, and Jackson walked around to meet her, carrying his swimming trunks.

The front door of the home opened up and Red walked out to greet them. He smiled and gave Giselle a hug, shook Jackson's hand, and ushered them both inside.

Giselle gushed over the typical Craftsman style architectural elements and trim work.

"This is beautiful, Red. When was this built, about the mid 1950's?"

"1956 to be exact. Look around all you want, or would you like me to give you a personal tour?"

"No, you guys talk, I can find my way around." After entering several rooms, she realized Red was another man with great tastes in furnishings. She wondered if he picked his the same way Jackson did, by choosing things out of a display. Something told her that wasn't the case.

She entered his study and had to smile at his shrine to the LSU Tigers. There were dozens of photographs of the baseball team on display. She screeched in excitement when she saw a picture of Jackson in a full wind up before throwing a pitch. Then she saw shots of Red putting someone out at first, both Jackson and Red at bat, and both of them sliding home.

She also saw group shots of the team with a huge trophy. It seemed like it should have been a joyous occasion, except that no one smiled. On second glance, she realized Jackson wasn't in the shot. She picked up the photo and turned it over to read a label placed on the back of the frame. 'The day we lost our pitcher, Jackson Broussard—a glum bunch of s.o.b's.'. There were also snapshots of Jackson with his arm in some sort of brace. There were dozens of shots with him in it. She surveyed the room which was such a contrast to the house Jackson lived in, where there were no photos of him displayed at all. It was almost as if Red had tried to make up for it.

"Find anything interesting?"

She turned to face Jackson, who'd slipped in quietly. "I'm getting over the shock of seeing you and Red as kids. Look how young you were, Jackson."

He smiled wistfully and walked around the room, staring at the different shots. He got to the "glum group" photo and picked it up to study it. "I didn't know it then, but this was the luckiest day of my life."

She approached him, placed her hand on his arm. "Why would you say that?"

He shrugged. "If I hadn't injured myself, I probably never would have met you or the girls."

She smiled. "That's very sweet of you to say so."

"I hope you don't think I said it just to score points with you, because I really feel that way."

"Do you? Really?"

He turned to her and nodded. "It's true; baseball was fun, but it didn't break my heart when I couldn't play anymore. I thought it would. Everyone around me assumed it did, but it didn't. That's how I knew it wasn't meant to be. If I was offered a chance to go back and have that career, and it meant never getting the chance to know you and the girls, I'd turn it down in a second."

She gazed into his eyes for several moments before asking the question that had popped into her mind. "What if he'd lived?"

He answered without hesitation. "I'd still turn it down. Knowing him changed me, in a good way. His was a friendship I'll always treasure."

Her eyes filled with tears at his confession, and he reached out to brush one that fell to her cheek. She reached for the large, gentle hand that had treated her and her girls with such care over the past seven and a half months, and her heart suddenly filled with tenderness for this man. Giselle traced his long lifeline with her slender fingers, and placed a gentle kiss on his open palm and closed his hand around it.

Smiling, she lifted her face to his, surprised at the emotion revealed in his eyes.

He pulled her body close, and rested his chin on the top of her head. He ran his fingers through her curls, massaged the back of her scalp in a way that made her want to close her eyes, and never move from his embrace.

"Are you still afraid?" he whispered.

She managed a small nod.

"Giselle," he said softly, "Will you do me a favor?"

She nodded again.

"The second you stop being afraid, will you let me know?"

Giselle smiled into his shirt. "I promise, you'll be the first to know." She pulled away from him, and cleared her throat. "So where's this fantastic pool of Red's?"

"Out back. There's a pool house back there, with everything you need." He led her out the back door.

Giselle's jaw dropped in amazement as she admired the lovely patio area. A covered gazebo centered between two pergolas bordered the huge, lagoon style pool on one side, while it opened up to a grotto area and waterfall on the opposite end. "Red, this is beautiful."

He beamed at her. "Thanks. I'm satisfied with it."

"You should be."

"Especially since he built it himself," Jackson added.

She looked at her host. "Did you really?"

Red shrugged. "I had some help here and there, but building things with my hands is stress relief for me. The landscaping around the grotto and waterfall really made the difference."

She shifted her shoulder bag. "I can't wait to get in there."

Red pointed out a building to the back. "You'll find everything you need in there."

The two men watched her disappear into the pool house.

Red turned to Jackson. "She seems as pretty on the inside as she is on the outside."

Jackson nodded. "She is, Red. If this doesn't happen for us, I don't think I could survive it."

"That bad, huh?"

Jackson ran both hands through his hair. "I used to think I'd be able to pick up and go on with my life, but the more time I spend with her and those girls . . ." His voice trailed off as he shook his head. "I don't know how she survived losing Toby."

Red stopped wiping down the grill to stare at Jackson. "It seems with some help from you," he said. "Giselle's a beautiful lady, and I'd be envious if I had the time for any kind of a relationship with strings involved, which I don't. You always were a worrier, Jackson. Why don't you try to relax and enjoy the moment?"

"Says the playboy with the Hugh Hefner grotto attached to his pool," Jackson snorted.

"Hey, you designed the damn thing, Broussard." Red threw a dishtowel at Jackson.

"To your specifications, McAllister." Jackson threw it right back at him. "Besides, I can't help but worry. They're too damned important to me."

"I'd stop worrying if I were you. You two have a real connection. I overheard a couple of women talking about you at the club. One of them wanted to ask you to dance, but her friend said not to bother, because you two were obviously a perfect match." Red slapped his pal on the back.

Jackson put his head back and placed his hands on his hips. "You can't imagine how good this feels after fifteen years of Chloe, whom we aren't bringing up today," he added.

"I didn't do it in the first place," Red commented. He focused on something just past Jackson. "Have you seen her in a swimsuit yet?"

"No, this will be the first time, but I've got a feeling."

"Two kids, huh?" He chuckled at Jackson's nod. "You are in for one hell of a treat, my man." He whistled one long, slow note as Giselle sauntered toward them.

Jackson turned, stunned by the sight before him. "H-h-oly crap." Giselle wore a solid white, halter style suit that dipped in the front just enough to show a little cleavage. Her tanned, shapely legs looked a mile long thanks to the high thigh cut of the suit. The halter style bared her long, lovely arms, as well as her shoulders. The contrast of the white suit on her tanned skin was sexy as hell. All in all, the first sight of Giselle in that suit wasn't something he'd likely forget anytime soon.

She smiled at the two men from behind her sunglasses. "Will I be the only one swimming, gentlemen?"

Jackson shook his head then grabbed his trunks off the table, and hurried to the pool house to change.

Red chuckled. "What's the rush, bro?" he called out.

Jackson was out in under a minute wearing black trunks and his shirt. His heart pounded. What was he? A gawky sixteen year old, trying to work up the nerve for a first kiss? His second glimpse of Giselle in that suit had him thinking he may as well be. She stood, her back to the pool, and talking to Red. "Ready to go in?"

She turned, graced him with a smile. "Can't wait. Are you coming in, Red?"

"I will after I marinade the steaks. You two go on in."

When Giselle turned slowly toward the pool Jackson nearly lost his breath at the sight before him. The low cut of the suit exposed her entire back to just above her *other* cleavage. He stared at the expanse of tanned, flawless skin that swayed gently with every step.

Giselle kicked her sandals off at the edge of the pool and walked around to the diving board. She stepped up, took two big steps, one good bounce, and executed a perfect dive as she sliced into the water.

"Very impressive!" Red yelled, clapping and whistling as she surfaced and swam easily to the edge of the pool. "Good Lord, the girl dives as well as she dances." He was still shaking his head as he disappeared into the house.

Jackson walked over and stood next to where she was hanging on to the edge of the pool. "So, Giselle," he said, casually crossing his arms. "Did you happen to teach diving, too?"

"Nope, but have I ever mentioned that I was an Army brat? I spent a lot of time at the pool as a kid and teenager. My dad re-stationed so often I never had a chance to make any real friends, but there was always the "Y" to go to, and a few of the bases had pools. Are you coming in, or what?"

He slipped his shirt over his head and threw it and his sunglasses down on the table. He turned around in enough time to see her mouth the word *Wow*.

"Thanks, but close your mouth. You're embarrassing me."

"You have been working out, haven't you?"

"Not as much since my bike came in. Before that, I needed the distraction. You see, this crazy woman couldn't seem to decide from one day to the next whether she was speaking to me or not."

Giselle raised her eyebrows. "You're blaming *me* for that?"

He nodded. "I guess I am."

"Oh poor, baby. Come here."

He squatted at the pool's edge just in front of her. "What?"

She reached up and tenderly caressed his cheek. "I'm so sorry for making you bulk up like that, and I'm especially sorry—for this!" She grabbed hold of the back of his neck and pulled him into the pool with her.

Jackson surfaced, spitting and sputtering. "I suppose I should have been waiting for that."

"Yep, all that Mr. Pitiful talk," she said.

"Come here, Giselle." He lunged toward her.

She screeched and dodged him, swimming off in the direction of the grotto. Jackson was the faster swimmer, and caught up with her easily. He grabbed her and pulled her under. When they came up for air, she hung on to his neck as he treaded water to keep them afloat.

Jackson watched her lick her lips. It would be so easy to kiss her right now, but he remembered the promise he'd made to himself, that she would be the one to go to him. He let her go, and swam toward the grotto. Once there, he climbed out onto the steps, and waited for her to catch up to him. When she did, she climbed out, walked over to the grotto area, and gasped loudly as she stood under the significantly cooler waterfall. She dropped her head back and smoothed her hair away from her face. Jackson watched the scene, thinking the entire time that it should have taken place in some tropical setting rather than in Red's back yard pool.

Giselle stepped to the other side of the waterfall and into the dark grotto. She wanted Jackson to follow her, even though she wasn't quite sure what she wanted to happen if he did. She walked all the way to the back of the remarkably cool grotto, and sat on the slate slab that served as a bench while her eyes adjusted to the darkness.

She studied the amazing construction of the man-made cave, and wondered who had designed it. She'd seen several of these waterfall grottos constructed for homes that Toby's architectural firm had designed. They kept a landscape architect on commission who specialized in this kind of set up, but she had never seen anything like this.

She examined the design, passing her hand on the coolness of the smooth stones. Giselle looked up as Jackson walked around the waterfall to the opening. He stood there, all tan and ripped, looking like a Greek god, with beads of water spotting his bronzed skin. Her fault, huh? Try as she might, she couldn't bring herself to regret the results.

"Came in here to cool off?" he asked.

"It does feel good in here. This is really amazing. It's a custom design, right?" Country music began to play softly from built in speakers somewhere inside the cave.

Jackson searched until he found the speakers. "Way to go, Red. He said he'd find the time to wire it for sound one day." He turned back toward Giselle. "He drew up a basic sketch, I designed it for him, and he built it. It's something, isn't it?" He leaned one arm against the wall of the grotto and crossed his foot at the ankle.

"You designed it?" She shook her head, wondering what else he could do.

"I just told Red what would and would not work from the engineering standpoint. We hammered away at a design until we were both satisfied."

"You ever thought about going into business for yourself? I know people who'd pay big bucks for a service like this."

Jackson shrugged. "I might get enough clients in a city like Lafayette, but Lake Coburn's only half the size."

"You don't understand. You wouldn't have to find clients. They'd find you. Architectural firms would kill to have someone like you to turn to. You and Red could make a huge profit off of this one design."

He shrugged like it was no big deal. "It's something to think about, I guess."

Giselle closed the gap between them. "I'm amazed at you, Jackson. Is there anything you can't do? You sing, you dance, you played baseball, and you design fantastic grottos. Your uncle says you're a natural horseman, not to mention the excellent engineering work you do. Is there anything else I should know?"

"I may have a few more tricks up my sleeve. I guess you'll have to stick around if you want to find out."

"I'm extremely impatient. How long are we talking about?"

He shrugged and gave her one of those sexy as hell lopsided grins.

"How long was that?" She inched closer as James Otto's sultry voice piped out Last First Kiss, one of the sexiest freaking songs she'd ever heard.

He gazed down at her, looking as though he was damn close to losing control. "I didn't say."

But damn close wasn't close enough for Giselle. She reached out a single nailed finger to trace from above his breastbone all the way down to the waistband of his suit. The look on his face was well worth her rare act of bravado. "What's wrong Jackson? You look surprised."

Jackson sucked in his breath and lifted both hands, an act of complete surrender. "Hey, you're the one in control. You're supposed to tell me when you're ready."

"Maybe I'm ready for just a little more." She hooked her finger into the waistband of his swimming trunks and pulled it forward. Before she could look down for a peek, he grabbed her hand.

Jackson backed her up against the smooth surface of the grotto then grabbed her hands and laced his fingers through hers. He raised them above her head, one on each side, effectively pinning her against the wall. Leaning forward, he brushed his mouth against her neck just below her left ear.

Her pulse quickened at the feel of his warm breath on her dampened skin. Instead of kissing her neck as she expected him to, he raised his head to speak softly in her ear.

"I have to tell you, Hon, I don't mind a little teasing every now and then, but I'm no masochist, and I'm sure as hell no saint. Here lately, being around you is agony."

"What's the matter big boy?" she gasped, trying to lighten the mood. "You afraid it's going to stunt your growth?"

The look Jackson gave her revealed he hadn't found much humor in this particular situation.

"What is it you want from me Giselle?" he whispered hoarsely. "I think you know how much I want you, but I need to know how far you're willing to take this little game of yours."

Giselle stared into the depths of his hooded eyes—eyes that had grown dark with desire. "In time—all the way. But we're not alone here, Jackson."

"Red's a grown man and knows better than to bother us. It's dark back here." He brushed his mouth lightly against hers.

She closed her eyes, ready to abandon all will, ready to give him whatever he asked of her.

He gently kissed one eyelid, then the other. He pulled back and watched, as she slowly open her eyes to look at him. He could go for it right now. He damned well could. She was every bit as hungry for it as he was. One good kiss and she'd be ready, Red or no Red. But did he *really* want her like this? Unfortunately, he already knew the answer. This scenario was far too 'first-time-in-the-back-seat' for Jackson. He respected Giselle entirely too much for that.

He groaned and dropped his head back in defeat then turned away from her. A moment later, he gasped as he walked straight into the waterfall. As the icy water took care of his current predicament, he saw a flash of white. He cleared the water from his eyes just in time to see Giselle's sexy, round bottom and bare back disappear into the deep end of the pool. He watched her swim underwater for a while, then surface, gasping for air. She treaded water until she caught her breath. She swam the length of the pool, turned, and did it again.

Jackson walked over to the table, grabbed his towel, and began to dry off. He looked up at Red, who was placing steaks onto the heated grill, tight-lipped and silent. "That waterfall sure is cold."

Red's face broke into a broad grin. "Every bit as effective as a cold shower." He shook his head as his gaze locked with Jackson's. "You two sure enjoy torturing each other."

Jackson watched Giselle's smooth, long strokes cutting a path through the water. "It seems to be the norm with us, Red. Nothing's ever cut and dried with Giselle. But, I'm willing to wait." He turned to his friend and gave him a wink. "In the meantime, it sure as hell makes life interesting."

Giselle swam for another ten minutes then climbed out of the pool. She grabbed her towel, and dried herself briskly before wrapping the towel around her waist. She walked over to the chaise loungers and collapsed in the one nearest to the grill, stretching out her legs.

"Giselle, would you like something to drink?" Red asked.

"A beer. A really cold one," she gasped, as she pulled her sunglasses from her leather bag.

"Any preference? I have several brands."

Jackson stood up. "I'll get it for her." He walked to the cooler on the other side of the built in bar area.

"How do you like your steaks?" Red asked her.

"Medium rare. Plenty of pink in the middle, please."

"No problem, it seems we all like them the same way."

She lifted her head. "You need help with anything?"

He shook his head. "Everything's under control. Rest, you look like you need it." Red glanced over at Jackson before returning his attention to the steaks. "He's a good guy, Giselle. God knows he's been hurt enough by—" He stopped suddenly. "By that crazy bitch he was married to. If you think this isn't going anywhere, break it off now, before he's in too deep."

She pushed her sunglasses to her head so she could see him clearly. "I hear you Red. It's good he's got you as a friend. He just lost one, and he'll need you more than ever."

Red nodded. "I've missed him over the years." He looked up as Jackson began muttering something unintelligible. "Hey! What the hell's taking you so long? Your lady is dying of thirst over here."

"Well, shit! Don't you have any American beer?" Jackson asked.

"My private stock is in the fridge in the kitchen. That's the 'Designer Beer' section. All of a sudden it's not cool to drink beer unless it's 'imported'", he growled.

Jackson disappeared into the kitchen and came out carrying three bottles of beer.

"What do you drink?" Red asked Giselle.

"Sam Adams, or MGD, if you have that."

He slapped a hand in the middle of his chest. "A girl after my own heart," he told Jackson as he approached. "Better watch out, I may steal her away."

Jackson handed Giselle and Red each a bottle of beer and kept one for himself. He smiled at Giselle as he addressed his friend. "Go find your own girl, Red. This one's mine."

Chapter Twenty

They ate steaks grilled to perfection, baked potatoes, and salad in the coolness of Red's gourmet kitchen. Lunch was followed by an afternoon of more swimming mixed with exchanging stories of teenage angst and tales of college. Red and Jackson laughed until they cried when Giselle told them several of the things the girls had said and done over the years, including how Lexie mortified her on a regular basis.

Red wiped tears of laughter from his eyes. "You should write that stuff down."

Giselle grinned at Red. "We call them 'Lexie-isms'."

"Jackson says they're beautiful. Got any pictures?"

"Sure I do." She reached down for her leather bag and pulled out school photos from the last three years.

"Look at those beautiful faces. Mackenzie must look like her dad, but that little one is a clone of you, Giselle."

"I can't get over how much they've changed in three years," Jackson murmured. "They've even changed since these last ones. Mac's face has slimmed down." He turned to Red. "She's going to be a knockout one day, man, and Lex," he smiled and passed his finger lightly over the snapshot. "Well, you said it best. She's a clone of her mama, and I think we can both see how well that turns out."

Giselle rummaged through her large leather bag, and let out a triumphant yell as she pulled out her digital camera.

"I've looked all over the place for this thing. I haven't used this bag since the birthday party at Bill's, and it's been hanging in my closet. I'm so relieved. I bought another one when the girls and I went to New Orleans, but this has all their ball game footage."

"Is it just pictures or video too?" Jackson asked.

"Both," she crowed.

"Perfect. We get to show Red our all-stars in action."

Red watched video of both girls playing ball. When he got to tournament video, they pointed out Carrie's granddaughters, Cathryn and Allie. "They're Gretchen's girls," Giselle said pointing out Carrie's twins.

"I saw them just a couple of years ago at a ballgame in Gardiner. Who's that adorable child Jackson's holding?"

Jackson puffed with pride. "That's Lauren's daughter, Ava Grace. She was all over me, man. She wanted to go home with me that day."

"He always was great with kids, Giselle. You should have seen him around my little sisters." Red shook his head in disgust. "If I brought him home with me for the weekend, I got totally ignored. It was all about Jackson."

Jackson grinned. "Hey, I can't help it if women under the age of eight find me irresistible. Look at Mac at bat, Red. It's just tee ball and she already has good form."

Giselle smiled at the pride in Jackson's voice.

Several videos and shots of Carrie and Sam with their grandchildren had Red contemplating their connections with Carrie. "It's a small world, isn't it? Who'd have thought we'd all have Carrie in common? My siblings and I were crazy about her. She was a drummer in the high school band, and she's the reason my oldest brother played. I can still picture her in hip hugger jeans with long, wavy hair."

"McAllister," Giselle murmured. "Hold on, I've heard her speak of Vivienne and Pete McAllister from Gardiner."

Red grinned. "That's my folks. They think the world of her. When I was just a little kid, I remember my brothers and me hiding so we could hear mom and dad talking about how Dave was screwing around on her. My dad wanted to go whip his ass."

Jackson looked at him in shock. "Not quiet, calm, Mr. Pete McAllister. I can't see him losing his cool over like that."

"Man, you don't know the half of it. Mom had to calm him down. None of us cared too much for Dave after that."

Giselle settled back in her lounge chair. "You must have seen her kids grow up, then."

Red chuckled. "Yep. Cute kids. When I graduated from LSU, Carrie came by the house with a gift for me. She was thirty-four and had just earned her Associate's Degree from a technical college in Lafayette. I don't think she'd hired on with the company in Lake Coburn yet."

"No, she started when she was thirty-five," Jackson said.

Red handed the camera back to Giselle. "The marriage with Dave had really taken its toll on her. She told us it was time for a change. I think they separated not long after that."

Jackson nodded. "I've heard that story enough times. She filed for a divorce, got a good job, moved to Kenton, and married Sam, all in a year and a half."

Giselle smiled at the two men. "If she were here, she would add "Thank God". Carrie sure loves her some Sam."

"My parents ask about her every time they see her mom, Mrs. Elaine. Carrie still visits them every now and then."

"I can't even imagine what it must have been like to grow up in families the size of yours and Carrie's," Giselle said.

Jackson groaned. "Man, it was a blast going to his house on weekends. His mom would stuff me with food from the minute I got there until the minute I left, and she's a hell of a cook. Ms. Vivi makes the best shrimp and okra gumbo, and she used to bake her own bread. I never left there hungry."

Red chuckled. "She always said Jackson was too skinny, and needed to put some meat on his bones. Wonder what she'd say if she saw you now."

Giselle smiled at Jackson. "She'd still want to feed him, it's a mom thing." She stood and threw her sarong on the back of her lounge chair. "I'm going back in the water. Who's coming?"

Another hour of pool volleyball had Giselle ready to take her wrinkled digits out of the water for good. After toweling off, she stretched out on the lounger to relax. She placed a hand on her growling stomach as Jackson and Red stepped out of the pool to join her. "Hey Red, is there a pizza delivery place around here? All this swimming has me hungry again."

"I'm getting there," Jackson said, as he draped a towel around his neck. "For some reason, I can't stop thinking about Ms. Vivi's shrimp and okra gumbo."

Red sat across from Giselle. "You know, as many times as I've tried, I can never get mine to turn out like hers, and I can't figure out why. I'm starting to think she's holding out on me. Leaving out some single ingredient that gives it that extra kick."

"Carrie showed me how to cook it. I guess I'll have to cook one and invite the two of you over."

Red leaned over to Jackson and whispered, "Watch the master in action." He turned back to face her. "Sure, Giselle, you talk big, but can you deliver?"

"Excuse me?"

"I mean, I've got all the ingredients for a gumbo here, if you're ready to prove it."

"Are you serious?" Giselle put her head back and laughed. "You know, Red, I love to cook. All you had to do was ask." She shook her head and mumbled, "Can you deliver? Has that line actually worked before?" She rose from her chair and laughed as she slipped a white gauzy cover-up over her head.

"The master. . ." Jackson clucked his tongue as the three of them entered the kitchen through the patio doors.

When Red placed all the gumbo ingredients on the counter Giselle held up a jar of store bought roux. "Don't tell me you use this."

"Why, isn't that a good brand?"

"I know your mom doesn't use roux from a jar."

"No, she makes her own, but I never learned how. It's the same, isn't it?"

"Haven't you ever heard that the beginning to every good gumbo is 'first you make a roux'?" she asked.

He shrugged a tanned shoulder. "It's flour and oil. There's no way in hell it could make that much difference."

Giselle grinned. "I'm gonna love proving you wrong."

Red's eyes rolled back in ecstasy after several bites. "Damn, that's just like Mom's, Giselle. It must be the roux."

"Good cooks don't cut corners, Red. I hope you realize that by now?"

"Yes, ma'am," he said, digging in to his meal. "So, how much do you know about Jackson's college days?"

"Nothing, actually. But I bet you could tell me some stories."

Jackson gave a low groan. "Watch out, now. Don't be soiling my reputation around this lady. I'd like to hold my head up once we leave here."

Red sent a wink Giselle's direction. "What's it worth to you, bro?"

"How about I don't kick your ass?" Jackson growled.

"Come on man. I fed you steaks and gumbo. Not even one story about you streaking across campus buck ass naked?"

Giselle's mouth gaped as she turned on Jackson. "You did not!"

"Of course not," he said. "You know Red's full of shit, right?"

Red burst into laughter. "Nope. No streaking, but we did put down a few beers."

"And Crown . . ." Jackson volunteered.

Red gave Giselle a lopsided grin. "And tequila . . ."

"And more beer," Jackson ended. "And then we'd have to run it off the next day."

"Oh God, until we puked."

Giselle made a face. "Sounds like a lot of trouble to me."

Jackson finished his gumbo and pushed his bowl aside. "Get a group of guy college athletes together and they suddenly turn into dumbasses—no matter how high the IQ."

Giselle gave a low chuckle. "You know, Red, before I saw that shrine to the LSU Tigers in that room, I couldn't imagine Jackson as a teenager. I couldn't see him cutting up, and drinking with the guys, but now I can." She looked across the table to Jackson as she pointed at Red. "I bet he was a terrible influence on you."

"Oh, please," Red snickered. "Nobody had to twist his arm when it came to drinking."

Jackson grinned at Giselle. "No, I liked my beer. I just didn't like it as often as he did. I actually had to study to make decent grades, so I couldn't spend *every* Monday morning recuperating from a hangover. Red could read through something once and he'd retain it. That's a 'Summa cum Laude' graduate right there, Giselle."

"Oh, yeah, Mr. 3.98 GPA—you really had to struggle to make those grades," Red interjected.

Giselle nodded in appreciation at the two men. "Summa cum laude—I'm impressed, Red. And a 3.9 GPA is nothing to sneeze at, Jackson. Carrie always said how brilliant you were, and how you were wasting your talents with the company."

"Speaking of the company," Red interrupted. "I know you're taking some time off, but how are you two going to handle it when you go back to work? I don't know exactly what's going on between the two of you, but—"

"Nothing's going on between the two of us." Giselle's comment, blurted out before she thought about it, had a devastating effect on the room's feeling of joviality. She caught the look of hurt in Jackson's eyes and rushed to explain. "Well, not yet, anyway, and the truth is, I'm not going back to work at all. I'm resigning."

Jackson leaned forward in his chair. "I know you mentioned it as a possibility, but I'd hoped to change your mind."

"I can't see how I'd swing it, Jackson. I can't leave town at 6:30 in the morning before the girls get to school. Their dad got them ready in the mornings. I don't need the money, and besides, I love being home with them. Since the accident, being a full time mother has become essential."

"I can see where that would be a problem," Red commented.

"To tell you the truth, it's a lot easier than I thought it would be to walk away." She saw the crushed look on Jackson's face and realized how heartless her words must have sounded.

"You've made up your mind then?" His tone was hard with disappointment as Red cleared his throat, uncomfortably and left the room. "Do you mind me asking when you came to this decision?"

"Well—" She rose slowly from her chair. "I realized it first on the dance floor last night, then again in the grotto earlier today."

"What the hell does that mean?"

"It's more than just the girls, Jackson. It's you and me. It would be too difficult to be around you at the office. To control ourselves around each other—don't you think?"

Jackson stood so suddenly his chair tipped. He righted it and stalked over to the sink. Turning, he leaned his hips up against the sink with both hands gripped tightly on the granite countertop. "What makes you think I couldn't control myself around you?" He spoke in a voice tight with anger.

A little put off at his tone, she brushed it off, knowing the reason for it. She sauntered over to stand in front of him and gave him her most seductive smile. "What makes you think I could?"

With full grasp of her meaning, he grabbed her shoulders, and spun her around until she was pinned against the cabinet.

She slipped her hands under his shirt, pulled his ripped body close. Giselle lifted her face, but he still held back. She dug her nails into his sides, heard his sharp intake of breath as she whispered hoarsely. "For God's sake, Jackson. Would you just do it already?"

He tangled his fingers in her hair, his voice rough with need. "There'll be no turning back for either of us."

"I know," she murmured, sensing his struggle for control.

He shook his head. "No, you don't, Giselle. You don't know how I feel about you. Don't ask me to do this if you're not serious. I couldn't take it," he groaned.

"I know that Jackson!" she snapped. "Are you going to kiss me or n—"

He cut off her comment—kissed her like a man who'd waited too long for this moment. Their mouths and tongues joined in a mad plea for attention. When it seemed as if he would break the kiss, her hands came up and pulled his head down harder, demanding more of him.

He complied, kissing her with renewed fervor. They finally came up for air, but even then, he held on to her, resting his chin on the crown of her head.

"*This* is why we can't work together," she gasped.

Jackson drew in a ragged breath. "I see your point. No way in hell would I be able to keep my hands off of you. It's been years since I've been this close to anyone."

She drew back to study his face. Saw the truth of it. His marriage to Chloe had been so terribly different from the one she and Toby shared.

He tore his gaze from hers suddenly, looking ashamed. She put both hands on his face and gently urged him to face her. "That's not your shame to bear, Jackson," she whispered. "I'm so sorry you had to live like that."

He lowered his forehead to hers then kissed her mouth gently, tenderly. He brushed a tear from her cheek with his thumb. "Don't cry for me, hon. Honestly, having you and the girls in my life has already made up for it." Suddenly, he dropped his head back, releasing a long, low groan.

"What is it?" she asked as she kissed his throat tenderly.

"I'm just thinking how difficult it's going to be when I'm around you, until we're ready to take this a step farther."

Giselle grimaced lifted her shoulders. "I know and I'm sorry. I don't know when I'll be ready for that."

He kissed her nose. "Don't apologize." They stood locked in an embrace, rocking, both of them coming down slowly.

He finally pushed her gently from him. "You about ready to go?"

She mulled it over and shook her head. "Not just yet." She wasn't quite ready to give up the freedom she had here, in a city where no one thought of her as Toby's widow. She moved away to clear their dishes from the table.

Red spoke warily from the hallway, "Hey, you two. Is it safe to come in?"

"Sure," Giselle said before he rejoined the couple. The three of them cleaned the kitchen in relaxed conversation. By the time they'd finished it was nearing seven o'clock.

"We need to go, Red. You've got a very successful club to run," Giselle said, gathering her things.

"Yes I do, but I've got plenty of time and reliable help," he said.

"I think it's time to go, anyway," Giselle said, stifling a yawn. "I'm not used to all this late night life."

They made their way to the front door, and Giselle gave their host a big hug. "Thank you so much for having me. You have no idea how much I needed this."

"I think I do." He hugged her back tightly. "You're welcome here anytime—with Jackson or without—if you ever feel the need to just come by and talk things over."

"And there's no reason for *you* to make yourself scarce around Kenton anymore, is there?" she said.

"All you have to do is call me. I expect I'll see a lot more of everyone over there from now on." He released Giselle and clasped Jackson in a one handed hug. "I'm happy for you, man," he grumbled.

Jackson nodded. "I know you are."

Giselle spoke up. "Next weekend your boy, here, will be playing in the company baseball tournament, Red. Sam will be umpiring. You think you can drag your butt out of bed Saturday morning to come watch him?"

Red flashed his white teeth in a grin. "Try and keep me away."

The air conditioning in Jackson's truck had a lethargic effect on Giselle. Fighting to keep her eyes open, she made a valiant attempt to converse with him. She finally buckled when he urged her to recline her seat and take a nap.

The next thing she knew, Jackson was waking her with a kiss.

From her languid state of semi-consciousness, she wove her fingers through his hair and groaned.

"Did you have a good nap?"

"Mmmm, I did, but my wake up kiss was better." She sat up and blinked several times, trying to shake off the grogginess. "I really passed out. Swimming always does that to me."

"Along with the dancing and the beer." He stifled a yawn.

She sent him an apologetic look. "It must have been difficult to stay awake driving."

Jackson smiled and leaned in to place another soft kiss to her lips. "Not so bad. If I got sleepy, I'd look over at my precious cargo." He took her hand and helped her out of the truck. She unlocked the door, and he set her bags down on the kitchen floor. He stood just inside the door, hands pocketed and looking a little unsure of himself.

"Please, don't go just yet?" Giselle waited for his nod before paying a visit to her master bath.

She washed her hands then rinsed her mouth out. Fluffing her hair, Giselle took out her compact, applied some powder and just a little eyeliner. She hadn't been gone from Jackson for more than ten minutes. By the time she walked quietly back into the living room she found him sound asleep on the couch, his long legs stretched out. His head propped on the overstuffed arm. Giselle knelt before him to watch him sleep. No way would she ask him to make the drive home tonight.

She tiptoed back into her bedroom and closed the door. Twenty minutes later she emerged, freshly showered, and dressed in a pair of shorts and a tank top.

Giselle slipped back into the living room and found Jackson in the same position. She sat on the edge of the sofa for a moment before taking a giant leap forward from her past with Toby. She stretched out alongside Jackson on the couch, wrapped her arm around his waist, and lay there watching him sleep. The urge to touch him called to her. She ran her fingers through his hair, used her fingertip to trace his features. Still he slept.

She couldn't stand it.

She inched her way towards him, kissed him softly at first, then a little firmer when he began to respond. Her arm tightened around his waist and suddenly he lifted his free hand to her face, cupping it lightly as the kiss grew deepened. Giselle pulled away, opened her eyes to see his hungry gaze on her.

Her breath caught at the look of stark need in his eyes. "Hey."

His gaze seared her. "Hey."

She sent him a shy smile, fighting to keep her hands from doing what they wanted to do; explore every inch of his taut body. "I guess I should have let you sleep."

He blinked, seeming to rouse himself. "I'm glad you didn't. I only meant to close my eyes for a minute. After that power nap, I'll be good for the drive home."

"Nope. I'm not risking you falling asleep at the wheel. Think you can handle spending the night here?"

He paused for a few seconds. "That all depends on where you'll be."

"Well, I thought I'd stay right here with you if that's okay. But if you can't handle it, I'll move to my own bed."

"You can stay here with me if you behave yourself. Otherwise I won't be able to . . . ensure your virtue," he finished.

She smiled as he used one long finger to gently trace a path down her nose to her lips. His hand moved to her hair. His fingers laced through her locks, every movement diffusing the soft floral scent of her shampoo.

"Mmmm, you smell delicious," he growled. "You must have showered."

"Yeah, chlorine and hair highlights aren't a good combination. Did you want to shower?" she asked him.

He nodded. "Would you mind? That might even wake me up enough to go home tonight."

She pushed him back suddenly. "On second thought, no. You're fine as you are."

Jackson's eyes crinkled with laughter. "Well, hell. I've got to admit, it's nice to be wanted."

She felt her heart expanding, growing to accommodate this man. "You are." His gaze softened.

"I'll stay, but we need to get some sleep." He inched backward on the sofa to give her more room. "Can you manage to keep your hands off of me long enough for that?"

She rolled her eyes and snorted. "I'll try." She turned so that her back was to his front, wiggling and squirming to position herself. Jackson released a low groan. She gasped, feeling his arousal on her lower back.

"For God's sake, Giselle, this will only work if you quit that squirming and try to keep some distance between us."

"Sorry." She pulled forward just a bit, until there was some space between them. But, even that couldn't erase the feel of his hardness from her mind. "That was quite—uh—you're really quite impressive, Jackson." Her entire body burned—not from embarrassment, but need.

"Hm. Thank you?" His tone indicated he was levitating somewhere between discomfort and bursting with pride.

"You're welcome . . ." *And obviously well-flipping-endowed.* She resisted the urge to push back against him—hard. "Maybe I should go sleep in my bed and leave you alone." She moved to sit up.

He laid an arm heavily on her shoulder. "Stay where you are, Giselle."

She settled back in her spot. "Okay."

"What do you want to do tomorrow?"

She smiled at his effort to change the subject. Let it go for his sake. "Ride your bike again?"

"If that's what the lady wants, that's what we'll do. Did you call the girls earlier?"

"Yep, but Gwen said they'd passed out watching a movie they'd rented at the hotel. They had a full day at the water park today," she said, stifling a huge yawn.

Within a few minutes, she'd drifted off into an exhausted sleep.

Chapter Twenty-One

Jackson dreamed that Giselle was asleep in his arms. The scent of her shampoo tantalized his sense of smell as soft curls tickled his chin. When she shifted, he could smell the soft, floral scent of her perfume. In his dream, she slowly drew her knee up and rubbed her delectably long thigh over the tops of his legs, until it rested on his groin.

He shifted, regained full consciousness.

No dream. Definitely not a dream. His eyes flew open as he struggled to get his bearings. He lay on a very comfortable sofa, flat on his back—with Giselle sprawled out on top of him, her head on his chest, and his right arm wrapped around her shoulders. If she hadn't yet felt his reaction to her close proximity, she would soon enough. He rubbed his hand softly along her shoulder and then began rubbing her back with light circular motions. She moaned, but didn't awaken. He raised his hand to her hair and began running his fingers through it, trying to tame the unruly curls. She moved her leg again, causing an even more intense reaction from his groin area. Her leg froze. Her entire body tensed, obviously fully awake now with the realization of what was happening. She slowly raised her knee and moved it down the length of his thigh without touching it, until her leg rested on the sofa cushion.

"Too late," he murmured. "Newton's third law . . ."

"What?" She sounded confused.

"For every action there's an equal and opposite reaction."

She looked down at his significant *reaction.* "Sorry."

"Don't apologize. This is the best dream I've ever had."

She used one hand to pat his chest. "Not a dream."

"Then it's the best morning I've ever had." He pulled her close. "Good morning beautiful. How'd you sleep?"

"Good, once I finally fell asleep. What time is it?"

He hit the backlight button on his watch. "6:05. When will the kids be back?"

"Late this afternoon. I haven't spoken to them since yesterday morning." She stretched slowly and sensuously next to Jackson, raising her arms and arching her back.

"Mmmm. You stretch like a cat. A long, sleek, sexy cat."

"You think I'm sexy?"

He groaned deep in his throat then pulled her knee to its former position, where the evidence still existed.

"Hmmm . . ." she purred.

"Uh huh." He removed her knee again. "So, does this mean we're ready to 'come out' in the light of day yet?"

She bit her bottom lip. "Jackson, when's the last time you lived in a small town?"

"Never, but I hope to one day." Kenton seemed like the perfect place to live.

"Let me tell you something about small towns. Word gets around fast and gossips can be ruthless and cruel."

"I don't think small towns have cornered the market on gossip, hon."

"I know, but it happens quicker. Adults talk, and kids overhear, and then kids talk. As cruel as adults can be, that's nothing compared to how cruel children can be. How would you feel if the child of some gossip went to school and said something to upset Lex or Mac? Something like 'My mom said that your mom shouldn't be dating already because your daddy hasn't been dead a year yet.'"

"Kids aren't that mean, are they?"

"Children don't understand how badly they're hurting someone. Believe me, Jackson. I've seen it."

"Okay, we'll be discreet, if that's what you want."

"Thank you. Now, I don't know about you, but I need coffee." She got up from the sofa. "Are you hungry? I'll cook breakfast."

"I'm starving. You mind if I take a quick shower first?"

"Not at all. How does bacon and eggs sound?"

"Like heaven." He kissed her then went to get his bag.

Twenty minutes later, Jackson entered the kitchen, freshly shaved and showered. "Mm, smells good in here."

"Sit down, here's your coffee, and here's your breakfast." She set down a plate of crispy bacon and scrambled eggs.

"Thanks, I'm starving."

Giselle sat beside him at the table, glad to have someone to share a leisurely breakfast with on a Sunday morning. The talk was casual and comfortable as they finished off breakfast and two cups of steaming coffee. "You know, the girls only have two more weekends before school starts."

"Already? This summer flew by, didn't it?" He stopped to gaze down at her curiously. "It's strange for me. I haven't had any means of measuring summer vacations since I graduated from college."

"I can see that. It doesn't really mean anything unless you're in school or have kids who are."

"Especially when you've spent over a decade avoiding any vacations, summer or otherwise, like the plague."

Giselle pulled her mouth down in an exaggerated pout. "Poor baby. We'll see what we can do about that."

He leaned over for a quick kiss. "You do that," he said, giving her butt a light tap. "Now, go get ready. I'll clean up because you did the cooking."

Giselle used the opportunity to change her clothes and apply a little make up. She fixed her hair and finished with a light spray of perfume. She entered the kitchen, finding Jackson standing at the counter watching the slideshow on the digital picture frame. She approached from behind and slipped her arms around his waist.

"I hope you don't mind," he said, "I love these shots."

"I took those the day before he died." Giselle reached out to touch the frame.

"You, Carrie, and I worked late on that turn lane project," he said. "I remember."

"I came home and asked Lexie where her daddy was. She said he was 'outside burning the steaks' like it was the most natural thing in the world."

Jackson's low chuckle resonated. "The girls have wonderful memories of him, but it's up to the rest of us to make sure they keep them."

Giselle smiled. "They had him all dressed up like a princess. God, it seems like an eternity ago." She studied one particular photo and laughed. "He looked good in that pink feather boa, didn't he?"

"He sure did." Jackson turned to gaze down at her. "I miss him too, you know." She nodded and he kissed the tip of her nose. It was an intimate gesture in front of the most recent snapshots of Toby. "Are you okay with this?" He gestured at the photo frame.

"The more I look at these, the easier it is. I was lucky once, and maybe I'll get lucky again." She smiled up at him.

Jackson squeezed his eyes shut, paused, as though contemplating the situation before speaking his mind. "Do you think someday I could be a part of this family?"

She relaxed against the kitchen cabinet and pulled him closer. "I think it's possible. Does that scare you?"

He leaned in for a kiss. "Not even a little."

She kissed him in return then pulled away. "It should, you know; with three women in the house, you'll be out numbered. Not to mention the fact that in about seven years, you'll have to deal with three different sets of PMS symptoms—all that crankiness and mood swings." She twisted her face into a grimace.

He nibbled on her neck. "Fortunately for you, I've been pre-conditioned to crankiness and mood swings."

She reached up, put her arms around his neck. "Yes, I guess you have." She inched her body as close to his as possible, wondering about their potential relationship. Giselle slipped her hands under his T-shirt to explore the soft, silky matting of fine black hair on his chest and lower abdomen. She splayed her hands on his highly defined abs, and gently traced the ridges and hard planes of his torso.

Nestling her face into the contours of his neckline, she tasted him with her tongue. He groaned low in his throat when she scraped his skin lightly with her teeth.

"You're making me crazy." He pulled away and she closed her eyes as he treated her to the same tenderness, tasting her, then lightly biting and nipping until she shivered.

"You see?" His breath was whisper soft against her neck.

She nodded, unable to speak, barely able to breathe.

He slipped his arms around to massage her back then moved his hands under her shirt to feel the soft skin of her sides and belly. She inhaled sharply at the touch and pulled him to her for a kiss, wanting more of him as his hands inched closer to her breasts. When he pulled away to bury his mouth on her neck, she was primed and ready for his touch. She moaned when his lips touched her hot skin, gasped as his fingertips brushed the décolletage of her lace bra. She let her head fall back as he brushed the back of his hands up the sides of her breasts.

"Jackson," she whispered hoarsely. "Please."

"Please, what? I don't know how far I can go." He pulled her roughly to him as she nearly sobbed in frustration. "I want you, Giselle, but I don't know if you're ready."

"Jackson. Please." She ached with need.

"Tell me what you want, hon. What can I do?"

"Please," she begged again, unsure how to ask him to do what she wanted him to do. "Hold me. Touch me."

He unbuttoned her shirt with trembling fingers then stood, as though contemplating what to do next. When she reached up to unhook her front bra closure, he covered her hands with his own, stopping her.

"Not yet," he said, giving her a slow shake of his head. "Not here. And not now." He cupped her breasts softly and began stroking the pads of his thumbs over the thin fabric covering her nipples. He rubbed in small circular motions, increasing the pressure.

In turns, Giselle mewled, panted with need, then groaned from the pleasure of having Jackson's hands on her. She arched her back to be more accessible to his tender touches. Jackson bent low, placed both hands under her thighs, and lifted her easily so that she rested on the counter top. He opened her legs and stepped between them. His hardness was right up against her heated core.

Giselle wrapped her legs around his hips and pulled him to her, demanding more. "Jackson," she moaned, desperate for some form of relief.

In response, he pulled her hips closer, grinding against her, thrusting his own hips forward. He kissed her, smothering her moans as he continued the circular motion with his thumb on her nipple, and grinding into her heat. Within moments, Giselle cried out with her release. He continued the motions, bringing her down slowly. Cupping her face in his hands, he kissed her, thrusting his tongue into her mouth with a furious need.

Giselle reciprocated, reached out to unbutton his shorts.

"No," he pulled away, gasping, moved her hands.

"But you need—" she began.

"Not like this," he said, cutting her off, his voice hoarse with need. "That was only for you."

"But Jackson . . ."

He gave his head a shake. "I'm fine." He trembled with the effort it took to control himself. "Or I will be in a few minutes. Just give me a few minutes," he gasped.

Giselle took his face in her hands and kissed him. She brushed back the hair from his dampened forehead and rested her head against his. "Jackson," she whispered.

They stayed in that position until they both came down from the sexual, emotional roller coaster ride. Until his breathing returned to normal. He pulled away, drinking in the sight of her, shaking his head slowly, his eyes warm with emotion. "My God, you're beautiful," he whispered, buttoning her shirt, adjusting her collar.

She laid her head on his chest, still able to feel the pounding of his heart. "I hate that you didn't get to—"

"Don't worry about me," he cut in. "I'm a big boy."

She glanced down at his package. "That, you are, Jack, and I have to admit, it's got me looking forward to—things."

"You should be. I promise, when the time is right for us, I won't disappoint you." He wiped the sweat from his brow again. "Until then, I see numerous cold showers in my future."

Chapter Twenty-Two

The shrill ring of the landline made them both jump. Giselle answered, shared a brief conversation then hung up. "That was Gretchen. They'll be home around 3:00. So, what do we do until then?"

Jackson wiped at his brow again. "Anything that gets us the hell out of here. Any ideas?"

She nodded. "Let's go get the bike."

He nibbled on her ear. "The sooner, the better."

"Give me a minute." She pulled away from him.

"Hey, bring your swimsuit." He grinned at her questioning look.

"I don't do rivers or lakes." She shook her head. "I hate snakes, and the thought of fish nibbling on my toes freaks me out."

"Just get your suit," he said, laughing.

They drove to Jackson's house, traded the Avalanche for the Indian, and rode for two hours. Around eleven, he turned into Bill's driveway and pulled up to the house. He unlocked the front door and ushered her inside.

Bill's home was a rambling log cabin style home, rustic looking on the outside. One step inside told her the home's interior was full of comforts and amenities. She surveyed their surroundings, her gaze landing on the huge leather sofas, either of which would make for a tantalizing setting for hot and bothered sex with Jackson. "This place is gorgeous, Jackson, but why are we here?"

"You'll see." He grabbed her hand and pulled her through the back door onto the patio area. There was another huge building to the rear of the home, with several windows along each exterior wall. He unlocked the building and led her inside. Giselle stood in awe of the huge indoor pool. The entire room was set up for entertaining and comfort, with several round tables surrounded by chairs, chaise loungers placed around all four sides of the pool, and several huge potted plants placed throughout the room, giving it a tropical feel. "I'm amazed. I had no idea this was here."

"When he bought the place the pool was here already. He decided if he was going to have one, he wanted to be able to use it year round. He had this built several years ago when he used to do a lot of entertaining for his oil company. Pre-retirement era. He swims every morning to keep in shape."

"Now that you mention it, he did tell me he swam laps every day. It never dawned on me that he had his own pool. Is it heated during the winter?"

"It's the same temp year round. You ready to swim?"

In seconds, Giselle had shimmied out of her shorts and slipped off her halter top. She stepped out of her sandals and dove in. She popped up and swam to the side. "The temperature's perfect. You coming in?"

"Be there in a minute." Jackson came out of the bathroom a few minutes later wearing his trunks and carrying two large towels. He walked to a corner of the room, pushed some buttons and country music played from a built-in stereo system.

Giselle was busy treading water as she watched him walk with deliberate slowness toward her. What the hell was he waiting on? Jackson stopped to pull the drawstring on his trunks then re-tied it. She kept her eyes on the two pads of muscle just above each hipbone where the trunks were hanging kind of low. One of her college roommates had a name for those pads. A little on the loose side, the girl had called it the "Make me stupid love handles". Obviously, it had. By the end of freshman year, she'd dropped out, pregnant and unmarried. Giselle had to admit that if she'd seen anything like this, she might have gone a little over the edge herself. God knows, she wanted to right now.

She lifted her gaze to his luscious abs and shoulders, all freshly bronzed from the previous day of fun in the sun at Red's. Their gazes met and she noticed the sparkle of hidden laughter in his eyes. So big boy wanted to play, did he?

She swam to the ladder and climbed out, swinging her hips seductively as she walked over to the diving board. She placed one delicate foot carefully in front of another, taking her sweet time to walk over to the end of the board. She glanced at him. He was every bit as captivated by watching her as she had been by watching him. She steadied herself then took several good bounces, cut a flip in the air, and sliced smoothly into the water.

The second Giselle hit the water, Jackson must have too, diving headfirst into the opposite end.

She broke the surface, wiped the water out of her eyes, and looked around, unable to spot him. He surfaced silently behind her making her gasp as he pulled her close. Giselle turned in his arms, looped her arms around his neck as he treaded water. He kissed her on the nose then dipped his head to kiss her deeply as their tongues did the exploring.

Jackson pulled back, admiring the woman in his arms. Her lids were half closed with desire. "God, you're beautiful."

She barely managed a whispered, "Thank you."

He kissed her again, and they sank as he lost concentration and forgot to tread water. Neither of them broke the kiss, but continued until he brought them back up to the surface. He side paddled to the edge of the pool where he could hang on and kiss her without having to work so hard. They became lost in each other, their hands all over one another until he finally forced himself to stop. "We have to slow this down," he groaned, "or I won't be able to."

"I don't want to slow down. I don't want you to stop."

"What . . ."

"Make love to me," she whispered, wrapping her legs tightly around his hips and pulling him close for a kiss.

With effort, he pulled back. "We can't take this back. Are you sure?"

"I'm sure," she panted.

"Yes. Giselle. Oh God, yes," he groaned as he buried his face in her neck and pulled her close.

Her breath came in short pants as she spoke in a hoarse whisper. "Make love to me, Toby."

Jackson's world came to a halt—a screeching, ice water down the front of his pants, knee to the groin halt—to put it mildly. He swore his heart skipped two full beats before starting up again at the pace and strength of a jackhammer. When she moved in for another kiss, obviously unaware of her slip, he put her at arm's length and kissed her lightly on the forehead. "I'm sorry, hon, but we can't do this right now." He avoided her gaze, didn't want her mistaking anything she saw there for rejection. She didn't call him by her dead husband's name to hurt him. But it didn't make it hurt any less. It was too damn soon for this.

"What? Why? What's wrong?"

"It's too soon," he explained patiently, climbing out of the pool to grab a towel. He didn't blame her for the innocent slip. Far from it.

She followed him out of the pool. Grabbed her own towel. "No, we need to talk."

"Giselle, for God's sake-just drop it," he pleaded.

"No! Why did you change your mind? We're both adults."

He knew she wouldn't drop it. Toby always said a bulldog had nothing on his wife when she was determined. The thought made his stomach lurch uncomfortably. Would he always think of her as *Toby's wife*? More importantly, would she?

He took a deep breath and braced himself. "You called me Toby."

"What? No. I didn't. Y-you must have misunderstood."

He turned to meet her gaze head on. "No way did I misunderstand the words 'Make love to me, Toby'."

Giselle covered her mouth with her hands and turned away from him. "Oh. Oh Jackson. I'm so sorry."

He paused, then walked up behind her and placed his hands gently on her shoulders. "It's fine, Giselle. It just means you weren't ready, that's all. It's too soon."

She turned toward him with tears trailing down her face. "I hurt you, and I'm sorry."

He pulled her close and wrapped a towel around her. "It's no big deal."

She stared at him in astonishment. "Jackson, if you'd called me Chloe when we're about to make love, it would have been a big deal. A *very* big deal, I promise you."

He grinned, adjusted her towel. "You owe me one, then."

Giselle did not look amused.

He placed his hands gently upon her shoulders. "Look, I would *never* call you Chloe. I'm not sure that I ever really loved her, and if I did, it's been too long ago to remember. But you adored you husband when he was taken from you. It's almost a compliment when you stop and think about it. Not quite," he said, a little uncomfortably, "but almost."

Giselle snorted and turned away from him.

He walked closer and spoke softly to her. "All I'm saying is that it's completely understandable. Maybe it's a sign from God—or Toby," he shrugged, adding a chuckle.

She turned, and stuck her finger in his chest. "Now see, *that* isn't funny." Jackson laughed, and she grinned at him, in spite of the situation. "You are entirely too understanding about all of this."

"Come on, let's go for swim." He swept her up in his arms then threw her in the pool.

She came up sputtering. "Okay, *now* we're even!"

Hours of swimming and bike riding later, found the two of them snuggled up on the couch watching movies. A little past 3:00 they both perked up at the slam of a car door. Jackson pulled himself up and her with him. "They're here."

She raced him to the back door just as her daughters barreled through.

"My babies!" Giselle clutched her girls to her, smothering them with kisses. "I missed you both so much."

"Mom, we had so much fun! I wish you and Jackson could have been there, though. Maybe we can go back."

"We'll make it a point to, Mac." Jackson ruffled the child's hair.

Gretchen and Caleb came in, both looking exhausted and lugging suitcases and various bags of souvenirs. They plopped the bags down at the door, and Gretchen gave Giselle a hug while Caleb shook Jackson's hand.

"I can't tell you how grateful I am that you took this on, man. You two saved Mac and Lexie's vacation."

Caleb exchanged a knowing look with his wife. "Are you kidding? We're the grateful ones. We got a vacation we couldn't have afforded and had a blast."

"The girls were perfect, Giselle—all five of them. I didn't hear a bit of the usual arguing or bickering from my two, and Bill and Gwen were awesome. I've never had so much fun on a vacation before."

After more profuse thanks from both parties, they left, leaving Jackson and Giselle alone with Mac and Lexie.

The girls talked non-stop about everything they'd done and seen. They couldn't wait to give Giselle and Jackson the souvenir coffee cups and caps they'd bought them.

Jackson helped Giselle empty the luggage and carried an armload of clothes to the utility room for her. He met her back in the kitchen. "I've got some things to do around my place tonight, but since I'd already taken tomorrow off, how about I take you and the girls to lunch and a movie?"

"You've got yourself a date, Mr. Broussard."

"I'll see you tomorrow girls. Go put your souvenirs in your rooms, okay?"

As soon as they were alone, Jackson turned to Giselle and pulled her into his arms for a quick kiss. "You were right about one thing, hon. Trying to act normal around other people is going to be a challenge. Can I call you later?"

"You'd better," she said, reaching up to brush a lock of hair from his forehead.

"I need to go." He took her face in both of his hands to kiss her then hugged her tightly.

"Jackson, please wait for me," she whispered.

He touched his forehead to hers, and tangled his fingers in her curly hair. "Forever," he whispered, before leaving her with one last kiss.

Jackson's keys hit the granite counter top as he closed his door behind him. He called Giselle to let her know he'd made it home okay, then called Bill.

He couldn't help but smile at the zip in his Uncle's voice. "How was the trip?"

"Outstanding. It was nice to be able to do something like that for them. Gwen's had to work hard to raise Alyssa. Things you and I take for granted are luxuries to them."

"I imagine they've had a rough time of it."

"Yep, but we did some talking when Gretchen and Caleb took all the kids for one night. Gwen and I have discovered we're 'compatible' in several different ways," he murmured.

"You don't say. So when's the wedding?"

"I was about to call you to talk about that. I've asked her, and she's said yes. Think you could be my best man?"

"Sure I will. I'm happy for you, for Gwen, and for Alyssa. They can't ask for better."

"Thanks, son. We've chosen the Friday night before Labor Day weekend. That way we can have a quick honeymoon. She's planning to ask Giselle to watch Alyssa for the weekend. You know," he took a short pause. "We've discussed trying for children right away." Bill's voice filled with emotion when he spoke. "Alyssa gave us her blessing and asked if she could call me daddy. You can't imagine how much that means to me."

Jackson held the phone to his ear and grinned. "Oh, I think I can. You don't have to tell me how those little girls can tug on your heart strings."

Bill chuckled at his nephew's comment. "No, I guess I don't. How was your weekend? What did you two do once Giselle got over the food poisoning?"

"Oh man, it was great. We rode the Indian a couple of days, went to Red's club on Friday and spent Saturday with him. I brought her swimming at your place this afternoon. By the way, Red's a little disillusioned that his bachelor mentor has gone over the deep end over a woman." Bill's laughter carried over the phone.

"Yeah?" he said. "Well you can tell old Red he doesn't know what the hell he's missing."

Jackson forced himself to wait until eight p.m. to call Giselle. Stretched out on his couch, he waited patiently for her to answer. She answered on the sixth ring, sounding out of breath. "I'd about given up," he said.

"Sorry, both girls zonked out on the couch, and I had to carry Lexie to bed. She's a lot heavier than I remember."

Jackson laughed. "Maybe you should have let her sleep on the sofa. I hope you didn't strain your back."

"Aw, I'm used to it," she drawled. "That's what us poor women folk do when we don't have a big, strong man around to do it for us."

Jackson hesitated. "Maybe one day you will again."

"Are you applying for the job, sir?" Her tone contained a hint of playfulness.

"Are you accepting applications, ma'am?" he countered.

"We're not exactly hiring at this time, but I'll definitely keep you in mind for any future openings."

He gave an exaggerated sigh. "Well, hell—I guess that'll have to do. Wait, will I need references?"

"Of course," she snapped.

"Well, then, I might be out of luck. My former employer didn't think too highly of me."

Giselle chuckled. "On second thought, I wouldn't worry too much about a reference. Your reputation is sterling around here, mister. Besides, I happen to know that your former employer was a very foolish woman."

He paused, wondering how much she really knew about the hell Chloe had put him through. "You think so?"

"I do."

Jackson closed his eyes, thinking those had to be the two sweetest words she could ever speak to him. He cleared his throat. "That means a lot to me, but I don't want to waste any phone time talking about—her."

"You didn't deserve to be treated like that, Jackson. Especially not by someone as horrible as she, whose name must never be mentioned."

He laughed at her reference, still determined to change the subject. "Yeah, well, I don't think I deserved to be called *Satan* for four years, either. That never stopped you." Jackson sat back and waited for the fireworks to start. He wasn't disappointed.

"I didn't deserve to get chewed out in a conference room full of engineers, either," Giselle huffed. "You hadn't asked *me* to put those memos in chronological order."

"I know," he admitted. "I remembered as soon as you stormed out of there. By the time I got back to our office, 'Ditzy Donna' had already walked off the job with no explanation."

"She handed me the folder, asked me to bring it to you in the meeting, and walked out. We never saw her again," Giselle added. "I had no idea you had asked her to organize it for the meeting. Are you telling me you knew all this time it wasn't my fault?"

"Of course I knew. I'm sorry, Giselle; I really am."

"Too little, too late," she snorted. "My reputation was sullied."

"No, it wasn't. As soon as you left, I told everyone it wasn't your fault."

"*That* would have been nice to know four years ago."

"But I so enjoyed seeing the fire in those green eyes flash with contempt anytime I entered a room." He waited through a prolonged silence. "What can I do to make it up to you?" He heard a light tapping on the phone, envisioned her tapping her nail impatiently. Several moments passed with no sound. Had she hung up on him? "Giselle?"

"Uh huh…"

"What are you doing?"

"I'm thinking about what to ask you for. I could totally make this work for me," she purred.

He laughed softly. "I have a feeling it would be difficult to turn you down for anything you asked for." He heard the sigh, prepared himself for what he knew was coming.

"You turned me down today."

"Giselle, I refuse to rush you into doing something you're not ready to do. I'll say it again, you're too important to me to screw this up."

Giselle was silent for several moments. "Jackson?"

He lowered his voice, wishing for a glimpse of her face. "What?"

"Please don't give up on me."

He smiled. If she only knew how long he'd already waited. "Never."

After spending the entire Monday with Giselle and the girls, Jackson returned to work on Tuesday. In comparison to the time spent with them, the rest of the week was a long, slow drag on his frame of mind. While the days were agony, the nights without them were torture.

Every afternoon, he drove straight to Kenton after work. Every afternoon, Giselle would run to meet him, doing what she could to avoid her nosy neighbor's prying eyes. If the woman was watching, she waited until he walked in the house before throwing her arms around his neck. If her neighbor was nowhere around, she attacked him when he was still in the truck, or on his bike.

Of course, if either Mac or Lexie were around, they kept it strictly G-rated. But those occasional moments when it was just him and Giselle—well damn, those made up for everything.

He wanted to tell her he loved her, but he'd had a few years to come to terms with his feelings, and he didn't want to scare her off. She still worried that people would think she was dating too soon after Toby's death. Carrie insisted it would come soon enough, but Jackson felt that every day without her was a massive waste of time.

On Friday afternoon, Jackson pulled up into Giselle's driveway, looking curiously at all the boxes in her garage. "What's all this?" She pushed him through the garage door into its dark interior, out of sight from snoopy Mrs. Cormier, who was watching from her porch.

"Kiss me first."

He backed her up against the wall of the garage and planted one on her, determined to show her how much he'd missed her. By the time he found the strength to pull them out of it, they were both nearing the point of no return. He rested his forehead on hers. "Hey, Baby."

"Jackson," she groaned low in her throat. "You make my toes curl when you kiss me like that."

"Then I'm doing my job." He smiled and kissed the tip of her nose. "How was your day?"

She stepped back and waved at the boxes. "Busy, I finally cleaned out Toby's half of the closet. All this is for St. Vincent's closet at the church. I've put a few items aside. I thought maybe you, Sam, and the rest of the guys may want to pick through some of his caps and things. Mac and Lexie each kept their favorite LSU caps for themselves, but he had so many. If it feels too strange, you don't have to." She made a funny face.

"I'd love to have something of his. As a matter of fact," he said, picking up the one item he'd been hoping to find, "This is what I'd like to have, right here!" He put on Toby's favorite old faded purple and gold LSU cap. "He always beat me in hoops when he wore this--claimed it was his lucky cap." He took the cap off and held it reverently. "I miss him Giselle," he said huskily. "Do you think he'd mind about you and me?"

"I think it's like you said months ago. He'd want to see me and his girls happy. So far, you seem to make us all happy." She placed the cap on his head then turned the bill to the back so she could kiss Jackson fully. "It figures you'd pick that one. You know why he has so many LSU caps, don't you?"

"No. This is a considerably large collection, for sure."

"The girls and I were always trying to get him to throw away this old ratty thing. We kept buying him new ones, but he always said this was his favorite."

"His coach gave him this after his last game at Tiger Stadium, right after he blew out his knee." Jackson fingered the faded brim reverently.

She smiled. "It figures he would have told you that, and kept it from me all these years. Keep the cap then, but do me a favor and take a couple of these others."

"Okay, I won't make you look at it all the time. How's this?" he asked as he tried on another one.

"Very handsome," she said as she kissed him on the mouth.

"But, can I wear the lucky cap for the tournament tomorrow? As out of practice as I am, I may need all the luck I can get."

"Somehow I don't think you'll need luck, but you can wear it anyway, the girls will get a kick out of it."

Chapter Twenty-Three

The next morning arrived with just enough cloud coverage to make the company softball tournament bearable during the morning hours. Jackson was introducing Red to some of the guys on his team when Mac and Lexie bombarded him.

He scooped them up into his arms. "There's my munchkins! Where's your beautiful mother?"

"Over there," Lexie sighed. "People keep talking to her about the ass-ki-dent. I hope they don't make her sad again."

Jackson hugged her. "She used to work with these people, sweetie. They care about her. She's okay."

Red cleared his throat impatiently. "Aren't you going to introduce me to these lovely young ladies?"

Jackson placed his hands on Mac and Lexie's shoulders and turned them toward Red. "Girls, I want you to meet one of my oldest friends, Mr. Scott McAllister, but you can call him 'Red'. Red, this is Mackenzie and Lexie Granger."

"Wonderful to make your acquaintance ladies," he said.

"Nice to meet you, too, Red," Mackenzie said.

Lexie looked up at Red, squinting one eye. "He doesn't look that old."

Mac turned on her sister. "What are you talking about, Lex?"

"Jackson said he was one of his oldest friends. I think Sam looks older'n he does."

"I meant that I've known Red for a long time, sweetie. Not that he's *old*."

"Oh. Well why didn't you just say so, then?"

Jackson's brow rose at Red's snort of laughter. "I thought I did, but I'll say it better next time."

Lexie stared up at Red. "I guess your mama throws big cows, too, huh."

Jackson and Red burst into astonished laughter.

Lexie pulled on Jackson's shirt until he picked her up in his arms again. "Did I say something wrong?"

Jackson stifled his laughter. "No, but—where did you hear that, Lex?"

"That's what Sam says when somebody is really tall—that their mama throws big cows."

"Oh. I think what he says is 'throws big calves'. That means—uh—well—I'll let your mom explain that to you, okay?" Jackson caught Red's amused expression.

Suddenly Lexie put her hand out to Red. "I don't care what kind of animal your mama threw down. Any friend of Jackson's is my friend, too."

Red wiped the grin from his face as he took her hand. "Thank you, ma'am. I'm honored."

She gave Jackson a serious look. "Maybe we better keep this to ourselves. I don't want mom to be mortified again."

Red burst into laughter, and Jackson shook his head as he set her down. "Oh, Lex, surely she's used to it by now."

"She is," Mac agreed. "Last night, when I told mom what Lex told Mrs. Cormier next door, mom said nothing she says surprises her anymore."

"Lex, what did you tell her?" Jackson almost dreaded her answer.

"I said her new puppy looked like her—wrinkly and a hunnerd years old."

"Oh Lex," Jackson groaned, trying to stifle a laugh, as Red covered his mouth and turned away.

"It's a hundred, Lex, and you don't even know how much that is."

"I know it's a lot."

Mackenzie shook her head in disgust. "I told mom to just be thankful she didn't tell Mrs. Cormier she has a big butt, too, because she says that all the time."

This time Jackson had to turn away.

"There's Sam and Carrie!" Lexie cried, as she and Mac ran to meet them.

Red turned to face Jackson and burst into laughter.

"What did we tell you? *Lexi-isms*. They're something, aren't they?"

"They are, and as beautiful as their mom," Red agreed.

Carrie and Sam approached the two men. "Red, I didn't know you would be here," Carrie said.

Red hugged her tightly. "I asked them not to tell. I wanted to surprise you."

"How are Vivi and Pete?"

"My folks are fine. I spoke to them yesterday and told them I'd be seeing you. They send their love."

"Carrie, you know Red already?" Lexie asked her.

"I've known him all his life, sweetie. I babysat for him when he was about your age, except I called him Scottie. Red, whistle at Giselle and wave her over here. She'll never get away from that one."

"Yes ma'am." Red emitted a shrill two-finger whistle, and when Giselle looked up at him, they all waved her over.

Giselle looked up at the sharp whistle, saw the group waving at her. She zeroed in on Jackson, looking hot as ever, even in shorts and a white v-neck T-shirt. She made her excuses and walked over to meet them. "Hey, Red." She gave him a hug. "Hey Sam, Carrie—Jackson." She passed behind him, letting her hand slowly caress his lower back.

"Giselle." His eyes lingered hungrily on her.

She pulled her gaze from him, to address Carrie. "Where's the rest of the gang?"

"Gretchen, Lauren, and Amanda are driving in together. They should be here any minute. Their guys are all taking the kids to the river today. Are you ready to play ball, Jackson?"

"Sure am. How many teams did we end up with, Carrie?"

"Only four, thank God. It's too hot for this," she said.

Sam got the team captains to draw numbers. Jackson drew the number one position, so they got to play the number two team. The two teams got their players on the field and it turned out that B & L's team was short a person. Nobody from the Jennings team wanted to sit out, so they asked the team captain to pick a volunteer from the stands. When Red volunteered, Jackson waved him down to introduce him to their team.

Sherri Dubois, the catcher for his team, also an LSU alumni, approached them with a question. "You wouldn't happen to be the same Scott McAllister that played first base at LSU on one of the winningest teams ever—would you?"

Red removed his cap to run his fingers through his short hair. "That would be me."

Sherri turned to her co-worker. "And we just happen to be short a player, huh? So, Jackson, who'd you have to bribe to stay home today?"

Jackson gave her a deep chuckle. "Nobody, it must be my lucky cap." He grinned at Giselle, sitting up in the stands, and waved Toby's old purple and gold cap at her.

Sherri laughed. "Good God, those poor bastards out there have no idea they don't have a snowball's chance in hell. Talk about a stacked team."

The first game went quickly. Jackson pitched, Red covered first, Tyson was on second, and Clayton played third base. Sherri was the only woman on the team, and they were fortunate to have her catching, a position she'd played in high school and college. They got three immediate outs with no runs scored.

Their team lined up to bat. After five batters, they had three points on the board and two on bases. Red hit a home run to stretch their lead to six points.

Jackson came up to bat and Mac and Lexie yelled at him to 'call it'. He turned, grinning at the three people who meant the world to him. The little girls screamed with laughter as he used his bat to point at left field. Just as he had done at Sam and Carrie's, he smacked one right where he'd pointed, for an easy run.

With no outs, they let the other team take their bat again. This time Jackson walked a couple of people so they could get on base. The next batter hit a grounder straight to him; he fumbled it a couple of times and threw it sloppily to Red who dropped it so that the runner could make it to first. The bases were loaded and it looked like the other team would finally score some points. When the next batter hit a pop fly to third base, Clayton caught the ball to put the batter out, along with the runner, who stepped off third.

Jackson shook his head in disapproval as the spectators laughed, obviously aware of his attempt to help the other team.

Clayton looked down sheepishly. "I'm sorry I caught the ball!" he yelled.

Jackson pointed at him. "Do that again and you're off the team, buddy!" The spectators burst into laughter.

Mackenzie approached the fence, hands on her hips, and called out to Jackson. "Why did you fuss at that man for catching the ball, Jackson? He's *supposed* to catch the ball and put them out, isn't he?"

Jackson took a knee in front of Mac. "Well, I was trying to give the other team a chance to score because our team is a lot better than theirs. It's called good sportsmanship."

Obviously not satisfied with how he'd answered her sister's question, Lex called down from the stands. "Well, somebody should have told that *other* team to pick better players," she insisted, garnering even more laughter.

Despite Jackson's efforts, they still beat the other team by a score of 14-2. After they finished, their team joined the cheering section in the stands to the sound of applause. As soon as Jackson sat down on the bleacher in front of Giselle, Lisa Benoit, the company's accountant, sidled in next to him. Lisa was a petite blonde, with a high pitched voice that got higher when a good looking man was around, and a laugh that had always annoyed the hell out of both Carrie and Giselle. She was single and always on the lookout for a man, married or not.

"Jackson, I didn't know you could play ball like that," she gushed, hanging on his arm. "Oooh, have you been working out?"

Jackson unwound Lisa's arm from his, and attempted to watch the next game. It was closer than the first game, but Lisa's chattering was a constant distraction. The woman's pitch was getting higher by the octave, louder by the decibel, and he'd had about enough.

"For God's sake, Lisa, give it a rest," Carrie groaned. Lisa looked back to see who had spoken, and Carrie looked down at her. "Yeah, it's me. You think you could turn it down a notch or two? The rest of us can't hear ourselves think."

"Well excuse me for trying to carry on an intelligent conversation with Jackson. Come on honey, let's go sit somewhere else." Lisa pulled on Jackson's arm.

Giselle straightened, her hackles rising at the woman's nerve. Red, who sat beside her, placed a restraining hand on her arm. She threw a glance in his direction in time to see him shake his head and give her a wink.

Lisa stood, took three steps down, and turned to face Jackson. Seeing he hadn't followed her, she moved to return to her seat beside him. Fortunately, Mac and Lexie had already scooted in smoothly next to him. He grinned at the girls and picked up Lex to set her on his knee as he made more room for Mac beside him.

"I'm sitting there, you two can move aside," Lisa screeched, her tone containing all the pleasantness of fingernails on a chalkboard.

"I don't think so, honey. You move it, you lose it," Gretchen said, leaning over to address Mac and Lexie. "You girls stay right where you are."

"Jaaackson!" Lisa stomped her foot on the bleacher.

"What?" he asked.

"Are you coming?" she whined.

"No." He completely avoided her gaze.

Lisa finally got the message and stomped off, while several people in the bleachers snickered. Jackson covered his face in embarrassment.

"Who is she?" Lauren asked.

"Lisa Benoit and she obviously wants *Jaaackson*," Giselle whined in a perfect imitation of Lisa, to several more chuckles. When Jackson turned in his seat to face her she refused to make eye contact with him.

Irritated at herself for letting Lisa get under her skin, Giselle tried to concentrate on the next game, which lasted a lot longer than the first one. By the time it was over, it was close to noon. Everyone took a break for lunch while someone played music from a portable sound system. Giselle climbed down from the bleachers, and stretched to get the kinks out of her legs and back. She walked over to Jackson's truck, where the drinks were located for their team. Jackson handed her an iced tea.

"Have you seen the girls?" she asked

"They're over there with Red. He's getting them chips and sandwiches. You ready to eat something?"

"No," she said, icily.

He pulled her around to the other side of the truck for some privacy. "Are you angry for some reason?"

"Should I be? Just because you let Lisa hang all over you for a full twenty minutes? You encouraged her," she seethed.

"I said two words to her—'what' and 'no'." He grabbed her arm when she started to turn away. "Are you jealous?"

"Of Lisa? Of course not."

He grinned and leaned in close. "You know, we wouldn't have this problem if we weren't keeping a 'low profile'. Then you could put your mark on me and make sure all the other females stayed clear."

Giselle glared at his back as he walked away from her, her mouth hanging open in shock. Her eyes narrowed to angry slits. "I know he didn't," she murmured. "You want to play, big boy? Game on."

Giselle sauntered over to Red. "Jackson must pay. Are you in or out?" A look of unspoken understanding passed between them, before Red nodded.

"Hey sweet thing, you want me to fix you a plate?" Red crooned.

"Would you do that, Red?" she asked sweetly.

"Anything for you, hon." He gave her his most charming smile.

She grinned. "Thanks Red."

"Anytime beautiful!" he answered loudly as he handed her a plate of food. He took Giselle's arm and turned her in the opposite direction toward the bleachers, his hand placed intimately on the small of her back.

Jackson stood there, his mouth gaping open as the two of them carried on a lively conversation during their walk to the bleachers.

"Aw, hell!"

"What's wrong with you?" Carrie asked from behind.

"I think I'm being punished," he groaned.

"You should be. There's no excuse for you letting Lisa hang all over you like that. If I hadn't told Mac and Lexie to scoot in next to you, she'd be fused to your hip by now."

"I didn't even talk to her," he hissed.

Carrie released an exasperated sigh. "Come on, Jackson. Do you want me to cut up your food into bite size pieces for you, too?"

He rolled his eyes, and turned to her. "All right, how do I fix this before it gets out of hand?"

"Treat Lisa the same way you treated Izzy. Don't put up with any crap from her and you'll be okay." She walked off.

Jackson got a plate of food and a drink. He walked toward Giselle and Red, catching the wink his friend passed him, a sure sign that Red was in on her game. When he was a few steps away he heard the most irritating of voices again.

"Jaaackson—there you are! I found a spot for us right over here," Lisa whined, pulling on his arm. Jackson glared at her, knowing Giselle, Red, and several other people were watching.

"Lisa, I'm not interested," he said, trying not to be rude.

"How do you know, unless you've had a sample?" she asked.

"Believe me, you don't have a damn thing I want." The line didn't work as well on Lisa as it had on Izzy. She wrapped both hands around one muscular bicep, and pulled on him again. He glared down at her. "And you never will. Let go. Now."

Lisa stomped off as the message finally seemed to sink in.

Determined to resolve this thing, he approached Giselle, his unwavering glare locked on her. "Are you happy now?" He dropped his plate unceremoniously on the bleacher, and swiveled, turning his glare on Red. "And you—Hef! Your role in this little charade is over, so go find someone else's leg to hump."

Red smothered his grin, picked up his plate and left them.

Jackson sat down, and began to eat in silence, determined to ignore the gaze Giselle had locked on him. When he couldn't stand it a moment longer, he looked up. "What?"

She simply smiled, one brow lifted, apparently amused at his aggravation. "That's more like it."

Jackson led his team to another win, beating the winner of the second game far too easily. After that blowout, the three other team captains converged to form one all-star team in order to give Jackson's team some competition.

By the time the game began, it was three o'clock in the afternoon. The temp had soared to a miserable one hundred degrees, with a heat index of around a hundred and seven due to humidity. The all-star team won the coin toss and lined up to bat. The first batter hit a double to center field. Jackson nodded in admiration as Todd landed safely on second.

"Alright, heads up gentlemen—and lady." He tipped his cap, acknowledging his catcher. "We have us a ballgame!"

The second batter hit a grounder to third and Clayton scooped it up but held it to keep the runner at second. The third hit a pop fly that Jackson easily caught. The one after that tipped a ball making it pop up. Sherri caught it for the second out and the cheering section went wild. Their next batter, Carrie's old buddy, J.C., hit a good, solid double, bringing one run in and leaving his team with runners on second and third. Their next man up hit a fast one straight up the middle, toward Jackson's face. His quick reflexes paid off as he caught it in his glove, saving himself a black eye, broken nose, or at the very least a busted lip.

Jackson's team performed beautifully at their first bat and by the time the second inning started, B & L's team took to the field with a solid 6-1 lead. The all-star team tightened up the score drastically in the next inning, pulling ahead by one.

By this time, every single one of the ball players was soaked with sweat. Jackson and Red walked over to the water faucet to drench their heads and upper bodies.

⚜

Giselle watched, in horrified amazement, as Jackson and Red removed their shirts and stuck them under the faucet.

"Oh my God," she murmured under her breath.

Carrie turned to her. "What's wrong?"

Giselle shook her head, sat back with arms crossed, and waited for the fallout. It wasn't more than a few seconds before she heard several women gasp as they saw the two men shirtless.

"Oh my God, would you look at that," Amanda murmured.

"Holy crap!" Tina leaned forward on the bleacher. "How long has Jackson been hiding *that* under those business suits and Polo shirts?"

Within seconds, every female in the park was drooling over Jackson and Red's bare, bronzed torsos. Giselle clenched her jaw as the 'oohs' and 'ahs' continued even after they wrung their shirts out and put them back on, causing steam to rise up from their heated bodies.

Jeanette leaned forward in her seat. "Carrie, who the hell is that guy with Jackson?"

"That's Scott McAllister, but everyone calls him 'Red'. He's from my hometown, and I used to babysit for him."

Jeanette's laughter rang out. "Lord have mercy, I'd like to babysit for him now."

Another woman murmured just loud enough for those around her to hear. "I'd like to have his baby."

That, in turn, lead to others chiming in.

"I'd have either one of their babies."

"Hell, I'd have *both* their babies."

Giselle leaned forward, placed her hands over her pounding temples, her jaw clenched so tightly she thought she'd break a tooth.

Carrie clucked her tongue. "Red might know, Giselle, but Jackson has no clue."

She faced her to ask what the hell she was talking about.

"Neither he nor his uncle have any idea how attractive they are to women. Not a drop of conceit in either of them." She leaned forward to whisper as the buzz of admiration grew to fevered pitch. "You can't very well blame them, can you? You'll just have to sweat this one out."

Giselle shook her head. "Not without a handful of aspirin."

Jackson and Red headed back to the dugout to wait their turns in the batting line-up. All the men followed their lead by drenching their heads and necks under the faucet. Hearing a buzz from the stands, Jackson turned to seek out Giselle's beautiful face. He found her all right; her face grim, tense, and looking like she was about to open up a can of whoop ass on someone. His stomach clenched at the sight of her rubbing her temples. His mind jumped to concerns of heat related illnesses. He pivoted, turning back to the stands. He caught her gaze as he neared. She shook her head and said something to Carrie before she jumped out of the bleachers and headed toward the parking lot. She was almost to her truck when he caught up to her.

"Giselle!" She stopped but didn't face him. He tugged gently on her arm to turn her. "Are you okay?"

"I have a headache."

Her tone stumped him. He couldn't tell if she was feeling ill or just annoyed. "Are you drinking enough water?"

"Yes. I'm not dehydrated, Jackson. It's just a headache."

"Do you have something to take?" He felt her forehead.

She nudged at his hand and pointed to her truck. "In my purse. Getting it now."

"You sure it's not heatstroke?"

"It's *not*. It's-it's probably just—stress."

"From what?"

She leveled her gaze on him. "Oh, for God's sake. Carrie's right. You have no idea!"

"About what?"

"Go, I'm fine." Giselle waved him off and continued to her truck.

Jackson stood there, his arms spread wide, totally stumped at her tone. "No idea about what?" His jaw dropped in shock as his sweet Giselle mumbled something and swore like a Marine. Confused as hell, he made his way back to the stands and paused next to Carrie's spot in the bleachers.

"Hey Carrie. Something's wrong with Giselle. Make sure she drinks enough water, would you?"

Carrie and her three daughters exchanged glances before dissolving into laughter. "She's fine, Jack. She's got to learn to adjust, that's all. She'll get over it."

"Adjust to what? Get over what?" Their amused snorts did nothing to ease his confusion.

"Go play ball, Jack," Carrie said, wiping tears of laughter from her eyes.

"Yeah, it's time to kick ass out there," Gretchen said.

"So we can go home," Lauren added.

"Because it's too damn hot out here!" Amanda threw in.

Jackson shook his head and started back to the field. He got about ten yards away from the stands when a loud whistle, followed by a woman's cat call, had him stopped in his tracks.

"Hey baby! I'd like to have that swing in my back yard!"

Jackson turned slowly, totally shocked that all eyes were on him. "What the hell?"

"Yep, I'm talking to you, good lookin'!" More feminine snickers followed the comment.

Jackson turned quickly back to the field, shaking his head as laughter erupted from the bleachers.

He entered the dugout, still somewhat in shock.

Red slapped him on the back. "What's the matter buddy?"

"I think I've just been sexually harassed." He grinned as everyone in the dugout gathered around.

"What did they say?" Sherri asked him.

"Um . . . Hey baby, I'd like to have that swing in my back yard." The dugout exploded with laughter.

Sherri snickered and shook her head. "Poor thing. Are you upset?"

"Should I be?" he asked as Sherri shrugged carelessly. "If any of us guys would have said that to you, they would have crucified us."

Sherri dropped her knee pads and catcher's mask on a bench inside the dugout. "Hey, if I'd have worn a wet tee shirt to play baseball, every damn one of y'all would have said I was asking for it, so get over it."

Red busted out laughing and slapped him on the back. "You just got burned!"

"I guess I did." He joined in the laughter as he turned to watch Giselle walk slowly back to the bleachers. She still rubbed her forehead as if she were in pain.

He put himself in her place, imagining how he'd feel if he had to sit through a bleacher full of men making lewd comments about *his* girlfriend. He winced inwardly, thinking he'd have had a massive migraine as well. Further contemplation had his frown turning into an ear splitting grin.

He chuckled, thinking this game couldn't end soon enough. Thankfully, the teams had decided to implement the ten-run rule, meaning if any team scored ten points more than the other, they'd call it a ballgame.

Jackson clapped his hands loudly. "Okay! I'm ready to get out of this heat. How about y'all?"

A round of affirmatives answered.

"Good! Get out there and hit the crap out of that ball. Let's score some points so we can all go home and cool off."

His pep talk must have hit the spot. They nearly made it through two complete rounds of their batting line up. His team was up by nine points, with two outs and the bases loaded. Jackson, highly motivated and primed for a much needed talk with Giselle, hit one out of the park. It ended the game with a satisfying, but energy draining 20 – 7 victory over the all-star team.

He walked off the field and caught up with Carrie and Sam at the faucet. Sam wet his bandana and used it to wipe his face and skull.

"Good game, Jack. You obviously haven't lost your skills."

"Thanks man. Hey, Giselle hasn't left yet, has she?"

Carrie grinned at him. "I don't think so. Wait, let me see that swing again."

"Your ass!" he threw over his shoulder.

"No, I believe it was *your* ass this time!" she said, her laughter following him out of the park.

He finally spotted Giselle standing at his Avalanche. The sight of her had his stomach cutting anxious somersaults. He approached, catching the girls picking out drinks from the two large ice chests in his truck bed.

Lexie saw him and jumped from the bed into his arms. "You did good, Jackson!"

He tossed her in the air, and gave her a kiss before setting her down. "Thanks, baby girl."

Mackenzie approached and gave him a one armed hug before wrinkling her nose in distaste. "Great game, Jackson. But pew-ee, you're all sweaty!"

"I know, but thanks Mac, that means a lot coming from a star player like you." Jackson pulled her just close enough to kiss the top of her head. He grabbed a bottle of water, twisted off the cap and gulped half of it down. "Man, that's good." He pulled a bandana out of his pocket and wet it with some of the cold water, and wiped his face. "Days like this make me miss wintertime."

"That was a good game. Congratulations," Giselle said.

"Thanks. How's the headache? Are you feeling better?"

"Some. It's still there, but not as bad. Ready, girls?"

He placed a hand on her shoulder. "Where are y'all headed?"

"Actually, I'm about to bring the girls over to Bill's to spend the night with Alyssa."

He leaned one hip against the truck bed and faced her. "Can you meet me at my house afterwards? I'd like to talk to you about something."

"Yeah, I guess I could do that. I want to catch up a little with Gwen and Bill, but I'll be there within the hour."

He nodded, pulling his shirt away from his sweat drenched torso. "Excellent. It'll give me a chance to get cleaned up. Thanks."

Red joined them, and Giselle stared at the two of them, giving her head a shake. "I see both your shirts have dried."

Jackson allowed himself to gloat just a little at her still visible signs of jealousy. "You do what you have to do to keep the body temp down." Her comeback was as sharp as any jab of a needle.

"I'll have to remember that. I can wear my *wet* T-shirt at next year's game. Better yet, I'll just come in my swimsuit."

Jackson sucked in his breath, getting a mental image of her barely there one-piece suit.

Red cleared his throat loudly. "I've got a club to run, so I need to pack up. Giselle, it was good to see you again." He leaned over to place a gallant kiss on Mac and Lexie's hands, making them giggle. "Little ladies, it was lovely to meet you."

Giselle gave him a quick hug. "Good to see you Red."

Jackson watched her departure while simultaneously helping Red load everything back into his truck.

Red's low chuckle got his attention . "I think she may be pissed at you for the shirt removal incident, bro."

"You took your shirt off, too. She didn't seem to be pissed at you." Jackson watched her Tucson pulling out of the park.

Red slammed his truck's tailgate and climbed inside the cab. "Could be because she's not in love with me."

Jackson turned his gaze on Red. "You think so?"

Red started his truck and nodded. "Yep, and it couldn't happen to two nicer people. Later, buddy."

Giselle pulled into Jackson's driveway in just under an hour. She entered the door he held open for her, still feeling a little miffed, though she'd tried to tell herself she was being silly.

"Did your headache go away?"

"Yes, finally." She winced at her snappish tone.

"Good, but listen up, Giselle—" He wagged his fingers back and forth between the two of them. "—this little arrangement of ours isn't working for me."

Her heart picked up a steady, uncontrollable pounding. "What do you mean?"

"I don't want to be friends with you," he said.

Giselle felt the icy fingers of panic creeping in and around her heart. She swallowed, biting back her fear. "I guess you can't help how you feel." How the hell was she pulling off this illusion of calm? Especially when all she wanted to do was scream, cry, beg him to reconsider. She walked sedately to the door, placed her hand on the knob. She felt the gentle touch of his hand on her arm, and turned, dreading his next words.

"I want to be with you, Giselle. I can't be around you and pretend that I don't." He closed his eyes and sighed. "I know what you're afraid of, but I'm begging you to reconsider. I only want you. So, what do you think?"

"Oh." Her breath released in a rush of relief. "I think maybe—we c-ccould try," she stammered.

His stance widened as he crossed his arms. "What does that mean?"

She pulled away, started a steady back and forth pacing in front of him. "Look, I spent all day at that park, first having to watch Lisa throw herself at you, and then later with all those women gawking and making comments." She stopped to face him. "God, it made me crazy!" She picked up the pacing again. "I had to keep my jaw clenched to keep from saying anything. That's how I got my headache. And you!" She turned and poked a finger in his solid chest. "Taking off your shirt like that in front of all those sex-starved women? The majority of those ladies live with men with pot bellies and bald heads. The only six packs they've seen in two decades are the ones in their refrigerators. What the hell, Jackson? What were you *thinking*?"

She shook her head at his smug grin, continued her ranting. "And then, as if the situation wasn't bad enough, once you put the wet shirt back on, there was *steam* coming off of your body. Honestly, it was like watching porn." She spread her hands out, remembering how helpless she'd felt at the time. "It just . . . it made me realize that I . . . I want you. All to myself," she finished, crossing her arms tightly to control her trembling.

Jackson had endured her tirade patiently, silently, one arm supporting his elbow and a hand covering his mouth. *Probably trying not to laugh his ass off at the situation.*

Slowly, he stepped forward to place both hands gently upon her shoulders. He dropped his gaze to hers. "Steam? Are you sure?"

She twisted her mouth in a crooked grin and nodded. "God, it was awful! You should have heard them." Her head fell forward.

He placed his hand on the back of her neck to pull her close, until her forehead rested on his chest. "So, does this mean we're a couple?"

She nodded, wrapping her arms around him. "If that tramp Lisa puts her hands on you again, you tell her you're taken."

"Or better yet, you can."

"I don't have a problem with that," she shot back.

His chest rumbled with laughter as he held her close, rocking her gently in his arms. "I'll tell her I already have the most beautiful girl in the world, and she's all I'll ever need."

She smiled, her face plastered against his broad chest. "You'd better."

"I thought it would take forever for you to come to me like this, baby."

She lifted her gaze to stare into those sexy eyes that invaded her dreams. "Jackson, I care about you so much. I just don't know about anything else yet."

"I know, but we have time for all that. Nothing but time." He gently lifted her chin and gave her one of those toe-curling kisses she'd been waiting for . . . All. Day. Long.

Chapter Twenty-Four

Giselle dropped off the girls at school and drove to Toby's old office. She knocked on Gordon's door, walked when his secretary said he was free.

Gordon moved around his desk to give her a bear hug. "Good to see you, Giselle!"

"You too. I'm sorry this took so long," she said. "I brought two big boxes. Do you think that'll be enough?"

"Probably—our boy didn't keep anything unless it was important to him. You think I could have a little something of his you're willing to part with?"

"Sure. By the way, I brought these for you."

He looked inside the bag she handed him, and grinned as he pulled out the caps. "Thanks Giselle; he did love those Tigers. I'll cherish them."

"Don't cherish them too much. He'd want you to wear them." Giselle entered Toby's office with the boxes and closed the door softly behind her. She stood in the center and pivoted slowly, regarding the area her husband had occupied for so long. She'd helped to decorate his home away from home, adding personal touches that said this was her husband's space. Everywhere she turned, she saw signs of Toby—with her—with their girls—with co-workers. Diplomas, certifications, awards, framed newspaper clippings of grand openings. Everywhere she looked she found more Toby.

Giselle only allowed herself a few minutes to get misty-eyed, before getting down to the business of packing his personal things. She began with the desk then worked her way around the room, methodically removing every trace of him from the walls, surfaces, and floors.

She examined the rack of rolled plans, all covered with a light layer of dust. She'd ask Gordon if she could keep them for her girls. Maybe one of them would follow in her father's footsteps. Even if they didn't, she wanted them to understand what he'd done for a living, how he'd provided for them. The very last set of plans she pulled from the rack turned out to be their proposed house plans. She unrolled it carefully, reverently, to study them. There were details in the floor plan that proved he'd listened to her suggestions; a room labeled *Giselle's craft/sewing room*, an area near the attached shed labeled *Giselle's potting bench*, etc. She smiled when she saw the notations in her husband's neat handwriting. Everything—every little thing they'd discussed, at one point or another, was here.

She wiped at her tear-filled eyes, sad that such a good man had been taken from this earth far too soon. "You did good, baby." She rolled up the set of plans, placed it carefully back into the tube, and placed it in a box. She surveyed the room. *That's it . . . I'm done here.*

She loaded the two boxes into her truck and pulled out a frame holding a shot she'd snapped of Toby and Gordon together when they'd all gone fishing in the gulf last summer. It was in a beautiful mahogany frame with a fishing theme, and she thought it would be just the thing to leave with Gordon. There was no one in his office, or at the secretaries' desk, so she went in and sat down to wait for him. She heard both secretaries return to their desks on the other side of the partition. She stood, intending to ask how long she'd have to wait to see Gordon, but the words from one of them carried through the open door, stopping her cold.

"Poor Giselle, do you think she knew?"

"No. There's no way. What was her name, anyway?"

"Chloe somebody, from Lake Coburn, I think."

"I remember Toby talking about a Chloe once. She was the wife of a friend of his from the gym—a Broussard, maybe? He called her 'Crazy Chloe'."

"That's it. Chloe Broussard. Her husband was a big, tall, good looking man. I saw them in that new restaurant in Lake Coburn once. She treated him awfully and caused a horrendous scene. He was so apologetic and polite but she was a flipping shrew. Honestly, some women are never satisfied."

"Some men either. Look at how gorgeous Giselle is. She and Toby always seemed so close. Are you *sure* he was sleeping around on her?"

"I saw them together with my own eyes about a month before he died. That tramp was wrapped around him like a stripe on a barber pole. Kept asking why he hadn't answered her email. One of those model skinny little blondes. Giselle is much prettier. Toby must have gone temporarily insane."

Thankfully, one of their phones rang and they both left to bring something to the meeting in progress. Weak and trembling, Giselle rose slowly from the corner chair—her stomach rolling with hurt and humiliation. She stood for a few moments, tying to steady herself. As soon as she could manage, she left the office through the back door, taking care to avoid any run ins with Toby's co-workers.

She sat in her vehicle, dazed and sick at heart. Toby and Chloe—having an affair. He wouldn't do that to her, would he? Her skin broke out into a cold, clammy sweat. A wave of nausea rolled over her. She fought it off, lowering her head onto the steering wheel until it passed. Fighting off tears, she made a mad dash to the cemetery. She threw her truck into park and ran to his grave, falling to her knees before the granite slab and headstone.

"How could you *do* that to me, Toby? To Jackson?" *Wrapped around him like a stripe on a barber's pole.* She placed one hand on her stomach as bile rose to her throat. She turned away from the stone, retching at the image of her husband with that vile woman. She faced the headstone, wiping her mouth.

"You son of a bitch. How could you?" She broke down, sobbing, crying bitter, devastated tears. Once the first wave passed she wiped her eyes and sat back on her heels. The secretary's comment about email had her recalling the small, leather bound pad she's seen. It held passwords to his various accounts, email and otherwise. Desperate to find information to disprove the accusation, she sped home and dug the book out of the box. She dropped in front of her computer and logged into Toby's local account. She typed his password with trembling fingers and hit the check mail button. The mailbox opened and

Giselle scanned the email. No message from Chloe. As a last resort she checked his recycle bin. Bingo. A discarded message from *Chloe3856-yolo.* She clicked to open, took a deep breath, and began to read.

Hello Lover-
Why haven't you emailed me? You know how I long to hear from you. Jackson still doesn't suspect a thing. That fool is absolutely clueless when it comes to my little indiscretions.
It was such luck running into you at the hotel. It made for a hell of an afternoon. I can't wait to do it again.
Catch you later lover,
Chloe

Giselle struggled for breath as the muscles in her chest constricted. "Oh God!" She pushed the mouse away and gasped, clutching at her chest where her heart was—where it would have been if her dead husband hadn't just broken it into a million little pieces. Tears streamed down her face as she struggled to collect herself. Blurry eyed and miserable, she managed to find the print button. She waited as the printer spit out the paper, folded it neatly and stuffed it in the pocket of her jeans. She grabbed her purse and keys, and hit the door. There was only one person in the world she could talk to about this. Only one other person who'd understand the depth of Toby's betrayal. She knew exactly where to find him.

Jackson pulled open his door, slightly surprised to see Giselle standing there. "Hey, Babe, you here to help me finish my deck?"

She took off her sunglasses, revealing puffy, red-rimmed eyes. "Did you know?"

"Know what? What's wrong?" He stepped forward and reached for her.

She avoided his grasp and walked around him. "Did you know about Toby and Chloe?"

"What about them?"

"They were having an affair. *My* husband and *your* wife."

Jackson stood there, shaking his head. "That's not possible." He reached for her and she skittered around, avoided him again.

"I overheard the secretary at his office say that she saw them at a hotel. She said Chloe was all over him. Did. You. Know?"

He forced himself to remain calm, wondered how far he'd have to go to prove her wrong. "That never happened, Giselle."

"Yes, it did. I have the proof!" She pulled the email print out from her pocket.

He read it and shook his head. "No, Toby was always faithful to you. I guarantee it. Oh, Chloe tried, but he turned her down. He's one of a select few of my so-called friends who did turn her down. She set Red up years ago, and he turned her down, too. She hated him for it, of course, and she hated me for believing him. I was stupid enough to choose her over his friendship, and that's why she wouldn't allow him to be a part of my life for so long and why she destroyed anything of mine that pertained to LSU. Red was a part of it."

"But I've got proof."

"This?" He shook his head and flicked at the print out. "All you've got here is the ravings of a lunatic who'd do anything she could to set someone up. She was counting on you to find this and jump to the wrong conclusion."

Giselle began to pace the floor in an agitated path. "I don't believe that. I'm so stupid. The last person to know. I keep thinking of him in that hotel room with Ch-Chloe and I just can't stand it. I could kill him if he was standing in front of me. I swear I could. I c-can't believe he'd do that to me, Jackson." She stopped, slapped her hands over her chest. "I'm so h-hurt that he'd do that to me. And to you, too. He claimed to love you like a brother. He did this to both of us." Her tears spilled over her lashes onto her cheeks. "He-he didn't think of his daughters. How can I talk to them about their father now? How can I do that without them sensing how hurt—how *angry* I am?" One agonizing sob escaped, then another. "I just don't understand it. I don't understand h-how C-Chloe even knew him. We didn't hang around the same circles. The only common denominator is you. H-he must have wanted her badly to do that to b-both of us."

Jackson took her in his arms, cradling her tightly. "Baby, please believe me. It never happened. I don't know what that woman saw, probably Chloe just doing what she did best. Believe me when I tell you that behavior was normal for her. But Toby would never have done that to you. You and those girls were everything to him. I swear to you, Giselle, he loved the three of you too much to jeopardize that."

She ripped the print out from his hands. "I know he d-did it! This email verifies that woman's story, Jackson. She emailed him and c-called him her l-lover. He d-did it! He did! And I hate him for it!"

Jackson pulled her close as she collapsed into tears. He rested his chin on her head and closed his eyes, as he listened to her heart-broken sobs. He couldn't stand by and see her in this kind of misery if he could prove Toby's innocence. Thanks to Chloe's letter . . . he could. Maybe—just maybe—he could convince her without actually showing it to her.

"Sit. I need to tell you something," he said, seating her gently on his sofa and kneeling before her. "Do you remember me telling you about a letter that Chloe left with our lawyer?"

She nodded. "V-vaguely."

"Well in that letter she talked about how she tried to get Toby to sleep with her, but that he wouldn't do it. She even said she followed him to that hotel and tried to set him up, but that he still wouldn't do it. She said he was the only one of my friends who hadn't. It was in the letter. Believe me."

Hope shined in her eyes. "Do you st-ill have the letter?"

Jackson squeezed his eyes shut. Why the hell had he kept it? Why hadn't he thrown it out? "Giselle, please. Just trust me. Take my word for it. Toby was faithful—always."

She sobbed again. "If I could just s-s-see the letter, J-Jackson. P-p-please!"
"Giselle—"
"If you have proof I n-need to s-see it. P-pl-lease!" she sobbed.

Here it was, the reason he'd kept Chloe's letter. For this very moment. To keep his dead bitch of a wife from hurting this woman with more of her lies. He nodded, knowing there was no way around this. Praying for the best, he pulled his wallet from his pocket, removed the letter and began to unfold it slowly.

She extended her hand and he pulled it out of her reach. "I need to tell you something first." He sat beside her, rested his elbows on his knees. "It's my fault that she tried so hard to get Toby to sleep with her. She hated you, Giselle." He winced at the ugly words, more so because he knew the absolute truth of them. "She hated you because of me."

Giselle shook her head. "That doesn't make any s-sense, Jackson."

Jackson reached up to brush the tears gently off of her face with his thumb and nodded. "It will." He handed her the letter and waited as she began to read.

Jackson-

If you're reading this, then I suppose I've keeled over somehow. Hopefully in the middle of hot sex with anyone but you. I never planned on going before you. I planned on you dying first and making me a very wealthy widow. I'd be able to spend your money any way I wanted without your oh-so-tiresome 'suggestions' as to what I should do with it.

Now that I have your undivided attention, I want you to know one thing. I never loved you. You were a means to an end and a constant source of entertainment. I never wanted children. Not yours. Not anyone's. I was not about to ruin my body by carrying around a growing lump for nine months. I've been on the pill for years. Shocked? I hope so. I do love it when I can shock you. You were getting desensitized to my actions. It was getting more and more difficult to shock you over the years. But, I digress. I just used getting my period every month as a handy excuse to perform the little act that I've perfected over the years. Tearing my hair out. Wailing about how unfair it was that I couldn't have a child to love. Keeping you desperate to console me.

I played you, Jackson, and you never even knew it.

I've slept with nearly all of your friends, and they enjoyed it. I even slept with your best man during our wedding reception. I bet you didn't know that, did you? Tanner Collins has proven to be of much use to me over the years. It's been quite a challenge to keep both you and his fiancé in the dark. Challenging, but such fun. There have only been two fish that wouldn't bite for me. Only two of your friends. That low class nobody, Red McAllister, and Toby Granger. I can't abide Red. He's always seen through me, and hated what he saw. That's why he had to go. Not even to hurt you could I swallow my hatred enough to sleep with that piece of small town white trash.

As for Toby, I've tried to lure him in countless times; I emailed him, called him, followed him, even to a hotel once to try and set him up, but still nothing. He stayed loyal to that cow Giselle—I hate that simpering little fool—and he stayed loyal to you, although I have no idea why he'd do that. Especially knowing what I know about you.

Giselle clasped the letter to her heaving chest and cried out. Her head fell back in utter relief, as she finally got the proof that Toby had remained faithful.

He reached for the letter, praying she'd give it back without reading the rest of it. She gazed up at him, looking so relieved, and he thought for a moment she would—and she'd never have to know the truth. Then he saw it. The question. The *why* of it, and knew she wouldn't stop until she had the entire story.

Jackson cringed as her head dropped to read the rest.

Did you think I didn't know? That's why I tried to get her husband to sleep with me. Because of your feelings for her. But they seem inseparable. The silver lining about all this is the fact that if I'll never have him, then you'll never have her. Ain't love grand, Jackson? That being said, it's still a mystery to me. How can one stupid, clueless woman have, not one, but two men madly in love with her? It boggles the mind.

Well, Jackson, it's been a pleasure screwing with your head. I guess I should say something about what I want done with my remains. I don't want any kind of church service and I sure as hell don't want anyone gawking over my poor dead body. Have me cremated and have my ashes sent to my mother in California.

I hope you never forget me. I hope you're tortured by the knowledge that you've wasted nearly half your life trying to please a woman whose greatest joy was to make you miserable.

See you in hell, loser!

Chloe

She lowered the letter, smoothed it flat, then refolded it. Jackson took a deep breath and prepared for the questions he knew were coming. He could practically see them forming in her mind. He didn't have to wait long.

"Is this true?"

He nodded.

"But, we were so happy, Jackson," she whispered.

He stood and turned away from her. "I know that. Believe me, had Toby lived, you never would have found out. Not by me, anyway. I couldn't help the way I felt."

"Why? When I treated you the way I did back then?"

Jackson stood, walked away from her. He ran his hands through his hair then turned to face her. "I don't know why. One day you put me in my place for something, and instead of irritating the hell out of me like you usually did, I realized I admired you for it. I'd watch you when you told stories about the girls and your eyes would light up. I didn't even know Toby at the time, but I was envious of the relationship you had with him. I'd see pictures of your family, and I wanted that life so badly, but one day I realized I didn't want it with Chloe, or any other woman. I wanted it with you—only with you."

"But, what about after you met Toby?"

He locked his gaze on his own feet. "After I met Toby, I knew why you were so happy with him. That man adored you and the girls. I met him at Carrie and Sam's one day and we immediately hit it off. I didn't *want* to pal around with him. It was strange at first. Too weird. Too damn depressing, knowing he had the only woman I wanted. But he kept pushing me, and I finally caved in. Toby became like a brother to me. I thought that being so close to him would change my feelings for you, but it didn't. After the accident, when I made my way to your truck and saw him—" He stopped, swallowed the lump in his throat. "When I saw he didn't make it, and you did, I knew how devastated you'd be. I couldn't walk away from you and the girls. I had to try to help you in some way." He wiped at his eyes.

She'd risen from the couch and walked over to him. "It must have been difficult for you. I was so awful to you."

"I couldn't stay away. I loved you too much, Giselle."

She looked up at him with tears streaming down her face. "Does anyone else know?"

"The only person I ever told was Red a couple of years ago. Carrie and Uncle Bill said they've known for years."

"Years?" She shook her head. "How did they know?"

This conversation was too much. He lifted both hands, tried to think of a decent answer, then let them fall helplessly to his sides. Overwhelmed by a sense of frustration and helplessness, he shook his head. "I don't know I. Don't. Know. I sure as shit never told them. All I know is that I felt bad for myself for losing my friend. You cannot imagine how confusing that was for me. Toby was a good man."

"He was," she sobbed. "And I should have had enough faith in him not to doubt that. I'm sorry Jackson."

He finally allowed himself to relax. "You don't have anything to apologize for." He reached for her, grasped air instead when Giselle backed away from his touch.

"But I do. I've rushed into this thing with you, and I shouldn't have."

Dread washed over him like a giant tidal wave. "Don't say that, Giselle."

She shook her head. "When I thought Toby had been unfaithful to me, I was so shocked that a man who'd been dead for eight months could still break my heart. I was devastated, and surprised, because I thought I was over him. Now I know that I'm not. The truth is, I don't know if I ever will be."

His hand came up to stop the words. "Don't! Don't do what I think you're doing. Please." He reached for her.

She took another step away from him, toward the door. "I feel so bad for not giving him the benefit of the doubt. For not trusting him. I owe him this, Jackson. I owe him. . ."

He shook his head, panic taking hold of him. "You owe it to Toby to be happy. He'd want that for you. I knew him, too. I loved him, too, Giselle. Both Toby and Red. They're the brothers I never had."

Tears flowed freely down her face, dripped off her nose and chin onto his bare floors. "I don't think I can do this right now. I'm sorry Jackson, I have to go. I have to get out of here."

"Giselle." He grabbed her hand when she tried to leave. He squeezed his eyes tightly shut before he pleaded with her one last time. "Please don't do this. Don't ask me to live without you. I can't go back to that."

"Don't try to stop me. I can't think like this." She pulled her hand from his and backed away from him. She paused just long enough to give him one last miserable look. "I'm so sorry." She left him then, closing the door behind her.

Jackson heard her drive away. Still, he stood with feet planted, both fists clenched, for a full, torturous five minutes after she left him. He stared at the door, hoping if he stared at it long enough, she'd walk back through to tell him she'd made a mistake.

Finally, he accepted that she wouldn't.

His one chance at happiness had just walked out of his life. Maybe for good. What kind of cruel God could let him see and experience that kind of happiness, only to pull it out of his grasp again? The same kind of God who had ripped Giselle's world in two when he'd taken Toby from her.

His mind flooded with memories of her and her girls. Ballgames, movies, yard work, sharing pizzas and chicken nuggets. He thought of the time he had spent alone with Giselle. Dancing, swimming, riding the Indian, and holding her beautiful body, kissing her beautiful mouth. Giselle—laughing, in pain, angry, and her eyes flashing with jealousy. Giselle—passionate, eyes closed, head thrown back in pleasure. How could he possibly go back to being alone when he'd already experienced a part of that life that he'd craved for so long? He couldn't.

He fell to his knees, pain slicing through his heart. "Oh God, please. Don't let her do this." Finally, he stood, drained of energy, his soul heavy with sadness. He gazed around at his silent, empty house through eyes a shade darker with sorrow. He had to get out of here. He'd suffocate if he spent another moment in this house alone. Grabbing his bike keys from the wall rack, he entered the garage, pushed the button to open the door and mounted his bike. He started it, buckled his helmet and headed out, hoping to outrun the pain. Out to the street. Out toward the edge of the city. Out past Uncle Bill's ranch. To the back roads where he could open up the Indian without with no other traffic. He turned onto the last route he and Giselle had ridden and accelerated. Kept accelerating until he felt the icy grip on his heart lessen with the increasing force of the wind blowing in his face.

Jackson saw the sharp curve up ahead in plenty of time, backed off the throttle. What he didn't see was the object blocking the narrow roadway, smack dab in the center of the curve. He tried to avoid the cow, but hit it with a force that sent him flipping through the air toward the grassy pasture. Completely airborne, a solitary thought crossed his mind.

At least he wouldn't have to live without his three girls.

Chapter Twenty-Five

Giselle shook with sobs the entire trip home, her heart racing with mixed emotions. On the one hand, relief that Toby had been faithful. On the other, racked with guilt over what she'd been so ready to believe of him. How could she have lost faith in her husband so easily? In her thirteen year marriage so quickly? Then there was the utterly hopeless situation with Jackson.

She let herself inside and walked straight to her bathroom to rinse her face and soothe her swollen eyes. She studied the reflection staring back at her. The bright yellow shirt she wore seemed too cheerful, a total contradiction of what she felt. She'd been such a fool to believe she could build a future with Jackson so soon after losing Toby.

Most people didn't find happiness like that once in a lifetime. It was too much to hope to find it twice. It wasn't allowed. She'd never done a thing to deserve being that happy. She was lucky as hell that Toby had walked into her life and had been her perfect fit.

And poor Jackson. First he'd been saddled with Chloe, and then had the misfortune of falling in love with a woman who couldn't be happy with anyone but her husband.

But she *had* been happy for a short time, when she believed she could move on. But, she couldn't yet, could she? He said he loved her, and that he had for years. *Don't ask me to live without you. I can't go back to that.* His tortured plea came back to her, caused a sick feeling in the pit of her stomach. Surely, he wouldn't do anything crazy. Would he?

She lifted her bedroom's landline phone, and dialed his home number. No answer. The voice mail beeped.

"Jackson, please call me when you get this."

Giselle dialed his cell phone. No answer. She left the same message on that one, trying to sweep aside a feeling of dread. She stopped her pacing and headed for her truck. *Keep busy, Giselle.*

She hauled the boxes from Toby's office into the house. *Stay busy—do something productive.* Seating herself at the dining room table, she began to go through the contents, sorting the objects, placing books in one pile, pictures in one, knick-knacks in another, etc. She pulled out his daily planner and thumbed through it, saw nothing of importance. Something to keep for the girls. She dropped it into a large manila envelope that had been inside his bottom desk drawer, caught sight of something at the bottom of it. She pulled out a snapshot and nearly stopped breathing.

Toby and Jackson stared back at her. Both sweaty and holding a basketball between the two of them. Toby's brown eyes crinkled with laughter as one hand gripped the brim of the old, faded LSU cap, the one Jackson had been so anxious to have.

Her hand flew to her mouth, biting back a sob. She collapsed in a chair, flipped the photo over to see Toby's scrawl on the back.

Me and Jackson, after whipping his ass in hoops again, thanks to my lucky cap. They don't make men any better than Jack! I'd trust him with my life.

"Oh Toby." She traced the photo with one finger. She studied his features for a moment, the coal black hair and warm eyes she'd found comfort in for years. God, she'd loved that man. Her eyes traveled to Jackson's image, not as buff as he was now, and paler. Despite the smile on his face, she detected the old familiar signs of stress and strain. Most certainly a by-product of life with Chloe.

But that Jackson had long since gone. She pictured him laughing with her girls, holding their hands, and helping them with baseball, school work, yard work. Helping Lex to ride her bike for the first time while she recorded the event.

She picked up her phone and viewed a picture she'd taken of him, Mac, and Lexie last weekend. They'd fallen asleep on her couch watching a movie together. Mac was curled up in front of Jackson, while Lex lay sprawled out on his hip, using him as her personal recliner. He'd wrapped one arm protectively around her so she wouldn't fall. All three were sound asleep. She hadn't had the chance to show anyone this picture, not even them. A sudden thought filled her with panic. *What if he never got to see it?*

Giselle held the phone to her chest. She cried then. For Toby, and for all the things he'd miss in his daughters' lives. For Jackson, who was somewhere, miserable and alone, thinking there was no hope for them. She cried for herself, for being such a fool.

Minutes later, she wiped her eyes, felt free, lighter than she had since Toby had left this world. She knew she'd love him forever, but also faced the undeniable fact that she did love Jackson. And her love for him was every bit as strong as it had been for her husband.

Jackson. Oh God. Where was he?

She pictured his tortured face, heard his tormented words. She felt sick inside from what she had done to him. She'd caused him such pain, and she had to take it back. She had to make it right.

She hit redial, getting the same result. At the voice mail prompt, she took a deep breath. "Jackson, I love you. Call me. I'm on my way to you. Please call me."

His cell number rang without an answer. Giselle picked up the photo, placed it carefully inside her purse. She grabbed her keys, and headed back to Lake Coburn.

She pulled into the driveway, relieved to see his truck parked inside the garage. A second later, she realized, no bike. That *could* explain why he didn't answer his cell. She tested the door to the utility room; it opened for her and she walked inside Jackson's home. Everything was exactly as it had been less than two hours earlier. Her gut twisted suddenly. Everything was *exactly* the same. Keys on counter, along with a bank statement and a couple of bills, his door unlocked, garage door opened. So not Jackson. She checked her watch . . . 11:00 a.m. Where was he?

Where would he have gone? She attempted to sit, to wait, but felt this desperate need to search for him. Find him. She called Bill. It rang twice before he picked up.

"Bill, this is Giselle. Is Jackson with you?"

"No, he isn't. Is something wrong?"

"Yes. No. I don't know for sure. Maybe it's nothing. I'm here at his house; his bike is missing and his house was unlocked, the garage door left opened, his truck and house keys left on the cabinet. All the things he'd never do."

"I don't think it's reason to worry."

She took a deep breath, thinking she'd better explain. "I left here about two hours ago. It's a long story, but I told him I couldn't see him anymore, Bill. I've realized how foolish that was, and I came back to tell him. He's not answering his phone. I don't know, but I've got a bad feeling. I think he needs help. Can you help me find him?"

"Sure honey. I bet he's just riding somewhere around here to clear his head. Why don't you come meet me?"

"I will. Start looking right away. I'll check some roads we've ridden on going toward your place."

She found a tablet to leave Jackson a note in case he came home. She wrote:

Jackson,
Everything I said was a mistake. I love you!
Giselle

She placed it on the table where he'd see it immediately. She ran out, filled with a dread that he'd never get a chance to see it. She drove to Bill's, using the same route they had, turning off on back roads instead of taking the highway. No luck. Within half an hour, she turned into Bill's driveway. She'd just hit the redial button to call him when she saw his truck turning in to the drive. She slid out of her vehicle with her purse, keys, and phone in hand. As soon as Bill's truck pulled to a stop she climbed inside with him. "Anything?"

"Not a thing. He doesn't answer for me, either." He headed back down the drive. "You know, he may be just riding and can't hear his phone."

She twisted nervously at her fingers. "He needs help, Bill. I know it. I can *feel* it. What's worse is that he doesn't know yet." She wiped an escaped tear from her face.

"Doesn't know what, hon?"

"That I love him. I love him so much, and I want to marry him. I want to have his babies, and I want us to be a family. One big, happy family." She shook her head anxiously. "Wherever he is, he's thinking there's no hope for us." She covered her eyes and pictured the tortured expression on Jackson's face when she walked out on him earlier. "When I left him, he was devastated,

Bill. He begged me not to walk away from him, and I did. I hurt him so badly.
I'm such a fool."

Bill laid a comforting hand on her arm. "Things will work out, you'll see."

"Where could he be?" She dug in her purse for a tissue, picked up the
picture and held it close, silently asking Toby to help her if he could. She
closed her eyes and concentrated, picturing their last bike ride and one of the
places they had stopped one morning.

"He and I went riding the other day and there was this pond. There were
cattle and a few head of horses grazing in a pasture, and ducks and geese that
stay there year round. Do you know where that is? Have you checked there
yet?"

"I know what you're talking about and I haven't checked there, but it's only
about five miles from here. Do you have reason to believe he's there?"

"No, it's just a feeling." She put her head down. "Oh God, keep him safe,"
she whispered, clutching the snapshot to her heart.

"What is that you have there?" Bill asked.

"I cleaned out Toby's office this morning and found this in an envelope. I'll
never forgive myself if . . ." Her voice trailed off, leaving the dreaded thought
unspoken.

Bill reached over and put a hand on her shoulder. "He'll be all right,
Giselle. He's strong."

She lowered her head and hot tears fell from her eyes. "But he's so alone.
And he thinks he'll stay that way."

Bill studied the snapshot with one hand. "The time stamp says this was
taken on February 28th. That's Jackson's birthday."

"That's right, it is," Giselle said.

"We'll find him, don't worry. Okay, this is the road."

"I remember it! How far is it to the end?"

"About six miles, but the pond is a couple of miles up."

She pointed at something on his dash. "Is this a GPS?"

Bill nodded. "If he needs help, they'll find us."

They stopped talking so they could keep watch for any sign of Jackson's
bike. They'd both been scanning either side of the roadside ditches when
Giselle turned to face the front just in time to see the dead cow on the road.
"Look out!"

He had to slam on his brakes and skidded off toward one of the ditches to
avoid hitting it. The truck came to a jerking halt. "Are you okay?"

Giselle didn't answer, just pointed at the ditch and jumped out of the truck.
She ran to the twisted heap of metal that had been Jackson's motorcycle. "He's
here somewhere, Bill!" She called his name every few seconds as she and Bill
began to search through the pasture's waist high grass.

You're in deep shit here, man. His injuries were that serious. He'd
managed to lift his head the first time he gained consciousness, just long
enough to see the compound fracture of his right leg—the bone protruding

nastily through the skin. He couldn't move his left arm, so he suspected it was broken, as well. Or dislocated. Or both. He knew better than to try to move but his symptoms—dizziness, the severe ache in his head, and blurred vision—scared the caution right out of him. With a good chance of a concussion, maybe even some swelling of the brain, he needed help. He'd worn his cap-style helmet. Could picture Giselle fussing at him, telling him it didn't offer nearly enough protection. It had taken the brunt of the initial impact, but had flown off after that.

He closed his eyes. Dreamed of Giselle—she was calling to him. Speaking tender words. "Where are you, baby? Please, answer me, I love you so much," she said. The dream seemed so real he opened his one good eye.

Something yellow moved through the tall grass toward him. Bright yellow. The sun? It couldn't be, it was moving too fast and making too much noise.

"Jackson!"

Not a dream. She was here. Giselle was here, and looking for him. His mouth went dry. He tried to answer but no words came out. Afraid she would leave without seeing him, he struggled to raise the arm that wasn't broken. It took all he had, but he finally did it. Please God. Let her see.

Giselle saw movement from the corner of her eye and saw him. "He's here!" She ran to him, turned just long enough to scream at Bill. "Get Air Med out here. Hurry!"

She kneeled down next to the bent and broken body of the man she loved, struggling not to cry. "Jackson! Oh my God, can you hear me baby? Can you hear me? Oh Jesus—look at you!"

He tried to say something, but no sound came out, gazing at her through the one eye that wasn't swollen shut.

"It's okay, baby! We're here now and help is coming. Listen to me, Jackson. I love you, and you have to come through this so you can marry me. Do you hear me? I love you!" She kissed him gently on the cheek that wasn't swollen. She thought she felt him squeeze her hand.

Bill approached, and the look on his face was almost more than Giselle could bear. She knew it was bad, but Bill's expression told her it was even worse than she thought. The compound fracture was bad enough with the jagged bone protruding through the skin. But his head, good God—his head injury looked extremely bad No telling what kind of internal injuries or bleeding going on inside him.

Bill kneeled next to his nephew. "I called in the GPS location. They'll bring them right to us."

"How long, Bill?"

He shook his head. "She said it'd be within six minutes. Jackson's strong, hon. If anybody can survive this, it's him."

She held his good hand and scanned his battered body, inventoried the injuries, known and unknown. *If* anyone can.

All they could do was be there for him. Talk to him, assure him. They did that, for five more agonizing minutes before they heard the Air Med helicopter's approach. Bill stood and waved his arms.

Giselle gave Jackson's hand one last squeeze before she moved aside to let the medics do their work. It took another couple of minutes to stabilize and load him into the chopper.

She leaned over to the man she loved and fought to keep from crying in front of him. "Jackson, you have to be strong now. Don't you give up. I love you! Fight for us. Do you hear me? Fight for us!" She turned to the nearest medic. "Where are you taking him?"

"The trauma center at St. Luke's is the best around. They're already waiting for him."

She and Bill ran back to the truck. She made phone calls while Bill broke every speeding law in the books. She called Carrie and Gwen, then Gretchen, Lauren, and Amanda. She thanked Amanda for offering to collect Mac and Lexie from the bus and take them to her place. After ending that call she turned to Bill. "Do you have Red's number?"

"I think Jackson programmed it in my phone for me."

She pulled up his contact list, found his name, and hit call.

"Red . . ." That's all she could manage before the lump in her throat stopped her from speaking. She handed the phone to Bill.

"Red, it's Bill Broussard. Jackson wrecked his bike. It's serious; he's got a bad head injury, a compound leg break, and surely some internal injuries."

"What the hell happened?"

"As far as we can tell, he hit a cow on one of these back roads around my place. The cow's dead, the bike's totaled, and it looks like Jackson flew about thirty feet into a pasture. I don't think he hit the pavement, and the pasture was pretty thick with tall grass. Maybe that softened the impact some. I didn't see a helmet, did you, Giselle?"

"Yes, it was that half helmet that he likes to wear. It must have flown off," she said, between sobs.

"Listen, I'll leave here in about five minutes. What hospital?"

"St. Luke's on South Ryan."

"I'll see you there. Put Giselle back on the phone."

Bill handed her the phone. "He wants to talk to you."

"Red?" she sobbed.

"You listen to me, hon. He's strong and he loves you. He'll be fine. I know he will."

"He has to be. I can't—" She bit back another sob. "I can't lose him, Red."

"You won't. I'll see you in an hour or so."

Before Bill's truck rolled to a stop, Giselle had jumped out and sprinted to the door of the hospital. She ran to the information desk. "Jackson Broussard was just brought here by Air Med. Bad motorcycle accident. We're his family. Can you give me us information?"

"Yes ma'am, they're prepping him for emergency surgery on the sixth floor. There's a waiting room up there."

"Thank you." Giselle turned in time to see Carrie rushing through the doors. "Sixth floor, Carrie. He's going into surgery soon."

Carrie took Bill's arm while they waited for the elevator. "How bad, Bill."

"It's serious." He described the injuries. "The medics suspected brain swelling from the head injury."

She seemed to take it in stride, nodded and turned to Giselle. "He's a strong man. He'll be fine, you'll see."

They took the elevator to the waiting room and began the long, agonizing wait for information on the man they all loved in different ways.

Giselle opened her purse. She rummaged around, growing more and more frantic. "Where is it?"

Bill pulled something out of his shirt pocket and held it out to her. "Maybe you're looking for this."

"Oh, thank you!" She hugged the snapshot to her. "I was afraid I'd lost it."

Carrie leaned forward. "What do you have there?" She inhaled sharply at the picture Giselle held up. "I took that—right before I told them they were stinking up my house. I'd forgotten I'd given one to Toby. It wouldn't have helped to give one to Jackson. He'd have had to hide the damn thing." She covered her mouth and suppressed a sob. "What happened, Giselle?"

"It's my fault, Carrie. If I hadn't put off cleaning out Toby's office for so long, none of this would have happened. I wouldn't have overheard the conversation I heard this morning."

"What conversation?" Once Giselle had filled them both in, Carrie put her two cents in. "That's ridiculous! Toby would never have done that."

"I know that now, but I guess I went a little crazy," Giselle admitted. "Besides, Jackson let me read the letter Chloe left him and it proved he didn't sleep with her."

"You read the letter?"

Giselle nodded. "It explained a lot of things. Like why Chloe was after Toby in the first place."

Carrie paused a moment before asking. "She knew Jackson was in love with you, didn't she? Of course she did. She was a mean little bitch, but she wasn't stupid." She glanced over at Bill. "If the two of us could tell, she had to have known."

Bill nodded as he took the photo from Carrie and studied it, even reading the back. "I'm sorry I never met him, he sounds like a wonderful man."

Giselle turned tear-filled eyes on him. "He was every bit as wonderful as Jackson is."

"This is a sign, you know, a sign that Jackson's going to pull through." He smiled down at her. "Jackson loves you and those girls more than anything. He'll fight like hell to live."

"He has to, Bill." Giselle allowed herself a final sniff, then wiped her eyes free of tears. She lifted her chin. "I will *not* lose Jackson."

He smiled and pulled her to him for a hug. "There's the spunky girl that Jackson fell in love with."

"How did you both know?" Her gaze bounced from Bill to Carrie. "He said the two of you have known for years."

Bill's eyes sparkled with laughter. "His eyes lit up every time he talked about something you did to put him in his place at the office. One day I asked him why he didn't apologize to you and be done with the whole business. He said it was worth keeping you pissed off at him just to see your beautiful green eyes flash with anger. That's when I knew he was in love with you."

Giselle turned expectantly to Carrie. "And you?"

Carrie sniffed then sighed loudly. "One day at the office you were telling Joan, Barbara, Tina, and Catherine a story about your girls. I think it was when Mac tied Lex up to your four poster bed in a sheet and told you to bring her back to wherever you got her."

"I remember. We were standing around Joan's desk. After I finished the story, I saw him leaning in the doorway of his office drinking a cup of coffee. I expected him to fuss at me for keeping everyone from their work."

Carrie shook her head sadly. "He was listening. I caught him watching you before you noticed him. The look on his face was so intense. I could almost hear him thinking how badly he wanted that, and suddenly I knew he wanted it with you. I started to pay closer attention after that, and all the signs were there. He was in love with you. There he was, trapped in that mess with Chloe, and he knew how happy you and Toby were. Then Toby and he became such good friends. He probably figured he could keep his feelings hidden as long as you weren't speaking to him." She released a long sigh. "Looking back on it, I wonder how he managed to put one foot in front of the other some days."

"When you've never had it, you don't miss it," Bill said. "They had a decent year of courtship together, but it blew up a couple of nights before the wedding. He had to choose her over his best friend. It didn't take him long to realize he chose wrong. Chloe knew it too, and never let him forget it. That was one sadistic little tramp."

Carrie shook her head. "He never lost Red as a friend, Bill. They got together every chance they could. Red always understood."

"It ate at Jackson. I don't know how he put up with her."

They turned, as a tall, blonde man in green scrubs walked into the waiting room through the surgery doors. "Excuse me. Is someone here for Jackson Broussard?"

Giselle jumped up to meet him. "We are."

Bill stuck his hand out. "I'm his Uncle, Bill Broussard."

"Of course, you look just like him," the doctor said. "Mr. Broussard, I'm Dr. Collins. I used to play ball with Jackson at LSU. An old teammate of ours called to ask if I could get some info to you. Scott McAllister?"

"Oh, Red—God bless him!" Carrie said. "What can you tell us? Are you his surgeon?"

"No, but I'll be watching to see what's going on and I'll come in here periodically to keep all of you informed."

Giselle stepped forward. "What can you tell us now?"

"He's got a compound fracture of the right tibia—that's the shin bone, a fracture of his left arm, and they're seeing some internal bleeding that needs to be taken care of. The most serious injury is his head. There's swelling in the temporal lobe of his brain. We don't know what's causing it yet, but they're going to remove a piece of the skull to relieve the pressure. Once they open him up, they'll be able to trace the bleeder and take care of it. After that's under control, they'll tend to the other injuries. This should take several hours, so don't get discouraged if the surgery goes on longer than expected. The good news is Jackson's in excellent shape and his heart is strong."

Giselle nodded. "Thank you so much."

Dr. Collins nodded and left the room.

Carrie touched her shoulder. "You see? It's because of you that he's in such good shape. If you hadn't made him so crazy, he wouldn't have gone to that gym every day. It was fate."

Giselle gave her a tight smile. "Maybe so, but it's also because of me that he's in here today."

Sam and Gwen arrived, swelling their numbers to five. After another thirty minutes, Giselle stood "I'm going to find the chapel." She raised her phone. "Call if there's any word."

She exited the elevator on the first floor, saw Red standing at the information desk. She called to him and he met her with an open armed hug. "Oh God, I'm so glad you're here."

"How is he, Giselle? Have you heard anything yet?"

"Dr. Collins came in and told us to expect a long wait." She explained the injuries and procedures as best she could. "He's a mess, Red. I don't know how long he'd been in that pasture, but he must have suffered horrendously."

"Is there a cafeteria or someplace we can talk?"

"I was about to go to the chapel—it's through this door." They entered the vacant chapel and knelt in front of the cross hanging on the wall. They made the sign of the cross and bowed their heads. After a few moments, the silence and solitude overwhelmed Giselle. She covered her face and began to cry openly, her shoulders shaking with uncontrollable sobs.

Red leaned over and hugged her tightly. "Just cry and get it out of your system. He'll need you to be strong."

"It's him that's going to need strength. If you'd seen him you'd know what I'm talking about. He must have been in unbelievable pain, and he was so alone. Before they loaded him into the helicopter, I told him he had to be strong and that he had to fight for us because I love him so much. He squeezed my hand." She looked up hopefully. "Do you think he heard me?"

Red nodded. "I know he did. That man has the constitution of a bull. I'm telling you, I've never seen him want anything as badly as he wants a life with you. He loves you, and I promise he'll do whatever it takes to get back to you."

Giselle jumped when her cell phone rang. She pushed the button. "Red and I are on our way, Carrie."

They entered the surgical waiting room at a run. "What's going on, Dr. Collins?"

"They've removed part of the skull and found a subdural hematoma inside the temporal lobe," the doctor said, before explaining the procedure for correcting the situation to the group. "It'll take a few days to know whether or not there's been enough significant damage to cause loss of function."

Giselle, more sure than she had been of anything in her life before, knew he'd be fine. "There won't be."

The doctor looked at Red and held out his hand. "Scott."

Red stared stonily at him for a few moments before extending his. "Tanner."

Their cold reception surprised Giselle. She had expected the usual round of backslapping between old friends; it seemed as if these two men barely tolerated each other's presence.

Dr. Collins assured them he'd speak to them again as soon as he knew more, and exited the room.

Red turned to Carrie and hugged her. "Hello, sweetheart."

She hugged him back tightly. "I'm glad you could make it here to suffer along with the rest of us."

"He's like a brother, I had to come."

Carrie stepped up. "What's the deal with you and Dr. Collins?"

"Wait!" Giselle's memory jolted with recollection. "Did you call him Tanner? Is that *the* Tanner Collins?" *The best man Chloe had sex with during their wedding reception?* One look told her it was.

Bill grunted. "I thought he looked familiar. He stepped in as best man when Chloe said you came on to her."

Red shivered, clearly revolted by the thought. "I didn't, you know."

"I know that, and so did Jackson. But why the hell would you call *him*?"

Red scowled. "I knew he worked here. I told him if he didn't do this I'd give him the ass whipping he deserved fifteen years ago."

Carrie pinched his cheeks affectionately. "You always were my favorite."

Giselle hugged him tightly. "Thanks, Red. But I don't want him doing any procedures on Jackson."

"Totally understandable." Red wrapped his arms around the shoulders of each woman and pulled them close. "Man, I love it here."

"As long as you're opening a club here, there's no reason not to move closer. Besides, our babies will need their Godfather around," Giselle said.

One of Red's brows arched curiously. "What babies?"

"The ones I plan to give him once we're married."

"Well, then. I guess I need to start looking for some property. I can't disappoint my Godchild; I'm looking forward to many years of watching him play baseball."

"God *children*, and the girl will play also," she corrected.

Red chuckled. "After seeing that video the other day, he's definitely going to need a baby girl in his life."

"I think you're right, Red. We'll have to keep trying until he has one of each."

Chapter Twenty-Six

Red tensed as Tanner pushed through the doors and sauntered over to their group. He listened as his old school 'buddy' reported that the surgeon had stopped the bleeding subdural hematoma, and was working on stopping the internal bleeding. He bristled as Tanner leaned in close to Giselle.

"I'll let you know when I hear more—Giselle, is it?" Tanner placed his hand intimately on her shoulder and squeezed, letting it trail down her arm.

Red cleared his throat as Giselle jerked away from the doctor. Stepping between the two, Red sent a warning glare in Tanner's direction. Tanner took a moment to send him a superior glare before making his exit through the same door.

Red turned toward Giselle, barely able to hold back his sneer. "That slimy S.O.B. will never change."

Giselle shuddered. "He's repulsive, especially knowing what I know about him."

"It takes a special kind of bastard to hit on a guy's girl while he's in surgery fighting for his life," Sam growled.

Bill shook his head. "Jackson was none-too-pleased when he stepped in as his best man. From what I gather, he continued to step in, in more ways than one."

"I'd just as soon not have to see him again," Giselle said.

Red seated himself. "You probably won't have to. I doubt he'll come back now that I'm here. He'll know I've blown his cover."

As it turned out, they didn't see Dr. Collins the rest of the day. It was another hour before the surgeon who operated on his lacerated spleen came into the room. He said it had been a simple procedure to remove it without any significant bleeding, and the orthopedic surgeon was preparing for the procedure to repair the compound fracture.

"How's he holding up?" Giselle asked Dr. Moss.

"Like a champ. That man's heart is some kind of strong." He wished them luck and exited the room.

Several minutes later, a young woman in scrubs pushed through the door. She was slim, around five and a half foot tall, with a blonde ponytail. Before Giselle could ask if she was there about Jackson, Red approached the woman.

"Excuse me, nurse. Are you looking for someone with Jackson Broussard?"

The woman whipped around, glared at Red with narrowed, accusing brown eyes. "Why would you assume I'm a nurse?"

"I don't know. What are you?"

"I'm Dr. LeBlanc. I'm the orthopedic surgeon who'll be repairing Mr. Broussard's leg. I need to speak with a member of his family immediately. Are you family?"

"No, but—"

"Then you're wasting my time." She turned her back on Red, leaving him wearing a dumbfounded look on his face.

Giselle approached. "Excuse me, I'm his girlfriend and this is his uncle."

"I'm Bill Broussard, the only family he's got, at least until he ties the knot with Ms. Granger, here. Whatever you say to me you can say to Giselle."

"Yes sir, I understand completely." She gave them both a pleasant smile. "Mr. Broussard's tibia has been seriously compromised; a compound fracture. An open fracture like his, is very easily susceptible to infection under the best of circumstances. He'd been lying out in a cow pasture for at least two hours, and there was serious contamination to the surrounding soft tissue. His tibia fractured in several places and there has been prolonged depletion of blood supply to the bone." She explained the best procedure to repair the damage, involving a brace and pins through the bones. They would have to monitor him closely to avoid infection, and dose him heavily with antibiotics. "You see, here, here, and here, I'd have to insert pins to keep the bones together." She showed them a print out of the ex-ray taken of Jackson's shin. "The brace keeps the entire thing stationary so it can heal and fuse back together."

"Man, in my day we only had casts," Bill commented.

She flashed him an indulgent smile. "We don't use casts when the bone breaks through the skin. Infections are too risky. We have to be able to check it often, keep it clean, and apply the topical antibiotics, as well as intravenous ones. It's common in cases like this. I need to tell you, however, in this instance, our best may not be good enough to save his leg. There could be serious complications, such as gangrene, in which case, I would have to amputate above the knee. I am seriously leaning toward amputation now just below the knee."

"Absolutely not!" Red's voice boomed from his position behind the surgeon.

She swung around. "Excuse me, I believe we've already established that you are neither a family member, nor a fiancé. So just who are you?"

"I'm a friend. His *best* friend, and I know damned well he'd want to do whatever is possible to keep his leg."

She turned her back on Red and faced Giselle again. "Even if it means having to amputate above the knee later on? It's a lot easier to maneuver a prosthetic limb when it's attached below the joint, rather than above it."

"Well, if you do the job you're paid to do," Red sneered, "that won't be necessary at all, will it?"

"Red—" Giselle began as he walked around the doctor to face her and Bill.

"Giselle, Bill, I'm begging you both. Do *not* let her do this. Jackson would want to at least try to save his leg."

Dr. LeBlanc turned an icy shoulder to Red, but her face softened once she saw how upset Giselle was. "I need to know what you want me to do. The timing is critical."

Giselle had grown slightly nauseous at the talk of infection, gangrene, and amputation. Knowing she had to make a decision, and now, she pulled Bill over to the window to talk.

Red hung back, stood his ground before the surgeon. "How old are you, anyway?"

She clenched her jaw with an audible 'snap', and turned to glare at him. "I'm thirty-six."

He jerked back, slightly surprised at her answer. "You sure as hell don't look it."

"Yeah? How old are you?" Her tone was tight with cynicism.

"I'm thirty-eight," Red countered.

"You sure as hell don't act it." She turned her back on him again.

Red glared at Ms. High and Mighty's ponytail then walked over to Giselle and Bill. He leaned close to Giselle's ear, "Can I say one thing?"

Giselle nodded silently, her eyes large and pleading, looking as though she were desperate for some sign from God on what to do.

"I know Jackson better than anyone in this world. I'm telling you, he wouldn't want you to give up on him—or his leg." Red brushed by the surgeon on his way to the elevators.

Giselle and Bill exchanged nods, in total agreement. She approached Dr. LeBlanc. "Do whatever you can to save the leg."

The surgeon bit her lower lip. "I can't begin to tell you how great the risk of infection is, but if that's what you want, I'll do my absolute best."

"I know it's what he'd want," Giselle explained.

Dr. LeBlanc smiled, and nodded. "I understand. I won't have the time to come out and give you reports, and I expect it to be a lengthy procedure. All you can do is wait it out. Any complications won't occur during the surgery, but afterwards."

"Dr. LeBlanc, please don't take this the wrong way," Giselle said. "I know looks can be deceiving, but it's just that you look so young. Have you done this procedure many times?" Dr. LeBlanc studied her, then looked as though she had decided not to take offense.

She smiled, and touched Giselle's arm in a reassuring gesture. "Ms. Granger, I've done this over a hundred times for many different hospitals in the area; I'm very proficient in this procedure. Like I told the other gentleman, and I use the term loosely, even though I may not look it, I'm thirty-six years old, and I've been a surgeon here for eight years. If *anyone* can save his leg, I can."

Giselle beamed at her. "I believe you can, Dr. LeBlanc. Thank you so much. Will you be the one to come out and tell us when this is all over with?"

"Yes, I will." She ran back through the doors leading to the surgical area.

Giselle watched her leave. "I've got a good feeling about her, Bill. I'll go find Red."

She searched the chapel and the atrium, and finally found him in the cafeteria. He sat alone, with his elbows propped on the table, and his forehead resting on his closed fists. She placed her hand on his shoulder. He looked up, his eyes questioning. "She's going to save his leg."

His head dropped back. "Oh, thank God! You and Bill made the right choice, you'll see. You want coffee?"

"I could use some."

He got a cup for her and seated himself. "Man, that Dr. LeBlanc's rough, isn't she?"

"I like her."

"She hates me."

"She doesn't know you well enough for that."

"Well, she sure as hell doesn't like me."

"She doesn't like the fact that you assumed she was a nurse instead of the surgeon. Was it because she's a woman?"

"No! She looked too damn young to be a surgeon. Four or five years of nursing school, compared to twelve years of pre-med and medical school, and however long she's worked here. It was deductive reasoning on my part. She only looks about twenty-two." He snorted, "She told me I was wasting her time."

"She's thirty-six."

"I know. I asked her when you and Bill were talking."

"Oh? How did you ask her?"

He repeated the conversation he'd had with the doctor.

Giselle particularly enjoyed Dr. LeBlanc's comeback about his age. She popped out a "Ha!" before she could stop herself.

"Gee, thanks, Giselle."

"Red, she's been a surgeon at this hospital for eight years. She's perfected this procedure and is confident she can save his leg."

"I don't have a problem with confidence, but I do have a problem with over confidence. She seems full of herself."

"She seems very capable to me, and when it comes to taking care of Jackson, that's all that matters." She stuck her finger in his face. "Don't you dare upset his surgeon by acting like a male chauvinist, I'm warning you."

"If I showed one ounce of chauvinistic tendencies, I'd get my ass kicked in seven different ways by my five sisters and both my parents." He threw his hands up in exasperation. "It was an honest mistake. She didn't have to be so damned rude!"

Giselle smiled, remembering a discussion she'd had with Carrie about a year ago. She'd said almost exactly the same thing about Jackson. "Red, try to see it from Dr. LeBlanc's perspective, would you? She's been performing complex surgeries for eight years, building a reputation in a male dominated field. I know she's the right surgeon for Jackson, and I want you to cut her some slack." Her eyebrow rose dangerously as he clamped his jaw shut.

"I'll try."

"You'll do more than try if you don't want to deal with me," she snapped.

He shook his head and laughed. "Remind me not to piss you off, okay Scrappy? I'm glad you're in his corner."

She sipped her coffee. "So which parent handed down the Red hair and blue eyes?"

"Dad, definitely. His father came to America from Scotland after WWII. My grandma called him her 'Red-haired, blue-eyed devil'."

"It must be wonderful to have that connection to family. Being adopted, I've never known that. I can't have a connection to the past, but you know what? I will have a connection to the future, and I can live with it, as long as Jackson's a part of it."

"He will be."

"Thanks, Red. Now I know why your mother is so terrified that you won't procreate before she dies. She wants more of you—another handsome, auburn-haired, blue-eyed devil, and who can blame her? We're gonna have to find you a lady friend."

He rose from the table, waving off her comment. "The only commitment I have time for are my clubs; the one I have, and the one I'm about to build."

"Yes, well life may decide differently—just barrel on through without getting your permission." She laughed at the face he made. "Tell me more about what it was like going to college with Jackson."

He traced the rim of his coffee mug. "I was a sophomore Jackson's freshman year. We were the only two underclassmen who started on the team, so we had a blast. Coach asked me to show him the ropes, and we became friends right away. After Jackson's injury, he buckled down and got serious about his studying. At first, I thought he was depressed about not being on the team anymore, but he didn't seem to be. Shrugged it off as if it never mattered to him in the first place. I, on the other hand, loved playing baseball. My sports scholarship served me well."

"So, you have a business degree and your club. What's next?"

"More clubs, I guess. It's what I do, for now. It keeps me from being bored."

"With your Hugh Hefner lifestyle?" she teased.

"Don't judge me because of my grotto pool. I'm not the dog Jackson thinks I am, you know. You do remember that I didn't have a date for my own club opening?"

"I'd wondered about that." Her phone chirped and she took the call from Amanda. After giving her updates she asked to speak to her girls. By the time the call ended, she was misty eyed.

"Mac and Lexie said to tell him they love him a bunch, a bunch." The tears rolled down her face. "That was something the girls and their dad used to say to each other before bedtime." She took a deep breath to collect herself. "I want us to be a family, Red."

His McAllister blue eyes sparkled as he gave her a nod. "You will be."

Chapter Twenty-Seven

The group spent more agonizing hours waiting for some word. Giselle stood when the surgeon scuffed in, still in her scrubs, head cover, and disposable shoe booties. Pulling the cap from her head to free her blonde pony-tail, Dr. LeBlanc motioned for her to stay as she approached the group.

"It went better than I expected. I believe we managed to clean up the area enough to stave off any bone infection, and the heavy doses of antibiotics will help."

The surgeon lifted one foot to slip off a bootie then stood on the opposite to pull off the other. The second one caught on her laces, and when she jerked it, she lost her balance and reached for the nearest arm to steady herself. It happened to be Red's. She glanced up at Red and seemed to suck in her breath.

"Oh, sorry."

"That's quite all right, doctor." His tone contained none of his former animosity toward the surgeon.

Dr. LeBlanc faced Giselle again. "His heart is in excellent shape, as well as the rest of him. He should do well with his physical therapy." Her eyes creased with a sincere smile. "Are you Giselle?"

Giselle nodded and wiped the tears from her face.

"I'm optimistic that the bones will fuse with no problems. From here on out it's vigilance that counts. Keep it clean, keep it immobilized, and keep him infection free. I don't know if the other surgeons told you or not, but he'll be here for at least a week. We need to monitor the head injury, the spleen, as well as the leg. As long as he's here, we'll have a much better chance of stopping any kind of infection before it gets out of hand. Before this is over with, his broken arm may be the biggest inconvenience for him because he won't be able to use crutches. Oh, and by the way, his arm is in a plain old cast—Just like in your day, Mr. Broussard." She grinned at Bill.

Giselle laughed through her tears and grasped the surgeon's hand. "Thank you so much Dr. LeBlanc. You've been wonderful. It was so nice to meet you."

The doctor flashed a brilliant smile at Giselle. "Oh, you haven't seen the last of me. I monitor my patients closely."

"Excuse me, doctor," Red interrupted. "I know you're not the surgeon who worked on his head injury, but maybe you'd know. Is there a chance he could be in a coma for a few days? My sisters tell me sometimes it's part of the healing process while the swelling goes down. They're not surgeons, but one's a physician's assistant, and one's a nurse practitioner."

Dr. LeBlanc cleared her throat, her eyes sparkling with amusement. "Normally I'd say your sisters are right, but not in this case. After I left you, we prepped him for his leg surgery." She turned to grin at Giselle. "He woke up, and told the anesthesiologist that he sure could go for a big, juicy steak—and some Giselle."

Giselle's mouth fell open in shock. "Are you serious?"

Dr. LeBlanc joined in with everyone else's laughter. "Absolutely. That's how I knew your name. The surgical ward's still buzzing over it."

"Jackson never liked to miss a meal," Carrie volunteered. "And we *know* how he feels about you. He'll be just fine."

Giselle exhaled slowly, releasing all the pent up tension from the long hours of waiting. "Can I see him?"

Dr. LeBlanc reached over and placed a hand on her arm. "He's still in recovery. As soon as he's fully awake, I'll come get you."

Giselle fought to control tears of relief. "I know you must be busy, you can send someone else."

"Are you kidding?" Dr. LeBlanc laughed and waved away Giselle's concern. "It'll be worth it to be the one to bring you back there. Besides, he was my last surgery of the day."

Red opened his arms to Giselle for a hug, and ended up spinning her in a circle. By the time he put her down she was still a little dizzy. But not too much to notice Dr. LeBlanc standing at the double doors watching them, a broad smile plastered on her face. She sent Giselle a slight nod before vanishing through the doors.

⚜

Dr. LeBlanc ushered her into a room where she could see a body covered with blankets except where his left shin, all wrapped up with surgical gauze, had a metal contraption sticking out of it. She walked quietly up to the bed, staring at the barely recognizable bruised and battered body of the man she adored. She'd take this sterile bandaged version of him over seeing him lying in a cow pasture any day of the week. She leaned close to speak to him. "I'm here, Jackson." He opened his one good eye and focused on her. "Hey baby."

It took him a moment to speak. "Giselle," he croaked.

"Yes, it's me." For a moment, she thought he'd lapsed back into sleep. "Jackson?" His next words proved her wrong.

"Will you marry me?"

She beamed at him and nodded. "Yes Jackson, I'll marry you. And don't think you can get out of it, either. I have all these witnesses." She waved her hand to encompass the hospital staff that'd gathered curiously.

"No way," he said, through a mouth still dry and fuzzy from surgery. "Let's do it now."

"No, babe, we're going to get you better first. Mac and Lexie said to tell you they love you a bunch a bunch."

He smiled. "Tell 'em—I love 'em too. A bunch a bunch. Tell Red—best man."

Giselle glanced up as a smiling Dr. LeBlanc told her it was time to leave. "I'll see you when they bring you to a room of your own. I love you, Jackson." She placed a soft kiss upon his swollen lips as he squeezed her hand.

"Love you, Giselle."

She left the surgical ward, but not before receiving several congratulations from hospital staff, including Dr. LeBlanc.

Giselle pushed through the double doors and faced the Jackson Broussard cheering section. "He looks like crap, but he's conscious and talking." She gave Bill the first hug.

"Did he know you?" he asked.

"I sure as hell hope so. He asked me to marry him."

Red chuckled. "Did you give him an answer?"

"I said yes, of course."

"Good!" Bill said.

She hugged Carrie, Sam, and Gwen then turned to Red, who wore the biggest grin of all.

"He said to tell you you're his best man, Red. Think you can make it this time?"

He sent her a wink. "You just try and keep me away."

Giselle shook her head. "I wouldn't dream of it."

To Jackson, it seemed like an eternity before he was settled in a room in ICU. It may have had something to do with the fact that he couldn't wait to see Giselle again. Giselle—his future wife. Nothing would stop him from marrying that woman. He didn't have to be told by doctors that he was in shit shape. He could see for himself. He didn't feel much, thanks to drugs and anesthesia still in his system, but that would change eventually. No matter. He was as determined as he'd ever been about anything that he, Giselle, and the girls were meant to be a family.

Finally she walked in with Uncle Bill. She came to him immediately, kissed him. He tore his gaze from her to speak to the man who'd raised him like a son. "Uncle Bill."

Bill nodded. "Son, you look a hell of a lot better than the last time I saw you. Listen, I just wanted to say that I love you, boy, but I'm going to give you and Giselle some privacy." He walked out, wiping his eyes discreetly.

The old softie.

Giselle leaned in close. "How do you feel?"

"Never better." He attempted a weak smile.

She laughed. "You are such a liar. The girls are thrilled at the prospect of having you for a daddy. They said to tell you they can't wait. Neither can I."

"Could get married—hospital."

She grinned as he gave her hand a squeeze. "We'll talk about it later. Red is here, so are Sam, Carrie, and Gwen."

Of course Red and Carrie would be here. The two biggest worriers of all, as well as supporters. "Send in Red and Carrie?"

She nodded and hurried out.

A minute later, they walked in. Red balked at first, enough for Jackson to see his condition through someone else's eyes. He *must* look like shit if McAllister was shocked.

Carrie walked right up to the bed and stood looking down at him. "Well, Jack, when you do it, you do it good."

He'd have shrugged if he could feel his shoulders. "No point, otherwise."

She beamed at him. "Congratulations are in order I hear. I'm the matron of honor."

He smiled, wondering if it even looked like a smile. "Cool. Thanks."

"Sure. I told her as long as she doesn't make me wear some awful shade of taffeta in a style made for skinny women."

He'd have laughed if it didn't take so much effort. He faced Red. "You?"

Red gave him a somber look. "I'm with Carrie. I draw the line at awful shades of taffeta, too. We're holding out for something both stylish and figure complimenting."

"Your ass."

Red laughed. "Just try to keep me away from this one. I'm happy for you, man."

Jackson gave a slight nod. Or he thought he did, anyway. Carrie wiped her eyes, drawing his attention from Red.

"You already know how I feel about it," she said.

"Always in my corner," he said.

Carrie busied herself smoothing his blankets. "Well, somebody had to be. Poor baby, you had it coming from both sides for a while, there. You deserve to be happy, dammit." Her voice cracked, and she mumbled a quick 'see you later' before turning away.

Jackson watched her leave and focused on Red. "Acts tough. Just a pushover."

Red nodded. "Hey, bet you didn't know that Dr. Tanner Collins works here."

Tanner—*bastard*. "He work on me?"

Red picked up the glass of water and put the straw to Jackson's lips. "Nah, I called him to tell him you were here. I told him to come in and give everyone updates, or else."

Giselle walked in. "It worked too."

Jackson had a vague recollection of a conversation between some of the nurses talking about a Dr. Collins.. "Heard nurses talk. He screws around on fiancée."

Red snorted, "I wouldn't expect anything else from him. Listen, I know you're just humoring the rest of us. You really just want Giselle in here." He gave him a wink. "I'll see you later, bro."

Red passed through the waiting room and hit the elevators, needing to be alone for a while. This thing had affected him in a strange way, sending the message that life could change in a single, solitary instant. Eventually, he ended up in a secluded area on the west side of the building.

He collapsed against a brick wall, taking the time to let things sink in—then offered up a silent prayer of thanks for his friend's life. He left an update about Jackson on his mom's voice mail, and was about to call his club manager., when someone pushed through the door. Before he could make his presence known, the sight of Jackson's pissy orthopedic surgeon, Dr. LeBlanc, stopped him.

For some reason, he kept quiet and watched—listened. Facing the opposite direction, she had no idea he was there. She pulled her satiny blond locks from its elastic band and gave it a fluff. She pushed a button on her phone and waited. After several moments, she lowered it, cursing softly, and pushed another couple of buttons. After a few seconds her head snapped forward, her entire demeanor tense. "Who the hell is this?" she demanded.

Red eased himself back to stay hidden from her.

"Tanner? Who's the woman who just answered your phone?"

Red's jaw fell open. Tanner? Dr. LeBlanc was Tanner's fiancée? He listened in, with renewed interest.

"I thought you said you had to go home and rest?" . . . "Then why aren't you at your apartment?" . . . "Tanner, I just called there. You're in a club." She sighed. "Yeah, whatever. Oh, in case you were wondering, your friend's surgery went well. Did you hear me? Hello? Tanner?"

Red leaned forward to watch her. She glared at her phone, shaking her head before muttering something about a cheating son of a bitch. She leaned against the wall and sniffed delicately before pressing both palms to her eyes. Red waited for the impending waterworks—she'd be falling to pieces any second now. Instead, she lowered her hands, wiped them on her scrubs. She stood, pulling her shoulders back, and walked inside without another sound.

Tanner nodded, admiring the woman's strength—her resilience. If he had to guess, he'd say Tanner's shenanigan's played a major part in her attitude toward men. The bastard had somehow coerced her into taking over his job of updating the family while he snuck off to play hide the bologna with another woman. From what he'd just heard, she probably suspected he was leaving to do exactly that. Definitely a mood crusher. He followed her inside, thinking he could forgive her snappishness. God knows, if he had to deal with that slimy son of a bitch on a daily basis, he'd be living in a perpetual state of foul moods.

Chapter Twenty-Eight

Jackson's two day stint in Intensive Care proved to be torturous for him, as well as Giselle and the staff. On Wednesday morning, once they moved him to a private room where he could have 'some Giselle' all day long, he transformed from surly to the perfect patient.

Red made the trip on Tuesday, and again on Wednesday afternoon, this time meeting Lauren at Sam and Carrie's place to pick up Mac and Lexie. At his arrival, the two girls came running, both excited to visit Jackson.

Lauren followed them outside, carrying Ava.

"Hey, twin, I bet you don't remember me." Even knowing he was to meet up with Lauren, Red still couldn't tell them apart.

"Sure I do. Gretchen and I cheered with your sister, Annie, in Gardiner. She's just a couple of years older than us."

"Yep, she's almost thirty and still living with my folks."

Lauren grinned at him. "I saw her last weekend at the festival in Gardiner. She told me she got her Physical Therapy license. I put a bug in her ear about moving to Kenton. We lost one of the two sharing a practice here."

"Keep bugging her, will ya? Mom and Dad could use the break." He gazed at the toddler she carried. I recognize this beauty from Giselle's videos. Hello, Ava Grace."

Ava looked shyly up at him, then flashed him a cheesy grin.

"She reminds me of you and Gretchen when y'all were that age, Lauren. Ava, I'm going to see Jackson."

At the mention of Jackson's name, the toddler's huge brown eyes lit up. "I go see Jackson!"

"You want to come with me to see Jackson?" He held his arms out. She nodded, and threw herself at him.

Ensconced on Red's hip, she turned to Lauren and waved. "Bye bye, Mama. I go see Jackson."

Red chuckled. "No wonder he fell in love with this one." Lauren used Red's phone to take a couple of shots and some video, before he and the girls drove to the hospital.

Jackson looked up when Red entered his room with Mac and Lexie.

Lexie hugged her mom then approached the bed, cautiously. She puffed out her breath and pointed her finger at him. "Jackson, you sure do know how to scare a girl. Next time you ride a motorcycle, you need to watch for cows on the road."

Mac stepped forward. "No! No more motorcycles. They're too dangerous."

Red lifted one, then the other so both girls could kiss Jackson.

Lexie crossed her arms. "Hey Jackson, I heard a rooma."

"It's a rumor, Lex, not a rooma," Mac corrected. "You're such a baby sometimes."

"I am not a baby. I'm five years old!"

"You are too. You can't say the simplest words."

"Mama, make her stop!" Lexie wailed.

Jackson smothered his laughter as Giselle held firm. "Girls, stop that." She sent him a glance. "There's still time to bail, babe. It only gets worse."

He sent her a wink before turning his attention to the younger child. "Lex, what is this rumor you heard?"

I heard a *rumor* that you're going to be our second daddy. Is that true?" Giselle thwarted her attempt to climb on his bed by lifting her to stand on a chair.

"It is, if it's okay with you and Mac," he said.

Lexie clapped her hands gleefully. "That's the best news I've heard since we got a Paw Paw Bill! You know, Jackson, my daddy was the best daddy in the world and I love him a whole lot. But, I don't like not having a daddy around. I think you're gonna be our next best daddy."

"Thank you Lex." He gave her a huge smile. "That means a lot to me, and I promise I won't let you down." He turned to the older child. "Mac, are you okay with this?"

"Actually," Mac said, in a very grown up voice, "I'm relieved. It was so hard explaining to my friends why Bill was my Paw Paw, but Jackson wasn't my daddy." She gave her eyes a dramatic roll. "This will be much better."

"Well, I'm glad, Mac. That's why I'm here, to make your life better." He caught Giselle's gaze. "I want to make all your lives better." The look she gave him could have melted butter. "And I can't wait to start."

After a twenty minute visit, the girls prepared to leave with Carrie. Giselle kissed them, saying she'd be home when visiting hours ended.

Mac looked at Jackson. "I'll go now, but when you get out of this place you're coming home with us. Nobody can take care of you as good as we can."

Giselle smiled at her daughter. "Don't worry, Mac. I'll make sure he comes home with us when he leaves here."

Once Carrie and the girls had gone, Red approached the bed. "Hey, I met Lauren's little Ava Grace when I picked up the girls. Take a look at this." He pulled up the photos and video as proof.

"She's a doll, isn't she?" Jackson gave Giselle his best hang dog expression. "Baby, can we have one? Please?"

Giselle laughed. "I'll see what I can do. You do realize we'll have to start from scratch, don't you? That means several months of midnight and 3 a.m. feedings, colic, teething pains, thousands of dirty diapers, and tons of other problems before they become that cute and that low maintenance."

"So, how long after we're married do we have to wait before trying for one?"

"I'm not getting any younger, so I'm ready when you are."

Jackson turned to Red and grinned. "That was easy."

"Too easy. She didn't even make you sweat for it." Red grinned at Giselle. "Watch out, hon. My sister's say if you start out spoiling them, they just get to expecting it."

Giselle leaned in to kiss him. "That's okay. We'll spoil each other, won't we Jackson?"

He beamed up at the woman he couldn't wait to start his life with. "Speaking of which, we need to get married before I leave here. I'm not staying in that house with you and the girls without making it legal first."

Her face fell. "Jackson, I want everyone to be there. My first wedding was Toby and I standing before the chaplain at LSU with a couple of friends to take some snapshots of us. I'd like to have friends and family around for this one."

He raised one hand to stop her. "Just hear me out, okay? How about if we get married at the courthouse as soon as I leave the hospital? Later, when I'm better, and can dance with my bride, we'll have a big wedding and reception out at the ranch and have it blessed. We could have everyone there, even Red's family. I really want you to meet them."

Her tension seemed to ease as, one by one, her excuses dissipated. She leaned over his bed until they were face to face. "You've got yourself a deal, big boy, but don't think I'll let you get lazy with your therapy. I expect to dance with my husband at our reception."

Red stepped out of the room to give the couple some privacy. Holding up the wall, he followed Dr. Tiffany LeBlanc's movements as she walked briskly towards him, her blonde ponytail swinging from side to side. He cleared his throat. "Hey Doc."

Tiffany glanced up from the clipboard, her steps faltering. "Are they changing linens?"

Red straightened to his full height. "No, she's just agreed to marry him as soon as he leaves the hospital."

"It's generous of her to give up the ceremony, the white dress, and everything," she said.

Red shrugged, before explaining about the legal ceremony followed by the later celebration. "This is the second marriage for both of them. Their spouses died in a pile-up on I-10 about eight months ago."

"I remember that. I didn't sleep for nearly forty-eight hours. It was one surgery after another." She frowned as she wrote something on a chart. "I knew someone who was killed in that wreck."

"Oh, I'm sorry. Was it a friend, or relative?"

"Neither, actually. More like a thorn in my side," she murmured. "She wasn't very nice, and didn't care whose husband, or fiancé, she slept with."

"Was her name Chloe Broussard, by any chance?"

Her head popped up. "You knew Chloe?"

"Not in the biblical sense," he snorted. "Although I hear plenty of other men did." He jerked his head toward the door. "That tramp was Jackson's wife. You only thought *you* had problems."

Her hand flew to her mouth. "I didn't know. I knew she was married, but I never met the husband." She pointed to the door. "Did I hear you say they *both* lost their spouses in the wreck?"

Red nodded. "Giselle's husband was killed instantly. They had a wonderful marriage, and two beautiful daughters. It was rough on her for the first few months, losing her husband so suddenly. Jackson, on the other hand, well, let's just say it set him free." He shrugged. "I guess you can tell I didn't think highly of her."

Her shoulders dropped. "I thought when she passed away that my life would get easier."

The disturbed look on her face told him it hadn't put a dent in her situation. Not surprising with the slimy son of a bitch she was engaged to.

She cleared her throat delicately. "How long have they been in there?"

"Long enough, but I'd knock if I were you, just in case."

She tapped on the door, waited a few moments, and entered the room. "Hey, I can see both of those big, blue eyes now. That swelling has really gone down since this morning. Let's hope the rest of your injuries heal that quickly."

"Did you hear the news, Doc? I'm getting married as soon as you spring me."

"Yeah, your friend just told me. Congratulations, although I don't know what kind of a honeymoon you'll have." She made a face then smiled at Giselle. "I need to change his dressing. You can stay or leave, whatever you prefer."

Giselle stepped forward. "I'd like to stay, if you don't mind. That way I'll know what to do."

"That's fine. How about you?" She looked at Red.

"I'll stay."

"Don't say I didn't warn you. It's not pretty." She washed her hands before removing the old dressing, and then donned sterile gloves and began examining the wounds carefully. She poked and prodded, checking the wound.

"How's it look, Doc?" Red asked, peering over her shoulder to watch her work.

"It looks good, no oozing around the area or on the bandage. It smells okay, color's good, warm to the touch, but not hot. So far, so good." She applied more topical antibiotic to the affected area with a sterile applicator.

Red was studying the strange looking pieces of metal protruding from Jackson's leg. "What's this called?"

"It's an external fixation system."

"So, how's it attached to the bone?"

"I had to drill into the bone to insert pins at different angles. The brace uses forced compression and distraction at the fracture sites to fuse them together."

Red nodded, fascinated at the mechanics of it. "That's impressive. Do you do many of these?"

"I perform the bulk of them in this area. Especially injuries this serious. Most wouldn't have attempted to save the leg."

"I'm glad you were around to do it, then."

"Oh, it was nothing. Just doing the job I'm paid to do."

Red winced at the sound of his own words being thrown back in his face. He cleared his throat, backed slowly away from the bed, as she finished tending to her patient.

She straightened and addressed Jackson. "I'll see you in the morning to check it again. It's looking good, though. Is the pain medication sufficient?"

"It's fine, doc. Thanks again."

"Are you finished for the day?" Giselle asked.

"I sure am. It'll be nice to make it home before dark. I've almost forgotten what my back yard looks like." She pulled her disposable gloves off with a snap, and threw them in the proper receptacle.

Red walked out first, holding the door open for her. She stopped to make a few notes on a clipboard, glanced up when Red cleared his throat.

He stood tall, fully prepared to take one in the nuts for the sake of making amends to Jackson's doctor. He certainly owed her that. "Look, Dr. Leblanc, I want to apologize for assuming you were a nurse a few days ago. I swear, I meant you no insult. I just thought you looked too young to have gone through twelve years of schooling already, along with internship and practicing."

"It's fine. You'd think I'd be used to it by now."

"No, it's not fine. All five of my sisters are in the medical profession, and my calling you a nurse wasn't meant as an insult, I assure you. I'm very proud of my sisters' accomplishments."

"Five?" she asked, finally looking up at him. "I thought you said two?"

"I only mentioned two. We also have a Registered Nurse, Respiratory Therapist, and Physical Therapist," he boasted.

She nodded. "Did I hear someone say your last name is McAllister? Did any of your sisters go to LSU?"

His chest puffed with pride. "We all went to LSU. It's kind of a family tradition."

"I had some classes with two McAllister sisters back when I was in the nursing program, Melissa and Bailey McAllister."

He nodded. "They're my sisters."

"Ah, small world, isn't it?" She gave him a tight smile. "They were so funny and sweet, it's hard to believe they're your sisters."

Red released his breath with a hiss. "I guess I deserve that."

"You certainly do," she said. "Melissa, Bailey and I hung out a lot my freshman year. Then I switched from nursing to pre-med and got too busy to do anything but study and work." She frowned in concentration. "I know they weren't twins, but I can't remember which one was older."

"Melissa is thirty-seven and Bailey is thirty-six."

"They got their degrees, then?"

Red nodded, thrilled with the chance to have a pleasant conversation with the good doctor for a change. "Melissa is the physician's assistant, and Bailey is the nurse practitioner."

Red wasn't at all prepared for the brilliant smile Dr. LeBlanc flashed him.

"That's wonderful, but I'm not surprised. Neither of them looked the type to quit something before they were done," she said.

Unfortunately, Red heard little of her comment. He'd been too busy staring at the way her beautiful brown doe eyes crinkled when she smiled. He spent the next few seconds wondering if he'd look like a dumbass for not answering some question she may have asked him.

"Tell them Tiffany said hello, would you? It'd be really nice to see them again." She tucked her clipboard away.

Red nodded, trying to get his cool back by taking charge of the conversation. "Do you have any siblings, Tiffany, or are you an only child, like Jackson?"

"One brother, two years younger—Mr. McAllister."

"Is he also a doctor?" Red totally recognized that she'd set a boundary he wasn't to cross..

"No, he's a lawyer."

"A doctor and a lawyer—your parents must be pumped."

"You'd think that, wouldn't you?" she murmured. "Give your sisters my message, would you?"

"I certainly will, Dr. LeBlanc." He couldn't help but wonder, as she made her way down the hall, if she'd show some interest by turning back. Unfortunately, another woman in scrubs stopped her to talk. He jumped when Giselle opened the door.

"Red, I need to run an errand. Will you stay with Jackson while I'm gone? I won't be long."

"Sure." He glanced back in time to see Dr. LeBlanc's ponytail disappear around the corner. He rejoined Jackson in his room after Giselle left in a flurry of excitement.

Jackson's voice boomed from the bed. "She's going to marry me, Red. How did I get so damn lucky?"

Red shrugged, figuring it was okay to give him a hard time now that he was out of the woods. "You nearly killed yourself. She only said yes because she felt sorry for you."

"Your ass!" Jackson launching a pillow at him with his good arm.

Red caught it and tossed it on the sofa. "Nah, this one really loves you. I'm a little jealous, but I'm happy for you."

"You, the career bachelor, jealous?"

"Hey, if I can find someone to make me as happy as you are, I wouldn't mind settling down and having a cute kid or two."

Jackson slapped Red's shoulder. "Your mom would be ecstatic."

"It may even earn me a reprieve from all that nagging."

"I don't have a mom to pester me so excuse me for the lack of sympathy. So get busy and start looking. Maybe concentrate on the good doctor? You could steal her from Tanner with one hand tied behind your back."

"Absolutely, if I was so inclined. I still can't fathom a woman with her talent and looks putting up with a class-A jerk like Tanner."

"I think you ought to do something about that."

Red recognized that gleam in his friend's eyes. He'd seen it before. The classic "I'm settled, so let's get you settled too" gleam.

"I have rules. I don't break up couples, and I sure as hell don't date women on the rebound. Those relationships never work out." He stretched out one leg on the vinyl covered couch, "I did discover she attended LSU with two of my sisters, though."

"LSU, huh?" Jackson perked up. "That explains why she's so good at what she does. Too bad you didn't know that before you practically accused her of being incompetent." He threw a second pillow at Red. "Smooth move, McAllister. Beaucoup smooth move."

Tiffany Leblanc sat with Giselle, giving her discharge instructions on how to care for Jackson.

"I've instructed a home health nurse to go once a day to tend to him, but you have to make sure he doesn't try to do too much. I can already see how he is," she said, glaring at Jackson. "I'm sending him home with crutches and a wheelchair. Hide the crutches from him until the arm cast comes off in two weeks. It's strictly wheels until then." She glanced up as Red entered the room then turned back to Giselle. "Will you have help, once you get him home? He's kind of a big guy for you to handle all alone."

Red stepped up. "I'll be there with them a good portion of the time. I can handle him."

Tiffany looked from Jackson to Red. "You'll do."

"Will he be good for a courthouse stop once we leave here?" Giselle asked.

"As long as you can get him into the wheelchair and keep him in it. You're still going through with the wedding?"

Jackson laced his fingers through Giselle's. "Absolutely. We have Red as one witness, but we were wondering, since this is your last stop of the day, if you'd be our second. I know it's a lot to ask, but, we'd really like you to be there. We owe you so much."

Tiffany smiled at the couple. "I'd be honored, as long as you give me enough time to change. I draw the line at attending weddings in scrubs. It should take at least another hour or so for your discharge, so can I meet you there?"

Jackson nodded his approval. "Perfect. Thanks Doc."

Giselle held open the thick door so Red could wheel Jackson into the Lake Coburn courthouse. Her gaze landed on Tiffany LeBlanc, standing off to the side. "Hey, have you been waiting long?"

"I've only been here a couple of minutes."

Giselle grinned at the woman she'd grown to like as a person outside her professional persona. She turned, wanting to witness Red's reaction to Tiffany, sans scrubs and athletic shoes. She nearly laughed in delight as the big, brawny man practically paled at the sight of "Doc" as Jackson had dubbed her. Tiffany's choice of a sexy, sleeveless sundress seemed to have made quite an impression on the eternal bachelor.

Giselle smiled devilishly as Red's blue eyes savored the good doctor's appearance, all the way down to the strappy, heeled sandals showcasing her quality pedicure. Giselle glanced at Tiffany, who straightened from checking to make sure her patient's leg was properly supported. Was she seeing things or had Doc applied makeup since she'd seen her last? Hmmm. Interesting. She watched and listened, waiting to hear what Red had to say.

"Hello again, Dr. LeBlanc. I almost didn't recognize you. You are truly stunning," he murmured.

Tiffany mumbled a polite thank you, before turning toward the couple.

Thanks again for doing this," Giselle said, grasping her hand. "You look fantastic, by the way. I want the name of the dress shop after the ceremony."

They found Jackson's friend, who had all of the paperwork prepared, thanks to a previous phone call. They obtained the license then stopped off at the judge's office for special dispensation of the three-day waiting period. Within twenty minutes of their arrival, the four of them were standing before the Justice of the Peace.

After the brief ceremony and everyone had put pen to paper, the document was stamped, signed and placed safely in her hands. Giselle turned to thank the witnesses, giving each a big hug.

The group exited the courthouse and gathered around Giselle's vehicle. Heat rose from the concrete parking lot in waves as the late August sun beat down mercilessly.

"Well, good luck you two," Tiffany said. "This was an honor."

"Thanks Doc," Jackson said. "I'll see you for my check up next week."

"You certainly will." She turned to Red and nodded. "Mr. McAllister."

He gave her a slight, but gallant bow. "Dr. LeBlanc."

Red loaded Jackson into Giselle's vehicle, and got in his own truck to follow them home.

Giselle buckled her seatbelt and gazed at her new husband, stretched out in her backseat to accommodate his leg brace. The man was a mess—head shaved, a surgical steel plate in his skull, and a metal brace with pins sticking out of his right leg. A cast covered his left arm, and black and blue bruises covered the rest of him from head to toe. Regardless, she couldn't help but smile at that crooked, boyish grin of his.

"Not much to look at, am I? Right about now, you're probably thinking you dove head first into the shallow end of the pool."

"I'm thinking I gained a wonderful husband. You're the one who should worry. You get a wife and two rowdy girls."

"Baby, this is a dream come true for me."

She slipped on her sunglasses and shifted her car into drive. "Let's go home."

Epilogue

October 25th

Crystal white lights twinkled and glittered in the luminescent glow of the evening sky, reflecting off the pond like bits of diamonds. Friends and family members gathered around to watch Jackson and Giselle as they walked gracefully to the center of the dance floor under the pavilion Bill had constructed for this night. It was the perfect night for a wedding—crisp, cool but not cold, with low humidity.

Giselle was stunning in an ultra-feminine, ivory, tea length wedding gown with insets of Brussels lace. She danced with Jackson, the man she'd just wed for the second time. Her new husband had so completely filled her life with love that, at times, she thought she had never been this happy. At other times, of course, she remembered she had been. She knew how lucky she was to have found love twice, first to Toby, and now to Jackson. This kind, loving, sexy man was her future and she prayed every day to spend the rest of her life with him.

She danced with her husband—tall, healthy, and handsome in his black tuxedo, holding him, loving him so deeply. They swayed to the sound of James Otto's deep soulful voice, singing their favorite song, *Last First Kiss*. A song about a couple finding the one love they hope is eternal, sharing a first kiss, one they pray will be the very last first kiss they ever share with another, and pledging their love for all time.

She gazed up into the piercing blue of her husband's eyes. "Sing to me Jackson."

He smiled, and did as she asked, singing the words she adored with the voice that made her melt. For the last verse, he slipped to one knee, acting out the words he sang in complete confidence, his voice rich and full.

Giselle laughed, as delighted at the show as their guests were. She let him have his moment, gloried in it, but pulled him up from his knee before the last chorus ended. Then and there, during their dance, in her husband's arms, she enjoyed her own moment. She wrapped her arms around his neck and stood on tip toe to whisper the closely guarded secret she'd saved for this day.

She pulled back to gauge his reaction—no disappointment there.

Jackson's eyes widened, his entire countenance filled with absolute delight. "Are you sure?"

She nodded, giving him a teary-eyed smile.

Jackson stared into the twin orbs of gold-specked green, loving her as he'd never loved anyone before.

"A baby? Are you sure?"

Again, she nodded, her eyes bright with tears and laughter. "Positive."

He wrapped her in his arms, treasuring this moment, holding her as if his life depended on it. He squeezed his eyes shut and held on to his wife, praying for the strength to protect her from all harm. He cherished this woman, as well as their daughters, Mac and Lexie. And now—now the new life growing inside her.

"I love you, Jackson," she whispered. "Are you okay?"

"I'm perfect. Everything's perfect. And I'm going to be a daddy again."

Other Work by Lori Leger

Fleur de Love
(Series set in southwest Louisiana)
Book 1: SOME DAY SOMEBODY
Book 2: LAST FIRST KISS
Book 2.5: HART'S DESIRE - A Novella
Book 3: BROWN EYED GIRL
Book 4: HEAVEN IN YOUR EYES

Halos & Horns
(Spinoff series: Where residents of Louisiana and Texas cross the state line to find romance.)
Book 1: GREEN EYED TEMPTATION
Book 2: SARAH SMILE
Book 3: MEAGAN'S MARINE
Book 4: ONE YEAR TO FOREVER

Seasons of Love
(Multi-authored Seasonal series by Cajunflair Publishing)
Book 1: HEARTS, HEARTHS & HOLIDAYS
("Bells Will be Ringing" by Lori Leger)
A short story about Bill and Gwen Broussard
(Jackson's Uncle Bill)

FULL CIRCLE LOVE
(Contains four novellas from Books 2-5 in the Seasons of Love series,
all stories about Cathryn and Zachary. Their story continues in RUNNING
OUT OF RAIN)

Prime of Love
(Mature characters finding love and laughter through the everyday twists and turns of growing older.)
Book 1: RUNNING OUT OF RAIN
Book 2: (Predicted Fall of 2015)
Book 3: (Predicted Summer 2016)

Non-Fiction Article in WRITING AFTER RETIREMENT
Publishers: Rowman & Littlefield

ABOUT THE AUTHOR

Lori Leger is a wife, mother, doting grandmother, and Mistress of Procrastination. She lives in Louisiana with the love of her life, her very own Studley-do-Right. He's earned his spot in the Keeper Husband's Hall of Fame by allowing her to walk away from an eighteen year career as an Engineering Technician in Road Design to stay home and write.

She adores writing stories set in her beloved south Louisiana, where good Cajun cooking, helping your neighbors, and saying y'all is as normal as hurricanes, heat, and humidity. She figures as long as she's not tunneling through ten feet of snow to get to her car, it's a perfectly acceptable trade-off.

Lori has nine novels published in two series: La Fleur de Love and its spin-off, Halos & Horns series. She has also contributed to, as well as published, short stories in each of the five Seasons of Love anthologies, an author collaboration series. She's contributed to the Sweet & Savory Cookbook of Amazon Authors, published by Top Ten Press. Lori also has an article published in the non-fiction book Writing After Retirement: Tips From Retired Writers, published by Rowman and Littlefield Publishers, and edited and compiled by Carol Smallwood and Christine Redman-Waldeyer.

Her latest book, Running Out of Rain is the first book in her Prime of Love Series, novels dedicated to mature characters finding love and laughter through the everyday twists and turns of growing older. She has a second planned for a fall 2015 release date, and a third set for the summer of 2016.

Lori Leger
P.O. Box 641
Kinder, LA 70648
cajunflair@lorilegerauthor.com
www.lorilegerauthor.com
www.facebook.com/lorilegerauthor
www.facebook.com/llegerauthor
www.facebook.com/CajunflairPublishing
Twitter: @LoriLegerAuthor